John Taylor was born in Ely in 1944 and raised in Littleport. He has been married to Elisabeth for 44 years and has three adult children. He has worked in 20 different countries and lived in England, Switzerland, Saudi Arabia, South Africa, New Zealand, Papua New Guinea and Australia. He now calls Cambridge home.

For Christopher, My Dear Brave Son.

28/11/1975 – 21/9/2016

John M. Taylor

I WILL FIND YOU

AUSTIN MACAULEY™
PUBLISHERS LTD.

A CIP catalogue record for this title is available from the British Library.

ISBN 9781787102798 (Paperback)
ISBN 9781787102804 (E-Book)

www.austinmacauley.com

First Published (2017)
Austin Macauley Publishers Ltd.™
25 Canada Square
Canary Wharf
London
E14 5LQ

Appreciation and Acknowledgements

The wonderful people at "Vanish" in Melbourne.

With great respect to the Indigenous
People of Western Australia.

Lorna Delanoy. MBE
Michael Delanoy. MBE

Dave Dawson. Chris Dixon.

My wonderful wife Elisabeth, for her help, patience
and encouragement.

1

Sitting in the red sand, on a shallow ridge beside the dry riverbed, Nick pondered his life. After his first fifteen years it had become no more than an existence that now left him surviving from day to day. Every day that passed was another day stolen from his future. Why did it have to be like this? What is more, it seemed the future offered little improvement. Any logic of the past remained elusive, and he was tormented with underlying anxiety and so many questions. His many hours of speculation offered no relief from the frustration of failing to find meaningful answers.

Where is it all leading? Is this it? Is this all there is in life? Maybe the Brothers at Clontarf Boys Town were right after all. Perhaps I really am worthless. Maybe no one ever did love me, care about me or want me. Will I really amount to nothing? Am I no more than the flotsam of life as they so frequently told me?

Again and again questions of doubt and self-worth attacked his consciousness from a dark place in his mind. His thoughts mingling with the sadness he now felt after the death of the woman who had taken him in and treated him as her own. He was upset and wanted to cry. He thought he ought to but the tears would not come, prevented by an underlying anger. It was an unnatural feeling and didn't feel right. Since his real mother, this kind lady was the only person who had shown him any great affection. It had been a sincere, non-judgmental and unreserved acceptance of him that had begun to heal his pain and help restore feelings of purpose and self worth. But now they flooded back. She was gone and his pain was raw. He wanted to scream and yell with anger and frustration. "Why?" There were always questions, so many questions with too few answers and now there were even more. Always asking why? Why am I here? What did I do wrong? And why did she have to die? Why now?

Nick felt betrayed by fate, lost and confused. He was sure that knowing his distant past would help him understand, provide substance and confirm that he was "somebody" after all. If he could only find his real mother he was sure his life would be so different. If only he knew more.

Most parts were just darkened gaps left by faded and lost memories, like dreams he sometimes had but couldn't clearly remember the next day. Many times he had tried to reach back for answers. But the fragments of his memories before coming to Australia were few and would not come to the fore. Now his name was Nicholas Michael Thorne. Where he came from in England had long since eluded him, leaving only distant shadows where memories should be. There had been occasions when his recollections had hovered just beyond reach, to elude and torment him. They seemed so tantalizingly close but he could not quite reach them to bring them forwards.

He believed he was born on 10th November, 1940 which he had discovered years before after seeing it on a file cover at the docks in Fremantle. In his mind's eye, Nick could still see the buff folder. It was proof that he was 'somebody' and it left a lasting impression.

He could hear his adopted Aboriginal brothers and sisters as they played in the dust bowl which only became a river for a week or two every few years. Although he could hear their excited shouts and screams he was not listening, and if they had called his name he would not have known. Putting his hands behind his head he slowly leaned back until his fingers touched the dusty red sand. He stared into the endless blue of the afternoon sky and became lost in its depths. Then, without even trying, he retreated into a deep, secret corner of his mind that was shut off from the rest of the world. Oblivious to the flies which scavenged for moisture at the corners of his eyes, his mind drifted. As he had done many times before and without moving his lips he asked:

"Where are you Mum? Where are you? I need you."

2

Robert Peter Spalding was a typical three-year-old boy, bright, energetic and enquiring. His fair hair, blue eyes and smile endeared him to most people. In 1943 there were many hardships and restrictions although he did not realise it or understand. Life was a nervous, testing existence for everyone. But Robert had no concept of hardship or worry. He had all that he needed, he was loved, cared for and had never known any different. So everything was normal to him.

He was "Robbie" most of the time but "Robert" or "Robert Spalding" when he had been naughty. He knew his father went up in aeroplanes, wore a smart blue uniform and sometimes a thick brown sheepskin jacket when it was cold. He had become familiar with his father's routine of sleeping until lunch time, then going to work later in the afternoon. He came home at varying times, usually very early the next morning. On a few occasions he was in bed and asleep before Robbie was up. Ross was always tired, very tired, and Robbie was told not to wake him. A few times his father didn't go at all, but it was not often.

"Why does daddy go to work at night?" Robbie asked his mother.

"It's what Daddy does dear. He flies in a big aeroplane in the dark."

"What sort of aeroplane?"

"It's a very big one called a Stirling Bomber," she replied.

"What does Stirling mean?"

"I don't know that it means anything dear. It's the name of a town in Scotland. Maybe they named it after that."

Robbie thought for a moment, frowned and asked.

"Where does daddy go?"

"I think he mostly goes to Germany, but he is not allowed to say," his mother replied.

"Where is Germany?"

"It's very far away over the sea."

Can I go with daddy one day?"

Amused, Anne smiled at her son's innocent notion.

"No sweetheart you wouldn't like it. It's very cold and noisy in the airplane, and Germany it's such a long way away."

Then after a moment of anxiety she quietly added "And very dangerous."

Most days Robbie's father would make a point of taking time to play with him before going to the airfield. They both had fun. For Ross it provided a time when he could escape from his underlying fears and sense of trepidation which he endured every day. Sometimes when he had returned from a mission, he was so tense and distressed that he could neither talk nor fall asleep even though he was desperately tired. Robbie had no idea and always wanted to get daddy out of bed to come and play the next day. Sometimes Anne would gently usher him away to allow Ross to rest a little longer. Many times when Ross was sleeping she would step back, look at him with love in her eyes and slowly shake her head as a little voice inside would say:

"You poor, dear man. Nobody should have to go through what you do day after day."

Then to dab her eyes as emotion rushed to the surface. Sometimes Robbie would carefully crawl into bed with his father whilst trying not to wake him. Ross's smell and radiated warmth was comforting enough. Wide-eyed

Robbie would watch his daddy and wait. But if Ross was already awake, he would pretend to be asleep for a minute longer. Then in mock surprise, waking would say,

"Who's this little scallywag in my bed?" As he tickled Robbie's ribs.

Robbie would fall into uncontrollable fits of giggling. He liked it just as much as when he crawled into bed with his mother. But that was for cuddles and occasionally serious talks. Sometimes before going to the airfield, Ross and Robbie would play football on the grass at the edge of the small orchard to the rear of the cottage. Ross would gently roll the scuffed old brown football towards Robbie so he could kick it back. He tried hard, sometimes kicking a tuft of grass from the uneven ground or missing the ball completely to fall over in fits of laughter. But when he was successful, Ross would sometimes pretend to miss catching the ball, letting it pass. They would both shout 'Goal' much to Robbie's excitement. Later he would take great delight in telling his mother how many goals he had scored. Ross would laugh and say,

"Robbie is very good Mum. He won again today." Pleased, Robbie would grin from ear to ear.

He loved to climb the apple trees but his nerve failed him on reaching the middle branches, and more than once he had to be lifted down to everyone's amusement. He especially liked the older gnarled tree that stood closest to the cottage where his father had made a swing with rope and an old car tyre.

For fun, Ross once gave Robbie an apple from that tree telling him it was really nice. The big green apple was so large that Robbie had to hold it with both hands to take a bite. Within a second of his teeth sinking into the hard flesh, Robbie winced and shuddered. His eyes involuntarily shut tightly as they produced a tear while the corners of his mouth pulled downwards. After a few seconds he opened his watery eyes to see his father in fits of laughter. Robbie opened his mouth to let a piece of apple fall from his tongue. He didn't find it funny and threw the apple away in disgust.

Anne came to the garden to ask what the fuss was about.

"Daddy gave me a big green apple to eat. He said it was nice but it was horrible," Robbie told her, pulling a face to emphasize.

Ross was still laughing.

"That's really mean! You jolly well know those are cooking apples," Anne said, chastising her husband. As a result Ross picked Robbie up and apologised to satisfy Anne as much as his son.

Robbie liked to be pushed on the swing but not when it twisted around making him dizzy. He laughed with excitement when he went high causing his tummy to tingle when he came down, and he always wanted to be pushed for longer.

When it was time to finish, his father gave him a cuddle and said,

"Must go now Skipper, look after Mummy till I get back."

"Can't you stay? Do you have to go?" Robbie begged.

"Sorry Skip, I have to go or the boss will come looking for me."

"Who's your boss?"

"No.75 Squadron. Or should I say The Royal New Zealand Airforce."

Robbie looked sad as though he was about to cry at his father leaving.

"Oh come on then, just one more minute!" Ross said.

That minute soon became ten and Flight Sargent Ross Spalding would probably be late for his crew's briefing. He gave Robbie another hug, went indoors, hurriedly gathered his things, kissed his wife, told her he loved her and that he would see her tomorrow. Then he left quickly on his bicycle hoping to make up time.

The next morning, as the sun was burning off the remains of a typical low Fenland fog, Robbie was swinging on the front gate waiting for his father who was late. Although impatient, he wasn't too concerned since it was not unusual. He saw a man in a blue uniform coming towards his house and ran out to greet him. But as they drew closer to each other, he could see the man was not his father. He hesitated, stopped and watched as the man continued to walk towards him. He ruffled Robbie's hair with his fingertips as he walked past, but there was no warm smile. Robbie instinctively felt something was wrong and followed him to the front door. The man knocked and Anne came out. Without being told, she instantly knew why Ross's Squadron Leader was there and uttered under her breath, "Oh no! Dear God no. Please just let him be missing." Tears instantly filled her eyes.

The Squadron Leader didn't stay long, but when he left the house Anne was crying. While leaning on the doorframe watching and listening, Robbie could hear the man's quiet voice as he held Anne's hand. Yet he could not hear clearly what was being said. As the man was leaving he didn't look down at Robbie, just firmly held his shoulder for a second as he passed. At the doorway the man turned back to say, "Anne, I'm so very sorry. If you need anything, or if there is anything I can do just let me know and I'll do my best for you."

She nodded while subconsciously twisting her wet handkerchief in her fingers and then turned back inside, dropping heavily onto a chair at the kitchen table. Her greatest dread had come this morning. She put an elbow on the table, pressed her handkerchief into her eyes whilst pulling Robbie close and sobbed deeply. Robbie had never seen his mother cry before and quickly became upset. Instinctively tears came to his eyes too. He clumsily climbed onto her lap, wriggling between her and the table, and put his arms around her neck. She held him close and squeezed him tight. Robbie could feel her deep convulsions as she sobbed.

"What's the matter Mummy?" Robbie eventually asked.

Discarding her tear soaked handkerchief, she reached for the corner of her apron and while wiping her eyes said, "Sweetheart, Daddy is not coming home again."

"Why not?" Robbie asked in alarm.

"His aeroplane has crashed dear."

June 3rd 1943 was a day that Anne Spalding would never forget.

With the limited wisdom and instinct of a child, Robbie knew not to ask more at this time. In that moment, Anne realised that she was not the only one to be affected – knowing she had to be strong for her son. After some minutes she lowered Robbie to the floor, stood, took a deep breath and said, "Right! A cup of tea. They don't call us Fen Tigers for nothing."

Anne hardly slept that night, just dozing for less than an hour before dawn. When she awoke Robbie was beside her. His head was on his father's pillow, eyes wide open watching her and quietly waiting. She embraced him, cried a little, then managed to regain her composure. After a few minutes she got out of bed saying, "Right young man, we have to get you some breakfast. What would you like? You can have toast and dripping, bubble and squeak or porridge with milk and a little sugar?"

Before leaving the room, she brushed her hair in front of the dressing table mirror. Then, as she put the brush down she said aloud, "Oh no!"

"What?" Robbie asked.

"It's Daddy's lucky charm."

His gold Kiwi tie clip was still there on the dressing table. She picked it up and clasped it to her breast before showing it to her son.

"Look Robbie."

Nothing more needed to be said as they both knew Ross would never knowingly fly without it. Like most aircrew, he had his share of superstition and had always worn his lucky charm.

Over the following months, Robbie missed his father greatly and wanted to ask about him but when he did, his mother always cried. Then he would cry too, so he learned to keep his thoughts and questions to himself.

Sometimes he would watch the blue uniformed airmen in the village hoping that one would turn around. Then, as if by magic, it would be his daddy. Anne tried to compensate with extra attention but it was difficult to be both mother and father. Her love for Robbie was more intense now although it had not seemed possible previously. She now loved Robbie with a sense of urgency and a mixture of pleasure and sorrow when she saw how many of his father's characteristics he had. Some she had not noticed until now. She knew she was becoming over protective but couldn't stop herself. Now he was all she had and she treasured him.

Anne became distressed most evenings when she heard the drone of the Lancaster and Stirling bombers, from the other side of the village, as they manoeuvred to leave on their nightly missions. Without fail she would say:

"Please God, bring them home safe and sound. Please don't take any more."

Occasional quiet evenings were a blessing for Anne.

Times were difficult and there were always shortages, even the locally grown food from the farms was subject to scrutiny and ration. Nonetheless it was common for a little to be spirited away now and then. Everyone did it but no one discussed it. A couple of onions in a pocket after a hard day of onion wringing would not hurt anyone. Most people in the village had gardens and allotments, each supplementing their rations as best they could with all manner of produce. Ration books rarely provided enough food to last the week. Fen soil was rich and there was no shortage of expertise in gardening. This industriousness became something of a joke in the village which started when someone in the pub had said, "They're only doing all that there diggin' 'cos they think they'll find King John's treasure."

So a few hours on the allotment became 'Looking for King John's treasure.' When anyone had vegetables to spare, they were given to older folks in the village who could no longer manage their gardens. It just became the thing to do. Some neighbours took over the cultivation of these gardens for a share of the extra vegetables. Quite often, produce was swapped for eggs, fruit or occasionally a rabbit or wildfowl, even a Pike or an eel or two. Nobody made a big thing of it, it just happened in the course of a deeper understanding and caring for each other in hard times.

Anne was lucky to have a small patch of rhubarb and an orchard which produced far more than she and Robbie needed when in season. Most of the ten trees were a mixture of eating and cooking apples but there was a pear tree and another that produced huge succulent Victoria plums. As the fruit was seasonal, Anne always bottled some for the winter. Then by wrapping apples in paper and putting them in a cool dark place, they lasted for many months. Well into Christmas. The remainder was given away so nothing was wasted.

Robbie would be sent next door to give Mrs. Boon a bag of apples or a few plums. Then without fail, next day Mrs. Boon would come round with a bag of potatoes or a jar of homemade Crabapple Jelly. Sometimes, to Robbie's great delight, an apple pie made from some of the apples given the day before. Returning the gesture was important as a matter of respect and gratitude. Folks had a variety of ways of showing appreciation, whilst a few people reciprocated only to satisfy their pride so as not to feel beholden to anyone. Although a different sentiment it was still appreciated.

When Mrs. Boon came round Anne would say, "I was just about to make a pot of tea. Will you stay for one?"

Mrs. Boon never refused although she knew Anne was not 'just about to' brew a pot.

"Oh alright, just a quick one then but only if you're making one. I can't stay long," she would say while settling onto a kitchen chair.

It was an opportunity for a chat and to catch up on village gossip of which Mrs. Boon took great pride in knowing all the latest details. The gesture of tea was always reciprocated by Mrs. Boon when Anne visited. Robbie liked it when she came because she always had a biscuit in her apron pocket for him. Mrs. Boon's biscuits always tasted better than their own.

As more men joined the forces, the demand for women to join the Land Army increased. This appealed to Anne and she decided that a little extra cash would come in handy. She was hesitant about leaving Robbie but hoped it would lift her sprits by mixing more often with other women. Getting started was easy but she had to make arrangements for Robbie to be cared for during the day.

Mrs. Boon suggested that Mrs. Sparrow might be worth a try. Standing barely five feet tall and carrying more weight than she would admit, she swayed from side to side when she walked. She was a kind old widow lady who clearly loved children. Mrs. Sparrow had never remarried after her husband's death in France in 1917, feeling she would be unfaithful to him and his memory. Yet she had a jolly, cheerful personality with a ready smile for everyone and prided herself on always doing what was right, even when it was not to her personal advantage. She had often said, "The Good Lord'll be my judge and I don't want to give 'im any cause to turn me away when the day comes."

It was agreed that for three shillings she would care for Robbie five days a week, give him his lunch and occupy him until late afternoon when Anne would collect him. The money was not important to Mrs. Sparrow but it would help, having seen hard times before and knew how to cope. Now she enjoyed looking after Robbie and relished his company. Her pride was boosted in the knowledge that she was not too old to be useful and be trusted with responsibility. By allowing Anne to work, she patriotically considered this as her contribution to the war effort. She fussed over Robbie with kindness and gentle authority, making it inevitable that he would became very fond of her in a short time. When Anne collected him each afternoon, Mrs. Sparrow would bend down with a little groan to give him a hug and kiss his cheek. The first time that Robbie responded by hugging her neck and returning the kiss, she became emotional. Anne, who was watching on, was touched. Mrs. Sparrow had wanted children of her own but she and her husband had decided to wait until World War One was over before starting a family.

It became a daily ritual for Robbie to get up early, wash, dress, have breakfast and ride on the special seat that had been fitted to his mother's bicycle. A wicker basket was strapped to the handlebars where Anne put her Docky Bag containing sandwiches and a Corona bottle full of cold tea with no milk or sugar. Robbie sat between his mother's knees with his feet on little footrests and holding tightly onto the handlebars he would yell, "Faster, go faster."

Anne peddled harder and they laughed as the wind rushed over their faces. On cold mornings, their eyes would stream and tears ran slowly back to Robbie's ears, leaving a faint white residue of salt. The morning ride was always fun for Robbie. Anne, wearing strong trousers tied at the ankles with string and a turban fashioned from a headscarf, they were a regular sight in the village. Robbie became used to getting up early, enjoying the stillness, which he filled with anticipation of the adventures he would have that day. Believing it was entirely his to do with as he pleased.

No time was wasted at Mrs. Sparrow's house. He was dropped off, given a hug and a kiss before being told to be a good boy. Then he watched his mother ride away. On the first day he was upset when she left. But Mrs. Sparrow was quick to get his attention with a few comforting words and the promise of a special jam tart she had made him. Taking his hand, she led Robbie indoors while he looked over his shoulder to see his mother disappear through the village.

Having grown up in The Fens, Anne responded well to farm work and enjoyed the company of the other women who were always ready to show her the ropes. But she hesitated at their occasional lewd jokes and comments. These were mostly about intimate moments with their husbands or boyfriends, things Anne thought might be remembered by a married couple but never spoken of publicly. Or 'the thing or two' they would teach an unsuspecting farm boy 'if they ever got him in the hay.' All idle boasts and bravado but Anne thought them in poor taste, often considering what their husbands would think if they had heard.

Before two weeks had passed, Anne was leading Clydesdales pulling carts. She loved the horses and was not intimidated by their size as some women were. She thought of them as gentle giants which never complained at hard work. Anne felt they liked her too, especially when she spoke to them quietly with words of encouragement, patted them and rubbed their noses. When in season, she brought them windfall apples from the orchard, a tasty treat they clearly enjoyed.

Within a few months, Anne had done celery pricking, potato picking, onion wringing, cob catching, sugar beet singling and even driven a tractor. On rainy days, it was usual to mend hessian sacks in a big timber barn. Anne was self-conscious at having never managed the pitch of voice that other Fen women had mastered, enabling them to hold conversations across the fields. In a short time, Anne's hands became hardened to the work. Her lips and the back of her hands were often chapped. Sometimes her back ached badly from constant bending. Like all the women, she accepted it as 'to be expected.'

Onion wringing paid the most and women worked hard to fill as many sacks as they could. Each was paid according to the number of full sacks they produced. No concern was given to the fact that their hands were sore and would smell of stale onions for days afterwards. Anne diligently pulled onions from her two allocated rows, wrung the tops off and dropped them into her cob. She occasionally stood with her hands on her hips leaning backwards to relieve the awful back pain of constantly bending over. It took five cobs to fill a sack. Trying as hard as she could, she was not able to keep up with the other women who seemed to consistently pull, twist and drop an onion in one swift movement. They had already finished their rows while Anne was only two thirds of the way along hers.

She asked Amy how they managed to work so fast.

Amy laughed saying, "Not used to farm work are you Anne?"

"Not really, although I know what to do, it's just hard to keep up with you girls sometimes," she replied.

"Well, have you noticed how the onions with dried out stalks wring off easily and the others are a bit tougher, so you have to give them an extra twist and pull harder. It all takes time you know. Look at my cob. What do you see?"

"A cob," Anne replied, unsure of what she was supposed to notice.

"Look here in the rim." Amy pointed to a single sided razor blade wedged into the weave.

"Now if you can't twist the top off in one go, push it down over the blade as you drop the onion in the cob." A cheeky grin appeared on Amy's face.

"But you can't let the boss or one of the men see you or you'll get the sack."

"Why?" Anne asked.

Amy looked about to see who might be listening before continuing.

"When you wring the stalks off, you twist and seal the stalk but when you cut'em, moisture can get in and they might rot."

Anne was learning that the 'old hands' knew many shortcuts.

Through the months, the days passed happily for Anne but there were times of distress in the early mornings and sometimes a tear when the later bombers flew low over the fields preparing to land. Sometimes she could see damage or a smoking engine, always thinking how brave those young men were and remembering Ross. The other women understood and left her to her inner thoughts as she stood in the fields staring skyward. Not all her evenings were sad as she and Robbie amused each other and talked about the day. Each bedtime carried the same ritual. Tuck him in, give him a kiss and say,

"Night, night."

"Sweet repose," Robbie would reply.

"If you fall out of bed."

"You'll squash your nose," He would add with contented giggles.

Then she would settle down with a cup of tea and listen to the wireless whilst doing a bit of sewing or knitting.

The weeks passed happily until the day Robbie waited anxiously at Mrs. Sparrow's gate for his mother to collect him. She was late that day. The picture he had drawn was in his hand ready to show her, but she didn't come. After a while another woman came, quickly dropped her bicycle into the privet hedge and hurried to speak to Mrs. Sparrow. To Robbie they appeared very serious and he got the same bad feeling he'd had the day the airman came to talk to his mother. When the woman left, Mrs. Sparrow could see Robbie's concern and struggled to get down on her knees in front of him, steadying herself with the edge of the table.

"Now there my Sunshine, your Mummy has had a bit of an accident and has been taken to hospital. Now don't you worry, she'll be alright soon enough, so for now you can stay with me."

Robbie had lots of questions and was clearly upset. Mrs. Sparrow hugged him saying:

"Now don't you fret my love, you'll be safe here with me until we know what's what."

"Where is my Mummy?" Robbie asked.

"I want to see her. What's wrong with her?"

"I don't know exactly my lovey. All I know is that she's had a fall and is in the RAF hospital at Ely," Mrs. Sparrow said with a deep sigh.

"When we know a bit more I'll tell you dear." But Robbie was still very anxious and wanted his mother.

"You'll be staying with me for a few days until your Mummy gets better dear." Mrs. Sparrow repeated.

"I want to see my Mummy." Robbie demanded.

Mrs. Sparrow distracted him saying, "You better tell me what you want for your dinner. I got a sausage or two? Now push that chair over here so's I can pull meself up."

The next day another woman came and spoke with Mrs. Sparrow for a short while. After she had left, Mrs. Sparrow told Robbie that his mother had been cob catching. As the cart floor was gradually covered with potatoes, she lost her balance and had fallen backwards, landing hard across the side of the cart. She had then toppled over into the field. Robbie was upset.

"I want my Mummy! I want to see her!"

"So you shall, but not just now my lovely. She might be hurt bad. It's her back you see, and she can't walk. You can see her after the Doctor says she's well enough for visitors."

After a moment Mrs. Sparrow added, "she sends you her love and wants you to be a good boy."

She felt guilty at making things up but knew Anne would say it anyway and it would comfort Robbie. Mrs. Sparrow heard speculation in the village that Anne may never walk again but did not tell Robbie.

The bed in Mrs. Sparrow's back bedroom was not as comfortable as his own. It was darker in there too, with the musty smell of a room rarely visited.

"Where is my Mummy?" Robbie asked at breakfast.

"As I said dear, she's in hospital and probably will be for some time yet if you ask me."

After a few seconds, the old lady turned and waddled away muttering to herself.

"Poor little mite, first his father, now this. I don't know."

A few days later, Robbie and Mrs. Sparrow climbed aboard an Eastern Counties bus for the trip Ely to see Anne. Robbie was both impatient and excited. The journey of only a few miles took far too long for him. Having to wait a while in Ely for a bus to Littleport which would stop by the hospital, only added to Robbie's frustration.

He noticed little about the hospital other than the clinical smell and a corridor that was so long he could not see the end. The pale green walls converged and seemed to touch in the distance. They turned right into a ward with about twenty beds in two rows of ten. Robbie hesitated a moment when he first saw his mother, surprised at the darkness under her eyes and her pale complexion. He ran forwards, threw himself at her and tried to embrace her. She smiled when she saw him coming then grimaced in pain when Robbie grabbed her. Mrs. Sparrow gently eased him away.

"Why don't you just hold Mummy's hand dear," she said.

Then she placed a copy of Woman's Day, along with a brown paper bag containing a few apples, on the bedside cabinet.

"They are off your own trees dear," she said as she stepped back to sit on the visitors' chair.

Anne was pleased to see Robbie and Mrs. Sparrow. They wanted to know what had happened but it was difficult for Anne to explain.

"I remember we had hardly started. There were spuds rolling around on the bottom of the cart. I must have stood on one and lost my balance. I don't remember much else after falling backwards, until I woke up in here."

Robbie sat on the side of the bed whilst holding his mother's hand. It was uncomfortable for Anne but she considered the extra pain was well worth seeing her Robbie again and to be so close.

"I hope you are being a good boy with Mrs. Sparrow?" She asked with a smile, already knowing the answer.

Robbie answered with a serious. "Yes Mummy."

Then Mrs. Sparrow said, "He's a proper little treasure e' is, and good company too. I got him shelling peas yesterday, did a lovely job didn't you sweetheart."

Robbie nodded while his mother smiled at him with pride.

The women speculated about how long Anne would be in hospital and about Robbie's ongoing care. Sometimes they spoke in indirect terms so as not to upset him.

"He can stay with me for as long as you like and don't you go worrying about paying nothing. He's a good boy an

29

we'll take good care of 'im. N' we'll come and see you as often as we can."

Anne was relieved and thanked Mrs. Sparrow.

After an hour, a nurse walked down the ward telling visitors that visiting time was now over. It had gone far too quickly. Anne reassured Robbie that she would come home as soon as she could, telling him to be a good boy and that she loved him very much. She thanked Mrs. Sparrow again for his care and for bringing him to the hospital. Finally she beckoned Robbie to her so she could kiss him good-bye.

Desperation overcame Anne as she watched them walk away. She missed her little boy terribly and would have given anything to go with them. Her anxiety heightened as she considered that she was the one who should be looking after Robbie, irrespective of how well Mrs. Sparrow cared for him. She wondered with some apprehension how Robbie was feeling at not seeing her every day, and questioned if he was anxious, unhappy, eating and sleeping properly even though Mrs. Sparrow had assured her everything was fine, as she would. Anne mildly consoled herself in the knowledge that Mrs. Sparrow would give him the best she could.

As they reached the door to leave, Robbie turned and waved. He looked sad and it upset Anne even more. A picture of him standing there, holding Mrs. Sparrow's hand, became indelibly imprinted on her memory.

Over the following months, Anne saw many sights she wished she had not. Injured airmen came and went. Some had bandaged heads, arms or legs. Others had a combination of them and the most awful burns. Each one upset her greatly, making her think of Ross and wondering how he had died. She prayed it was mercifully quick, that he was not in pain whilst plummeting earthward, knowing that he was about to die.

3

In the following month Robbie saw his mother twice each week. It was a tiring trek for Mrs. Sparrow, and one that did not go unnoticed. She did not seem to have the strength and enthusiasm she once did and looked tired. Anne wondered if she would be able to cope with Robbie much longer.

Robbie was sitting by Mrs. Sparrow's front door trying to make his brightly painted clay marbles stay in a straight line on the step. A polished black car with painted white rimmed mudguards pulled up outside the gate. He watched inquisitively as a man wearing a dark suit and spectacles climbed from the driver's seat followed by a lady from the passenger side. They came through the gate, up the short garden path to the front door and knocked. Robbie quickly moved his marbles away so they would not get crushed. The man ignored Robbie but the lady looked down and smiled. Her smile was not warm but a gesture of perceived obligation. Her lips curled but her eyes showed little emotion. Mrs. Sparrow invited them in; she had clearly been expecting them and was very nervous.

Robbie discretely hovered in the background trying to overhear their conversation. He didn't understand what was being said but instinctively knew they were talking about him. Occasionally, they glanced his way with a purposeful look. He became worried and a little afraid. The man showed Mrs. Sparrow some papers and asked her to sign one, which she did with an anguished look. Robbie managed to hear only a few words which were spoken throughout the conversation. Although he recognised his mother's name, hospital, visits, and approval, he could see that whatever was happening, Mrs. Sparrow was not happy about it.

Before another fifteen minutes had passed, Robbie was being hugged by Mrs. Sparrow as she said goodbye. With a sad look she had explained that he was to go with the man and lady. They would look after him until his mother came home from hospital. Mrs. Sparrow's eyes glazed as she said a final goodbye and wished him well with her parting words, "Now you be a good boy for these nice people and everything will be fine. You'll see."

They waved to each other as the car drove away, Mrs. Sparrow dabbed her eyes as she returned to the house which now seemed strangely empty.

Robbie was unhappy and confused. His small brown suitcase was on the seat next to him in the back of car. It contained his clothes, a Boy's Own Annual that he could not read but he enjoyed looking at the pictures, his colouring book and a few crayons. He clutched an old worn shoe polish tin containing his clay marbles. He liked the tin because it had a picture of a Kiwi on it, just like his father's tie clip.

"Where is my Mummy? Are we going to see her?" Robbie asked.

"Sorry son, no," the man said.

"Where are we going?"

"To Dr. Barnardo's."

"But I'm not sick, I want to go home," Robbie replied.

The lady looked over her shoulder and smiled at the innocence of his reply, but nothing more was said.

This was only the second time Robbie had been in a car. For the rest of the journey he sat quietly, full of apprehension as he stretched to look out of the side window. In the far distance he could see a huge building with a tall tower standing above everything else, even the trees. He thought it looked like a big church, specially put there so it could be seen from miles around. He had asked what it was when they went past it on the way to the hospital. Mrs. Sparrow said it was a Cathedral. It must be the one he had heard people talk about when they said they hoped it would not get bombed.

After driving for almost an hour past flat fields of dark earth, which to Robbie seemed to stretch for ever, they were in a town with lots of people, shops and old buildings. Some probably as old as the Cathedral, Robbie thought.

The car stopped outside a large Victorian house where they all got out. Whilst the man locked the car, the lady ushered him through the front door to a chair in the entrance hall.

"Wait here Robert," the woman said as she walked further down the corridor.

Robbie felt helpless, afraid and apprehensive as he looked around. From his position just inside the front door, he could see the man and woman in conversation with another man further down the hall. He received occasional glances and nods of apparent agreement in his direction. Robbie felt vulnerable and desperately wanted his mother. He considered running out the door but didn't know where to go or what he would do. Looking at the dull, austere interior of this big house, he was close to tears even though he could hear the distant sounds of other children, happy sounds, which ought to have been comforting. After a few minutes a big lady with a warm smile approached him.

"So you are Robert are you dear?" She rhetorically asked.

Robbie responded with a simple nod as he clutched his case even closer.

"I'm Mrs. Fletcher and I'm going to be looking after you from now on. Come with me dear and I'll show you where you'll sleep. There are other boys and girls here so you will have lots of nice new friends."

This was the first sign that he was not going back to Mrs. Sparrow and a feeling of trepidation welled up within him. She took him up three flights of stairs to a room at the top of the house containing six beds in two rows of three. The sides of the ceiling sloped to a flat portion in the middle above a single window at the end of the room. Robbie was shown to the bed closest to the window. After the stairs Mrs. Fletcher struggled to get her breath but managed to tell him this would be his bed. Later Robbie was pleased when he discovered that if he stood on the bed, he could see outside to the trees and lawns below. His small suitcase was taken from him and he was told to leave his treasured round polish tin and book on the bed. Seeing his reluctance Mrs. Fletcher said,

"It will be quite safe there dear."

But he never saw the tin again. He didn't care about the marbles, only the tin.

The large house was sombre and dull with many rooms and high, ornate yellowing ceilings. Mrs. Fletcher took him to the kitchen where he was given a sandwich and a glass of strange tasting milk before being taken to see a doctor.

"Now then young Robert take your clothes off, you can keep your underpants on. Let's take a look at you," the doctor said.

"Now come and stand in front of me over here."

The doctor sat forwards on the edge of his chair while Robbie stood between his knees. He thought this must be the Doctor Barnardo they had told him about. The Doctor poked and prodded him and made him say "arr" while his tongue was pressed down with the tail of a teaspoon. He tapped his chest and back with his fingers, then put a cold stethoscope on his front and back, followed by a quick look in his ears. Next Robbie was asked to sit while the doctor gently tapped each of his knees with a strange little hammer. Robbie smiled in surprise at the involuntary response of each leg as it jerked up. He didn't know that would happen and was amused. The doctor held each ankle in turn and stroked the underside of his feet with the edge of the spoon, making Robbie flinch, his toes curl down and almost laugh at the sensation.

Robbie had no clear idea what was going on and was apprehensive of what might happen next. He just wanted his mother, or even Mrs. Sparrow, to be hugged and told everything is alright.

"I want my Mummy," he said almost involuntarily.

The doctor looked at him, smiled and said, "All in good time my boy, all in good time."

It had been a big day for a Robbie, so much had happened, starting with his 'Bubble and Squeak' breakfast with Mrs. Sparrow, before being taken away. Now he was in a strange house, in a strange town and about to sleep in a strange room with five other boys he didn't know. He was afraid and confused.

Yet that night he slept surprisingly well after the other boys had talked to him for what seemed a very long time. Even after the lights had been switched off and they had been told to be quiet. They wanted to know all about him, so Robbie was bombarded with questions.

"What's your name?"

"Where are you from?"

"Why are you here?"

"Do you have any brothers or sisters?"

"Is your dad in the war?"

"What does he do?"

"Has he killed any Germans?"

"Do you have a mother?"

"Where is she?"

"Has your dad been killed in the war?"

It seemed that Robbie had little opportunity to ask questions of his own but shyly did his best to answer others.

Eventually he fell asleep leaving his own questions until another day. That night he heard one of the boys crying before falling asleep and Robbie, to his great embarrassment, wet the bed, something he could not remember doing before.

The routine of the house was easy to learn and he settled in quickly. He became good friends with a dark haired boy named Jeremy who was a little older than himself. His bed was across the room immediately opposite Robbie's. Their friendship provided solace for both of them and muffled their anxieties which grew fewer as a result. However Robbie was unable to adjust to the absence of his mother. He missed her greatly, longed for a loving word, to feel the soft warmth of her body when she hugged him and her light scented smell. Sometimes he tried not to think of her because he knew he would get upset and might cry. It made him feel guilty but he didn't want to be seen crying, not even for his mother, knowing the other boys would tease him. Yet his efforts had an adverse effect and he only thought of her more.

Jeremy was beyond his years with his compassion and understanding and would suggest quiet places where they could talk alone. They shared their fears and desires, would talk about the past and what the future might hold. Discussing experiences in confidence strengthened their bond. Their friendship proved a great comfort since now both had someone to turn to who was not an authoritarian figure, someone who would listen, understand, not judge them or brush their concerns aside. They soon became special to each other.

Jeremy had been evacuated from London to live with foster parents in the country for the duration of the war. He had been happy and enjoyed living with his temporary mother and father, even though they were much older than his natural parents. Then, unknown to him at the time, his parents had been killed in a bombing raid. A month later his surrogate parents received a letter telling them that Jeremy was to be taken to a Dr. Barnardo's Home. They were upset since they had come to love Jeremy and hoped to adopt him as their own. However it was not permitted due to their advanced age.

"After proper consideration by the authorities a decision had been made and it was final. What is more there will be no further discussion on the matter." They had been told.

It was only a matter of time before Jeremy was collected and escorted to the big house in Cambridge where he eventually met Robbie. Both boys missed the warmth and love of their mothers.

Once or twice Robbie thought he had detected his mother's fragrance on the lady who made the beds. Although he didn't see her every day, he was still drawn to her. She was always too busy to respond to him or any of the boys. But seeing that Robbie liked to watch her, she would give him a warm smile. Once she put her arm around his shoulder as she brushed past to get to the other side of his bed. His heart leapt, he felt like holding onto her, wanting her to hug him the way his mother had.

There are but three events which Robbie would clearly remember from that time. The first was when Mr. Robertson, who was in charge, had ordered all the boys to stay in the assembly room after morning prayers. He was a big man with a full, red face and a big belly that tried to escape between the buttons of his waistcoat and roll over the top of his belt. His fat round face reminded Robbie of a Toby Jug that sat on Mrs. Sparrow's sideboard.

On this occasion he had a very stern face and gave the boys an angry lecture about honesty. He was so cross that he frightened some of the younger ones. Vowing to catch and severely punish the boy who had taken a jar of homemade jam from the kitchen, saying, "It is war time and such items are very precious. How would the good ladies of the church feel if they knew the produce they had toiled over and donated to the orphanage had been stolen?"

The word 'orphanage' startled Robbie. He knew what it was but only now did he realise with some degree of shock that he must be in one.

"Orphanages are for orphans! Am I an Orphan? I can't be. I have a mother, only she's in hospital!" He later told Jeremy.

The more Robbie considered, the more upset he became and eventually asked one of the cleaning ladies if Dr. Barnardo's House really was an orphanage.

"Well…yes dear, you are all orphans here."

Robbie was upset and indignant.

"But I'm not an orphan," he retorted.

The second event took place the day they were taken for a picnic to a place called 'The Backs.' Robbie remembered the name because he thought it was a silly one to call a place. It was a large grassy park like area by a river. On the opposite side were old buildings, just like those he had seen when he had first arrived.

There they played games, laughing and shouting with the fun of it all. Some boys had tried to play cricket but the grass was too long and they could not bowl properly so decided to play Rounders instead. This led to excited shouts of instructions to run to the next corner when the ball was struck. Later they were told to sit and were given sandwiches followed by small homemade cupcakes. Jeremy had commented how strange it was that the same sandwiches, as in the home, tasted so much better at a picnic. Robbie agreed.

When they had grudgingly taken a mandatory rest, which they all thought totally unnecessary, the boys decided to play football whilst the girls picked buttercups and daisies. Some girls made daisy chains. It was a challenge to avoid the cowpats scattered in the grass. But in his excitement, Jeremy accidentally stepped in a fresh one and had dark green cow dung over his sandal and foot. It could not be cleaned or the smell removed by wiping it on the grass so Jeremy went to the river to wash it off. Robbie thought it hilariously funny and exaggerated the awful smell by holding his nose as he shouted "Poo." In reaching out to the water, Jeremy lost his balance and slipped in. None of the grown-ups had noticed since their attention was captured by the screams of excitement from the girls now playing 'What's the time Mr. Wolf'. Even when Robbie called for help, his voice was lost amongst their screams. He ran to the river and was frantic as he saw Jeremy disappearing under the water.

After a second or two he reappeared, shocked and spluttering, standing up to his neck in water amongst the lily-pads. Fortunately a man in a punt had seen him slip, so with a long wooden pole, he reached out to Jeremy providing him with something to hold onto. Whilst coughing up brown water, Jeremy scrambled onto the river bank, helped by Robbie's outstretched hand and the timber pole.

Robbie told the housemother what had happened whilst Jeremy stood next to him picking his cold, wet clothes away from his body. He told her it was an accident in the hope it would lessen any possible punishment. She was angry with both of them saying they should have stayed away from the river. She reminded them of her warning at the outset, which she repeated for effect.

"Now don't go near the river I said. We don't want anyone falling in. Do you remember that?"

The boys nodded sheepishly.

She spoke in a manner suggesting that, in her opinion, she had totally fulfilled her obligation of care by telling them, even though she and the other housemother had failed to see the boys go near the water or hear Robbie's calls for help.

Other children quickly gathered around to see Jeremy in his wet clothes and hear the story. The girls giggled and made teasing remarks but were quickly silenced by a housemother and told to get back to their games. Jeremy began to shiver as his nose and lips turned blue.

"Well I suppose we had better get you back and into dry clothes before you catch pneumonia and die," the woman angrily barked.

So Robbie, Jeremy and the housemother walked back through the town to the Dr. Barnardo's Home. She was clearly upset with them, saying very little along the way and rarely relaxing her pinching lips and scowl. The boys were not sure if it was because of the inconvenience and extra work they had caused her or that she might be in trouble with Mr. Robertson, who may hold her responsible for not paying attention.

The third event that Robbie remembered, which had raised his hopes that his mother would come for him, was when the children had all been taken to the main hall where a wireless had been installed for the occasion. There was a sense of excitement as all the children sat crossed-legged on the floor. Mr. Robertson stood by the wireless whilst other staff sat on chairs around the room. Then a few minutes before 3pm he called for silence in the room. He informed everyone, with much pomp and authority, that they were about to hear something of great importance, 'an historical event no less'. There was murmuring and fidgeting amongst the children as the wireless was turned on. Everyone waited for it to warm up and for voices to be heard. Mr. Robertson turned a dial on the front to make the words clearer and louder. Again they were told to settle down and be quiet.

Sitting silently, they listened to Winston Churchill announce that Germany had surrendered and the war in Europe was over. The boys all knew that it was important but did not comprehend the true magnitude of the event.

Mr. Robertson listened intently, hanging onto his lapels with his thumbs pointing upwards as he stood motionless staring into a far corner of the ceiling. Mrs. Fletcher sat with her hands in her lap occasionally dabbing a tear in the corner of her eyes. She reminded Robbie of Mrs. Sparrow when she had said goodbye. After Mr. Churchill had finished, the wireless was switched off. Mr. Robertson inhaled, expanding his chest with pride as he turned to the gathering and announced.

"What a wonderful day this is for all of us, VE Day. We all have good reason to rejoice and be happy. We will now have a better world, one of hope and love where families will be reunited again. Today sees the start of a new era of better understanding in the world. I have asked the ladies to organize a party to celebrate."

The children's excitement was reflected in their smiles and murmurings, more so for the news of a party than anything else. Mr. Robertson talked for a while longer but Robbie was not listening. His imagination had already been captured and his thoughts were elsewhere. He didn't understand what 'VE' was but hung onto the words "families will be reunited again."

Robbie was convinced this meant his mother would now come for him and was overjoyed. They were all asked to stand whilst Mr. Robertson led them in a prayer of thanks.

Some years later Robbie learned that it had been 8th May 1945 and calculated that he must have been four and a half years old.

Over the following days he expected his mother to walk in at any moment and his excitement flared every time a visitor came. When a week had passed and his mother had not come, he started to get anxious. A week was a long time for a little boy, full of hope and longing. In anticipation of his mother coming, Robbie asked his housemother for his suitcase back.

"Good heavens boy, whatever for?" She asked.

"So that when my mother comes for me, I'll be ready."

"My, my young Robbie, you really are anxious to leave us," she said as she walked away.

He was annoyed and just wanted his suitcase. Such a simple request he thought. Later he told Jeremy what had happened.

"Nothing has changed since that 'VE' day, not one thing. It's just the same as it always was. I don't know what all the fuss was about!"

His mother had not come for him and there was no better world' in Robbie's mind.

The following months were uneventful as they followed their daily, somewhat regimented, routines. Robbie and Jeremy fitted their adventures around their chores. Occasionally they helped in the kitchen with simple chores like peeling potatoes or scraping carrots. New potatoes were always fun to peel as they were placed in a bucket of water and stirred vigorously with a heavy stick until all the fragile skin came off in little pieces. Although they never did any washing themselves, they were required to carry the clothes baskets to and from the clothes lines on washdays, a task Robbie and Jeremy usually did together by holding a handle at each end of the basket.

Robbie began to experience new conflicting emotions. He was sad and upset that his mother had not come for him. Yet the more he considered it, his sadness would turn to anger and frustration. He began to question her love for him even though he knew full well she had once loved him. However the conflict didn't last long. It was more comfortable to believe she really did still love him.

Mr. Robertson had been keen on sport and exercise so encouraged the boys to take part whenever they could. Robbie liked cross country running, even if it was only through the parks and along the river towpaths. It gave him a feeling of space and freedom that was exhilarating. He felt he could run all day long, and he never wanted it to end. Sometimes he stretched his arms out and imagined he could fly, dipping and turning like a swallow. Free at last.

A few days following Robbie's fifth birthday, his housemother took him aside saying.

"Well young Robert, you are a big boy now, so after Christmas you'll be going to the school in the big room."

As he was now a 'big boy', he hoped he would no longer have to take the daily dose of Cod Liver Oil. However it was not to be since it was given to every child as a matter of routine, in the evening just before going to bed. The horrible taste lingered until he fell asleep. When he could get away with it, he would deliberately avoid cleaning his teeth. Then after swallowing the Cod Liver Oil, he would tell his housemother that he had forgotten, expecting to be sent to the bathroom where he would find the round tin containing a hard block of pink toothpaste, which he could use to rid his mouth of the awful taste. Robbie was inwardly amused when Mrs. Fletcher told him off for forgetting to brush his teeth, but he always apologized with great sincerity, enhancing his sense of achievement.

School started in the middle of January and was welcomed since he enjoyed doing something different and more stimulating. First he learned the alphabet, the sounds of letters, to print his name and to count beyond ten. He also learned how to tell the time. Some evenings he would take a pencil and paper and pretend he could write by connecting loops and letters together at random. He secretly wrote letters to his mother ending with 'Love Robbie'. Although illegible, he would read them back to himself, giving the letters meaning to match what he wanted to say. Writing 'proper' letters to his mother motivated him to learn how. Sometimes he wrote letters from his mother to himself, reading them back many times, reciting the things he wanted to hear her say.

"I am getting better, I love you, I miss you, I will come for you soon." Always followed by kisses.

Robbie was soon ahead of the class in English and was enthused by what he could discover from reading. He particularly liked stories that allowed his mind to escape into an adventure. Huckleberry Finn and Treasure Island were his favorites. He read so much that he was soon proficient beyond his years.

One of the privileges of going to school was to be given a small bottle of milk every morning. He and his classmates would compete to see who could drink the whole bottle fastest. They were always given a straw but Robbie found he could win if he drank straight from the bottle. The boys discovered a game with the foil top. If they could get it off the bottle still in shape, they would hold it between the tips of two fingers and flick it, making it spin and float away like a miniature flying saucer. The impromptu competition was to see who could make one fly the furthest.

One lunch time in late spring, he, Jeremy and four boys from his dormitory were told to report to Mr. Robertson's office immediately after school. They thought they had unknowingly done something wrong and were worried all that afternoon, speculating with apprehension as to why they had been summoned.

It was with trepidation that they knocked on Mr. Robertson's door and waited to be invited in to stand in a line before him. Mr. Robertson was seated behind his big oak desk, making him appear even more squat and fatter than he really was. Robbie's image of a Toby Jug returned. Mrs. Fletcher and another man, whom none of the boys had seen before, were sitting side by side on a worn Chesterfield sofa. Mrs. Fletcher was clutching her handkerchief, anxiously twisting it through her fingers.

Mr. Robertson spoke first.

"Well boys, as a reward for your good behaviour, diligence at school and excellent attitudes, you have all been chosen for a great adventure. You would like that wouldn't you?"

With the relief of not being in trouble, the boys eagerly nodded their agreement.

The question assumed acceptance and there could be no other reply than "Yes." Mr. Robertson raised his eyebrows to the man on the sofa inviting him to speak.

"Do you boys know what adoption is?" He asked.

Two of the boys had vacant looks and shook their heads whilst the others nodded saying, "Yes."

"Well it means that you could leave this Dr. Barnardo's Home and be taken in by a family. You would have a proper mother and father and live just like normal boys."

Two things immediately went through Robbie's mind. First, he had never considered himself to be anything other than normal. Second, he already had a mother. What would she think if he now went off to live with someone else, and how would she find him? Here at Barnardo's she knew where he was.

The man took a breath and raised his voice a little saying, "Well boys, you are very lucky indeed to have this chance."

None fully understood the full extent of what was to happen to them but they were asked if they had any questions. Robbie immediately spoke out.

"My mother won't be pleased if I'm adopted. I want to go home, to my own home please."

"And your name is?" The man asked.

"Robert Spalding Sir."

The man shuffled through the six files on his lap and opened one. He paused for a few moments and said in an assuming manner, without feeling.

"But you do know that your mother is dead, don't you?"

Robbie was horrified and unable to respond. He just stood there, frozen like a shop mannequin, in a fixed stare, trying to comprehend what he had just heard. Mrs. Fletcher saw his shock and felt his pain but said nothing, resisting her instinct to embrace and comfort him. She might do that later in private. She knew that Robbie had never been told, and saw this was a cruel way to find out.

Tears streamed down Robbie's cheeks. He wanted to shout at the man.

"She is not dead! She 'will' come for me!" But he was unable to make a sound.

Mr. Robertson took over the procedures again, telling the boys they were especially lucky because they were going to Australia where their new homes and families were waiting for them. Both Robbie and Jeremy had little idea where Australia was but knew it was where kangaroos lived and that it was very hot.

That evening brought confusion, worries, questions and excitement to the boys in their little dormitory. Robbie just wanted to be left alone to ponder and grieve. Jeremy understood and let him be. Robbie quietly cried himself to sleep that night.

In the morning they had breakfast, went to the regular morning service and school as usual. Robbie was pensive. One of the boys asked the teacher where Australia was. A globe was produced showing them it was on the other side of the world. It seemed a very long way to go.

"But my mother will never find me there!" Robbie said. There was no answer.

"What is it like there Sir?" Jeremy asked.

"Well, I have never been there myself of course but I know it's very big, quite hot and dry. I understand it's a wonderful place to live with plenty of open space and with lots of beaches. They have millions of sheep and wild kangaroos, grow lots of oranges and bananas too. Oh yes, they produce good cricketers too. You boys who are going there are very lucky, and I'm certain you will be very happy there."

Over the following weeks, Robbie and Jeremy fell back into their usual routines although Robbie continually thought of what the man had said about his mother. The pain never went away. He was upset, angry and confused. In his heart he could not, would not believe his mother had died. He would never accept that. Never to see his mother again was too much to comprehend. His heart played tricks confusing his mind.

4

The day before the six boys were due to leave for Australia they were summoned to Mr. Robertson's office for the last time, and were introduced to a lady named Margaret who would accompany them on their journey. They were told it was necessary to change their names as it would be better for them to have the same names as the families they were going to in Australia. Robert was to become Nicholas , James Thorne, and Jeremy would be Christopher Norman Cole. The other boys were given their new names and all were told to start using them immediately.

"I don't want to change my name. My mother won't be able to find me," Robbie pleaded.

"Now then young Robert, I mean Nicholas, you know that your mother will not be looking for you, don't you," Mr. Robertson replied.

"She will, she will! And I will always be Robert Peter Spalding underneath!" Robbie retorted.

He understood what was said to him but still did not accept his mother's death.

The boys were unhappy about changing their names but the explanation seemed logical, and they knew they could do nothing about it.

Mr. Robertson gave a short speech about the pride he had in them as ambassadors of the orphanage and hoped they would all continue to be a credit to Dr. Barnardo's. Finally, he wished them well for the future and shook their hands. It was the first time Robbie had shaken hands with anyone. Mr. Robertson's hand felt very large.

The journey to Tilbury the next morning was interesting but uneventful. On the train to Liverpool Street Station, they were reminded to use their new names. Both Nicholas and Christopher knew this was an important day in their lives and that nothing would ever be the same again. It prompted Nick to ponder his more distant past, before Barnardo's, when he was Robert. In his heart he still was and always would be Robert. He became frantic as he considered how his mother would ever manage to find him again, especially with a different name and living on the other side of the world.

As the train rumbled on with a repetitive clatter, Nick's mind began to wander. Try as he might, he could never recall exactly what his father looked like. He thought it odd, as though he was betraying his memory. It left him feeling guilty. Mostly he remembered the blue uniform and the small gold Kiwi tie clip he always wore. He called it "My Lucky Kiwi." Nick knew his father had been killed in the war and often wondered how he had died. In frustration he would ask himself, "Why did it have to happen to 'my' father?"

He was sure his life would be quite different if his father was still alive, and his mother would have been happier too. The memories now seemed distant and far off as if they were from another world, another time, and could have belonged to someone else.

When the boys first saw the S.S. Asturias they were in awe of its great size, having had no idea ships could be so big. Painted all white, it was impressive and the boys were excited. They were asked to stand in groups to have their photographs taken with the ship in the background. Once on board they were taken to their shared cabins. With great relief, Nick and Chris were together. An hour later they were taken to a place on deck where they were shown how to put a life jacket on and told to remember this place because it was their muster point in an emergency.

The S.S. Asturias sailed on the high tide that evening. Crowds of people had gathered on the quay and when the ship began to move, people waved and called out across the widening gap. However, the boys could not understand why some people looked happy and others cried. A band played on the quay and people on the ship threw streamers down while the horn sounded. It was so loud and deep that it made their tummies vibrate, much to their amusement.

Nick was sick for the first two days and found it more bearable if he lay down. He didn't eat, only drank. Chris was fine but would have preferred to have had Nick with him when he explored the ship.

"You'll be fine in a couple of days when we've crossed Biscay," a steward told him.

Later Chris was able to play tour guide when Nick was feeling better. Their first port of call was Tenerife. Nick and Chris were surprised at how warm it was. High up behind the town they saw their first ever glimpse of a mountain, like a big grey cone reaching for the sky. While they were talking about it, a lady passenger overheard them and said it was an extinct volcano, not a mountain. This made it even more exciting.

Some local boys, not much older than themselves, paddled out to the ship in little boats, calling up to them, but Nick and Chris could not understand what they were saying. One of the adult passengers tossed coins into the clear water and the boys dived to retrieve them. When they surfaced they held the coins aloft with big grins on their faces, shouting for more. Nick and Chris were amazed at how long the boys could hold their breath and tried to hold theirs for the same amount of time. As a boy dived, they took deep breaths which they held for as long as they could. Yet well before the diver returned to the surface, Nick and Chris burst for air, gasping and laughing at the same time.

opened his mouth to let a piece of apple fall from his tongue. He didn't find it funny and threw the apple away in disgust.

Anne came to the garden to ask what the fuss was about.

"Daddy gave me a big green apple to eat. He said it was nice but it was horrible," Robbie told her, pulling a face to emphasize.

Ross was still laughing.

"That's really mean! You jolly well know those are cooking apples," Anne said, chastising her husband. As a result Ross picked Robbie up and apologised to satisfy Anne as much as his son.

Robbie liked to be pushed on the swing but not when it twisted around making him dizzy. He laughed with excitement when he went high causing his tummy to tingle when he came down, and he always wanted to be pushed for longer.

When it was time to finish, his father gave him a cuddle and said,

"Must go now Skipper, look after Mummy till I get back."

"Can't you stay? Do you have to go?" Robbie begged.

"Sorry Skip, I have to go or the boss will come looking for me."

"Who's your boss?"

"No.75 Squadron. Or should I say The Royal New Zealand Airforce."

Robbie looked sad as though he was about to cry at his father leaving.

"Oh come on then, just one more minute!" Ross said.

That minute soon became ten and Flight Sargent Ross Spalding would probably be late for his crew's briefing. He gave Robbie another hug, went indoors, hurriedly gathered his things, kissed his wife, told her he loved her and that he

Other small boats came too, mostly manned by adults or older boys and girls, selling all manner of things from fruit to sun hats. They were only in the Canary Islands for twenty-four hours, just long enough for the ship to take on provisions and fuel. Nick and Chris were fascinated by the whole scene. It was after this port of call that Nick and Chris tasted fresh pineapple for the very first time.

It seemed a long time before the ship docked in Cape Town. As they drew close, the view of Table Mountain behind the city impressed the boys. They were allowed to leave the ship in supervised groups and were given a tour of the city. They saw Lion Mountain and as a special treat were taken to the top of Table Mountain. This exceeded the boys' expectations and was especially exciting after the confinement of the ship. From the top, they could see the S.S. Asturias, which looked tiny, like a toy. It occurred to them that South Africa would be a nice place to stay. They thought it hilariously funny when seeing horses wearing straw hats with their ears sticking through, pointing and laughing every time they saw one.

Nick and Chris had never seen so many black people before, especially in one place. Between them they could only ever remember seeing two. But here they all looked very poor. Their clothes were mostly ragged and few had shoes, including those who worked on the docks. Nick was struck by the forlorn, sad look in their eyes. None of them smiled.

Life on board was quite different from anything they had experienced before. Every day activities were organised to amuse and stimulate them. Sometimes in the afternoon, magic shows and quizzes were organized especially for the children on board. There was a good library and they read all the Enid Blyton books they could find, especially The Famous Five, and any other books that appealed to their adventurous spirits. Margaret taught them to play chess, which they enjoyed immensely. When enough boys and girls were proficient they organized their own tournaments. Every morning they were taken for exercise on deck where they met other groups of children. The ship was so large they might not see many of them again until the next morning. Chris estimated there must be at least a hundred and fifty on board. Not all came for exercise at the same time but it was always fun, as the activities were often games and races. On many evenings there were concerts which they were allowed to go to if they were not showing too late. The food was the best they had known and varied from day to day.

They liked Margaret as she was kind, spoke nicely to them and was always thinking of what would please and occupy them. Her occasional hugs were wonderful and Nick always wanted them to last longer, but they made him miss his mother more.

Margaret was an Australian nurse returning home to Sydney after two years' training at Great Ormond Street Children's Hospital in London. Through a friend, she had heard that suitable people were being sought to escort groups of orphaned children to Australia. Given her profession, she was considered highly suitable for the job, and for Margaret it could not have been more opportune. For her it was a labour of love, and she received a modest fee with free passage to Australia.

Nick had his seventh birthday on board and Margaret organized a birthday cake with candles. His friends gathered around when the cake was presented to him. He was not sure what to do as this was his first ever birthday cake. Margaret led the other boys in singing "Happy Birthday." Which made Nick feel special. She told Nick, "you have to blow all the candles out with one big puff. Then you can make a wish but you can't tell anyone what it is or it won't come true."

Nick filled his lungs and blew as hard as he could. When the candles went out they all cheered. Nick squeezed his eyes tight shut, turned his face to the ceiling and silently wished.

"I wish that my mother will find me and take me home."

5

As the S.S. Asturias was docking in Fremantle, the boys saw no impressive mountains or city buildings. Everywhere looked quite ordinary, especially the large corrugated iron sheds along the quayside. Everyone noticed how very hot it was and some of the adults on board complained.

They could see people waiting for friends and loved ones to disembark. A few were calling out and waving. Some excited passengers waved back. It reminded the boys of leaving Tilbury where there had been lots of people waving and some crying, even a brass band had been there to see them off. Now, six weeks later, their fears and apprehension returned once more. A new phase of their lives was about to begin and none had any notion of what was to happen. Speculation was rife amongst all the children as to the sort of homes they would go to. It seemed all too strange, almost unreal to arrive in another country far from all they had known and be expected to accept complete strangers as a new mother and father. Maybe even brothers and sisters too.

Margaret told the boys in her group to neatly pack their belongings into their suitcases and get ready to leave. An air of excitement and cautious expectation lingered within the group. They didn't need to hurry but they packed immediately, such had been their conditioning at Dr. Barnardo's. It was only a short time before the boys were all clutching their suitcases and waiting with other groups on the deck for further instructions.

Nick and Chris were apprehensive. Nobody had told them what to expect, or anything about their new homes. They were left wondering if their future guardians would meet them off the ship. Of greatest anxiety was the thought of being separated, although deep down Nick and Chris thought it was inevitable at some time. However neither had mentioned it until now.

"I wonder what sort of family we'll go to," Nick contemplated.

"I don't mind as long as we can still see each other. We'll still be friends won't we?" Chris asked.

"Yes of course we will. I hope we will live in the same town."

Chris agreed and they both took comfort from the notion.

As they waited, two ladies were discussing the children. One commented that there had been one hundred and forty-seven "of these poor orphans" on board. Nick still hated being referred to as an orphan.

Before long Margaret ushered them down the gangway. Then as they congregated on the quay, she asked them to stand still, pointing at each in turn as she counted them. In her other hand was a brown attaché case. Two priests wearing black cassocks approached, introduced themselves and shook Margaret's hand. After a moment or two they pointed to a large black corrugated iron building and instructed the boys to follow them though the big sliding doors. Inside, one of the priests waited with the boys, whilst Margaret and the other priest went to a table at the far side. Wide-eyed and nervous, none of the boys spoke, nor did the priest speak to them. It was hot in the metal building but a breeze blew through the open doors on each side making it more bearable. They watched Margaret open her briefcase and take out a bundle of buff folders, each one tied shut with a piece if tape. The group watched as the priest shuffled through them and signed some papers which were given back to Margaret. In less than five minutes Margaret returned with the priest, who now carried the briefcase containing the folders.

The priest who had been with the boys counted them again as Margaret announced she was now going to leave them in the good care of the Christian Brothers. When the priest stopped counting, he told the boys to acknowledge their names as they were called out. When all were seen to be present, he nodded his acceptance to Margaret. Seeing the worried looks in their eyes, she assured them they would be fine, saying that she was certain they would have a wonderful new life in Australia and wished each one well with a hug before she left.

As she disappeared through the doors into the bright sunlight, the boys began to murmur. Everything that had been familiar to them was now gone. It was struck from their lives and again apprehension laced with fear crept in.

The priests did not introduce themselves, say where they were from or tell the boys where they were going. When they spoke, it was only to give instructions. They never smiled and referred to each other as 'Brother'. The boys were ordered to stand in line in front of the table to have their fingerprints taken by the police.

"They must think we are criminals or something!"
Nick said to Chris, deliberately loud enough for anyone else to hear.

"Silence!"

One of the priests shouted whilst staring at Nick as though trying to remember his face for some future recourse. The piercing stare unsettled Nick. All murmuring in the group stopped as they stared at the priest in shock. No one had ever spoken to them that way before.

One by one each of their fingers were rolled on an ink pad, then to be pressed onto marked squares on a sheet of white paper bearing their names. A piece of rag was provided for them to wipe the surplus ink from their fingers but the stain remained.

As each boy left the table, he was directed by name to one of two trucks, told to climb into the open back and sit quietly on wooden benches. Once all the boys had been processed, a priest climbed into the passenger side of each truck. Nick's truck shook and rattled as its engine begrudgingly clattered in to life, filling the air with blue smoke.

As they drove out of the huge shed, the boys observed everything around them with intense interest. After ten minutes, the trucks parted company going their separate ways. At that moment Nick and Chris were happy that they had been placed on the same truck. It was an uncomfortable ride and the boys would be pleased when it was over. Their journey lasted less than half an hour with the last one hundred yards along a dusty unsealed track.

When they had passed between two tall, white painted gate pillars with stone crosses atop, they knew their journey was almost at an end. Nick caught sight of a small plaque on one of the pillars. He could not be sure what it said, but it looked like 'Boys Town.' They were driven towards the largest building which was straight in front of the driveway, facing the gate. Chris said it looked rather like some of the big white buildings they saw in Cape Town, especially with the palm trees nearby. The other buildings were of a variety of styles and ages. They could see that a few were still being built, or being pulled down, they were not sure. There was an avenue of palm trees to the main building and areas of grass beyond, which clearly struggled to stay green in the hot sun. Nick caught a distant glimpse of a river. Of all the buildings the most appealing was the largest white one with a terracotta roof. It had a row of arches supporting a covered veranda across the front to offer protection from the sun.

When the truck stopped in front of the arches, the priest and the driver got out. Then, seemingly from out of nowhere, groups of boys gathered to see the new arrivals. They were poorly dressed and most did not have shoes. The driver went to the back of the truck to lower the tailboard then beckoned to the boys to climb down. The new arrivals were hot and thirsty as they looked about. No one spoke as several more priests came. One in particular seemed to be in charge and gave instructions to the driver. He was fat and wore a wrinkled black suit that looked too small. Once all the boys were off the truck, the driver immediately raised the tailboard and drove the truck out of sight.

There were no introductions or welcoming words from the priests, only commands.

"Leave your bags, cases and your jackets on the veranda and follow Brother David," A Brother shouted.

Another much younger priest raised his hand signaling that they were to follow him.

Pleased to be out of the sun beneath the arches, Brother David led them towards the end of the verandah where there was a wooden chair, a Jerry Can and a bowl. The boys were told to remove their shirts and make a line in front of the chair.

Each boy took his turn to sit on the chair and was told to tip his head back to prevent kerosene from running into his eyes. A boy of about fourteen years of age slowly poured the smelly liquid over their heads. Dripping and smelling, their scalps were scrubbed sore with vigorous combing by a second boy. Brother David said it would rid them of lice and they would need to get used to it. Nick was both offended and humiliated. He had never had lice and didn't have them now, but knew better than to protest.

After all the boys had been deloused, they were taken to a wash room, ordered to strip naked and wash themselves. Cold water and carbolic soap made their heads sting even more. The rectangular grey stone sinks were quite big enough to sit in if needed. Each had a single brass tap above it which the smaller boys could hardly reach. Eventually they would learn that after a few hours of sunshine, the first boys to wash would have hot or warm water since the pipes to the washroom ran along the outside of the building in the sun. It was the same in the showers. There were only a few pieces of soap and the towels were pieces of cloth that did not absorb moisture well, leaving the boys damp. Every boy took this opportunity to take a drink of water. They had been given nothing to drink since leaving the ship.

One of the Brothers monitored their progress as they washed, telling them not to take too long and occasionally shouting washing instructions. Another Brother took their clothes and shoes away. It was impossible to remove all the kerosene so the smell lingered.

Nick and Chris wondered what sort of place they had come to. This is not what they had been expecting and was surreal. They were directed to a room close by where they were given clothes. Although clean, they were old and worn. Shoes were not provided.

Nick asked Brother David if they could fetch their suitcases now. He responded with a curt 'No' without an explanation. They had already been taken from the front verandah and the boys would never see them again. This upset them as their luggage had contained keepsakes from their family or friends and other little familiar treasures. Especially upsetting was the loss of photographs of parents or of family groups with brothers and sisters. The last vestige of their past lives was removed and they were now at the mercy of the Christian Brothers.

By early evening they were tired, hungry, fearful and bewildered. Soon they were taken to a large dining room in another building. On entering in single file, they were told to be seated together and remain silent. The boys sat on forms against large rectangular tables capable of accommodating at least six boys along each side. All had been placed end to end in four long rows down the length of the hall. At the head of the hall were two similar tables that had been placed across the room in a single row with chairs on the far side.

As they sat silently waiting, other boys entered in orderly lines to sit at the tables. Nick estimated their ages to range from about four years, through his own age and up to fifteen years. They mostly stayed in their age groups and didn't speak but they all stared at the new arrivals. Within minutes the tables were full and watched over by strategically positioned Brothers who paced up and down the rows. Nick found it odd that one of the boys flinched and ducked as a Brother, in passing, raised his hand to scratch his nose.

There was a sudden tension in the air as the boys stood to become motionless when more Brothers entered the hall. Nick, Chris and the other new boys followed suit as it seemed the right thing to do. The last person to enter was a big man with a heavy, jutting lower jaw and a large stomach held in place with a wide leather belt. His tall boots almost reached his knees, reminding Nick of Desperate Dan, a comic book hero who always appeared on page three of The Dandy comic. However, he didn't have a gun like Desperate Dan. Instead, he carried a strange looking stick with a lump on one end. The Brothers treated him with great respect, or maybe they were afraid of him and moved quickly to make way. Nick thought he must be in charge.

When he reached the end of the room, he stood behind the middle of the head tables, laying his strange stick down. Then without introduction, facing the boys, he raised his voice and said, "some new orphans arrived today. See they know what is expected of them, our rules and routines and what happens to those who do not obey or cause trouble. To the new boys I say, if you follow our rules we will all get along fine. Now we will say a prayer of thanks for our sustenance."

They closed their eyes and put their hands together while a Brother said a short prayer. Immediately the "Amen" was said, everyone sat and began to chatter. Some fumbled with their spoons as older boys brought in stacks of empty bowls, while others delivered plates. Each boy was given a bowl. Three plates of roughly cut white bread were placed on each table. The older boys who were serving then left, only to reappear minutes later with large containers of soup, each boy was given a ladle full and took a piece of bread.

"Yuk! What is it?" One of the new boys asked aloud.

An older boy sitting diagonally across at the next table stared in earnest at the boy who had spoken to get his attention. He raised his forefinger vertically to his lips and holding the stare, gently shook his head.

Nobody spoke, they just pulled disapproving faces. The soup was very thin, did not taste good and the pieces of cabbage smelled strange. As unpleasant as it was, Nick noticed that none of the existing boys had picked it out to be left on the side of their bowls as some of the new boys were doing. A patrolling Brother noticed and slapped an offender's ear as he barked instructions for them to eat it all. When the soup was finished, the bowls and plates were taken away and each boy was given an apple for dessert.

"I thought the soup was just a starter," Chris said.

They noticed that the priests sitting at the head table were eating, what the boys called, with resentment, 'proper food'.

Nick and Chris soon learned the routines of meal times but they never got used to the food. Not that it was always this bad, although it often was, and never more than very plain and simple. There was never enough to satisfy the boys' hunger and little variety. Soon they could tell the day of the week from the boring routine of the menu.

Not until all the boys had finished were they allowed to leave the dining hall and mingle. Two older boys came to where the new arrivals were sitting and introduced themselves as Roger and Peter. A few of the new boys gave their names.

"So where are you all from?" Roger asked.

"England," someone said.

"A lot of us came from England too," Roger replied.

"Well, most of us really, a few are from Malta and some from Ireland. But where did you come from in England?"

There were a variety of answers but Nick did not comment, wanting to ask more about where he was now.

"What is this place?"

There was a moment of silence. Peter and Roger looked at each other before Peter replied.

"It's called 'Clontarf Boys Town' but some people just call it Clontarf or Boys Town."

In that second the body language and the tone in Peter's voice carried a message that said, 'caution, be careful here'.

"Who was that really big man who spoke to us before dinner, the one with that funny looking stick?" Chris asked.

"That's Brother Flannery. He's in charge. You want to stay well out of his way, he's a bastard," Peter said.

"That's a shillelagh he carries and he'll wallop you with it just for looking at him. You don't have to do anything wrong, just be in the wrong place at the wrong time. Nobody wants to get on the wrong side of him, even some of the Brothers are afraid of upsetting him."

"Is dinner always as bad as we just had?"

One of the new boys asked, noticing the contrast with what they had been eating on the ship.

Peter gave a wry smile as he answered, "Pretty much, that was about average. Breakfast is especially boring, a cup of cocoa then only ever porridge with no sugar, or maybe semolina. I hate semolina. Sometimes, as a punishment, they put salt in the porridge. You are not allowed to leave anything on your plate. You have to eat it all. It tastes horrible but no matter how bad it is, you have to eat it or get a beating. Any leftovers in the kitchen are brought back at the next meal, even if it's the next day. It usually comes with a lecture about waste and a reminder of how lucky we are. That's a joke!"

The new boys sat wide-eyed in silence, listening intently.

"How long have you been here?" Nick asked.

"Five years."

"Me too," Peter added. "We came from Castledere, which was like a strict boarding school for nippers. It's not far from here."

"We won't be here that long. We are going to be adopted," Chris interjected.

"Oh yeh!" Peter cynically jeered.

"We were told that before we came too, but here we are, still stuck in this place. Sometimes people come to see if they can adopt one of us but the Brothers always turn them away saying we are not available for adoption."

Nick and Chris exchanged worried looks. Roger continued as he clearly had more to say.

"But because we are older, we get to go out. Two or three days a week we go to a farm to work. Soon we'll be there full time. We are supposed to be learning about farming but mostly we just work. We're just cheap labour but I suppose we do learn something. They said we have to repay our debt for being brought to Australia and for being so lovingly cared for. Huh! That's rich that is! One of the Brothers told us we might be going to Bindoon quite soon. He said it's a special training farm in the country. Lots of the older boys go there. It's got to be better than here."

Roger hesitated then enthusiastically added, "we'll get two shillings a week for the work which is good because we get nothing at all for working here. Once a month we are allowed to go into town with Mr. Con on his truck. He's a Greek man. His last name is too hard to pronounce so he told us to call him Mr. Con. Now everyone does. He's really a stonemason or builder, not sure which. He shows the boys how to build but does lots of other things around the place too. He probably brought you here on his truck. He usually brings the new boys. We like him, he's nice to us but only when the Brothers are not around."

"Why does an orphanage need a stonemason?" Nick asked.

"To show us how to do even more work."

The resentfully toned answer came from another of the older boys.

Chris pointed to the lectern that stood on the raised platform at the end of the hall saying, "see that stand up there? Across the front it says 'Suffer the Children.' What does it mean?"

"Well, it's really part of a quotation from Jesus in the Bible but it means something quite different to the Brothers," Roger explained.

"What does it really mean?"

"The full quotation is 'Suffer the children to come unto me."

"So what do they think it means?"

"You'll find out soon enough," Peter scoffed.

They didn't see Brother David approaching and before Roger or Peter could say any more, he interrupted.

"Come along you newcomers, I'll show you where you are going to sleep."

They scrambled away from the table to follow Brother David through to the rear of the building and onto a verandah where there was a row of iron framed beds.

Brother David raised his voice.

"You may choose whichever bed you wish but you must always use the same one."

Nick and Chris looked at each other in surprise and disbelief at being told to sleep on the veranda.

Again Brother David spoke up, "You will sleep here for the next few weeks until some of the older boys leave, when you will be moved into their dormitory."

"Come on Chris, down to the end, let's stay together," Nick said.

Chris took the bed at the end of the row and Nick the next one in. On each was a striped flock mattress, a blanket that had clearly seen better days, a yellow stained pillow and a thin folded sheet. Brother David walked along the line telling the boys to make their beds. Nick and Chris found it easier to help each other in turn. Several boys had unsuccessfully tried to make their beds by themselves. Then they noticed and did the same with the boy next to them. When Brother David saw them he shouted, "Stop that! You must learn to make your bed by yourself!"

All the mattresses were heavily stained and smelled of urine. Some had small tears, and most had half the leather buttons missing. They noticed the sheets had pale stains in the middle that faded to the edges. All the boys had feelings of dismay and concern. Trying to maintain a brave face Chris said, without expecting an answer, "it might be fun sleeping on the verandah, but what have we come to? What sort of place is this?"

"Dunno," Nick answered in a low tone, reluctant to discuss it.

His heart was bursting with emotion. He had a lump in his throat that prevented him from saying more. He wanted to scream and yell out, "I want to go home! I don't want to be here! I want my Mum! Where are you Mum?" Then said very little for the remainder of the evening. Even now he still did not, or would not, allow himself to believe his mother had died.

Some of the older boys, who had been there a while, came to investigate the new arrivals. There were many questions from both sides. Some of the new boys went with the old hands to be shown around the place and learn more of the rules and routines.

"The Brothers won't tell you what's what here but they'll expect you to know, and if you don't know and do something wrong, you'll get a cut or two with a strap. They rely on us to tell you and show you where things are," one boy said.

Nick and Chris walked to where they had seen a river earlier and sat on the bank to ponder their future. They speculated on what this Boys Town really was, wondering if it could be a place where boys stayed until adopted or was this to be their home for the next few years? Then they fell silent for a while, each with their own thoughts. Eventually, to lighten the atmosphere, Chris said.

Do you remember when I fell in the river in England?"

They both smiled at the memory. Then Nick replied, "It seems such a long time ago."

They were quiet again for a few minutes until Chris broke the silence.

"Hey Look! The swans are black. I didn't know there were such things as black swans." They sat and watched the birds in fascination for several minutes until Nick casually said, "come on, we'd better go back. We don't know what time they'll want us to go to us to bed."

Getting to sleep was difficult. They had never slept in the open air before and were bothered by the occasional mosquito. Two of the boys had cried until they had fallen asleep. It was the familiar sounds of the night so Nick and Chris let them be, leaving them to work through their sorrows in their own way.

6

The next morning they woke to the sound of voices and bright sunlight. It took a few seconds to become orientated and remember where they were. The previous day had been long, tiring and stressful but they had slept soundly even though the flock mattresses were uncomfortable.

It was six-thirty. Brother David was now hustling the boys to get up, make their beds and wash.

"Go and wash before exercises in the yard, then to morning service in the main hall before breakfast," he commanded.

Almost all the boys needed the toilet first.

"Come on hurry up. Get on with it!" Brother David was impatient.

As he paced the veranda, he noticed a small puddle under one of the beds.

"Whose bed is this?" He bellowed angrily as his face reddened.

The boys froze like statues, frightened. They had never heard or seen such rage from a grown-up before, least of all from a priest. Slowly they turned to look at where Brother David was pointing. There was silence for almost five seconds which felt like an eternity to the boys.

"Well? Someone slept in this bed last night, who was it?" Brother David demanded.

"You might as well own up or it will only be worse for you when I find out, as I most definitely will."

A small fair haired boy of slight build, named Craig, slowly raised his hand and said, "it's my bed Sir."

Frightened and embarrassed, he tipped his head forward as if looking at Brother David's feet, not knowing what to expect next.

Brother David grabbed Craig's left ear, twisting and holding it hard.

"You don't call me Sir, do you hear. I'm Brother David to you. Do you understand?" he shouted with great emphasis on 'Brother'.

"You are a dirty, nasty little urchin. What are you?! How old are you?" Brother David barked as he marched the boy to an open door leading into the building. He didn't wait to hear Craig's answer of "five."

Craig squealed with the pain. His head was tilted to one side, stumbling as he tried to keep up. Brother David didn't release his grip on his ear, only raised it higher to cause more pain and forcing Craig to walk on tiptoes. The boys were shocked and frightened, no one spoke. But then, as Craig and the Brother disappeared, and as if a silent command had been given they, simultaneously and as quickly as possible, made their beds and waited.

It was only a few minutes before Brother David re-appeared still clutching Craig's ear. Tears ran down Craig's cheeks as he clumsily skipped along at the side of the priest with his head still forcibly tilted to one side. Another Brother followed them, a big man the boys had not seen before. Yet another Brother brought a wooden chair into the yard placing it in front of the boys. Brother David instructed Craig to remove his trousers. He had no underpants and was embarrassed in front of the other boys. As he tried to cover himself with his hands, he was made to lean forwards over the back of the chair with his hands towards the seat. The back of the chair pressed hard into his armpits. The big man raised his voice as he flexed a stiff leather strap with both hands.

"We do not tolerate bed wetting here. Boys who do it are disgusting, smelly little creatures and are severely punished. So let this be a lesson to all of you. This boy will receive ten cuts to teach him a lesson, as will any other boy who wets the bed."

Chris and Nick could not believe what they were seeing as this big man stepped to the side of Craig's bare buttocks, whacking them so hard it caused him to grunt with every stroke. Craig yelled with the pain as his tears dripped onto the chair seat. Again and again he cried out as each stroke tore a path across his buttocks. Brother David told him to shut up. Long red welts immediately appeared. Craig was sobbing deeply now, as were some of the boys who were made to watch. They flinched with each stroke, feeling Craig's pain. On the eighth stroke, a stream of urine ran down Craig's leg as he fainted. His knees gave way and he slowly slid down the back of the chair to settle at the priest's feet.

With rage in his heart and without regard for the consequences, Nick charged forwards to help Craig. Brother David grabbed him, holding him back. The Brother who had brought the chair pulled Craig up by his wrists and draped him over the chair again, holding him down whilst the final two strokes were delivered. Nick tried to free himself but Brother David was too strong. The priest holding Craig, partly dragging, partly carried him back to the verandah and through a door into the building. Craig was moaning as tiny beads of blood oozed through the angry raised welts on his buttocks. The Brother who had administered the punishment turned to Nick, pointed the stiff strap at him and looking down its length saying, "now young man, we will have to teach you a lesson for trying to interfere with discipline, won't we. Take your trousers off!"

Half naked, Nick was made to lean over the chair and received five strokes across his buttocks. Each stroke hurt more than the previous one. Anger and outrage overwhelmed Nick's natural reaction to cry out as each stroke seared his bottom. Raising his head he stared at the distant trees without blinking. The rage in his eyes was now joined by defiance. Gritting his teeth and remaining silent with every stroke was hard. He was determined not to let the Brothers see his pain. His defiance did not go unnoticed, especially by Brother David.

"Let that be a lesson to you boy!" the priest growled with the satisfaction at a job well done and authority maintained.

Nick was told to return to the group of watching boys. Chris took his hand as he whispered under his breath, "Bloody bastards!"

That was the first time he could remember swearing but his outrage was not for himself but for Craig.

Craig reappeared after about fifteen minutes. He was pale, trembling and all his hair had been cut off, a practice the boys would soon be familiar with, being designed to advertise that he was a bed wetter and cause humiliation. It made them easy targets for the Brothers and some of the older boys to pick on, publicly taunting them and calling them names, adding to their shame and embarrassment.

It was obvious to Nick and Chris that Craig would not cope well here. He was a quiet, shy boy and easily intimidated, making him a prime target for an accomplished bully. His nervous disposition made his circumstances especially stressful and it was difficult for him to handle such harsh treatment. Whenever he was asked what was the matter, or if he wanted something, his usual answer was,"I want my mother. I want to go home." Then he would cry.

All the boys knew that he was certain to wet his bed again, as most boys who were prone to did. So they decided that if either of them were to wake during the night, they would take Craig to the toilet if he needed to go or not.

Craig agreed and it worked well for the first two nights. He regained a little confidence and was pleased with himself. The Brothers concluded their punishment had worked and were satisfied.

On the third night Craig wet the bed again and was terrified as he stood by his bed, trembling with fear when the other boys woke. Chris got a cloth and attempted to wipe the floor dry before Brother David arrived, but was caught in the act.

Craig was given a few whacks across his head and verbally abused. But this time there were no strokes across his buttocks. Even the Brothers realised he could not handle a second flogging. So he was made to stand on a box outside, in the middle of the quadrangle, naked and in full view of everyone with his wet sheet draped over his head. He was to stand there until it was dry or wait until a Brother allowed him to get down. Not only was it humiliating but he was not to move, sit, drink or eat until after he was permitted to get down. Remaining motionless was very hard. Should he move a little and a Brother see him, his ankles or the backs of his legs were whacked with a stick or strip of weighted leather, specially made for thrashing boys. Nick and Chris watched as two Brothers walked past Craig, each giving him a jab with a stiff forefinger, simply because they could, saying "Smelly animal."

Craig couldn't see the jab coming and almost fell off the box which earned him two more pokes while being told to stand still.

The next night Craig wet the bed again and was so terrified that he vomited and shook as he stood by his bed.

Nick and Chris looked at each other knowing they had to do something. So they told two other boys to clear up the mess and if Brother David came they would delay him somehow.

"They'll give him a thrashing and make him stand on the box again, but he can't do it!" Chris said.

"I know. We can't stop him getting a walloping but we can help him with the sheet," Nick replied.

Craig received a few random strokes of the strap across his calves, making him dance and leaving angry welts. There was no chair to lean over this time. The Brothers had refused to lose face by not giving him his final strokes that first time, even though he had passed out. However it had given them a fright. Not for Craig but for themselves with the thought of the possible repercussions.

Craig was weak, pale and in tears. But he was still made to stand, trembling on a box in the quadrangle, with his sheet over his head.

At the right moment, Chris watched out for any Brothers whilst Nick swapped places with Craig under the sheet. Nick was the shorter of the two and less likely to be noticed. The other boys quickly took Craig and hid him in one of the outbuildings. Within an hour the morning sun would dry the sheet and they would have to make the switch back.

Chris gathered half a dozen boys together and went to fetch Craig, telling them all what to do as they went. Craig was feeling a little better and inconspicuous in the group as they walked to where Nick was standing on the box. As they neared, Brother David appeared making his way to check on who he thought was Craig, under the sheet.

"Get ready Nick," Chris said urgently as he walked past in the direction of Brother David. The other boys in the group stopped near Nick and waited.

"Brother David," Chris called out, "can I ask you something please?"

The priest stopped and looked towards him.

When they had reached each other, Chris asked if they were allowed to swim in the river. The priest said that some boys go after school, but he did not give a direct answer of approval. Chris engaged the Brother in conversation about safety in the river as he manouvered himself to face the group, who were at the box. Brother David now had his back to the boys. When Chris could see that the switch was complete, he excused himself and Brother David proceeded to the box to release Craig, telling him if he wet the bed again there would be worse to come.

There were many mornings when they saw the chair brought out and were forced to watch some poor soul get thrashed for his mishap in the night. Nick and Chris's anger never diminished but they did manage to control it since it made no difference to the punishments. Often Nick was too upset to eat his meagre breakfast, giving it to the other boys who eagerly accepted the additional food.

Nick and Chris bonded as never before, as though their very survival depended on it, always caring and looking out for each other. They were already discovering the characters and moods of the Brothers. Which ones were approachable, those who were not and those who enjoyed punishing boys for trivialities.

Without consciously realising it, they had identified four groups at Clontarf Boys Town. First were the Brothers who hypocritically controlled with fear and arrogant self-righteousness. Then a group of the older boys, known as 'Pets and Squealers,' who had divorced themselves from the other boys by doing 'favours' for the Brothers in return for privileges and the freedom to torment, punish and tease the younger boys. They were hated and despised by all the boys for their treachery. The Brothers did not respect or totally trust them either but enjoyed their willingness to betray other boys, do their bidding and report misdemeanours. Third were those who appeared to play the game by getting along within the system, yet who took advantage of situations as they arose, mostly without getting caught. The final group was the most vulnerable, being the younger and weaker ones who were easily intimidated and taken advantage of. They suffered most without daring to complain, and were easy pickings for the

Brothers to take to their rooms at night. Some, as they got older and wiser, migrated from this group.

An invisible line had been drawn in the sand. On one side was the Brothers and the Pets and Squealers, on the other the boys. From now on, they would stick together, abiding by an unspoken code of comradeship.

7

It didn't take long for the boys to learn the ropes at Clontarf. The first important lesson was to 'never be found out' as punishments were severe. The next lesson was to learn which Brothers were fair in their dealings, which were brutes and those who 'liked little boys'. One or two were sympathetic towards the boys, but none would ever openly do or say anything in their defence. Nick and Chris soon discovered who they could and could not trust amongst the boys. At first the Pets intrigued Nick. He was not sure what they did for the brothers because they were not seen to do anything. Yet some Brothers had their favourites and gave them privileges.

Nick asked Peter and Roger about them.

"They do personal favours for the Brothers, especially at night. A Brother will come to their dorm after dark and take them back to their own room."

"What sort of favours?" Nick asked.

"You don't want to know. Just hope they leave you and your friend alone. They pick on others too," Roger said.

Nick pondered a while and thought of the many times he'd heard a Brother walking along the row of beds after dark and picking a boy to go with him. He still didn't fully understand but he knew the boys hated it and would never talk about it afterwards. For reasons unknown to Nick, neither he nor Chris had ever been picked, assuming it was because they would be expected to rebel.

75

They wore the same clothes for a week at a time, but on Saturday mornings they lined up to be inspected. Dirty clothes were exchanged for clean ones, except for underpants which were changed once a month. The clothes were always worn, never new. Shoes were rarely provided, and then to only a few. The remaining boys went barefoot. Summer days were always very hot, especially until early afternoon when a cooling breeze blew in from the ocean. Winters were relatively short but it was cold often at night. On colder days they were each given a jumper which most boys wore in bed as well as the daytime.

The winter brought a new fear for smaller boys. That of being picked to warm Father Flanagan's bed. Boys were selected to lay naked in the sheets to warm them until Father Flanagan was ready to retire for the night. Sometimes a boy was told to stay. On other occasions he might be made to lay inside across the foot of the bed for Father Flanagan to warm his feet on.

All the boys had regular chores and responsibilities which ranged from cleaning, doing laundry, scrubbing floors and gardening, to working in the kitchen. Many of the older boys were selected for building work because of their strength. Kitchen duties were considered the best as they could sometimes sneak a little extra to eat. Yet it was the Squealers and Pets who got the best jobs.

School at Clontarf was a new experience. Many boys had difficulty with the strict regime and were constantly in fear. However, most boys adjusted quickly out of necessity, afraid of making a mistake or not keeping up with the class. Punishments were brutal and often unforeseen. A stroke with a leather strap or from a cane from behind was common. A Brother silently wandered behind their desks, peering over the boys shoulders at their work, and if it was not correct in every respect or untidy, the Brother would strike. Boys dared not to look up and in time they developed an instinct for knowing where in the room the

Brother was at any time. English, Mathematics and Religion were the main subjects, with a little Geography and History now and then. There was always punishment for errors but never praise for achievement. It was expected and taken for granted.

Brother McFee was an unusually short man who always wore a cassock. The older boys said he cut the shape of his heels in pieces of cardboard and put them inside his shoes to make him look taller. His black hair was greased and combed to sit in a wave high above his forehead giving the illusion of extra height. The boys were amused at his strange walk, as if he had springs under his shoes to help him see over a fence as be bounced along. He stretched his head upward to raise his eyes and chin in an effort to appear taller. His students mockingly called him "Brother Isaiah" but never to his face or be overheard. It was considered fun to imitate his walk and gestures but never when he might see. His reputation was that of a cruel bully and he was one of the Brothers who took pleasure in using his authority to administer punishment.

Most boys disliked Brother McFee, and he appeared to dislike them. He would be the first to call them stupid and worthless idiots. Yet he seemed to tolerate Nick and Chris better than most. Nick believed it was because they could read better than the other boys in the class and always kept up with their work. Such was the legacy of their schooling at Dr. Barnardo's. As a result Nick or Chris were often asked to read the Bible aloud. They always read slowly and carefully so as not to make a mistake, in fear of being poked or hit with the half broomstick Brother McFee carried. He jokingly calling it his 'Mark1 Motivator' but the boys did not find it funny. Brother McFee would use it to point at things on the blackboard or slam it down hard on a desk with a loud bang to get their attention, frightening the boys. He clearly enjoyed patrolling the classroom with the stick resting on his shoulder, ready to slam down or poke an unsuspecting victim.

Nick had never liked him from the first day at school. They had been given a slate board and a piece of chalk and told to write their names on it. After a moment or two, there was a loud bang and a cry from the back of the room, followed by the sound of a boy crying. No one dared turn around to look. Brother McFee had brought his stick down hard across a boy's left hand, so hard that it broke the slate in two.

"Writing with the left hand is the work of the Devil and it will not be tolerated!" Brother McFee bellowed.

The boy's knuckles quickly swelled to twice their normal size. He was told to 'stop blabbering' and was later chastised for the poor handwriting he had presented by using his right hand. Apart from a bandage, he received no proper treatment or sympathy for his broken fingers and was expected to continue as normal. Professional treatment for such injuries was rarely, if ever, sought from outside Boys Town. The Brothers were afraid of the causes being revealed.

Nick and Chris were lucky. They had learned to read at an early age, which helped them with all their subjects, so were considered bright. Consequently, they were not picked on often.

They had come to like Craig who was innocent and vulnerable, being in need of friendship and protection. They felt sorry for him, yet frustrated that they could do little to lift his spirits for more than an hour or two at a time. He easily fell into depressed moods, especially when he would talk of his mother, desperately longing for her to come and take him home.

After dinner Craig went down to the white stone pillars at the gate where he sat and waited for her. It became a regular occurrence as he was convinced she would come for him one day, he just didn't know when. So Craig spent every evening waiting by the gate, returning just before dark. Sometimes he had to be brought back by the other boys. The Brothers learned of Craig's activity and told him to stop. But the next evening he was back at the gate again. When the Brothers realised he had disobeyed them, he was prevented from leaving the buildings after dinner, with chores as punishment and to keep him occupied; most were in the kitchen where he washed dishes and cleaned. Consequently his days were mostly fourteen or sixteen hours long. After two weeks, Craig became so tired that he would almost fall asleep in class the following day.

The first evening Craig discontinued his kitchen duties, he went back to the gate to wait for his mother again. The Brothers were outraged that he would dare to disobey them so blatantly and to openly challenge their authority. A Brother was sent to bring him back. He grabbed Craig by the shirt collar dragging him to his feet.

"What do you think you are doing?" The Brother demanded.

"Nothing."

"Nothing! It's a funny place to do nothing boy! I'll tell you what you are doing. You are being disobedient, that's what you are doing. You can expect to get a darn good thrashing!" The priest shouted.

"But I'm waiting for my mother," Craig said in frightened desperation.

"Your mother? Your mother! You utterly stupid boy, you don't have a mother anymore! She sent you here because she didn't care about you or want you. She didn't even like you. That's why you are here. She's never coming for you, you idiot boy!"

Craig was devastated and turned on the Brother, lashing out with both fists. The Brother easily defended himself against Craig's rage while holding onto him.

"You have really done it now my boy, just you wait and see! Attacking me is the worst thing you could have done," he growled.

Craig was locked in a dark, empty cupboard for the rest of that evening and night, all the next day and night. On the second morning he was not given breakfast but was taken directly to the assembly hall.

It was Friday, when morning assembly took on a different air, one the children hated. Father Flanagan would take the service himself. Then afterwards came the "crimes and punishment" session which successfully administered pain, embarrassment and humiliation.

A chair was placed on a raised platform like a stage. Boys would be called by name from the assembly to the platform where Father Flanagan would describe his crime. Punishment was pompously pronounced according to the crime but it was never less than five cuts of the cane or strap across bare buttocks. Nobody was spared the humiliation.

On this day, Father Flanagan raised himself with an air of great authority saying, "Craig Johnson, come forward."

Craig had not expected this, thinking he had already been punished. Frozen with fear, he had to be taken forward by a Brother. Father Flanagan told Craig to drop his trousers and lean over the back of the chair whilst his crimes were described.

"This boy has repeatedly and deliberately disobeyed clear instructions and is also guilty of striking, nay attacking, a Brother. Both demand severe punishment. He will receive five cuts for each crime." With that he turned to a Brother holding a cane and nodded. Craig gritted his teeth while trying not to cry in front of everyone. "Boys don't cry," he had been told. But he did.

There were murmurs of fear for Craig through the hall. Father Flanagan turned and yelled, "Silence." The hall became quiet, apart from the swish of the cane striking bare flesh.

Nick and Chris felt Craig's pain and wanted to shout for the strokes to stop. Nick could not watch for more than the first two seconds. He turned away and surveyed the hall, noticing the Brothers who lined the side of the assembly. Some seemed to enjoy the scene while others had self-righteous expressions. Others showed no emotion at all. Then Nick's eyes fell on the words across the lectern which now took on an intense meaning.

Craig was told to return to his place, which he did as he adjusted his trousers. Chris offered him a few words of comfort whilst someone they didn't see muttered, "one day we'll get these bastards for you mate."

After the assembly and before school, Craig bathed his buttocks in cold water. They stung and were very hot. At school he was allowed to kneel upright rather than press his bottom onto the hard wooden bench. Craig hardly spoke all day and seemed to become more pensive and withdrawn as the day wore on. The pain of his whipping and public humiliation was not as great as the words from the Brother about his mother.

The next morning it was seen that Craig's bed was cold but had been slept in. Yet he was not there. Questions were asked and a search of the grounds was organised to find him but there was no trace. Thinking he had run away, which was not unusual at Boys Town, the Perth Police were notified to look out for him.

That evening the police telephoned to say that a boy's body had been found by a fisherman in Canning River, downstream at the tributary with the Swan River. Craig Johnson was buried in a corner of the grounds at Clontarf.

8

In the following months the boys became more familiar with the daily routines and regimes of Clontarf, including learning a few tricks. However, the undertones of fear and insecurity never diminished. Exasperating their plight was a feeling of helplessness and frustration in having no one to turn to.

"Who would listen to us? Who would even believe the things that went on here?" Nick had once said.

The day the Mayor of Perth, the Chief of Police, other dignitaries and a representative from The Department of Child Welfare were to make their annual visit, made it obvious to the boys that the Brothers knew they were doing wrong.

"Otherwise why would they go to such lengths to put on a special show to cover up the reality?" Nick had told some of the boys.

At morning assembly, after announcing the visit was to take place in two days' time, Brother Patrick gave strict instructions, pausing for effect after each one.

"The day after tomorrow there will be an inspection by local and Government dignitaries. So!" There was a long pause, then, "you will all be on your best behaviour, every one of you, every minute of the day. You will not fight, argue, tease shout or scream. You will walk smartly everywhere. You will not run. You will keep yourself, your beds and dormitories spotlessly clean and tidy. You will not engage the visitors in conversation. If you are spoken to, you will smile, answering politely in as few words as possible. 'Yes' or 'no' Sir or Madam will be quite enough for you to say on almost all occasions. And remember... if you are asked, you like it here!"

Finally he stated, "This is not a social visit. It's an inspection of us all, and you are to be judged by the authorities."

There was a murmuring amongst the boys whilst leaving the hall. Some of the older boys were pleased. Nick and Chris asked Peter why?

"You wait and see," Peter said excitedly.

"We'll get better clothes and everyone will get shoes. The best part is that we'll get decent food, so make the most of it."

Peter looked down and slowly, more seriously, added.

"Pity it's only for one day a year. Whatever you do, don't complain to the visitors or the Brothers will kill you. Well, not exactly but you'll be really sorry you did. Last year a new boy from Malta was asked if he liked the food. He lied and said "yes" but added that he wished it was like this every day. The visitor then asked Father Flanagan what the boy meant. Well, I can tell you the boy got the thrashing of his life, was locked in a broom cupboard for a week and was only given bread and water. It took him a long time to get over it. He was never the same again, a bit of a wreck if you ask me. It was the broom cupboard that did it."

At assembly the next morning, they were reminded again of the instructions of the previous day. This time it was Father Flanagan who spoke, adding a greater sense of importance to the occasion. However he did not let the announcement pass without repeating the threat of punishment for anyone who failed to comply. Then went on to say, "today will be a day of cleaning and preparation. You will meet with your respective Brother outside your dormitory immediately after this assembly. He will assign your duties which you will perform well and without complaint."

Nick knew that Brother David would give him the worst jobs. He disliked Nick, having been cautious of him since that first morning when he showed defiance at his whipping. Nick had found he was able to keep Brother David at bay with looks that unsettled him. When Brother David was administering threats or punishment, Nick would hold a piercing stare into the priest's eyes who, on catching Nick's stare, would find it hard to break away, so tempered his words and actions. On occasions, the priest had privately cursed Nick and decided not to look at him whilst giving a beating or tongue lashing. But he was drawn to Nick's eyes like a moth to the flame. Brother David had discussed Nick's perceived insolence, as he saw it, with another priest who had agreed to be cautious around him saying, "he is just the sort of boy who would likely make trouble later on."

Nick and Chris were given a cloth each, a scrubbing brush and metal buckets after being assigned to clean the washrooms and toilets. Not an easy job with boys coming and going all day but it had the consolation of being out of the sun. Walls were washed down, the grey stone sinks and toilet basins were scrubbed, as were the floors, which hurt their knees, but they knew better than to complain. By mid-afternoon they were finished and brought Brother David to approve their work.

"What do you call this?" Brother David demanded as he pointed to the stained brass taps above the sinks. But before there was a chance to explain he shouted, "clean them, clean them all. I want to see them sparkling like new when I return."

The boys had nothing that would clean them well enough and pondered a while deciding what to do. Then Chris said, "I remember once talking to Mr. Con, he said that in the outback when water was scarce he cleaned his billy with a damp cloth and sand. He said it came up like new with a bit of elbow grease."

So they brought clean sand from the edge of the river, wet their cloths and dabbed them in the wet sand. Then with vigorous rubbing, they began to remove the dark brown and green stains to eventually reveal bright yellow brass. Feeling pleased with themselves and proud of their ingenuity, Chris went to fetch Brother David for his approval.

"So you think you have finished do you?"

The priest grumbled in a manner suggesting a foreknowledge of a job that would be poorly done. He neither criticized nor praised their efforts. Praise of any kind was rare at Clontarf.

"I suppose that will do," he said in a resentful tone.

From his expression, Nick and Chris thought he had been looking forward to chastising them. He did not ask how they had achieved the shine and no explanation was given.

"There are footprints on the floor. People have been walking on it. Wash it again and keep off it until it's dry!" He commanded.

The next morning, breakfast and assembly was earlier than usual. They were all told to take turns, by order of their dormitory, to form a line at a storehouse where they would be provided with fresh clothes. These clothes were not new but were much better than their current ones – similar to those they wore when they first arrived. After so long without shoes, it felt strange, and some boys had difficulty walking due to a poor fit or chafing.

Wearing a cassock, Father Flanagan told the priests to form a line in front of the main building ready to greet the visitors. At 10 am, three shiny black cars came through the gates and up the dusty driveway to halt in front of the waiting reception. With an insincere welcoming smile, Father Flanagan stepped forward and shook hands with each of the visitors to welcome them. The other priests remained in line, knowing this was Father Flanagan's day. None were introduced.

The visitors looked about as they were politely ushered indoors. Two of the Pets had been chosen to serve tea and biscuits, which had not been seen since Father Flanagan's birthday. The Police Chief was an old friend of Father Flanagan and monopolized his time in jovial trivialities unrelated to Boys Town. Not all the Brothers were invited to take tea with the visitors but those who were, smiled, chatted and politely answered casual questions. Father Flanagan explained what they would be seeing today, and asked if there was anything else they wished to see. He hated surprises.

First they were shown the kitchens where there were piles of fresh vegetables. All being processed by older boys in white aprons.

"This is all part of our process of providing a rounded education. It does not all happen in the classroom, you know. The boys are encouraged to contribute to the common good, which in turn gives them a sense of satisfaction. Such are the Christian attitudes we instill here. Most boys find they enjoy the kitchen and aspire to become chefs one day. So you could describe this as an introduction to a formal apprenticeship in a restaurant or hotel. We do as much as we can to help them on their way. Isn't that right boys?"

Flanagan said bursting with pride. The boys smiled and nodded their agreement, exactly as they had been instructed.

Next the entourage went to the classrooms where Nick, Chris and other boys were working. Brother McFee had pre-arranged that Nick would be standing and reading aloud as the visitors entered the room. The group stood and listened for a few minutes before offering their approval to Brother McFee and turned to leave, suitably impressed.

Nick was thanked and asked to sit while Brother McFee teasingly ruffled his hair saying, "well done my boy, well done indeed."

Said loud enough for the dignitaries to hear, and to note the kindly gesture but they did not notice Nick flinch at Brother McFee's touch. Such an acknowledgement and gesture had not been seen in a classroom before.

Lunch in the big hall was the best they'd had since they arrived. Fresh carrots, potatoes, cabbage, a piece of chicken and gravy followed by sliced bananas in cold custard. This was normal for the Brothers but not for the boys. Making the most of it, they ate like the hungry orphans they were. Guests were given the same, and asked to approve the quality and standard.

"You will see that we all eat the same here," Father Flanagan told the visitors.

This was the first time Nick and Chris could remember when Brothers did not patrol the rows of tables. They didn't need to as all the plates were scraped clean and everyone was well behaved. Tea was served to the guests and priests whilst the boys were given orange juice before quietly filing out of the hall.

Eventually the visitors were taken outside to where a game of cricket was underway. Father Flanagan said with a smile, "cricket, a game for good sports and gentlemen, don't you think?"

The group agreed. After watching for a short time, they strolled to the river where swimming races were being organised. Again Father Flanagan provided a commentary.

"Competition is as good for the spirit, as exercise is for the body."

Once more there was agreement.

The day wore on in a similar fashion until the visitors left satisfied in the mid-afternoon. Only a few Brothers saw them off and those who did left the talking to Father

Flanagan, other than to smile, shake hands and say goodbye with a "thank you for coming."

The next day at morning assembly, Father Flanagan was in a wild rage, one that none of the boys had witnessed before. He was known to have an uncontrollable temper, causing the boys to be terrified at such times. He would lash out, striking them for no reason and they knew to keep well out of his way. On a past occasion, he had knocked an unsuspecting boy unconscious with his shillelagh. Father Flanagan had walked away leaving the boy on the ground.

Now, red-faced, he loudly announced, "Yesterday, someone gave a visiting official a note complaining of ill treatment here. I want to know who it was! I demand to know! So come forward right now! I'll teach you about ill treatment!"

Father Flanagan paused to get his breath but was unable to stay composed. His eyes bulged red, the veins on his neck stood out and his jutting lower jaw quivered with rage as he waited, slapping his shillelagh on the side of a high leather boot.

"If the culprit does not come forward right now, you will all be very sorry, each and every one of you!" He shouted. Yet still nobody came forward.

"Right!" He bellowed, in a tone suggestive of impending doom. Then he marched across the raised platform and out of the hall. For the first time ever, even the Brothers were visibly shaken.

The boy who had taken the initiative was far too afraid to own up, fearful of the consequences. So for a week the boys were worked much harder and for much longer hours , than usual, often on unnecessary tasks. Free time was not allowed, some meals were denied and they were only given water to drink. Father Flanagan was as upset about not discovering the culprit as he was of the note being delivered. Even the Pets and Squealers with their bullying and hollow promises of rewards, could not discover the author of the note. Father Flanagan felt it an affront to his authority and hated the thought that a boy had the better of him. Brother McFee asked to see the note in order to compare the handwriting with that of his students, only to discover that it had been printed in capital letters making identification almost impossible.

Father Flanagan resolved the issue with the authorities by a carefully worded letter, suggesting it was inevitable that there would be at least one boy in so many who was disgruntled from time to time over one matter or another. That it was impossible to please them all, all of the time. Perhaps the boy had recently been chastised for some misdemeanour and was resentful. Further, that the visitors were in the best position to judge the treatment and care accorded to the boys, having recently seen it with their own eyes. There was no inquiry and no more was heard of the matter. So regime at Clontarf continued unabated.

Nick and Chris finished school in September 1952, two months before Nick's thirteenth Birthday. Officially they were considered well educated for their ages and were reaching the limits of what the Christian Brothers could teach them in class, with the exception of religion. They had enjoyed the stories and philosophies from the Bible but not the interpretations and hypocrisy the Christian Brothers practiced, causing them to question God's motivations.

On one occasion during religious instruction, Chris had carefully asked, "if God loves everyone so much and controls everything, why does he let bad things happen like wars and people dying in accidents or from terrible diseases?"

He wanted to add something about the cruelty at Boys Town but didn't dare. But it did not pass without other boys thinking the same.

"Ah, you must understand that God moves in mysterious ways," the Brother had answered.

This did not satisfy Chris's questioning mind. He thought of it as no answer at all, believing the Brother did not know why. They found The Old Testament more appealing and with greater credibility, liking the historical aspects best. Yet they agreed with the New Testament teachings on Christianity in the way we see others, treat them and conduct our own lives. Chris's final thought had been, "perhaps the Christian Brothers should read the New Testament."

Brother O'Brien, who they previously had little contact with, wanted to see them after lessons. They met in the assembly hall as they had been told, nervously wondering what they may have done to be summoned for punishment. When they introduced themselves, Brother O'Brien looked them up and down, then with a strong Irish accent he said, "well look at yourselves there will you now. Two fine strapping lads."

He walking behind them before continuing.

"Oh yes, you'll do fine, just fine. We'll make farmers of you yet, we will."

Nick and Chris relaxed, realising they were not there for punishment but for the assessment to work on a church farm.

9

Nick, Chris and four other boys were driven on the back of Mr. Con's truck, on a journey that took most of the day to a church farm many miles north of Clontarf. The trip reminded them of the day they first arrived in Australia. The last two hours of the journey were on unsealed roads so the little truck lifted clouds of dust as it trundled along. By the time they arrived at the farm, they were filthy and could even feel the grit between their teeth. Their hair was dry and itchy, feeling like straw, but they didn't mind. This was an adventure and they were out of Clontarf into wide open spaces for the first time since they had arrived six years earlier. Now they were experiencing the illusion of freedom.

None of the boys knew what to expect but they hoped of better things to come. The truck turned onto a track leading to a group of small timber and corrugated iron buildings. Mr. Con stopped near the largest one, went to the back of the truck and lowered the tailgate for the boys to climb out. As they did, two men and a heavily built woman came from the building.

"Right you lot, over here in the shade if you don't mind," one of the men ordered.

They stood under sheets of corrugated iron which looked precariously balanced on top of eight vertical posts making a shelter. Football sized rocks had been placed on top to hold the sheets in place. Although there were rough benches beneath for seating, they remained standing.

"I'm Brother Connolly and I run the farm. This is Brother Michael and this is Mrs. Butcher. You can think of her as your House Mother."

Brother Connolly, who was wearing a grubby white shirt, baggy khaki shorts that reached below his knees and heavy army style boots, stepped closer.

"We have a great deal to do here every day and you are expected to pull your weight. Malingering and laziness are not tolerated. The same disciplines that apply at Clontarf apply here too although you might find you are less supervised and may have a little more freedom. Some of the older boys left the farm a week ago to take up work on commercial farms and outback stations so there is a lot to catch up on. I will tell you what to do but it will be up to you to see that work is completed properly and on time, even if you have to work all night to do it."

With just one hand he removed his dusty straw hat and scratched his balding head before continuing.

"Mrs. Butcher will show you where to wash and where you'll sleep. By the look of you, you'd better wash before you do anything else. Take them to the showers first Mrs. Butcher."

Without speaking but with an air of great authority, Mrs. Butcher led, like a mother duck with chicks, to a large concrete slab beneath a round corrugated iron water tank that perched on four legs fifteen feet above their heads. Two rusty shower nozzles, each with a string attached to a lever, hung from the tank. A crude corrugated iron screen was attached to each of the four wooden pillars supporting the tank. These rusty panels offered some privacy on three sides but left knees and shoulders visible from outside.

"Here's where you wash and shower every day boys. Sorry, but there's no soap at the moment," she said, maintaining an air of uncompromising authority.

This was the first close encounter the boys had with a woman in many years and it did nothing to endear them to females. Some boys were disappointed, having hoped that a little feminine kindness might ensue. Mrs. Butcher looked over her shoulder to see the priests returning to the larger building. When they were out of sight she smiled and said, I'll fetch you some towels and see if I can find a bit of soap my lovelies."

The boys looked at each other in amazement and relaxed with smiles as they watched her large body waddle to one of the buildings. Nick and Chris immediately saw how it was and gave each other a knowing glance. Mrs. Butcher returned with an assortment of worn towels all lightly stained from the red soil but clean.

"Oh dear, we seem to be out of soap just now. I'll show you to your beds when you are ready boys," she said, as she gave each one a towel and stood waiting for them. The boys were hesitant to remove their clothes in front of her but said nothing. Mrs. Butcher realized, saying with a chuckle, "oh all right my lovelies, don't you mind me. I've seen more bare bums than I care to remember. They all look the same to me."

The boys were accustomed to seeing each other naked, even in front of the Brothers who often hung around in the showers, supposedly to supervise them. However they had never been naked in front of a strange woman.

"I'll come back in a few minutes then," she called.

The boys took turns to shower in the lukewarm water, then shook much of the dust from their clothes before dressing. Mrs. Butcher returned saying, "Right my lovelies let's show you where you will sleep."

She led them to one of the wooden huts with rusty red roofs. As there were no windows, it appeared dark inside and their eyes took a moment or two to adjust from the sunlight to the dim light of the hut. They soon saw six beds in two rows of three.

Mrs. Butcher stiffened as she heard Brother Connolly's voice from the doorway behind her.

"Everything all right here Mrs. Butcher?"

"Yes Brother."

Then she raised her voice and spoke more firmly so Brother Connolly could hear.

"You can select your own bed and no arguing! Do you hear? You have over an hour before dinner so you can use it to find your way around the farm."

Satisfied, Brother Connolly left her to it and the atmosphere relaxed once more.

"Now boys, go to the big hut when you hear the bell, that's where you'll eat, and try not to be late," Mrs. Butcher kindly instructed before leaving.

The beds were similar to those they had become accustomed to at Clontarf although the frames were a little more rusted. After twenty minutes Nick and Chris had seen as much as they thought necessary of the immediate farm area. Some distance away was a collection of smaller buildings surrounding a wind pump. On investigating they found pigs in a small pen, chickens and a basic blacksmiths shop which didn't look as though it had been used for a while. Further away was a slightly larger, open sided building where two working horses were tethered. Satisfied, they returned to the shaded benches and waited. Chris spoke quietly.

"You know what? I can't believe how lucky we are."

"What do you mean?" Nick asked in surprise.

"Well, to still be together after all this time. Even in England we could have been separated."

Nick agreed. In a moment of contemplation they realised that they only had each other and the depth of their friendship. Chris turned to face Nick, looked into his eyes and speaking in a low sincere tone said, "we are more like brothers than friends. We are the only family each of us have."

Like a reflex, Nick thought, "no, I have a mother somewhere." Yet he still looked back at Chris, nodded his silent agreement and after a moment or two speculated.

"We could still be separated. Let's make a plan, call it a pact, a promise to each other to meet up again somewhere if we do get separated."

Nick totally agreed, so they set about deciding on a date and place, agreeing it was important to pick a time when they would have the freedom to travel if need be, and a place easy to find. Nick said that he had read that people sometimes meet outside the main Post Office in Sydney.

"It's a big Victorian building in Martin Place right in the centre of Sydney. I've seen pictures of it. Neither of us could miss it."

Chris said he thought it was too far away. But Nick speculated they could be coming from anywhere in the country or even already be in Sydney itself. Also that transport to Sydney, from anywhere, should be easier than to many other places.

So it was agreed that it would be an easy place to find, planning to meet at midday on Nick's 21th birthday, on the 10th November 1961. Although neither one ever thought they would lose contact with the other, this would be their contingency plan. They sat quietly again for a while before Nick asked, "what do you want to do when you leave here?"

Chris didn't hesitate.

"Well I've been thinking and pretty well decided to join the army."

Nick was shocked, then reacting in an surprised voice.

"Why? You would just be swapping one institution for another!"

Chris didn't respond to Nick's surprise, he had expected it when he eventually told him.

"Well, apart from you I have nobody in this world, no proper family, no mother, father, brothers or sisters that I know of or that I could ever find. What's more, when we eventually leave here, neither of us will have any particular skills to get a decent job. I don't want to end up as a nothing person. I read that the army will teach you things and give you skills. They feed and clothe you as well as provide somewhere to live. I only know institutional life, disciplines and structure so it will be perfect for me."

Then he jokingly added, "and there won't be any beatings either."

"You won't be old enough to join the army when you finish here," Nick exclaimed, to argue against Chris' decision.

"I'll try and join as a cadet or a boy entrant, or whatever they call them. If not I'll work somewhere until I'm old enough. Anyway, I read that men in the army are like brothers and feel part of a special family, just like you and me."

Chris paused then asked, "what about you? What are you going to do when you leave here? You will have to get a job and earn a living somehow."

Nick thought a moment before replying.

"To be honest Chris, I really don't know what I'll do for a living, but I really want to find my mother."

Nick was feeling awkward as the question had not previously crossed his mind and especially as Chris had already worked his future out. Nick had frequently longed to be free of the care of institutions but had not given much thought to earning a living later on. Chris understood from Nick's tone that he didn't want to pursue the subject and asked no more questions.

At 5.30 pm an old American Style Ford utility trundled from the fields into the yard, stopping in a cloud of dust. Six tired, dirty boys, just a little older than Nick and Chris, climbed from the open back and made their way to a tap near the showers. Each took turns to drink and some splashed water over their heads. It ran down their faces marking its passage through the day's dust and dirt. The new boys watched in silence as the workers walked towards them.

"Are you the replacement kids?" one asked.

"Guess so," someone said.

"Okay, they'll expect us to show you what to do. The Brothers will tell you but won't show you. We'll show you the ropes tomorrow. Now we have to shower before dinner, see you there."

Some dispersed to the showers and others to their huts.

The evening meal was surprisingly only a little better than those at Clontarf. They had hoped for better given this is where much of the food came from. At the very least, they expected to get enough but there never was. Prayers of thanks for what they were about to receive were strictly adhered to. However the existing boys had changed the words to:

"O'Lord, please give us better food than last time and more of it. Then we will be truly thankful. Amen."

Their prayers were not answered. A stew smelling of old meat was served although only shreds of it were actually found but the potatoes and carrots were obvious. There was no dessert, just a mug of weak tea.

After dinner Nick and Chris went into the yard to sit on the benches in the corrugated iron shelter. They were met by some of the older boys who they had seen briefly earlier.

"I'm Tim and this is Bill, Jeff and Mike. We've been here a while and expect to leave soon," Tim said.

"Where have you come from?" Jeff asked.

"Clontarf," Chris replied.

Tim drew breath through his teeth, looked down and shook his head. The others were silent.

"Clontarf or Bindoon, much the same," Mike then added.

"I bet you have never done farm work before?"

Tim stated in the manner of a question he already knew the answer to.

"No," Chris replied.

"Well you'd better learn quickly or you'll cop a beating with old Michael's cricket bat. He don't care, bash you as soon as look at you he will."

"Out of the frying pan into the fire then!" Chris muttered.

Nick and Chris looked at each other. Nick was always outraged at the punishments handed out by the priests, often for little reason or no real crime at all, simply because they could. They called it maintaining discipline or administering justice. Nick had learned to hold back the tiger inside and not protest so making matters worse.

The new boys quickly understood there were two separate things to learn, both of equal importance. One was farm work and the other was survival.

Work consisted of managing the animals and what to do with crops at appropriate times. Brother Michael, with his cricket bat, would make sure things were done properly. Survival was mostly staying out of Brother Michael's way and knowing how to get extra food without being caught. The latter carrying an element of cunning excitement.

There were opportunities to supplement their basic diet with fresh produce that the older boys knew all about. The first was to volunteer to collect the chickens' eggs each morning. Nobody would ever know how many eggs had been laid. They were difficult to carry away concealed, so a fresh raw one was often on the menu in the hen house. The important thing was to dispose of the shell, which usually meant burying it or putting it in a pocket to be discretely discarded later in the day.

Bandicooting was popular when potatoes were ready to harvest. The boys soon learned how to burrow in from the side of the heaped row and extract a single potato without affecting the plant. Although bitter, it was usually eaten raw. Carrots were easy to get and tasted sweet. Pull one out from a clump in the row, break the top off and stick it back in the ground. The underside would decay and the top die. If it was checked, it looked as though it had been attacked and eaten from underneath.

The most exciting escapade was to raid the morning truck which brought bins of pig food from a nearby town. It could only be done when the boys were working in the right area. The driver would collect leftovers and waste from cafés, restaurants, greengrocers and bakers, bringing them to the farm. He was obliged to stop at a padlocked gate before reaching the pig pens. The boys would spit on a handful of dirt and push it into the lock through the keyhole. Then throw a handful of the dry dusty dirt over the lock. It would be dry by the time the truck arrived at the gate. The lock looked as though wind had blown dirt into it. Consequently, it took the driver a few minutes to open the gate during which time the boys would emerge from hiding, scramble onto the back of the truck and pick out edible food which was often better than what they were given at meal times. Sweet cakes were considered a luxurious delicacy.

Nick, Chris and four other boys were chosen to help build a small chapel not far away. They were happy with the variation of work and to learn something different. They were also pleased to see Mr. Con again who had come with a set of plans and tools to supervise the work. Under Mr. Con's guidance, they learned about building and stone masonry as this was his trade. He enjoyed building and his enthusiasm rubbed off onto the boys. The work was heavy and hard. They were grazed, scratched and their hands were sore. By the end of each day they were extremely tired and their limbs ached from heavy lifting. Shaping stone blocks by hand and mixing cement mortar with spades was back-breaking work. Yet they did it willingly with a sense of pride at their achievement. It was motivating to see their labours grow into something lasting and worthwhile, feeling they were worthy of something good and not just 'a waste of space' as they had been previously told.

Once every two weeks a Brother from Clontarf came to check on their progress. The boys tried to stay away from him, busying themselves when he was near. Mr. Con sensed the tension and was pleased to see him leave, also feeling he knew more of what was to be done than the priest and wanted to be left alone to get on with it. The boys worked harder and were happier when Mr. Con was the only authority there. He encouraged and motivated them with kindness, congratulating them when a job was done well. He was good to them and especially nice after the Brother had gone, and so to relax them, he'd say,
"it's alright now men, he's gone."

They liked being called men.

Mr. Con knew what went on at the institution but said nothing for fear of losing his job.

10

Nick became worried when he heard that some boys were to return to Clontarf to help with building work there. He hated the place, despised the Brothers and was desperate not to go. In bed at night he fantasized about running away, never allowing himself to think of being caught and punished. It would spoil his daydream. But where would he go? Where would he live? The more the answers eluded him, the more frustrated he became. He knew nothing of life outside the farm and Clontarf Boys Town.

In their last days at the chapel they were to tidy the site. Building waste was moved to a hole about fifty yards behind the chapel and buried. Some of the rocks were kept to mark a path around the building. Others defined a pathway over the dry terrain leading to the door of the chapel. Mr. Con had scratched a line to show where they were to be placed. Nick thought they would look better whitewashed. Mr. Con agreed but there was none to use.

Before leaving for Clontarf the truck was brushed clean, the tools loaded and bench seats placed along each side. Two Jerry Cans of water were put in the back for the journey, one for drinking and the other in case the truck overheated.

As they drove away, Nick and Chris looked back with a sense of pride at the little chapel they had worked so hard to build. Nobody spoke for the first ten minutes when eventually someone said, "oh well, it's back to Hell again."

Nobody responded, but Nick felt a wave of panic flush through his mind.

They bumped along the dusty road in the heat for what seemed like hours. The rattle and drone of the truck was hypnotic while the boys sat quietly pondering what the future might hold for them on their return to Clontarf. Nick simply didn't want to go back, and that was all he could think of. He was stressing over it when the truck suddenly swerved to miss a dead kangaroo that Mr. Con had not noticed until almost too late. The bench on one side fell across the truck spilling one row of boys onto the other. There was a lot of shouting and noise so Mr. Con stopped the truck.

The bench was repositioned and the boys re-seated. Some were in pain with minor cuts and bruises but none complained. Mr. Con decided there was nothing seriously wrong, and after apologising, continued. Soon the drone of the truck took over again. With every minute that passed, Nick continued to become more desperate not to return to Clontarf.

After two more hours, they pulled off the road. Mr. Con got out, walked to the back of the vehicle and called,
"OK boys, time for a pee-break. Anybody who wants water can get it now. And don't go wandering off. I don't want you getting lost out here."

He then went to the front of the truck and lifted the bonnet, allowing the engine to cool.

Welcoming the opportunity to stretch their legs and drink, the boys clambered from the back of the vehicle. Most relieved themselves at the side of the road before drinking. Others were already pouring water from a Jerry Can into metal mugs. Mr. Con produced packets of sandwiches that had been brought from a station a few miles away. Nick looked around. They had stopped in a rocky depression which looked as though it had been cut when the road was made. It was lined with large boulders that had presumably been pushed aside after blasting. He wandered back along the road behind the truck to explore and stretch his legs.

He was startled by an Aboriginal boy hiding behind one of the larger boulders. They looked at each other without speaking, Nick in surprise and the boy in fear. There was a pregnant silence in what seemed a longer time than it really was.

"Who are you? What are you doing?" Nick asked.

The boy had a worried look on his face as he reluctantly muttered, "hiding."

"Why?" Nick asked.

"White-fella Police."

"Why? What did you do?"

"They want to take me. I hid because I heard the truck and thought it was them."

"You can't stay here, there's nothing around for miles. You'll die out here," Nick replied.

"Narr, I know how to get along in the outback. I live out here and I got friends too," the boy said.

"Where are you going?"

"Home, miles and miles through the bush to the north east. Take a lotta days but I can find the way. And I got water, look."

The boy held up a dirty Darwin Stubby half full of water."

Nick had seen this boy's haunted, frightened look many times before. That alone caused Nick to empathize and want to help him. He didn't know why, it was just a willing desire. Perhaps it was the sorrowful look in the boy's eyes. Institutions unwittingly instilled feelings of comradeship and resentment of authority amongst its boys. Nick knew the unwritten rule that you never turn another boy in, no matter what. You never tell tales on another boy or blame him to the priests and if he needs help, you give it. For Nick, those rules now applied everywhere.

"Give me your bottle. I'll fill it up for you," he said instinctively.

The boy clasped it close to his chest. He looked fearful, a white person had never offered to help him before. Nick saw his concern and said, "Come on, I won't steal it and we've got plenty of water, clean water too."

The Aboriginal boy took a swig from the bottle before cautiously handing it over. Nick quickly went back to the truck, while pouring a little of the Aboriginal's water into his hand. It was dirty so Nick poured it away and filled the bottle with clean water from the Jerry Can. A boy asked what he was doing. Nick looked him square in the face without replying, giving him a look that suggested he didn't need to know. Before heading back down the road Nick took Chris aside and whispered, "this is it. I can't go back to Clontarf and I might not get another chance, I'm off! Are you coming?"

Chris was taken by surprise and without thinking said, "no. What's going on? What are you doing?"

Typically he wanted to know more before deciding. Chris was always the more cautious of the two.

"No time, it's now or never," Nick replied in earnest.

He quickly embraced Chris before he had a chance to ask any more questions and was on his way back down the road to disappear behind a boulder. Nick's heart was pounding with the knowledge of what he was doing. At last, this was his chance to escape the tyranny of the Christian Brothers. He didn't stop to reconsider this opportunity, he just took it, now crouching behind the boulder at the side of his new comrade. Nick gave the bottle back while making a point of smiling. The boy returned half a smile and nodded but his eyes remained fearful.

"What you doing?" The Aboriginal boy asked.

"I'm hiding like you," Nick replied.

Back at the truck, the boys had watched Nick wash and fill the bottle then run along the road to eventually disappear. When he didn't reappear after a minute or two, they looked puzzled and struggled to contain their excited speculations. Chris gestured to them to be quiet. Mr. Con called for the boys to get into the back of the truck, and just before driving off called, "Everyone on board?"

"Yes," the boys responded as a rabble.

Chris stared at the boulder until it disappeared in the distance. He had a lump in his throat and was afraid for Nick.

Nick heard the truck move away making his heart pounded faster. There would be no turning back now.

"Where are you going?" Nick asked.

"Home."

"Which way is that?"

The boy hesitated before standing and pointed to the north east.

"Longway, a long way, another place."

"What place?"

Nick asked showing urgency and a little frustration. Then aware that he was pressuring the boy, he checked himself. Nick had spent many years around frightened boys and understood, so didn't want to push him. The Aboriginal boy was clearly afraid of Nick and it was a new experience for him to have a white boy as his perceived equal. Nick was careful not to appear dominating, not wanting to be guilty of causing another boy's fear. He'd come to despise those who created fear in others. Nick reached out and gently touched the boy's arm before gesturing to shake his hand. The boy was reserved but his hand moved towards Nick's as if by a slow reflex. Nick shook it firmly and deliberately smiling to appear friendly and unthreatening said, "my name is Nick. What's yours?"

"Gidga." The boy said quietly.

"I'm pleased to meet you Gidga. Can we be friends and travel together? I'm going your way too."

Nick was carefully nurturing his new relationship. His veins were full of adrenalin and his heart was pounding. He was both excited and apprehensive, not knowing where he would go or what would happen. But he was free and felt he could fly. Tagging along with Gidga seemed like a good idea, especially since Nick had little knowledge of where he was or how to survive out here.

11

Nick and Gidga waited until the truck was out of sight and could not be heard before walking out of the cutting. It was early afternoon and the sun was high and hot. Neither of them was wearing shoes. Nick was dressed in old shorts, a half decent shirt and a well worn bush hat. He felt sorry for Gidga who wore the remains of a shirt and threadbare shorts which were all he had. Clutching his bottle of water, he looked a pathetic sight. His skinny frame and legs, big knees and large flat feet did nothing to improve his image.

"We'd better get going," Gidga said.

They started to walk to the north, back up the road Nick had just travelled. He was simply following Gidga with absolute trust that this Aboriginal boy knew where he was going.

In an effort to relax Gidga, Nick told him about himself, where he was from and why he wanted to leave. Gidga listened patiently then said, "You white fellas are strange lot. You got priests what act like that and you call us black fellas Bastards."

Nick was surprised at the comment and agreed with the irony. He was pleased that Gidga was beginning to talk without being prompted each time.

Gidga pointed out a track that cut across to the road north to Koolyanobbing.

"Want to miss Southern Cross, there's a white fella copper there. They always nosey, got a lotta questions and treat you like you dirt."

They headed off the road to the right. Then after a few minutes they heard a vehicle back on the road, so they crouched to hide in a circle of tall spinifex grass and watched a truck go by about four hundred yards away.

"Why are you hiding from the police?" Nick asked.

"I think they looking for me."

Surprised, Nick asked why.

"Long story."

Gidga paused, he would continue when he had decided where to start. Nick remained silent and waited. Once the truck had disappeared, they started walking again.

"I come from up Lake Disappointment way. Well that's what white fellas call it anyway, maybe not that far. But long way, long way on the old stock route, takes days to get there. Weeks if you gotta walk all the way."

"So what are you doing here?"

Now Nick was even more curious.

"Couple a years ago my mother went with my sister to Newman to live with her sister. Just for a little long-time. Newman is over to the sunset. Government made proper houses for Aboriginals there, from proper new iron and put a water pump in. Her sister got a cleaning job in the town there too. But one day a couple a white fellas and a copper come, they took my sister away. She cried and screamed cos she don't want to go. My Ma tried to hold onto her but a white fella copper pulled her away. She was crying hard. The white fellas took my sis away in a car and we never seen her again."

"What for? Why?" Nick asked.

"Dunno. My aunt went to the copshop and asked. Said they were taking her to Perth for her own good, didn't say no more. But my mother was so upset, she cried for days. So when I got older I promised to go find my sis and bring her back."

"And did you find her?" Nick asked with interest.

"Narr. I got to Perth all right. Bigger place than what I thought. It took a couple'a weeks with lifts and a lotta walking to get to Mullewa. From there I sneaked a lift on a goods train to Geraldton. That was good, only took a couple'a hours. So I thought that was the best way to get to Perth. I hid in a wagon and a day and a bit later I was there. It was slow and I had to be careful not to get nabbed.

Perth was a big place, I never been there before and I didn't know where to look. I got no money and nothing to eat. I went to the cop shop to ask where my sister was. They didn't know, didn't care, just ask a lotta questions about me. I think they wanted to keep me there but it was too much bother, so they told me to bugger off. Then I got caught taking tucker from back of a café. It was only stuff what they throwed out. But the boss fella called the coppers and said I was thieving. As soon as I could get away I ran off before the coppers arrived. I didn't want to get locked up. Makes us black fellas go crazy see."

"So where did you go?" Nick asked.

"I hid under a bridge. Didn't know if white fella coppers were looking for me or not. I waited till it got dark and went out of town. I fell asleep in some bushes. What waked me up was a bloke from a truck what had stopped, he was cussing while he changed a wheel. A skinny sort'a bloke, dunno if he was Aboriginal or a white fella, could'a been a bit of both. Anyway, he comes to the bushes for a piss, sees me and asks what I was doing. He seemed alright so we got talking, said he was going to Kalgoorlie. He'd bin to Fremantle docks collecting stuff for the mines. So I got a lift off him."

"So what are you doing by the road back here, Kalgoorlie is in another direction?" Nick enquired.

"I heard a lot about Kalgoorlie, lotta mines and plenty people with a lotta white fella coppers. So later when he stopped and got out to check the wheel again, I grabbed the bottle and run off. I never did go near Kalgoorlie. The wrong direction anyway like you said, but I got away from Perth."

In an attempt to relieve Gidga's concerns Nick said, "I don't think the police would be looking for you over a small thing like taking a bit of thrown out food."

"You whites would think that, but you not black."

Then Nick suddenly thought. 'but they will look for me, being a runaway white boy from an orphanage.' Now he hoped he had not placed Gidga in danger of being detained and investigated.

Gidga stopped to take a mouthful of water and offered the bottle to Nick who took Gidga's lead by taking only one mouthful although he felt he could drink more. They walked on at a steady pace along the track that led through a dusty red plain splattered with spinifex and an occasional small struggling tree. It was hot, and after about two hours they sat under a rare shade tree for a while. Again, they each took one mouthful of water. In the shimmer of heat, they could just make out a mob of kangaroos.

Gidga started to laugh and Nick asked what was so funny.

"Do you know how kangaroos got their white fella name?"

"No," Nick replied.

"Well, when the white fellas first come to our land and sees one of them he asks a black fella. "What is it?" The black fella say 'kan-ga-roo.' That means 'I don't understand you.' But the white fella went and called it a kangaroo."

Gidga laughed harder and Nick joined in. Clearly Gidga had a good sense of humour and Nick was beginning to like him. Neither boy had much to laugh at before now. After a few minutes they got to their feet to continue their journey. Gidga asked Nick where his father and mother were. With a lump in his throat, Nick could only say that his father had died in the war. He didn't know where his mother was but that he believed she was still alive somewhere. For a few moments he felt very low. Then to deliberately change the mood, he asked Gidga about his own mother and father. Gidga said that not long after his sister was taken, his mother had returned to their small outback community of about 100 people. His father had died three years before.

"How did he die?" Nick asked.

Gidga did not want to discuss it although after a pause he said, "the Rainbow Serpent took 'im."

Nick did not understand but asked nothing more.

They walked on for some hours, taking only short occasional breaks. Eventually Nick said he had to stop for a little longer. Gidga reluctantly agreed but insisted they only stop where and when he said.

The duo had stayed in one place too long and should never have fallen asleep. The gully was good for only a short stop, just long enough to regain some strength and composure. If anyone was looking for them, this is where they would be expected to hide. But they were exhausted. Nick thought that Gidga had the stamina of three men and could walk forever. He knew he was physically stronger and more athletic for his age but he did not have Gidga's stamina. They would have been vulnerable in the open, to both the scorching sun and the searching eyes of the police. They had to leave the relative comfort of the gully soon or they might be found if a search had already been started.

"We gotta go."

Nick didn't reply, just nodded through a tired look. Gidga was clearly anxious.

"Listen, if the white fella coppers were just looking for me, one little black kid, they wouldn't look for long. They would give up plenty quick. But for a white fella kid they would look for days, even weeks, get on the wireless and tell all the stations to look out for him too. They'd use a black tracker fella who could easily follow us and one what knows this area better than us," Gidga said.

Nick was now worried and more eager to leave. After a short silence, Gidga looked at Nick almost apologetically and said, "We go now, or we get caught real soon."

"Which way?" Nick asked.

Gidga pointed to the north east and said, "There, long way, where my people live. They will keep us from the white fella coppers. But we gotta go now!"

Gidga knew that with an Aboriginal tracker to help them, the police would not be far behind and it was no good trying to cover their tracks. It would only make them more obvious to the tracker and cost precious time. They might fool a white policeman but not an Aboriginal tracker. The simple repositioning of the sand, or a pebble in any way, would not escape the notice of a skilled tracker, and the police only ever used the best. Gidga had lived in the bush all his life and knew how good Aboriginals were at tracking. For generations they had learned their skills hunting in order to live. Some police said they were even better than dogs. They could follow a trail just as well, explain what had happened in any particular place and sometimes predict what was going to happen. They could think ahead, take shortcuts and move at night to get ahead of their quarry and wait. A dog could only follow behind and it could lose the scent if the quarry went through water or along a creek. Then it might take hours for the dog to pick up the scent again. But an Aboriginal tracker could soon follow without difficulty.

Gidga reached for Nick's hand to pull him to his feet.

"I dunno what is worse, a dog or an Abo tracker? Dog you can maybe fool but the bloody thing will tear you to bits if it gets you. White fella copper will let it just to teach you a lesson. But a black fella tracker is smarter than a dog. He always gets you, if he really wants to," Gidga sighed.

They came to an area of gravel which they had to cross, the stones hurt Nick's feet even though he was accustomed to not wearing shoes.

"Don't walk normal. Lift your feet high and put your feet down level so as not to move the stones," Gidga instructed.

"Why?" Nick asked.

"When you walk normal you turn the stones."

Gidga picked up a pebble to demonstrate.

"Look, see the side on top is whiter from the sun and the bottom is dark. If you turn the stones a tracker will see the dark side stones like they was footprints in clean sand."

Gidga said their best chance was to get onto hard rock. Even then their movements might be followed. But with care, they could make it more difficult for a tracker.

"Come on, we got a chance if we get to Dingo Gorge. It's about four miles. Plenty places to hide tonight, and water there too."

They peered over the far side of the gully, anxiously looking in the direction they had come from. Then they climbed out to stand up straight. Still looking back, Gidga's posture demanded silence and attention. He stretched his neck forwards and squinted into the distance.

"Bloody hell! They coming, look!" Gidga said as he pointed.

Nick followed Gidga's finger but all he could see was a wisp of dust about a mile away across the flat terrain.

"Gidga it's just a dust devil."

Gidga instantly replied, "no, they following us. See the wind comes from one side. That makes the devil move sideways. This is not moving that way, only towards us. I tell you they following us."

They ran from the gully towards the north east. After about a quarter of a mile they stopped, both panting heavily. Nick leaned forwards and put his hands on his knees while gasping for breath.

"Where are we heading? We seem to be running further into the bush with nowhere to hide. If the police have a tracker they'll follow us easily, even I could follow our tracks," Nick panted.

Gidga heard but he was not listening. He was already thinking of what they could do to escape. After a moment he said, "look we can't lose them in this stuff but we might on the sandstone in the gorge. All we can do now is slow 'em down. See them blue hills on the horizon?"

Nick nodded.

"OK, now see the highest one in the middle?"

Nick nodded again while still trying to recover his breath.

"Good, now we gotta split up. They got one tracker and he can't go two ways at one time."

Gidga pointed to the right and said, "you go that way, run for about a thousand steps, keep the mountains on this side of you."

Gidga touched Nick's left shoulder.

"Then turn to that big mountain, go straight to it. Before them hills is Dingo Gorge. Hide there but don't climb all the way down or cross it, stay this side. That way I find you cos I only got half the places to look. On the other side they will see you easy, so stay away. Go part way down on this side and hide under a ledge and keep still so they won't know where you are from above. I will find to you."

"What are you going to do?" Nick asked.

"I do the same, only go the other way. Don't run too hard, breathe slow and easy as you can, that way you won't get tired so quick. If you see water at the bottom of the gorge don't go down to drink it, don't touch it, stay away. Tell you why later. Now go."

The boys set off in opposite directions. Nick had no idea how long it would take to reach the gorge or even if their plan would work, but he was happy to follow Gidga's instructions. He seemed to know what he was doing and obviously knew more about the bush than he did. Nick settled into a steady rhythm but found it difficult to control his breathing as Gidga had suggested due to the psychical exertion and adrenalin that was pumping through his body. He clenched his fists in determination while he concentrated on counting his paces. Each time he reached one hundred, he released a finger from his fist. When all ten digits were extended he knew he had done a thousand paces. It was easier to count that way and the concentration took his mind off his aching limbs, dry throat and burning lungs. He was feeling vulnerable now, alone in this vast country for the first time. It came home to him how much he now relied on Gidga for his survival.

The sun was lower in the sky now, just over Nicks left shoulder and not so hot. The distant hills were beginning to take on a pinkish blue hue. Almost immediately after Nick had turned towards the hills, he ran past a dingo that was sheltering from the sun under overhanging spinifex.

They were both startled and Nick's heart beat even faster from fright. The dingo leapt back, wide-eyed as it darted away. It eventually stopped and looked back to see what had so rudely woken it. On seeing Nick running away, its instinct was to give chase, which it did. But for only a few yards before giving up, its bravado satisfied. The chase was not worth the energy so it stood intently watching Nick for several minutes before it relaxed and slumped down into the dirt again.

Nick didn't dare to look over his shoulder to see what the dingo was doing. He thought it would be great to be able to bounce like a kangaroo. Then he'd get away from the dingo and cover the distance in no time at all.

The hills that had seemed so far away before were now closer and turning a darker blue. As the sun lowered to the horizon a light chill wafted up from the gorge. Nick could see that it was easily two hundred yards across and about a hundred feet deep. The edges were rocky with protruding horizontal ledges. If he was careful it would not be too difficult climbing down. At the bottom he saw the glimmer of water in small pools, reminding him of his desperate thirst and of Gidga's instruction. He was so adamant about not going near the water that Nick felt obliged to comply.

Nick searched for the best way to climb down the side of the gorge whilst carefully traversing narrow ledges until he could reach the next one. The sides of the gorge were a mixture of sandstone, ironstone and loose sandy dirt with little vegetation. Great care was needed as it was easy to slip or overbalance. He tried not to look down but concentrate on where he was putting his feet. To his left about half way down, he could see a sandstone outcrop. The sedimentary sandstone ledge protruded far enough to conceal him from any searching eyes above. The loose sandy soil on the wall beneath it had eroded away to create a recess, and a layer of sandstone below protruded enough to create a hiding place.

From his vantage point beneath the ledge, Nick had a good view in both directions along the gorge as well as to the bottom. He would be able to see Gidga coming and make himself seen without their pursuers knowing. After brushing away animal droppings with his hand, he sat under the ledge and waited. As he recovered his breath, he looked at the pools of water below while being aware of his thirst. Some pools were a dark sandy colour and some green whilst others were clear. It suddenly came to him how hungry he was.

As darkness approached, deep blue shadows crept up the walls from the bottom of the gorge. Nick began to worry if Gidga would be able to find him in this light. He stiffened once as he thought he heard sounds from above. Not daring to breathe, he concentrated on listening but there was nothing more, only the distant squeal of an animal or bird.

Gidga was already in the gorge, working his way to where he expected to find Nick. He was careful to stay close to the southern side using the features of the gorge and shadows to hide his movements from above. Like Nick, he was thirsty but their bottle had long since been empty. The temptation to go to the middle of the gorge and drink from one of the pools was great. Knowing it could mean declaring his presence and position if he were seen, he would wait until dark. As he made his way further along the gorge, he constantly scanned the walls above for signs of Nick expecting him to be about half way down under a sandstone outcrop.

Sensing he must be close now, he looked up and spotted Nick forty feet above him and about thirty yards ahead. They saw each other simultaneously. Nick was relieved and waved. Gidga waved back and held his forefinger vertically in front of his lips, instructing Nick not to call out. In a few minutes the boys were together on the ledge, smiling at each other with relief and a sense of satisfaction. For the first time today they were genuinely both happy.

In a low voice Nick said, "my mouth is as dry as a Pommy's towel. I've got to have something to drink."

An expression he had picked up at the orphanage. Gidga grinned as he asked, "what's a Pommy? What do you mean?"

Nick smiled as he told Gidga that English people are called "Poms" in Australia, and have a reputation of not washing very often.

"Yeh," Gidga replied. They say the same about us black fellas, only they call us Abbos or Black Bastards. They forget we don't always have enough water to wash."

They shared a low chuckle then Gidga said it would be dark soon and they could go down to the pools, drink and fill their bottle. Nick asked why he didn't want him to go to the pools earlier.

"Well first, a white fella or tracker might see you from the top. Then if you drink from the wrong pool, you get sick real bad. The clean water is in the middle and you leave tracks in the sand. Yeh, an you stir up the water. Any tracker would see that through one bad eye from up there. An I bet you don't know what is good water or bad."

Gidga was right. Nick answered by asking if they could go down.

"Soon, let it be darker first."

Nick was developing a great respect for Gidga's common sense and knowledge, so was becoming more confident.

"There's a cave nearer the bottom below us. I saw it when I come up. We'll drink, fill the bottle, then sleep in there tonight. Come on, be quiet, don't talk and don't knock any rocks down. The sound echoes in here, you can hear it for miles at night."

Gidga lead the way down. It was tricky and not easy to see in the evening darkness. They passed the cave and Nick was relieved to reach the bottom. Then cautiously they made their way to a pool that Gidga had noted earlier. Gidga tasted the water and said it was okay.

Nick gulped water down as if they were competing against each other. Gidga drank more steadily.

"Not so fast or you'll be crook," Gidga whispered.

When they had their fill they sat back and looked at each other with contentment, neither speaking. Both boys burped and quietly giggled. Nick filled their bottle, poured water over his face, rubbed his eyes and sat with his feet in the pool. How wonderful it felt.

"I'm hungry," Nick said very quietly.

"We might be able to catch a Goanna or trap a Rock Wallaby. But we can't cook it. I know how to make fire but the white fella coppers would know where we are quick smart. They'd smell it from miles away."

Gidga cautioned as he produced a handful of berries he had stuffed into his pocked back near the gully. It was a habit the Elders had taught him in bush survival. Take it when you can. The berries were bitter making Nick wince and his eyes smart.

Gidga laughed.

"They good energy tucker mate. Come on, we can't stay here."

They got to their feet and clambered up to the cave. By now the moon was lighting up the gorge with a clear, eerie blue hue. Although it was darker at the bottom, they could still see the way as they scrambled upwards to the cave. It looked deep and dark inside. Neither was happy about going in very far, so they sat inside the entrance. The moon had now risen high in the night sky but its light did not reach the cave entrance where blackened rocks and gray ash from many previous fires lay. Silhouetted in white around the walls, were hand shapes of all sizes. Gidga said they told him it's a safe place, that they were the marks of his ancestors who had passed this way before.

They sat in the cave entrance marveling at the brightness and clarity of the stars and moon, while the pools at the bottom of the gorge offered perfect reflections of the stars to create a strange illusion. The boys had no idea they were not alone in the cave.

"My mother will worry about me tonight," Gidga lamented.

"Why tonight?" Nick asked.

Then after a short pause.

"Doesn't she know where you are or what you're doing?"

"That's why she worry. My name, 'Gidga' means God of the Moon.

She called me that cos I was born the night of a big moon like this, it remind her of me. She look at the same moon as us and see my face, maybe she looking right now.

That makes us close. She like the name Gidga because her name is Arana, that means moon. Them names make us closer, see."

Nick sat back and wondered if his own mother was looking at the same moon on the other side of the world. Was she thinking of him? The thought was comforting but it came charged with unwelcome emotions. He understood Gidga's sentiment better than Gidga would ever know. A lump had started to grow in his throat, and the emotion was upsetting, so he forced himself to stop thinking about her.

In low voices they talked about what they would do the next day and decided to leave the gorge before it got light to avoid the possibility of being seen. Both were concerned about their inability to carry enough water. So they agreed to drink their fill before they left.

"If we could find emu eggs, we could suck out the inside for tucker and fill them with water. But there won't be emus down here," Gidga said.

They slept fitfully in the cave, were cold and the floor was hard beneath a thin layer of fine sand that had never been washed by rain. Gidga was comforted by the many white silhouetted hands on the walls, saying they would keep them safe here.

Deep in the back of the cave an Olive Python stirred. It had been aware of the intruders as soon as they had arrived. High on its sandstone ledge it had detected the boys scent all night long. The ledge was long enough for it to move almost to the entrance of the cave without touching the ground. It had not eaten for more than two weeks when it had devoured a rock wallaby whole. Driven more by curiosity than hunger, it silently and slowly moved its twelve foot bulk along the ledge towards the boys, resting just above them.

Gidga woke first, having set his body clock to wake him an hour before dawn.

It was colder and darker then. The moon had gone and the sun had not yet risen. It was much darker in the cave than when they had fallen asleep the night before. Nick was still sleeping as Gidga rose to his feet. He raised his arms above his head, stretching and arched his body backwards, almost losing his balance. He didn't see what suddenly entwined his left arm in a vice-like grip whilst sinking its teeth into his shoulder to hold fast.

Gidga shrieked in shock and pain, not understanding what was happening. Nick woke in alarm, rubbing his eyes, and adjusted his sight to see what was happening. He could see very little at first, only hear the pained commotion. Using leverage from the hold on Gidga's shoulder, the python threw its entire sixty pound body at him, knocking him off his feet then immediately held his torso in coils of contracting muscle. Nick tried to drag the monster away by the tail but the harder he tried, the tighter it constricted around Gidga's body.

Gidga yelled. The pain in his shoulder was excruciating and the pressure on his ribs was increasing. He knew the snake would keep squeezing until he could no longer draw breath and suffocate. Nick tried to pull the head away but Gidga yelled with even more pain as sharp teeth dragged into his flesh. Nick found it was hopeless trying to pull the snake away or to uncoil it from around Gidga's body. Both boys were now fighting the snake, thrashing about in the dust. Out of desperation, Nick grabbed the tail again and pulled it, but to no effect. Gidga could no longer draw enough breath to yell. He could only moan and gasp. Nick was frantic and tears of desperation welled in his eyes.

They had rolled across the middle of the cave to where the old firestones were. Nick could see that Gidga's wide unseeing eyes were bulging. He felt helpless as Gidga slumped and passed out. Nick reached for one of the firestones and pounded the snakes head. It opened its jaws releasing its grip but did not relinquish its prey from the suffocating coils. With both hands, Nick raised a firestone boulder high above his head for a last desperate, mighty blow to the animals head. But he was pulled off balance and fell backwards.

12

Senior Constable Mike Williams had been in the outback six months. He was getting bored and disgruntled having originally hoped for greater stimulation from some outback adventure or, at the very least, one day that did not involve sorting out family arguments amongst Aboriginal families in the larger settlements. All an inevitable legacy of alcohol and the poor acceptance by western society they were now obliged to rely on. S.C. Williams was always annoyed with the persistent flies that irritated him with their incessant attention. He was sure they lay in wait for him outside his door.

There were two police officers at Watchit Creek. Constable Doltry was seven years Williams' junior, had been raised in a small country town and was more comfortable in the outback, preferring it to city life. To his advantage was an understanding of Aboriginals and their culture, but he sometimes became frustrated with their problems and considered them all lazy.

The Watchit police station was a basic three roomed brick building with a corrugated iron roof. One room was the lock-up. Another tiny room, cynically known as The Kitchen, contained a sink and a power point that an electric kettle was permanently plugged into. The third room was "an apology for an office," as S.C. Williams called it. The lock up had only been used once and the poor Aboriginal soul inside had gone crazy. S.C. Williams learned a valuable lesson about Aboriginals, so the cell was now used for storage. Yet this was his first command and he was quietly proud of it.

The two-way radio was always switched on, being more reliable than the telephone and it could reach remote places where there was no phone line. For most working cattle stations and communities, it was a lifeline. The seemingly conscientious S.C. Williams got agitated when asked to relay domestic messages. But he did it anyway, mostly because he knew that policing relied heavily on the support of local folk and that being part of the community was important. It was the way of the bush.

At about 6pm, the radio crackled into life, just as S.C. Williams was about to leave for the day. He immediately reached for the blue Pye microphone. It was Sergeant Mills from Regional Headquarters. Just as he acknowledged his boss, the small diesel generator by the backdoor rattled into life. He turned the volume up to hear his boss say as a statement rather than a question, "bet you was about to bugger off for the day, hey Williams?"

"Just about Sarge."

"Yeh, well sorry to muck your evening up but we got a runaway kid on your patch'o dirt. Seems he ran off from a truck taking him and some other kids back to an orphanage over at the coast. Get your local O.S. map and I'll tell you where to start looking." Sergeant Mills commanded.

He directed S.C. Williams to a reference point on the map where the boy was last seen.

How old's the kid and what's his name?"

"Not sure of his age. I think about thirteen. His name is ⸱ Nicholas Thorne, he answers to Nick," Sergeant Mills replied.

"Why did he run away? There's nothing out there but rocks, dirt and bloody flies."

"Yeh I know, but he won't have got far. You might even find him along the road feeling sorry for himself. You'd better get down there and bring the little bugger back. It might help if you take a tracker in case he's done a runner away from the road. You'll be quicker finding him, we don't want him wandering about all night. Take that lazy bastard Jacko if he's still around. According to the driver they stopped for a piss in a cutting, that's when he buggered off," Sergeant Mills said.

"Did any of the other kids see him bolt?"

"Nar, or if they did the little bastards are not saying."

"Alright Sarge, I'll get to it. I'll let you know when I've got him. Over and out."

For the first time in a while, S.C. Mike Williams felt motivated. He called to Constable Doltry, who entered the tiny office a few seconds later.

"Yes Boss?"

"We got a runaway kid down on the main road about ten miles out. Go and find Jacko."

As Constable Dolty was leaving, S.C.Williams called after him, "and tell that old black bastard that he's going tracking."

Constable Doltry was no friend of Jack's but he respected him for his knowledge of the outback and his tracking skills. He had once told S.C. Williams that what Jack didn't know about the bush was not worth knowing. It took only a few minutes to drive the half mile to where Jack lived on the edge of Watchit Creek settlement.

Although Jack had a government sponsored hut, he liked the old traditional ways and was dozing in his humpy when Constable Doltry arrived. Jack didn't speak but deliberately took his time. It was his way of saying. 'You don't own me', knowing with satisfaction that it would annoy the policeman.

Impatient, Constable Doltry called to Jack again.
"Come on Jacko, move your arse. The boss is waiting to take you tracking."

Jack continued to move at his own pace, first putting on his cap then picking up an old army water bottle.

"We got a runaway kid, a boy, down the main track and the boss needs you to go with him to bring him back."

Jack didn't need to ask if the boy was black or white. He knew he would never be asked to track an Aboriginal child. He sauntered over to Constable Doltry's ute and climbed in, not saying a word until they got to the police station. As they arrived, S.C. Williams was putting a one gallon can of water in his Land Rover. He didn't expect to need it for himself or Jacko but he thought the boy would most certainly need it. Nonetheless, carrying water had become a habit.

"Come on Jack'o, get in here and I'll tell you what we're doing as we go."

"Yes Boss."

S.C. Williams called to Constable Doltry.

"Stay by the radio mate. I might need you later."

It took half an hour to get to the main road and little was said between the two until they arrived. S.C. Williams pulled off the road at the start of the cutting saying, "We'll start here Jack'o, we are looking for a white boy, so he's probably wearing shoes."

"Yes Boss," Jack replied.

He didn't much like S.C. Williams and was reluctant to engage him in conversation. Nothing really bad had happened to make him dislike the man, it was just the way he was spoken to, always telling, never asking and sometimes rude or disrespectful. It left Jack feeling cool towards him. He also sensed resentment from S.C. Williams because he could do things the police officer could not. It seemed to Jack that the policeman felt his authority was being undermined. Which Jack quietly enjoyed.

S.C. Williams walked a few yards with Jack then left him to go on alone. It was not long before he identified where the truck had stopped. In the dust at the side of the road were tyre marks and as many as half a dozen other different footprints. One was an adult set, made by someone wearing boots. The others all belonged to white kids with no shoes. Jack decided they were made by boys in their early teens. Being fresh tracks it was easy for him to determine the events that took place. A truck had stopped and later rejoined the road. There were dry crusted splash marks in the sand where liquid had been spilt, and more crusting at the base of rocks where liquid had run down into the sand and dirt. Jack took a pinch of sand from each location and sniffed it. He waved to S.C. Williams, beckoning him to come to him. Jack pointed and said.

"They stopped here, boss. Look, tyre marks, today, lots of bare feet, all white kids except one grown up with boots, water marks here, they pissed agin the rocks over there."

"Are there any kid's tracks that lead away from the road?" Williams asked.

"Yes boss, two tracks go away, both from the same kid, one walking one running and the same one walking back again. I reckon he went away, come back then run away."

Jack started to make his way further along the road. Fifty yards from where the truck had stopped, he found more footprints in the dirt to the side of a large boulder. One set was clearly that of the same white boy without shoes. Yet the others belonged to an Aboriginal boy, also without shoes. Neither was an unusual sight to Jack but together they were a puzzle. He looked to the back of the rock and saw a pair of Aboriginal boy's flat footprints that had been ground into the dirt. Immediately behind them was the shallow smooth imprint of a boy's buttocks. Jack accurately read the events of the day in the sandy earth. In his mind's eye, he could clearly see an Aboriginal boy squatting, hiding behind the rock and a white boy standing in front of him. Then to one side he could see where a white boy had also squatted.

Again he beckoned to Williams.

"Someone hid behind here boss."

Jack didn't say that an Aboriginal boy's prints were there too. He didn't know the circumstances and was instinctively protective of the Aboriginal, whoever he was. Williams correctly assumed that the white boy had hidden here while waiting for the truck to leave.

"So it looks like he's a runner, not just left behind. Bugger! Where did he go from here Jacko, down the road or into the bush?"

Jack didn't reply but again went his own way. The cleanest prints always told what happened last, and Jack noted that they led back onto the road. He crossed over to see if they reappeared on the other side but they did not. Jack slowly walked to the end of the cutting and crossed back over the road looking for signs as he went. He noticed two sets of footprints leading from the road. They were identical to those he had seen by the boulder. Narrower prints of a white boy and the wider spread soles and spaced toes of an Aboriginal boy. To Jack they were obviously travelling together.

He walked back to S.C. Williams and said he had gone north east into the bush, still not mentioning the Aboriginal boy.

"Now I suppose we got'a go bloody walkabout. Little Bugger!" S.C. Williams cursed.

Jack stood silently waiting for the inevitable instruction.

"Well come on Jacko, let's get to it."

They walked back to the Land Rover where the police officer radioed to Constable Doltry, telling him where they were, and that they were going to follow tracks north east into the bush for a while and that they expected to be back late. He then added as an afterthought,

"You'd better call Sergeant Mills and give him an update."

They took a rucksack and two water bottles from the Land Rover. S.C. Williams slung a rifle over his shoulder and they returned to where the tracks had left the road. He didn't think he'd a need the gun but didn't want to leave it in the vehicle. He paid little attention to the tracks, preferring to leave that to Jack.

"How far do you think the little bastard has gone?"

"If he walks steady, don't stop, maybe eight, nine miles at most," Jack replied.

"Christ Jacko, it'll be dark long before we get to him." S.C. Williams complained as though it was Jack's fault.

"Yes boss," Jack responded quietly.

He was used to this and didn't object. Had he done so, he would expect to receive a few words of sarcasm.

It took only minutes for Jack to see that the boys had crouched in a circle of Spinifex. Then the tracks showed a steady walking pace to the north east. Jack told S.C. Williams there was a gorge some miles ahead and that would probably be as far as the boy would get today. After a half hour of steady walking, the policeman considered the prospect of darkness, not carrying any swag and being poorly equipped for a longer trip. So he decided to return to the Land Rover telling Jack to keep going, saying that he would return in the morning with swag and basic supplies. He knew Jack would cope easily out here alone overnight and even enjoy it.

"The Land Rover will get across this stuff alright. So I'll see you an hour after sun up at the gorge," he told Jack.

After handing over the emergency rucksack, S.C. Williams headed back to the Land Rover while Jack continued to follow the boy's tracks to where they separated. The Aboriginal boy's tracks went west and the white boy's went east. Jack smiled, realising they knew they were being followed. The split was clearly to slow or confuse a tracker and force the police to choose to follow one track or the other. Jack had to follow the white boy, but in the certain knowledge that the tracks would eventually meet up again. Yet he hoped they would not, since the

Aboriginal boy could then escape whoever he was running from. It also worried him, believing the white boy could not survive out here alone.

Jack would never mention the Aboriginal boy's footprints, and nobody would be any the wiser. So he followed Nick's tracks east and eventually to the north. Just as he had expected, they lead directly towards the highest peak on the range ahead, an easy landmark to aim for. He now knew exactly what their plan was. He smiled again knowing they would spend the night in the gorge, probably in one of the caves or under an overhang. Saying to himself out loud, "these Joeys are not stupid, they getting shelter and water."

It was getting dark by the time he got to the edge of the gorge, so he decided to sleep before searching further. He intended to rise before the moon disappeared in the morning, knowing the boys would leave early to escape the gorge without being seen. Jack lit a fire not far from the rim of the gorge. The breeze was from the northwest, blowing the smoke away from the gorge, so the boys would not know he was close. He ate the meagre rations from the rucksack and quietly hummed Aboriginal ballads. Jack was home again and at peace with the land. He woke an hour and a half before dawn, just as he had told himself he would. He was cold and stiff so did a few energetic arm swings to get his blood moving and warm his body. Standing at the rim of the gorge he waited, listening as a light hue of the approaching morning rose from the east. The only sounds were those of nature waking around him.

The gorge was still in a deeper darkness as he made his way down. Part of the way there were sandstone ledges with natural overhangs and recesses where the boys might hide. He knew of a cave close by.

He stopped suddenly hearing a sharp, pained cry that was not an animal or bird, coming from about twenty yards further ahead. There was a hollow, muffled echo that told him it had come from a cave. Jack hurried towards the cave where in the dim twilight he could make out two figures, one white and one black, rolling on the floor of the cave appearing to fight. The white boy had a rock in his hand looking as though he was ready to strike the Aboriginal boy. As Jack rushed forwards he could see the truth of the situation and quickly pulled out a clasp knife. He grabbed the white boy's shoulder, pulling him out of the way, and reaching out he grabbed the back of the serpent's head with his left hand and with a single slash, he cut the snake's throat as deep as he could. The huge snake thrashed in convulsions and contracted its coils one last time around Gidga before falling back into the dust to writhe once more before becoming limp.

Jack pulled the snake from around Gidga's torso, then put his ear against his nose to listen for sounds of breathing and feel his breath. There was none. Quickly he rolled Gidga over while apologizing for the pain he was about to inflict. Then with a few hard, sharp compressions of Gidga's chest, he shocked his lungs and heart into action. Jack continued the compressions less vigorously until Gidga stirred.

Jack stood back, looked at both boys, shook his head and said nothing for a full minute, before asking, "what the bloody hell are you two Joeys doing out here?"

Neither boy answered, both still in shock. Nick was more concerned with Gidga, who was too shaken and weak to reply. Jack dragged the python out of the cave to throw it down the gorge, a movement made clumsy by the length and weight of the reptile. Then he produced a small bottle of antiseptic and a dressing from a pocket in his rucksack. He washed Gidga's shoulder wound and applied the dressing, awkwardly holding it in place with a bandage.

"Good job them bloody things are not poisonous. I'm surprised an Olive would go for you. Did you startle it or something? Or maybe it felt threatened, they usually placid beggers. But you can still get crook from infection. Now are you gonna tell me what this is all about?" Jack asked in a relaxed but demanding tone.

The boys looked at each other to see who would speak first. Before either could say anything, Jack added, "I know about you White Joey, I'm supposed to take you back."

Then in a more sympathetic tone he asked Gidga what he was running from. Gidga replied weakly in his native language. A huge smile crossed Jack's face to reveal two uneven rows of brilliant white teeth with a few gaps. While they talked, Nick was concerned about what the tracker would do with them. After a few minutes, Gidga looked at Nick and said, "It's OK, he knows my people. I told him you are my friend. He won't dob us in to the white fella coppers."

"But you can't let on to nobody," Jack quickly added.

Nick relaxed and offered Gidga some water. Jack and Gidga talked on for almost half an hour and it was almost light by the time Jack helped Gidga to his feet. Gidga held his ribs but didn't complain.

"Are you alright?" Nick asked.

Gidga winced and groaned a little as he said, "a bit sore, and I got a funny taste in my mouth."

The boys stood together as Jack spoke to them.

"The boss white fella copper will be back soon. If I turn my back I won't see you Joeys leave. Go to the bottom of the gorge and fill your bottle. Here take this flask as well. Go along the gorge towards the sun for a mile to where it gets shallow, climb out on the other side and go north for three miles. You'll come to a track the quarry trucks use. Go left on the track for five miles until you come to a gate. It says 'Robertson Station' on it. The road crosses the station and the driver gotta stop to open and close the gate. Hide away from the gate and climb in the back of a truck when it stops. It'll be empty cos they going back to a quarry for another load. The truck'll cross the station in about three hours but it would take you all day on foot and you might get seen. So you'll get a long way, see."

The boys nodded.

"Now I'll go up to the top and wait for the boss copper, and I'm not gonna look back, OK."

Nick helped Gidga scramble down the rock terraces while Jack went over the ridge to disappear in the direction he had come from. It was barely an hour before Jack saw the telltale dust from an approaching vehicle. Ten minutes later, S.C. Williams stopped beside Jack who closed his eyes and waited for the cloud of dust to pass.

"Did you find him Jacko?" S.C. Williams asked.

"Not exactly Boss. Tracks went up and across the gorge. They was easy to follow, went up to the quarry road, must'a got a lift cos his tracks disappeared where a truck going south had stopped."

"OK Jacko jump in, there'll be no more walkabout today."

The police officer sighed in relief as he reached for the radio microphone. He called Constable Doltry telling him they were on their way to the truck depot at Wenting, about forty miles away, to see if Nick had turned up there. Then he gave instructions to radio Sergeant Mills with an update and to call ahead to the truck depot, telling them to look out for a white boy with no shoes.

"It'll only be a matter of time before we find him," S.C. Williams mumbled.

"Yes boss," Jack replied.

13

Nick and Gidga soon found the shallow part of the gorge that Jack had described and clambered up the north side. Gidga was in pain and Nick helped him when he struggled. At the top they had to stop for a minute or two for Gidga to rest before following his directions across the flat scrubby terrain.

"How do you know which way is north east. It all looks the same to me out here?" Nick asked.

Gidga smiled.

"But I know. See them termite hills, not like normal round ones but flat. They look like someone stuck a giant hand in the ground with fingers together pointing up. Look, some are taller than me and you. They all face the same way, north and south. The sun comes up on their east side so you always know where north is. They like a compass," Gidga said as he pointed to the horizon.

Nick was impressed and was pleased that Gidga really did know where they were going.

"How did you know that?" Nick asked.

"My people know lots of things," Gidga replied with a smile.

"We could watch the direction of the sun and how long our shadows are to know where north is and know the time of day. They teach these things when we kids. My father and the Elders taught me. Like where to find water, what to eat and about the birds and animals. My father was real good. He could tell the colour of a snake's eyes just from looking at its tracks."

"Oh, come on," Nick said with amused disbelief.

Gidga deliberately didn't look at Nick so as not to be seen grinning.

"Do you believe he could tell what sort of snake it was from its tracks, if it was a Black Head, a King Brown a Desert Adder or what?"

Nick hesitated for a moment then said, "well yes, I suppose so."

Gidga faced Nick and looked him in the eye.

"Well, don't you think he would know what colour eyes they all got?"

Nick started to laugh realising that Gidga had been pulling his leg. Gidga joined in but quickly grabbed at his ribs. He said nothing but his face described the pain. Nick put his hand on Gidga's shoulder and looked enquiringly into his eyes showing concern. He didn't need to say anything. For Nick this was a defining moment. He now understood much more about his new friend. Gidga had a sense of humour, could be playful, teasing and was beginning to trust him. Nick felt a wave of compassion for his suffering, and admiration for how wise he was in this environment. He was not just a skinny Aboriginal boy that Nick had met along the way. A comradeship was developing between them, which they both could feel.

Nick looked carefully at Gidga's torso through his torn shirt. Large angry bruises had appeared around his ribs. He noticed a row of small vertical scars across his upper chest, back and down his arms to his elbow, maybe twenty or thirty in all. They were not random, looking as though they had been made deliberately for a purpose.

"What are these marks?" Nick asked.

"When the Elders first see you got a little fluff on your face, you get circumcised and they mark you to show you are now a man. The ceremony teaches you to handle pain.

Circumcision was the worst. Not so much when they do it cos you away with the spirits but when you piss for days afterwards it stings like hell," Gidga replied.

Even with the exertion of the walk, Gidga was beginning to feel better. Although sore and badly bruised his strength and stamina were returning. They sat for a few minutes under one of the few Koolaba trees they came across, drank a little of their water and massaged their feet. The arches of Nick's feet ached, and even though his feet were hardened, he began to get blisters under his toes from the burning sand. A Big Red Kangaroo came looking for a shaded place to rest. On seeing the boys it hesitated, stood tall to observe, ears perked high and forwards before bounding away. It stopped after 50 yards to look back in disgust that its shady spot had been taken. Nick continued to massage his feet.

An hour later they arrived at a dusty sand road. Pleased, the boys looked at each other with a great sense of achievement. Then without speaking they turned north to follow the track towards Robertson's Station. The road surface was covered in fine dust which was much more comfortable to walk on than the stony scrub.

"Walk in the tyre tracks," Gidga said.

"Them trucks drive in the same tracks so as not to get bogged in the soft stuff at the sides. When the next truck comes through it'll kill our footprints."

Nick did as he was told, trusting Gidga's bush and tracking skills.

As they walked, Gidga periodically looked over his shoulder for the telltale cloud of dust that would let him know a vehicle was coming.

They were forced to hide a number of times as trucks went by. Being low on water, Nick was concerned. Gidga said he didn't expect they would find a billabong along the way but thought there would be water somewhere at the station. Perhaps a wind pump and a trough put there for cattle.

"We could always find Woolumbully roots if not. They got bulbs on them with water inside if you squeeze 'em."

Their walk along the track to the gate of Robertson's Station was long and mostly uneventful, apart from passing trucks. They broke leaved twigs from the scrub to waft away the flies but it was a constant battle. Searching for the boys' perspiration, they covered their backs to get what they could before the sun could evaporate it. Of special annoyance were the fly's persistent search around their lips and the corner of their eyes.

The rusty iron gate was closed and a chain, pretending to hold it closed, was draped over a side post. Half a dozen giant dust covered aloes were scattered within a few yards of the fence.

"When the truck comes we'll hide behind them, over there on the left side so the driver don't got much chance of seeing us. When he gets out on his side we'll go to the back," Gidga said.

Nick agreed. While keeping an eye open for an approaching truck, Gidga broke off one of the giant leaves from an aloe. As it dripped white sap, Gidga licked it and tried to squeeze more from the spikey, fibrous leaf which was over a yard long.

"Good tucker this stuff. Try some," Gidga said.

"My people use it a lot. Good for your guts if you got problems. You can survive on it for a while too. Got moisture and a lot of, what you white fellas' call, vitamins and stuff."

Gidga crushed more of the leaf between rocks and allowed the juice to drip on his wounded shoulder where the dressing had rubbed off. He spat on his fingers and gently massaged it in before allowing more sap to drip on the puncture wounds.

"It helps to heal and stop infections too."

He broke off another, smaller piece of leaf giving it to Nick, saying, "here, try it."

Nick tentatively put his tongue onto the broken part and cringed at the taste. Before Gidga could comment, he spotted a cloud of dust back down the track.

"Come on Nick, get behind here quick."

Nick noted this was the first time since they had met that Gidga had called him by his name, causing him to feel a growing kinship. It was only minutes before the quarry truck pulled up at the gate. As soon as the boys heard the driver's door open on the far side, they dashed to the back and clambered in. There was a grunting noise and the sound of liquid being poured into the dirt. They peered over the top to see the driver urinating, causing them to struggle to stifle their giggles.

After more than two very uncomfortable hours in the back of the hot, open truck, they were pleased when it stopped. Peering over the side they could see they had arrived at a gate to leave the station. They quickly climbed over the tailgate and dashed to nearby scrub to hide. Within a few minutes the truck had disappeared ahead of a cloud of dust heading away from the station. Not far from the gate, they saw a windmill pump, just as Gidga had thought there might be.

"Let's go and see if there's water. I'm thirsty and we might be able to fill the bottles," Nick suggested.

A small flock of budgerigars, which had been drinking from where the cattle trough had overflowed into the dirt, left in protest as the boys approached. The cool clear water that dribbled from the spout was, they thought, the sweetest they'd ever tasted. After bloating themselves with water and filling the bottles, they returned to the track and continued their journey. Gidga knew they had to go north east but the road led directly north. He also knew of an old stock route that went off to the north east but was not sure of exactly where it was this far south. If they could only find its route, it would provide wells along the way, eventually leading them close to Gidga's home area.

They tried to ration their water supply but the searing heat made it difficult. It was so hot that sweat evaporated from their clothes and body almost as soon as it appeared. Nick now understood how quickly a person could die out here without water, and thought that half a dozen pints each day would hardly be enough.

They continued north and eventually, by luck, came across the old stock route. It was late in the day and the boys were tired and hungry. Luckily, the first well was not far. On removing the corrugated iron covering from the old timber lined structure, they found clean and fresh water a few feet down, drank and filled their water bottles pouring it over their heads.

There was little point in continuing now as the sun was already low in the sky, and the distant hills were swathed in purple. They sat side by side leaning back on the shaded side of the well to relax.

"I'm hungry," Nick said.

"We'll find something soon don't worry. At least we got water, that's the most important." Gidga replied.

After a few minutes of silence, he whispered.

"Look, tucker!"

"Where?" Nick asked, confused since there was no food to be seen anywhere.

"Over there, look." Gidga said as he pointed to a clump of low bushes.

"They Witchetty Bushes mate."

"What? Can you eat the leaves? Do they have berries?" Nick asked.

Gidga shook his head and grinned.

"You white fellas would die out here cos you don't know nothing about the bush. Come on, I'll show you.

As they walked over to the bushes Gidga picked up a flat stone before kneeling at the base of the largest bush.

"Okay, now dig around the roots and look for Witchetty Grubs."

"Grubs! What do they look like?" Nick asked.

"Like big white maggots about the size of your finger."

"Yuk!" Nick replied in disgust.

"Don't complain, they keep you alive when you starving."

They dug with an old can and a piece of wood left by previous travellers and soon had half a dozen of the large white grubs wriggling on the large flat stone.

"Sorry Gidga but I can't eat them!" Nick complained.

"Up to you."

Gidga replied as he picked one up, tipped his head back and dropped the wriggling grub into his mouth. Then after chewing, he swallowed it. Nick looked away in disgust.

"Sure you don't want one?" Gidga asked, laughing as he offered the wriggling grub.

Nick pulled a face and replied with a positive shake of his head, deciding he'd rather remain hungry.

That evening they slept side by side in a shallow depression a few yards from the well. It was cold so they moved closer to share their warmth.

Neither boy slept well, it was the screeching of Galahs that brought their attention to a new day. Nick was fascinated by their vivid pink and grey plumage and amused at their playful behavior. Gidga spotted a goanna that was foraging for food before the day became too hot. He chased it down with a stick. Two sharp blows and it was dispatched. Then breathlessly Gidga proudly dropped it at Nick's feet.

"What's that?" Nick asked as he jumped back.

"Breakfast," Gidga said with a grin.

They looked for sticks, old bits of timber and anything else that would make a fire. Nick was enthralled as he watched Gidga quickly spin one stick against another. Within a few minutes, smoke was drifting from the tinder.

Gidga knelt and gently blew on it to produce a small flame that grew as more scrub sticks were added. Nick knew it could be done but had never seen it before. The goanna was dropped onto the fire whole and Gidga turned it several times to help it cook it evenly. Forty-five minutes later the boys were eating a breakfast of soft white flesh. Satisfied, they filled their water bottles, covered the well again and set off up the track.

"I know this track, I been here with my father. There's another well twenty miles up, we should get there in plenty time before dark," Gidga said.

The hours passed with little conversation beyond comments after spotting an emu, dingo or a kangaroo. Gidga showed his knowledge by explaining that the emu and the Kangaroo were similar as their legs worked backwards. Their knee joints were in reverse so they could only kick up forwards and that they were not able to walk backwards. Nick was very impressed.

They rationed their water to last the day but ate only the few remains of the goanna making their hunger grow. The wind was in their faces to combine with the sun to crack their lips. Stopping suddenly, Gidga put his arm out to stop Nick in his tracks.

"Listen! It's a truck. Quick, get off the track."

They ran to the thickest scrub to hide. But they were not quick enough to avoid being seen. A tattered old ute stopped beside their hiding place. It had once been white but was now stained red to almost match the colour of the landscape. It had no hubcaps and the tyres were badly worn and not fully inflated. One headlamp was missing and a front wing flapped against the passenger side door frame. The rear tray was overloaded, forcing the suspension down to a dangerously low level. The driver didn't get out but called from his open window.

"Come on out, I ain't gonna eat'chu."

Gidga peered through the scrub and recognized the man, then slowly showed himself.

"Come on. Where's your mate? I saw there were two of ya," the middle aged Aboriginal man called.

Gidga walked towards the ute while Nick cautiously followed a few paces behind.

The man was surprised to see a white boy out here and asked Gidga what they were doing. They talked for several minutes in an Aboriginal language. Nick could only guess what they were saying. He trusted Gidga and relaxed as their body language and tone suggested the man was friendly.

Gidga turned to Nick.

"It's okay, he's from a village a few miles up the track from mine. I know him, his name is Ed. He knows my mother and knew my father, says he'll give us a lift the rest of the way."

The man got out of the ute, almost falling to the ground as his legs took the enormous weight of his body. He was the fattest man Nick had ever seen. He had a broad pockmarked face, a large brown strawberry nose, deep set bloodshot eyes, and a shallow forehead. Nick looked at his belly as it pressed to free itself from the constraints of shirt buttons while it had won the battle to hang over a restraining belt. The man smiled at Nick while struggling to arrest his trousers which were only being held up by his huge buttocks.

"I'm Ed, well that's what they call me now. 'Ed the Trader'. They used to call me 'Big Ed' but I told 'em I didn't like it. If ya see what I mean. An don't look so worried mate I won't dob you in." He chuckled, making his jaw tremble and multiple chins ripple.

"Anyway, you two Joeys might come in handy if we get bogged along the track. Come on, we'll make some room for you."

Ed supported himself with one hand on the side of the ute as he made his way around the back, and forwards again to the passenger's door. It opened with a crack and a squeal while Ed hung onto it to gather his breath.

"You can get them slabs of stubbies off the seat and into the back so's you got somewhere to sit."

The boys cleared the seat and floor of five cartons of beer, putting them in the back to join a Jerry Can of water, three with petrol and several others containing paraffin. They moved four battered suitcases bursting with clothes and some cartons of tinned and dried food. A half dozen spades and axes lay at random across the cargo, all causing the ute to sink to the bottom of its rear springs.

Ed eased himself back into the driver's seat, his bulk spreading to rob Gidga of space on the bench seat, forcing him to lean onto Nick who was squashed against the door. As they settled in the cab, Ed told them to slam the door hard to stop it from falling open.

"We don't wanna to drop you out along the track!" He said laughing.

Gidga winced as Ed's great bulk pressed against his ribs. The steering wheel rubbed on Ed's belly, which drooped down between his legs to rest on the seat. Stretching forwards with a grunt, he turned the ignition key. There was a low grinding sound for a few seconds followed by a loud clatter as the engine started. The exhaust pipe had become detached and the noise made it difficult to talk in the cab without shouting.

After a short while Ed said, "tell you what young Joeys', I gotta go to your place sometime this trip for deliveries and orders so I'll drop you off there first. It'll be two days yet though."

The boys were pleased to get a lift, as uncomfortable as it might be, but it was a luxury compared to walking. They would get to the village in only two days, all being well.

Nick was especially pleased, thinking that the police would never believe he could have got that far in such a short time.

The day was mostly uneventful as they trundled along at twenty miles an hour or less, leaving a constant cloud of dust and blue smoke in their wake. Twice the boys were obliged to dig and push the ute out of soft sand. Ed was especially pleased to have them along as he would otherwise have had to do it himself. Given the noise of the ute, there could be little conversation other than on essential matters. But they were amused to see startled Big Reds standing tall, like an audience of old ladies, looking on in amazement as they passed.

Two wells further on they stopped for the night. They ate well as Ed had produced bread and tins of beans and bacon, all of which he was willing to share. It was dark when they had finished eating so the metal plates were left to be cleaned in the morning.

Nick was surprised that Ed had not asked him why he was in the outback with an Aboriginal boy and believed Gidga must have explained it at the outset. Gidga's earlier wince had not gone unnoticed by Ed, so he asked what the problem was. He told him how he had got bitten and crushed but made no mention of Jack. Ed took a paraffin lamp to the back of the ute where he rummaged for a few minutes to produce a bottle of antiseptic from a carton of twenty-four. He removed the cap and poured some over Gidga's wound. Nick was surprised how well it looked after the aloe treatment. As Ed topped up the antiseptic bottle with water, he noticed Nick's surprised look.

"No worries Joey, they'll never know the difference," he said chuckling as he put the bottle back into the carton. While at the back, Ed took a stubby of beer saying,

"Just one, can't drink all the profits."

Nick asked Ed what he did. He laughed saying.

"Oh, a bit of this, an a bit of that."

Then more seriously he added.

"Well, I started out doing a mail run once a month for the Post Office, out to the villages and a few stations. Most of the post was for the stations, not too many letters but a few parcels. Then some stations asked me to take stuff back into town to deliver or post. I didn't charge at first, then I got smart. Most of the time the truck was only part full so I didn't mind collecting stuff to bring to people. But as I got asked to do more I thought I could make a business of it. So now I buy stuff in town what I think they want and sell it to em. An I charge a bit to be a courier for 'em.

There's not a lot a money out here so I started to barter for paintings that I could take into town. Its good business now but it worries me a bit."

"Why?" Nick asked.

"Some traders in town ask me for paintings to sell to tourists. But they take advantage and offer peanuts, then sell the work for top dollars what would take the artist a year to earn even if he worked eighteen hours a day. Not only that, it worries me I might be trading away my people's beliefs and culture in the paintings. They all tell a story you know. But the white fella tourists only see patterns. They are all very special to us Aborigine people."

Nick tried to understand what Ed meant, while Gidga sat by taking it all in.

"Another long day tomorrow," Ed said, wanting to change the subject.

He always carried a full swag for himself and gave the boys a blanket each to help them sleep. Although they were warmer and more comfortable than the previous night, they found it difficult to sleep given Ed's loud snoring. Joking with Gidga, Nick said that he was sure he could feel the vibrations through the ground. So they spent several hours staring at the bright night sky looking for shooting stars before being overcome by sleep.

Ed was up long before the boys and had lit a camp fire, prepared a breakfast of porridge and Billy Tea each with lashings of tinned milk and sugar. Nick had never tasted porridge so good.

Within a short time they were on their way again, sitting silently in the cab as Ed navigated his way through sandy ruts along the track. Nick sat next to Ed today but Gidga still got jolted and bumped when the vehicle hit a hole or hump. Ed eventually gave up apologizing for the rough ride. The motion and heat made them all tired. The boys closed their eyes as their minds drifted to linger somewhere between awake and sleep, a place that could only be reached when feeling safe and contented. At midday Ed stopped at the next stock well. Removing the cover he could see two dead birds and a goanna floating in the water. His only comment was, "Bugger! We can't drink that."

He drew a bucket of water and took it to the ute. Lifting the bonnet and trying not to get burnt or scalded, he slowly released the radiator cap through an old rag. Nick and Gidga stretched and explored the immediate area. After only minutes they returned to see Ed violently shake his hand then suck his fingers as he cursed. When the steam had dispersed and the radiator cooled, he filled it again and replaced the cap. After eating bread and cheese and drinking lukewarm water, they continued their journey, stopping only for a pee and a drink. The temperature was dropping and the sun had almost touched the western horizon when they arrived at Gidga's village.

14

Noise and clouds of dust announced their approach long before they appeared. A vehicle of any kind arriving in the settlement was an occasion not to be missed. First to greet them were the children, who ignored the clouds of dust to run alongside the ute for the final fifty yards. A dozen or more excited children of all ages gathered around. Ed prized himself from his seat making the ute groan as it raised itself three inches on the driver's side. The children were excited to see Gidga get out of the other side. They jabbered and shouted such that nobody could have clearly understood what any of them were saying. Gidga walked away from the ute as they mobbed him with greetings and questions. Two girls ran to tell Gidga's mother that he was back. Then one by one they fell silent as they noticed the white boy still sitting in the passenger seat. They stood in a semi-circle inquisitively watching him and waiting.

Gidga broke the silence.

"It's okay, he's my friend. He's gonna stay with us. His name is Nick," he told them.

There was a murmuring amongst the group. Gidga had created more questions than answers. Ed deliberately changed the atmosphere with a handful of lollies that he tossed in the air for the children to catch and scramble after. He always did this when he first arrived at a settlement, calling it 'marketing,' because it created attention, and folks liked him for it. Even the adults thought it amusing to see their children scramble after these rare treats. Ed laughed aloud making his whole body ripple. When the dust was settling and the squabbling just about to start, he asked, "who didn't get one?"

Those with a raised hand were given a lolly to turn their disappointed looks into huge grins. Someone tried to cheat to get an extra lolly but the others were quick to tell Ed that the boy already had one. Adults were beginning to gather and those seeing Ed's antics thought him a kind generous man. Thus a good atmosphere was created for trading, all be it with goods at greatly inflated prices.

Nick got out of the ute, feeling out of place as he waited. In less than a minute an Aboriginal lady hurried towards them. She made straight for Gidga, calling his name. They embraced, speaking a few words of affectionate greeting in an Aboriginal language. Nick thought this must be Arana, Gidga's mother. She looked a little strange, being only slightly taller than himself with a rounded, overweight body and a flat bust that rested on her stomach, all supported on thin straight legs and large, flat feet. But he felt a wave of emotion as it struck him that Gidga had a mother, someone who loved and cared for him. Nick longed to be greeted like that by his own mother and a lump came to his throat.

"Did you find your sister?" She asked anxiously.

"No Ma," Gidga said quietly, feeling awkward.

"I'll tell you about it later."

Then he pointed and said, "this is my friend Nick. I want him to stay with us Ma."

Arana looked puzzled, and was confused as she stared at the white boy.

Nick moved nearer to say, "hello."

She did not look happy and offered no reply or acknowledgement. He could see her features now and noticed similarities with Gidga. Her skin was dark and wrinkled. In the middle of her round face was a small button nose that seemed too small. Her slightly bloodshot

148

eyes were deep set under a heavy brow. Other people watched to see and hear what the white boy was doing there. Arana said something to them that Nick did not understand before they drifted back to Ed.

"I need to explain lots of things to you Ma," Gidga said.

Arana turned and walked back to her shack without speaking. As Gidga walked beside her, he turned and beckoned Nick to follow. Once inside they sat on rickety chairs. Nick waited to be invited to sit.

Gidga described the events of his aborted search for his sister, why he could not stay in the city, how he had met Nick and why he had brought him here. His mother was clearly not happy and scolded him knowing the police would eventually be searching the area for him. Gidga disagreed, believing they would not expect Nick to have got so far. Then, still in her Aboriginal language, Arana said, "He can't stay here. He'll bring us trouble."

Gidga pleaded, saying Nick was his friend and he had helped save his life, showing her the python's teeth marks. She shook her head at the sight of his shoulder and wanted to fuss over him but Gidga was more concerned with Nick staying. Arana relaxed and became thoughtful. Then she said, "Well, let's see what the Elders have to say about it before we decide what to do with this white Joey."

Again Nick had no idea what was being said.

So the matter was closed for now. She had already set an old black kettle on a paraffin burner which had now come to the boil. Arana made a strong brew of tea, produced hard crusty bread and stringy pieces of meat. The boys were hungry and ate with relish.

While Arana went to see what wares Ed had for sale, Gidga explained the situation.

"My Ma's not happy. Problem is that if the white fella coppers come looking and find you, we all got trouble. An them coppers don't much like us anyway. My Ma is going to ask what the Elders think. It's proper in our ways they should decide."

Arana chastised Ed for bringing a white boy to their village but thanked him for bringing Gidga home. Ed could only reply saying, "What else could I do Arana? Was I supposed to leave him out there to die by himself?"

Thoughtfully, Arana replied quietly, "I suppose not. Well, if the coppers come, we'll say you saved him and we was looking after him until they come for im."

The Elders had told Arana they had already decided on a meeting for the next morning. In the meantime she was to look after him. The boys slept well in the two room shack that was Gidga's home.

They woke to the jabbering of young voices close by, all eagerly waiting to hear of Gidga's adventures in the city and to know more about the white boy. Arana was beginning to warm to Nick. There was something about him she liked. Partly because he was vulnerable, appealing to her motherly instincts, and partly from a feeling of moral obligation for his helping save her son.

At mid-morning they were summoned to an Elders' meeting under the Billy Goat Plum and Eucalyptus trees that grew by the river bed. Rugs were spread out for the Elders to sit on. Smoke from smoldering leaves was waved to cover the gathering in its fragrance, purifying the air for the meeting.

The Elders sat together facing the village folk. First, Gidga was asked to explain how he had met Nick, and why he brought him to their settlement. Next, Arana explained her feelings about accepting him into her home. The Elders listened patiently without interruption. Nick was not asked to speak or asked if he wanted to stay. He had not understood the discussions and didn't know how many of the gathering spoke English. Once Arana had finished, the Elders talked amongst themselves. Eventually, they turned to face the gathering, and a middle-aged Elder began to summarize their collective view.

"The question is what do we do with this young white fella? He is not supposed to be here. He's running away from the white bosses and the coppers. He will bring us trouble. The white fella coppers will come looking for him, unless they decide he's wandered into the bush got lost and died of thirst or something else. We got a choice of three things. We can tell the white fella coppers to come and get him. We can keep him safe until they come looking for him and hand him over, or we can keep him and hide him here. If we keep him, we have to accept that if he is found there will all be trouble. So when the coppers come we will have to hide him."

There was more subdued talk amongst the Elders and chatter amongst the onlookers. Sitting back from the Elders was a man, much older than any of the others. His dark heavily wrinkled skin contrasted with his long white hair and bushy white beard. He had not spoken or involved himself in the previous conversations, only watched and listened. After some minutes, he cleared his throat. Everyone stopped talking to listen with reverence and respect.

"I hear a lot of talk about what to do with the white fella boy and what is best. If you listen to your heart and remember our traditions, they will tell you what to do. So listen. The Rainbow Serpent decided the daughter of Arana would be taken from her by the white fellas. As they tell us, it's to give her better education. Better white fella's doctoring and to learn to live the white fella ways. They did not think of what Arana and the girl wanted, the pain they would feel or even respect our ways. Now the Serpent has brought Arana one of theirs in return to repay her, and punish the white fellas."

He waved his hand towards Arana and saying, "Arana, you must obey the Serpent and accept him as your own."

There was no further discussion, only silence as the gathering absorbed what the old man had decreed. Each person nodded out of respect and obligated agreement. Gidga knew that Nick would not have understood what the old man had said. So as the gathering dispersed, he nudged Nick saying, "It's okay, this is your home now."

15

In the following weeks Nick adjusted to a way of life that did not involve hard labour, regimented routine or harsh punishments. He began to learn a few words of the local language which caused amusement amongst the younger children when he made an error. He didn't mind and joined the laughter when they corrected him.

Nick was bonding with Gidga but not in quite the same way that he had with Chris, whom he often thought of and dearly missed. Chris would be worried about him and Nick wished he had come too. Yet he was always the more cautious of the two, rarely giving way to impulse the way Nick did. It seemed as though Nick had always known Chris and he was a major part of his life. They had shared so much and being apart only heightened Nick's brotherly love.

For the first time that he could clearly remember, Nick was experiencing a resemblance of a family life. He had a surrogate mother who cared for him and a brother, both of whom had accepted him into their humble lives. They shared their meagre existence with him without reservation or question.

Their home had been provided by the Government and consisted of two rooms. It was made from corrugated iron on a timber frame that got very hot in the daytime and cold at night. The largest room was sparsely furnished with cheap furniture that had seen better days. In the other room they slept on the floor with blankets although Arana had a foam mattress. As humble as it was, Arana took pride in trying to keep it clean and as nice as possible. In the shaded area outside the door was an old threadbare carpet that Arana shook every morning to create a cloud of dust that drifted across the village. Every day she said the same thing.

"We can't have people sitting in the dirt can we, it wouldn't be decent."

The atmosphere was friendly and it was not long before the novelty of Nick's presence began to wear off, making him happy here.

He was always respectful and spoke kindly to Arana. Yet she never fully understood why he had been sent to her of all people. There were many other Aboriginal mothers whose children had been taken away. Why not an Aboriginal boy or girl in return, why a white boy? It all seemed so very strange to her but she accepted the Elders' decision without question. She had been surprised at first when Nick had offered to help her with chores, in contrast to Gidga who had to be asked or told. Nick liked her and he responded to the warmth she gave him. It was the loving warmth a mother gives her son. Part of him wanted to call her 'Ma' as Gidga did but he was too reserved. It was his own mother he wanted to call 'Ma' or 'Mum' and to bestow that title on someone else felt unnatural.

Gidga enjoyed having a brother more than a sister. Nick was much more fun, even though he loved and missed his sister. He was deeply upset for his mother because he had not found her and brought her home, vowing that he would find her one day. It was as much for his own self-respect as for his mother's happiness.

Five weeks after Nick arrived in the settlement there was a defining event. An event that confirmed he was safe and with friends. Ed returned to the settlement, and without stopping to amuse the children, he quickly went to Arana's house looking very serious.

"Arana, them white fella coppers were at my place last night looking for the white Joey. They asked me if I'd seen him on walkabout. I said I didn't know nothing about any white fella kid. They poked around a bit looking for him then left. They went to Cabberoo village and said they'll come here tomorrow morning. You gotta do something with the boy."

"But there's nowhere to hide him here," Arana replied.

She called Gidga.

"Go and fetch the Elders, run be quick."

Within minutes two Elders came to the house and asked what was going on. Ed repeated what he had told Arana. They all agreed they had to hide Nick, but where? Everywhere they could think of the police would surely look.

"I could take him away with me now. They have already been to my village and won't come back," Ed said.

One of the Elders cut in.

"No, what if you meet them on the track? They would see him and you would be in trouble. Anyway, we said we would keep him here. We should not panic at the first sign of trouble. When we took him in, we knew what we were doing and have to deal with it here. But thanks for the warning and your offer," the Elder said.

Then the old Elder with white hair spoke.

"We will hide in full view, where the coppers will not see him."

Everyone looked puzzled, so he explained.

Gidga, Nick and two others were immediately sent three miles up the river bed to fetch a lot of white ochre. They returned almost two hours later puffing and panting. While they were away the Elders had collected as much animal fat as could be found. The white dry ochre was given to Arana and the other women who crushed it to a fine powder. In the morning it would be mixed with the fat to make a sticky paste.

The Elders gathered all the boys together from the settlement and explained they were going to practice a Junba dance, and to teach Nick how to dance at a Corroboree. Also, that it was part of the plan to hide Nick amongst them.

An Elder then spoke to Nick.

"Now young Joey, we gonna teach you to dance like an Aboriginal. But this is serious work. It's not just jumping about in the smoke and stamping the dirt with your feet. This is to hide you from the white fella coppers, make you invisible to them. Later when you understand the song and the music and get your heart in time with the rhythms, you will mix with the Dreamtime Spirits."

Nick was serious, simply nodding his understanding of the importance.

The boys had gathered at the edge of the settlement waiting for Nick and the Elder. Two men were already there, one with a didgeridoo and another with clapsticks. The boys listened to the Elder intently as the seriousness of what they were about to do was impressed upon them. Three men sat as the dozen or so boys formed a rough circle. The Elder nodded and the man with the clapsticks set a rhythm. Within a few seconds the didgeridoo released its low haunting sound. Nick watched in fascination at how he could keep blowing without seeming to take a breath. He just kept blowing. It looked impossible. As the boys danced, an Elder called instructions to help correct and polish their performance.

Nick was then shown the basic movements and told what they meant, which helped his interpretation. The music started again and Nick was told to join in. He looked stiff and awkward at first, so an Elder called to Nick.

"Relax, close your eyes and let your body and spirit mingle with the sounds. Relax and feel the rhythm in your soul."

The longer they practiced, the more in tune he became. Soon he was enjoying the dance with a renewed feeling of confidence. The Elders were pleased with his progress and proud of their teaching, especially to a white boy who wanted to learn their ways. So the Elders praised him.

"You done well white Joey. If you forget tomorrow, just follow the other boys and keep moving like them. Don't stop or the coppers will pick you out. Whatever you do, don't look at them straight on or they will see your blue eyes. Just look at the earth. And when the boys sing don't make a sound, just pretend to sing, your voice is not like our singing voice, and we don't have time to teach you. Hear me?"

"Yes," Nick replied.

Early the next morning the boys gathered by the eucalyptus trees where two women mixed the ochre and fat into the sticky paste. The Elders then smeared and painted it on all the boys' bodies, faces, arms and legs. They ignored traditional patterns to get maximum coverage. One of the Elders commented.

"Them white fella coppers won't know the difference."

Next fibres from aloe leaves were used to tie grey green foliage around their heads, upper arms and torsos. It would hide Nick's straight hair. Some boys had leaves hanging over their faces, as did Nick. By the time the make-up and costumes were complete, Nick was indistinguishable from the other boys. The Elders and the women were satisfied.

It was decided to have the dancing next to the river bed with good reason. To inspect the dancers, the police would have to walk the short distance from the settlement to the river. The wind would blow smoke from smoldering leaves their way making it uncomfortable, and they would not want to scramble down to the river bed to avoid it. A girl was sent along the track to watch for the signs of an approaching vehicle. Fire stones were laid where the centre of the dance circle would be. Some dry grass, sticks and lots of green foliage was placed nearby. Finally Nick was reminded not to look at the policemen. They were now ready.

Almost two hours later the lookout came running.

"They coming! They coming! Be here in minutes."

The fire was immediately lit, burning quickly. Green foliage was placed on the top to make smoke. The clapsticks started to beat time as the boys gathered to be dancing as the police arrived.

Two policemen in a Land Rover drove to the senior Elder's hut where the old man sat outside waiting for their arrival. The officers knew enough to respect the Elder by visiting him and asking permission before looking around, even though they were resentful of the custom. The policemen were wearing light khaki uniforms and police issue Akubras. Both carried firearms.

"G'day old fella. How'yer going?" the Sergeant asked.

Then without waiting for a reply, "we're looking for a white kid, about thirteen years old, seen him about?"

The old man shook his head but did not speak.

"Well, we'll take a look around just the same if you don't mind," said as if the Elder had no choice in the matter.

"What's going on over there?" He asked as he pointed to the smoke and sounds of the didgeridoo.

"Tomorrow we having corroboree. The boys are practicing the Junba. Elders over there showing them how," the old man said.

"Yer well, we'll take a look around now we're here." As they wandered off.

The old man thought them arrogant. Their last comment was a statement, when to show respect, it should have been a request for permission.

They looked in each hut asking the same questions and getting the same answers. Nobody had seen a white boy. They peered inside two humpies that could have concealed a boy but found nothing. As they walked towards the dancers, the smoke was deliberately made thicker to help mar their view and deter them from staying long. The Sergeant and his Constable stopped and watched for a minute or two, mostly out of interest, and partly to see if the white boy was there. It did not occur to them that he could be one of the dancers. The smoke got in their eyes. The music, singing and chanting was loud and they soon became irritated.

"Can't you stop that racket for a minute?" The Sergeant shouted.

"No way boss. Not now or the spirits will be angry and bring us bad things," the man with clapsticks replied.

"Suspicious bastards. Well at least the smoke keeps the bloody flies away," the Constable mumbled.

They waited and watched for several minutes. Nick was aware of them and tried hard to concentrate on dancing and resist the temptation to look at them. He kept his eyes to the ground like the other boys, and turned his back to the policemen as often as he could without raising suspicion. Those few minutes seemed like hours.

Before leaving the settlement, the policemen returned to the senior Elder who sat quietly outside his open door and with a straight face playfully asked, "Find him?"

Unimpressed, the officers ignored the loaded question.

"If you see the kid or know anything about him you better tell us or you'll be in the shit for sure old man!"

The Elder didn't flinch, change his expression or answer, which added to the Sergeant's frustration. They returned to their vehicle where the Constable, leaning in the doorway, spent a few minutes on the radio reporting there were no sightings of a white boy in the area. As they climbed in he said, "The truth is that the buzzards will have picked his bones clean by now. We are wasting our time out here Sarge."

The boys continued to dance until the policemen were out of sight. The old man afforded himself a smile and, with a twinkle in his eye, he asked the officers a rhetorical question they would never hear.

"We not so dumb after all are we?"

Everyone was excited with their sense of achievement in saving Nick and at tricking the police.

Gidga showed Nick more of the ways of the bush and encouraged him to learn their language and beliefs. In return Nick began to teach Gidga to read and write English. After working in the open on the farm, chapel and now living in the outback, Nick had a deep dark tan and his blond hair had developed an orange tint from the iron oxide in the soil and dusty air. Apart from his hair being straighter, it was now almost the same colour as many of his younger Aboriginal friends, who he was surprised to see were fair haired at an earlier age.

Nick became more and more fascinated with the knowledge the Aboriginal people had of their surroundings and how they made the best of it, asking many questions in his eagerness to learn. He was beginning to understand how they had been able to successfully survive here for tens of thousands of years. His interest was noticed by the Elders who, with pride, included him in their teachings. Nick learned that Aboriginal history, mythology and traditions were handed down by word of mouth from one generation to the next, never being written down. Sometimes Aboriginal mythology and history were displayed on cave walls or depicted in the artwork. Arana had a friend who specialized in painting historical events in the Aboriginal dot style. When the woman explained the symbols, each story became clear. Nick marveled at the extent of the knowledge the Elders held in their heads, and their sense of importance to pass it on to future generations.

He quickly began to see that these people of the outback were not as backward as many white people believed. They knew as much as white people, but it was about different things. Nick decided they simply did not understand Aboriginal culture, traditions and society. Likewise, Aboriginals did not understand the European way of things. Different values were placed on events, wealth and ownership, especially land. They believed that people were only its custodians and could never own it. The only permitted interpretation of ownership was that the land belonged to everyone including their ancestors and future unborn generations. But the Elders told Nick that some of the old values were changing as white people's ideas were being adopted.

Nick enjoyed his new found freedom but still missed Chris, wondering where he would be at any one time and what he would be doing. He knew the Brothers would have questioned Chris about his disappearance. Yet with equal certainty, he knew that Chris would say nothing. He reminded himself of their pledge that they would eventually meet in Sydney, wishing it would be much sooner. In melancholy moments he longed for his mother, trying hard to understand what she must be feeling, wondering if she was thinking of him, and if she was trying to find him. In dreamy moments he imagined what it would be like to meet her now. There would be disbelief, relief, joy and more tears than he could imagine. But these were just fanciful daydreams.

Yet Arana considered Nick her son, caring for him and chastising him when needed. There were no special favours or privileges, just the love of a mother to an adopted son. Neither colour nor origin mattered. Nick felt it and grew to love her in return. As time passed, he grew closer to Aboriginal ways and philosophies, finding them basic, yet profound. He loved the stories of the ancient Rainbow Serpent and how it had made the land, trees and animals. He came to understand and respect why their heritage and history was so important in their culture and folk law. Nick spent many hours listening to the Elders, who named him Migaloo, an Aboriginal name for white fella.

They enjoyed talking with Migaloo as, unlike many of the Aboriginal children, he did not only listen and absorb but asked many questions, showing a greater interest. Each question led to yet another story and another question.

Nick asked with curiosity why their predecessors had not invented a wheel of some sort as most other cultures had.

"After all, lots of Aboriginal tribes were nomadic. Wouldn't it have been easier to move and carry things? I know some white people laugh at Aboriginals for it, saying you were not intelligent enough."

The Elder smiled confidently.

"That's easy young Migaloo. First, as I told you, our ancestors didn't believe in possessions, so had nothing to carry except hunting spears a boomerang, a turndum and perhaps a didgeridoo. They lived off what the land provided wherever they were, so why drag a cart around in this rough, hot country?"

Nick agreed.

"As for not being intelligent enough. I heard them say that too. Sometimes they even say we are stupid. Now I ask you to imagine that forty thousand years ago a white fella was given a piece of wood from a tree, then told to make it so if he throws it away it would fly back to him in a big circle so he could catch it. A white fella would not know where to start, but our ancestors did. Look at the cut through shape of aeroplane wings, you see the same shape as a boomerang. We made that wood fly longtime before any white fella even thought about it. Now them new plane wings even look like a boomerang. So we not so stupid are we?"

Nick was impressed and again had to agree.

"There are lotta things like that. We learned to send messages with smoke and sound that could be heard miles away thousands of years before the white feller did."

Migaloo learned many skills, from peeling paper bark without killing the tree, to catching food and what can and cannot be eaten. What is dangerous and what is not, where to find water and how to survive. He learned to mimic the movements and sounds of animals and birds, amazed that he could sometimes call them to him. Given his new found talent he found it easy to emulate the Aboriginal accent while speaking English. He often did it for fun when teaching younger children to speak English, making them laugh.

It was a great adventure for a boy. But he knew he could not do this for the rest of his life and that one day he had to leave and try to find his real mother. Gradually, piece by piece, Arana came to know all that Nick could remember of his past. Sometimes she secretly cried for him and wanted to hug him to make everything better. She could not understand why white people would treat their children so badly and so became upset for them all. She understood Nick's anxieties over finding his natural mother. Something she knew he had to do if his spirit was to ever be at peace. As a mother with a daughter who was taken away, she also understood only too well how his mother would be feeling.

One evening, after listening to Nick's stories, she went to the river bed where she sat in deep thought whilst gazing at the stars that seemed extra bright. She was lost in their splendor, letting her mind drift away. It was the distant howl of a dingo that returned her mind to the present.

Struggling to her feet, she collected dry sticks and twigs to make a small fire to smolder eucalyptus leaves. Sitting in the smoke and waving a small leafed twig across her face, she began to sway back and forth and lightly chanted. It took an hour before a trance was slowly induced and she was gone. Arana did not know where she was, only that it was in a white woman's bedroom in a foreign land. A dark haired woman was sleeping in the bed and was beginning to wake. Then she was clearly startled. Arana spoke softly telling her not to be frightened.

"I come to tell you that your son is safe and well, in another place, but you must go to where he can find you if you want to see him again."

Then the image in Arana's trance began to fade.

The strain on her was great, and as the embers of her little fire died, she began to return from the Dreamtime. The next day Arana told Nick she had seen his mother, that she was alive and well, but in a foreign land. Arana said she had told her to go to where he could find her. Adding that she did not know where that was or where his mother is now. Then after a pause said, "your father will lead you to your mother."

Nick did not understand the comment. At first he thought she was simply trying to console him, but over the following days he asked the Elders about Dreamtime trances and what could be done. They told him to believe Arana and not to question her spirit. He still had doubts but desperately wanted to accept it, as it seemed to reinforce his belief that his mother was still alive.

Within a year Nick had become fluent in the local language and was able to hold lengthy conversations. He felt he knew as much about Aboriginal ways as any fourteen-year-old Aboriginal boy. Yet he still continued to learn a little more each day. The Elders were so impressed that it convinced them Nick was truly sent by the Rainbow Serpent and they had to formally adopt him into the tribe. The old Elder agreed.

Nick was told, and the preparations were made. He was both honored and pleased until an Elder told him he would have to be circumcised. He asked what happens. The Elder told him that a small piece of skin at the end of his penis would be cut off by the Medicine Man in a special ceremony. Nick was frightened and told Gidga he didn't think he'd want to join the tribe after all.

"You can't refuse. You don't have a choice if the Elders have decided."

"Does it hurt much?" Nick asked.

"Like Hell for days, especially when you pee."

"But if you can stand it without complaining, you'll become a man. The cutting is quick but what really hurts is later when they hit it with a stone knife to split it. Sometimes boys pass into Dreamtime when they do that. But it's okay, they can't feel anything cos the spirits are taking care of them."

Nick looked shocked and Gidga laughed saying, "but they don't do that no more."

Nick didn't care. He told Gidga that no way was he going through that even if he did upset all the Elders.

"You have to do it," Gidga said.

"Here look at mine. It's not so bad when it's better, see! Get yours out and I'll show what they do."

Nick reluctantly dropped his ragged shorts and Gidga began to laugh out loud again.

"What's so funny?" Nick asked feeling offended.

Gidga found it difficult to stop laughing. He couldn't make up his mind if he should tease Nick more or not. Nick indignantly raised his shorts again.

"Come on, what's so darn funny?"

"Migaloo, you already been done!"

"You mean I'm already circumcised?"

"Yes."

It must have been done when I was a baby because I don't remember it," Nick said in great relief.

"Yeh," Gidga said, still laughing.

"But you still have to have to get the tribal marks."

"What are they?" Nick asked.

"Nothing too bad, there's a ceremony when they make cuts on your back, front, arms and your bum too. You've seen mine. That's when you become a real man of the tribe."

165

Nick was wondering what he had got himself into and was beginning to regret it.

The news travelled around the settlement within an hour and with much excitement, a corroboree was arranged for the next big moon in five days. Nick felt he had not been given a choice or even been asked and was apprehensive. Even with his fear, he was determined to go through with it honourably. The Medicine Man told Nick what would happen at the ceremony, and that his preparation would begin the day before. A mixture of ash and crushed leaves from the Acasia bush would be placed behind his ears and must not be removed before the corroboree. It would help him enter Dreamtime, and the spirits would protect him throughout the ceremony. Also, that he will be given Pituri from the Head Man's cup but only a little because it was very strong.

"I give it to the Head Man Elder to help his Dreamtime, and it will make it easy in your mind too," the Medicine Man said.

"I will ask the Elder if we must mark you all the way or not, as you were not born from our people. I think you will be what white fellas call an honourary member."

On the fifth day in the late afternoon, as the sun neared the horizon, a fire was lit in the river bed. Everyone from the settlement gathered around to watch or take part. The men had been painted with red and white ochre and carried branches of eucalyptus up to a yard long. Arana was there, both proud and anxious at the same time. She didn't know if her Migaloo could stand up to the ceremony or not. Nick remembered the control he had summoned the first time he was whipped at Clontarf, when he had withstood the pain from sheer determination. Now he would grit his teeth and summon the same strength and control, even if he was afraid.

An Elder had told Nick it was good to be afraid. It was what protected him from danger, so he should not be embarrassed.

"If you do something you are not afraid of it means nothing. But if you are afraid and still do it, then you are brave."

The mixture placed behind Nick's ears had gradually made him feel intoxicated. A faint nausea lingered in the background and his anxieties faded. His balance was not as good as it was and he twice bumped into things noticing that he hardly felt it.

The Elders shuffled slowly around the fire chanting and stamping their feet every three steps to evoke the Dreamtime Spirits of their ancestors. After twenty minutes other men joined in. While the Head Man sat cross legged, he swayed and chanted himself into a light trance-like state. Next he asked for Migaloo to come forward and be recognized. The steady movement around the fire gradually increased and the chanting got louder. Green leaves were thrown onto the fire to make smoke. They stamped their feet in a frenzy, whipping themselves with their eucalyptus sprigs before stopping suddenly to fall silent.

The Head Man beckoned for Nick to be brought closer to the fire where he too was purified in the smoke. A large piece of paper bark, measuring several feet square, had been placed between the fire and the Head Man. Nick was told to sit facing him where he could feel the warmth of the fire on his back. The old white haired Elder sipped Pituri from a cup that was then given to Nick to finish, making things go hazy and unbalanced. The Head Man chanted and swayed for several minutes before looking Nick in the eye and with two fingers pointed to his own eyes. Nick had already been told that he must hold the Elder's stare until released.

As they sat transfixed in each other's gaze, the Medicine Man waved a large leaved twig over Nick's body while he quietly chanted. Then he produced a knife and began making small, shallow, vertical cuts into Nick's back above his shoulder blades, five vertical cuts in a row. Nick felt no pain, just a sensation followed by mild stinging. At first, he was not aware that he had been cut. Next his chest received the same treatment. His upper arms and buttocks were not marked. Nick saw small trickles of blood run from his chest, and only then did he weaken. He took a deep breath as he remembered the priests and their whips. Then it was over.

Women took him away to wash the blood from his wounds, which were now sore. Nick was proud of himself, relieved and thinking it was over. The Medicine Man reappeared, congratulated Nick and started to rub something into each of his cuts. It made Nick wince with pain.

"What's that stuff? Do you have to do that?" Nick pleaded.

"Yes," the man answered.

"It's washed sand and Bloodwood sap. The sand makes the wounds stand out when they heal and the sap will stop them going bad."

Nick could hardly wait for him to stop.

It was three days before the wounds sealed and stopped weeping, then a month to cover with skin but they were still tender. It was a difficult time for Nick, but he was proud of the honour he'd been given. For the first time in his life he felt that he belonged somewhere and he could prove it.

Gidga and Nick were summoned by the Elder who had officiated at Nick's inauguration ceremony.

"Gidga, now Migaloo is one of us, he can see our sacred sites. Take him to Lala-ma, tell him why it called that way and explain what is there."

Gidga was honoured to be trusted with such an important mission but the Elder saw it as part of Gidga's training to pass on their history and culture.

"Go along the river and get white ochre on the way. You know what to do with it," he said.

Nick and Gidga took a bottle of water and headed west up the dry river bed. After almost three miles they came to white ochre deposits which they scraped up and put in their pockets. Continuing west for another mile, they reached a rocky outcrop about two hundred yards back from the river.

"That's it. Lala-ma, it means rock to sleep," Gidga said.

As they approached, Nick could see a thick overhanging layer of sandstone that created a shallow cave beneath it. The sheltered back was covered in white and red Aboriginal art and hand stencils. Nick stood back in admiration asking, "Who did this?"

"All who pass or sleep here, mostly ancestors," Gidga explained.

"When they came this way they rest here at night and out of the sun in the day. See here, this symbol means 'resting place', this one means water. Maybe the river was running when this fella was here. They paint on the walls to tell what they seen or about their journey. Sometimes they cut symbols and animal shapes into the rock, they last longer or maybe they didn't have ochre. Look at this, it says four men sat here and they left their marks, see their hand marks red ochre."

Nick was fascinated.

"Now we have to put ours here too. I'll show you."

Gidga took a smooth stone and ground the ochre from their pockets on a smooth rock, then mixed it with water to make slurry.

"Okay, now we put it in our mouths and blow it out over our hands like we was blowing a didgeridoo."

Gidga placed his hand on the wall of the cave, spread his fingers and sprayed it white to leave a silhouette. Nick did the same and Gidga explained the significance of this place. They sat for a while in the shade admiring their handy work, washed their mouths out and drank the rest of the water. Gidga noticed a thin dark line on the horizon and said he could smell rain.

"Come on, we better go now before it gets here. It will be an hour or more but we got a way to go."

They followed the river bed back towards the village as the storm gained on them from behind. The thunder was now much louder and the temperature had dropped. A dark grey band of cloud was almost above them when there was an eerie calm. The birds stopped chirping and nothing moved. In front of them was bright sunshine and to their back dark shadows. That moment lasted only seconds and the sun was gone. A clap of thunder shook the ground and lightening cracked as Nick had never heard before.

"Come on, run, get away from these trees, stay low in the river," Gidga shouted.

Minutes later they were squatting in torrential rain at the side of the river bed.

"We have to stay low so as not to attract the lightening like the trees do," Gidga said.

They were afraid as the storm crashed about them with lightning strikes every few seconds. They watched as a small tree, two hundred yards ahead, exploded into a shower of sparks as a finger of lightening momentarily clung to its tip. They looked at each other seeing fear in their eyes.

The violent storm lasted only fifteen minutes then they were able to resume their journey. The unfortunate tree still smoldered, giving off a pungent smell as they passed. The dry grass at its base was now burned black and grey. Gidga stopped as he noticed what looked like a tiny meandering stream that appeared to run from the base of the tree. It was only about an inch wide and just over a yard long. Nick was puzzled, never more so than when Gidga carefully picked it up in one piece.

"Looks like water hey!" He said.

Nick was intrigued.

"When Mungi gets angry he strikes the ground and it's so hot it makes sand into glass."

The river bed was wet and sloppy but before they reached the settlement it was firm again. The sun had dried their clothes and warmed their bodies. They saw few signs that it had rained here, and Arana said they had seen the storm but it had passed them by leaving only a few spots of rain behind.

Instinctively Nick knew the day would come when he would have to return to a European society and wondered how he would cope. His previous experiences had done nothing to educate him into white society, given him any social graces or equipping him to live comfortably in a white community. Nor was he street wise to white people's ways.

Another year passed. Now fifteen he was feeling a need to move on. It would be an enormous wrench, but he had to go to find his mother and see Chris again. He was afraid to tell Arana of his decision since he knew she would be upset, so he had to pick his moment carefully.

One evening he steeled himself for the emotional effort of explaining to Arana that he had to go soon. He finished by saying.

"Ma, I love you and would never want to hurt you, you know that."

Arana interrupted emotionally. "Oh, I have waited for ever for you to call me Ma."

Nick suddenly felt guilty that he had waited so long. So in that moment he said, "I may not have called you Ma before, I'm sorry, but since I have been here I have always thought of you as my Ma. I can never say thank you enough times or repay you for what you have done for me and the love you have given me."

Arana raised a finger to stop him and said, "My son, I have always known this day would come. I understand that you must do what you have to do and find your birthmother. The Serpent brought you to me, and now he takes you away to the rest of your life. I know he will look after you."

Nick was humbled by Arana's grace and understanding. She had made it easier for him and in that moment he felt her love intensify, as his did for her.

"When will you go?" she quietly asked.

"I don't know, there is no big hurry but soon I think."

"I have been thinking about going to see my sister over near Carnarvon soon. Will you wait until I get back?" Arana asked.

Nick was quick to say he would.

"I'll be gone a few weeks," she added.

Nick confirmed that he would not leave without saying goodbye to her and asked when she was going.

"I was thinking of going the next time Ed comes. It should be in about three, or maybe four weeks. He said he would give me a lift part of the way."

They talked on for several minutes until Gidga entered.

"I'm going to see your Aunty Margaret soon. I might be gone for a few weeks," she told Gidga.

"Ed has promised to take me to Meekatharra, that's as far as he's going on his next trip. I know people there and I can get a lift to Glenburgh up Gascoyne River way. I'll wait there until the weekly bus to Carnarvon comes."

The next few weeks went by quickly and it seemed no time at all before they were saying goodbye and wishing Arana a safe journey. Tied in an old sheet, her meagre luggage was bundled into the back of Ed's ute along with his wares. She lowered her rotund body into Ed's passenger seat and Ed eased himself in beside her. The ute groaned as it's springs stressed under the weight. The engine roared and they were gone, leaving a lingering cloud of dust and fumes in the still air.

With the exception that now they had to do more for themselves, little else changed. Gidga continued to do the male chores as he usually did while Nick took on some of the domestic tasks. There was not a great deal to do as the other women had taken over without being asked. This was a community that shared and looked after each other. Arana was missed after only one day and the boys already looked forward to her return. Their life became less disciplined, eating what they liked and exactly when they felt like it. If they killed a wallaby or a large goanna, they gave it to other families knowing they would be invited to join in the feast for bringing the gift.

Seven weeks passed. Nick and Gidga had been out collecting Bush Honey and were casually wandering back along the track with their golden treasure when they noticed a vehicle approaching. They stopped, standing to one side and waited for it to pass. A dark green, ex-military World War II truck with a faded canvas covering pulled up next to them. Two weathered looking white men sat in the front, both were smoking.

"Need a lift fella's?" The driver called.

Nick pretended to shield his eyes with a hand and managed to cover part of his face, Gidga replied.

"Where you going?"

"Up the track to the Abo settlement. Is that where you're from?"

"Yes," Gidga replied, then asked, "What you doing there?"

"Not a lot mate, we's government contractors come to check that ya windmill and ya water pump's working okay, maybe give it a bit of a grease up. Do'ya wan a bloody lift or not?"

The boys nodded. They didn't need a lift but the novelty of a ride in the back of a big truck was too tempting.

"Jump in the back and bang on the cab when you're there," the driver shouted. Then after a pause added. "and don't pinch nothin!"

Nick and Gidga climbed in. It took a few moments for their eyes to adjust to the dimmer light under the dark canvas but they were pleased to be out of the sun. They could make out pieces of machinery, boxes of tools and swag. An Aboriginal lady was sitting on the swag. She smiled and said, "it's me, your mother."

The boys stretched their necks forward and squinted to peer into the semi-darkness, which their eyes had not quite adjusted to yet.

"Ma!" They said excitedly as they made their way forwards to hug her. Nick then reached through a canvass flap and banged twice on the cab. The engine was revved, gears crunched and the truck lurched forwards.

"What are you doing in here?" they asked.

"Oh, I saw these fellas about a hundred miles back down the track. They from Mingoo Station. Said they work there all the time but government men paid the boss to send them out and check windmill pumps and wells. Anyway I asked them where they going, here was on their list so I got a lift. Lucky hey!"

They were pleased and excited that she was back and bombarded her with questions about her trip, often not waiting for a proper answer to a question before asking another.

"You two young Joeys got too many questions, just wait till we get home and I'll tell you everything, we nearly there now anyway. But what you been up to? No trouble, I hope."

Although the boys had been fully occupied whilst she was away, they didn't have a great deal to tell that was out of the ordinary. Only about their hunting successes as they showed her their haul of honey. Nothing special had happened in the village worth reporting.

The truck pulled into the settlement, stopping close to the windmill. The driver's mate appeared at the back of the truck and lowered the tailgate.

"All right, time to get out," he called.

Excited, inquisitive children had already gathered around the truck. Nick and Gidga jumped out, then helped their mother to climb down, after which Nick reached inside to get her bundle. Arana was unsteady on her feet at first but soon regained her balance. She thanked the men and walked to her hut as Villagers shouted their greetings.

"Ooo! I gotta sit down for a minute. I don't feel quite right, must be the journey, took four days and a lot a walking you know. Think I must be getting old."

The rest of Arana's day was taken up with questions, answers and explanations which were often repeated as more people came to welcome her home. It was fortunate that the boys had found Bush Honey today of all days, it was a prized specialty and was shared to celebrate their mother's return. The boys laughed at the sticky mess they made of themselves while eating the honey from the paper bark containers they had made. Arana ate slowly, savouring the sweetness and taste. Knowing its medicinal properties, she hoped it would make her feel a little better. By the time the sun was setting, she was exhausted and wanted to sleep.

In the morning she had a high temperature, coughing often, her eyes watered and her limbs ached. She struggled to go about her daily chores and at midday she returned to her bed. Gidga brought the Medicine Man and Arana explained her symptoms. He listened intently then sung a few chants before leaving, saying he would return soon.

Worried, Nick asked.

"What's wrong with her?"

"She got bad fever, real bad. Maybe she got a white fella's disease. I gotta do some medicine. You young'uns can help. Go get some Murrin-Murrin bush, eucalyptus twigs with lot a good leaves and some Billy Goat Plums. Now go and be quick."

They dashed across to the creek and beyond, first to get the plums and eucalyptus, taking them back to the hut.

They had to go further and scavenge far from the settlement for Murrin-Murrin bushes but managed to gather everything in an hour.

When they got back the Medicine Man was there, lighting a small fire in the doorway of the hut. He took two twigs of eucalyptus leaves, set them smoldering and took them inside. There he waved them about as he chanted, calling on the spirits to help.

Nick was surprised and impatiently asked, "what good will that do?"

Gidga was annoyed at Nick's doubts and would not look at him as he abruptly said, "Eucalyptus is good for pain and fever."

The Medicine Man heard the boys talking.

"Keep that fire going and keep them leaves smoldering. We want that smoke to come in here."

The old man took the prickly Murrin-Murrin leaves and placed them in a small Billy Can of water. He crammed as many in as he could and left the can by the fire for the leaves to infuse to make bush tea. When it was ready, he produced a small jar of eucalyptus oil and pouring some into the tea, he gave some to Arana telling her to sip it until it was all gone. Later he gave her a Billy Goat Plum to eat. Nick asked what it was for.

"To make her better!" the old man said impatiently.

Then realizing that he may have been too blunt, he apologised.

"We been eating them since our ancestors' time to cure fevers. Once a white fella Doctor come here and said they are good for that. He said they got fifty times more Vitamin C than oranges. I don't know about Vitamin C but I know they help. Now keep that fire going."

Arana didn't improve that day and was no better the next, even though the Medicine Man visited several times to administer his tea and chants. Nick and Gidga took turns to care for her throughout the day and night, bathing the sweat from her brow and giving her sips of water and the special tea. She was never alone, and the boys became more worried about her as time passed.

By the third day her fever had increased and she perspired more than ever. Yet there were times when she said she was cold. Her deep chesty cough had worsened and she was now coughing up thick green mucus. In spite of what the Medicine Man did and said, her condition was clearly getting worse.

Nick told Gidga that he would fetch a white doctor.

"No, it's too far, take two and half days at best to get help. Better if I go, I know the way. It's too dangerous for you. Besides, what if they find out you are a white fella underneath."

Nick reluctantly agreed but still wanted to go.

Arana had heard the conversation and pleaded. "Don't go Migaloo, stay with me. I like it best our traditional way. No white man's doctoring. Please don't go. Anyway, I want you near."

Nick became emotional and even more afraid for Arana.

By the sixth day their mother was finding it hard to breath. She gasped for air and her shallow rasping could be heard from outside. The hut was under constant vigilance by the local people who sat nearby for many hours at a time. Some quietly chanting, calling on the spirts to heal Arana.

On the seventh day Arana asked for the tribal Elders and both boys to be present. As they entered Arana was again coughing up mucus. Nick could not help but notice that it was mixed with threads of blood. He was now frantic with anxiety. The gathering stood around Arana's bed and waited. After a minute or two, in a weak breathless voice, she told them,

"I have seen the Rainbow Serpent. He told me not to be afraid, said he would come for me in a few days. I must

177

honour our traditions with a passing the way of our ancestors if I am to enter the Dreamtime."

Arana relaxed and closed her eyes. Gidga sat next to her holding her hand in his. The gathering dispersed. Once outside Nick spoke to an Elder and the Medicine Man begging.

"Please don't let her die."

"She has been visited by the Rainbow Serpent. He will take her. It is his will. There is nothing we can do," the Elder said.

"There must be something?"

The Medicine Man shook his head saying. "no."

"What did she mean about 'passing the way of her ancestors'?"

"She wants a traditional funeral. We have to honour her wishes and obey the Serpent. If we don't she will never enter the Dreamtime World, and her spirit will never rest."

There and then Nick decided to fetch a white doctor, as doing nothing was not an option. He gathered a blanket, some food and a bottle of water. Confident in his bush skills, he was certain he would survive a few days in the outback by himself. So without giving anyone an opportunity to talk him out of going, he started westward along the track. Sustenance along the track was sparse, but he was able to find enough Bush Figs to provide energy and moisture. After walking fast at the beginning, within an hour Nick had settled into a steadier more sustainable rhythm. The days were not too hot, so he was able to' maintain a good pace with few rests. His mind wandered and occasionally he talked aloud to himself. It was as though he was two separate entities. His legs knew only one determined purpose, while his mind thought only of Arana and the urgency of bringing a doctor.

It was two and a half days before he saw signs of civilization again. He was desperately tired and wanted to rest but pushed on, calling on reserves of adrenalin to keep him moving. The constant flies and thirst were insignificant compared to his urgent determination that he had to save his Ma. He didn't know what to expect when he reached the station and didn't want to reveal his true identity if he was questioned. So he thought up a story in advance, but his priority was Ma and the risk of discovery was worth it.

Nick arrived at the main gate to the station not expecting they could help Ma directly, but that they would have a radio to call for help. After fifteen minutes he arrived at the homestead buildings. He had been seen coming, and a woman met him a few yards from the house. She looked stern with a frown on her weather- beaten face. This was the first white woman Nick had seen in a long time, and he was hesitant.

"What do you want?" she demanded.

"I need help for my Ma. She's very sick."

The woman looked hard at him and said, "You are a white boy!"

Nick realised his lapse and immediately changed to speaking with an Aboriginal accent.

"No Missis, only a little bit. I'm from the settlement up by Gumtree Creek."

"Yes I know it. How did you get here? Gumtree Creek is miles away."

"I walked Missis, three days. Please help my Ma. She real bad sick, maybe gonna die if we don't get help."

The woman accepted Nick's story believing no white boy could walk that far in the outback and survive.

"What's wrong with her?" the woman asked.

"Dunno Missis, but she real bad sick, said the Serpent is coming for her soon. She needs white fella medicine real bad," Nick replied.

"All right then. Wait here and I'll get on the radio to the doc at Meekatharra, but don't get ya hopes up cos he might not want to come all this way for an Abo Sheila."

Nick was offended but said nothing.

"If you're thirsty, there's a tank over there by the windmill."

The woman went inside to return after ten minutes. Nick quenched his thirst and returned to the house to wait for the woman.

"You are in luck young'n. He don't have much on just now. Too late to leave today though. He'll leave early tomorrow morning. All being well he should be here about midday."

Nick relaxed. "Thank you missis, thank you."

"You can doss in the shed with the other Abos tonight. Grub's up at dusk. You'd better chuck some water over yourself first, get rid of some of that muck and dust."

Then said in a lower tone as she turned away, "there's something bloody odd about you mate. It'll come to me soon enough."

By this time two Aboriginal station hands had sauntered closer to see and hear what was going on. When the woman went in, they approached Nick.

"Where you from brother?"

"Up Gumtree Creek way."

Nick replied in the local Aboriginal language. The men grinned showing rows of bright white teeth. They were inquisitive, but didn't ask any more questions now. They would come later.

"Don't worry about the Missis. She's got a rough tongue for us bros', but she's not as bad as she makes out. Come on, we'll show you around here."

Nick followed the men to a shed. There they showed him where to sleep and eat. Although the roof was made from corrugated iron, it was cool inside as a door at each end let a breeze through. There were no windows, just square holes with shutters propped open with pieces of wood. Nick was tired. He lay down in a vacant bunk and was soon asleep. He didn't know how long he had been sleeping when he was awakened by one of the station hands.

"Tuckers ready mate."

Two more men and a boy, not much older than himself, had arrived while he was sleeping.

Food was served on benches beneath a lean-to shelter at the side of the sleeping shed. This was the first meal he'd had in days and he ate too fast. There was a large piece of meat of a type he had never tasted before, boiled potatoes, beans and thick slices of homemade bread and butter. To Nick this was a king's banquet. As he was finishing, a white man appeared.

One of the hands greeted him.

"G'day boss."

"G'day Jess. Where's the kid that came in today?" He asked with an air of authority. Before anyone could speak Nick was on his feet, standing as if to attention – a legacy of care institutions.

"Come out here mate. I want to talk to you."

Nick went outside with the man and waited for him to speak as they examined each other for a few seconds. The boss's face was permanently tanned and wrinkled from the sun and weather. When he lifted his hat to scratch his almost bald head, Nick noticed the great contrast between his face and the white of his scalp. It looked odd. As he patted his hat back onto his head, he asked,

"Yep, the missis is right. There's something different about you young fella. What's your name?"

"Nick."

Now where do you say you are you from?"

Maintaining his Aboriginal accent Nick replied.

"Like I told the missis, up Gumtree Creek way. There's a small settlement there."

"Yes I know, I know. But you don't look like no Abo kid to me. Not with that straight hair, narrow nose and them blue eyes."

Nick was pleased he had thought his story through in advance.

"My real name is Migaloo but everyone call me Nick. My Ma said my Pa was from a place called Germany. He come here to prospect then worked on the mines. He met my Ma in a town, but later when he saw she was gonna have me, he cleared off. Ma often says I look like im. But I rather look like my brothers and Ma. I cop it from both sides, see. I don't fit proper nowhere."

"Mmm, that could be it." The man said. "I thought you might be that white kid the coppers were looking for a while back...but you you can't be... I suppose.

The station hands had been listening from the tables and Jess interrupted saying, "he's more Abo than any white kid boss, we seen his marks."

"Well how come you were left with the Wunambal people? These days most half-chats get taken away for resettlement with white folks."

"My Ma and the Elders hid me from white fellas until I was old enough for'em not to be interested. They didn't know about me anyway."

Nick's answers came with so little hesitation that the boss was convinced he was telling the truth. He returned to the homestead and rubbed his chin. The station hands had heard all they wanted to know and asked no more questions. Nick slept well that night.

Breakfast was toast, eggs, bacon and a mug of strong tea. Nick had never had bacon before and asked what it was. The station hands laughed as one said, "pig's arse," and they laughed even more.

It tasted good, and they were all eating it so Nick just laughed with them and enjoyed the meal.

He spent the morning tidying the yards and sheds as instructed by Jess, who was in charge of the buckaroos. By midday Nick was anxious for the doctor's arrival, but it was two more hours before he appeared. The doctor was a slim, late middle-aged man with an accent that Nick had not heard before. He stood aside as the doctor explained to the boss's wife that he had been delayed with a flat tyre. She called for Jess and told him to get one of his boys to fix the doctor's spare, then invited him in to refresh himself. Nick waited anxiously outside. It was a half an hour before they reappeared.

The woman called to Jess who came running.

"The doctor's tyre fixed yet?"

"Yes Missis, all done," he said.

"Good. Put it back on his truck."

The doctor thanked him, then turned to Nick.

"I'm Doctor Stewart laddie. You had better tell me what this is all about. It must be serious if you walked three days to come and get me."

"It is!" Nick said urgently.

"Well then, tell me all about it."

They sat together in wicker chairs in the shade of the timber veranda while Nick explained Arana's symptoms. The woman fidgeted and clearly didn't like Nick sitting in one of her chairs but would not offend the doctor who had invited him to sit.

"It seems to me she might have a serious case of pneumonia but I can't be sure until I see her. You did the right thing to get me, even if it is such an awful long way," the doctor said.

"She said the Serpent was coming for her soon. Is she going to die?" Nick asked.

"Oh! It's that serious is it? We'll do our best for her laddie," the doctor sighed.

"It's too late to go on today. I'm not one for driving on outback tracks at night. We'll leave first thing tomorrow morning."

Nick was pleased the doctor had come yet frustrated they were not already on their way. He wanted to go now without delay, so his second night at the station was restless.

Nick was sitting on the edge of the veranda before the grey light of dawn began to creep in from the east. Jess was already up and attending to his horse and saddle before breakfast. He couldn't chase the Jackaroos up if he was not ready himself.

"What are you doing up at sparrows fart?" He asked Nick.

"Me and the doctor are going early. I'm waiting for him."

"Good luck mate, it'll take most of the day to get there. I hope the doc can fix your Ma up."

In less than fifteen minutes Nick and the doctor were on their way.

"Have ye had breakfast laddie?" The doctor asked.

"No I got up too early."

"Well, we can't have you fainting for lack of food can we? Here take one of these sandwiches the lady kindly made up. You'd better take a sip of coffee from the flask too while you are about it. It will make a change from water."

Nick was pleased to accept. The sandwich was strange with lots of butter and a dark bitter tasting substance spread over it. There didn't seem to be a proper filling but the flavour was strong. The doctor saw Nick pulling a face at the taste.

"Have ye no had Vegemite before laddie?"

Nick didn't know what it was, just that he didn't like it and responded with a simple "no."

"Well ye have'na lived then." The doctor said laughing.

"Eat it, it's good for'ye, it's full o' vitamins, it will put hairs on your chest.

Little was said for the next hour until the doctor's curiosity got the better of him.

"I noticed right away that you have blue eyes. Are ye no a full blooded Aboriginal?"

Nick repeated what he had told the boss back at the station.

"Aye, there's a bit of that about in these parts," the doctor said.

"So your poor mother had to bring you up all by herself, did she?"

"Yes, but our people follow traditions so the other women helped and men brought food after they been hunting, the same way if her man had died."

The doctor was warm and friendly but was not completely convinced of Nick's story. It was logical and any other possible explanation seemed very unlikely, especially given the tribal marks he had noticed across Nick's chest. He asked no more questions but moved the conversation along.

"Aye, we have a lot to learn from you folks," the doctor lamented.

"I'm always amazed at how you all survive out here and have done so for forty thousand years or more. Us white folks would die out here in no time at all."

As the doctor was a kind, understanding man, Nick felt guilty for not telling him the truth. In order to try and avoid more questions about himself, Nick asked the about the doctor.

"Why did you decide to be a doctor?"

"Well, to tell you the truth, I don't think I decided. My father was a doctor in Perth, and it was always expected that I would follow in his footsteps. Oh, that's Perth in Scotland laddie. Do you know where that is?"

"Yes I think so. It's next to England," Nick replied.

Dr. Stewart was surprised that a boy raised in an Aboriginal settlement, many miles from the nearest school, would know such a thing and it added to his suspicions.

"So when I was old enough I was sent to Edinburgh to study medicine. At first I worked in a hospital then in my father's wee practice."

"Why did you come to Australia?"

"Och well, when the war started I joined the Army Medical Corps and found myself in the Far East. I came here on leave and liked it. I decided there and then I'd come and live here when the war was over. So here I am."

They arrived at the village in the early evening. As usual, the younger children were the first to greet the vehicle.

Gidga walked out to greet Nick. It was not the happy reunion Nick had hoped for. Gidga stopped short in front of him. His eyes were tired and his shoulders drooped. He didn't speak, just gently shook his head.

"What's the matter?" Nick asked fearing the worst.

"The Serpent took her Nick."

"When?"

"Two days after you left. You missed her ceremony, but we did what she wanted, and she is going the traditional way. The Medicine Man did his job and we wrapped her in paper bark. See, over there beyond the river."

Nick could see her funeral parcel resting high on a rickety pole platform that stood above head height. The four slim poles supporting the platform hardly looked strong enough to carry her weight. Nick breathed heavily and tears filled his eyes as he embraced his brother. Nick cursed himself for not bringing the doctor when he first thought of it. Now he felt very guilty.

Having read the body language, Doctor Stewart came forward and put a hand on each of the boy's shoulders saying.

"It's good to grieve. Aye, I'll leave you to it."

Then he turned to the children and asked where he could find the Head Man and Medicine Man, who he hoped could tell him more of Arana's condition and death.

Afterwards he decided to stay for a day or two and examine the local people, starting with the children. It was his habit to always carry his swag, a small tent and a good supply of medicines on his trips out of town. First, he had to ask the senior Elder's permission and involve the Medicine Man so that their status in the settlement would be maintained.

Sitting in the red sand on a shallow ridge beside the dry riverbed, Nick pondered his life. After his first fifteen years it had become no more than an existence that now left him surviving from day to day. Every day that passed was another day stolen from his future. Why did it have to be like this? What is more, it seemed the future offered little improvement. Any logic of the past remained elusive, and he was tormented with underlying anxiety and so many questions. His many hours of speculation offered no relief from the frustration of failing to find meaningful answers.

Was it true? Was he really the flotsam of life? He had never believed it before and was determined to prove the Brothers wrong, but he could not do it from here in the outback.

Nick's thoughts were abruptly brought back to the present by unusually loud, excited shouts from the children and a far distant rumble. He looked up to see a clear blue sky, everything about him was still. Then again he heard that distant rumble from the northwest. Nick squinted as he focused on the far horizon to see a dark line of clouds. Over the next two hours the clouds came nearer and the thunder became louder. Long before the clouds arrived, he could see vast columns of water falling from them. Angry ragged flashes of lightening randomly struck the ground to announce the storm's approach, then loud cracks and rumblings as if the spirits demanded recognition. It was both frightening and exciting, bringing the first rain to the village in two years.

The sharp contrast between the bright blue sky and the deep blue grey edge of the clouds was startling. As the storm drew closer the children became more excited. Then again, as if by some unseen command, when the edges of the clouds were straight above, there was calm. The galahs stopped their excited screeching, even the children hesitated and looked about in the eerie silence, and the dogs took cover. The first spots of rain hit the hot metal roofs with loud taps to then disappear in miniature puffs of steam before they had a chance to run away. Those that landed in the dirt appeared to hesitate for a second like transparent pearls before sinking away to leave wet shadows marking their passing. It was only seconds before a deluge overcame the earth's resistance, transforming the dust and sand into a red mire. Plants and trees that had previously been pale and tinged with the red dust now looked greener for their rinsing. Small streams of water meandered at will between the buildings making their way down the gentle slope to the river bed.

After Mungi and Murungat had passed, the steady rain continued. Excited children ran, splashed and dragged their feet through the water making channels of their own. Dark young bodies glistened in the rain, and their wide grins revealed rows of teeth that now seemed unusually white. Nick had gone to Arana's home to wait out the storm knowing Gidga would already be there.

"The river will flood in a few hours if this rain keeps going up country," Gidga said.

"Will the water last?" Nick asked.

"Maybe three days, maybe a week. It depends on how much runs down from higher ground. It won't be deep but it will be fast, then sink and run away. Now it's rained once there might be more in a few weeks. It's the wet season, but sometimes we don't get the season for three or four years."

They sat looking out of the door watching the children enjoy themselves. Before long some were exhausted and just sat in the water. Others had taken to splashing each other with the sloppy red mixture. The younger children had never seen so much rain and were excited as they stood under streams of water that ran from the corrugated iron roofs. Some people had put out pots and buckets there to catch the soft clean water.

Nick took this opportunity to tell Gidga he was planning to leave soon.

"Why? Don't you like it here?" Gidga asked.

"I do, I do. This is the only home I have, and you are the only family I know. You are my brother but..."

"So why go?" Gidga interrupted.

"I have to find my birth mother. I don't know who I really am or where I'm from. I can't settle until I know. I have to know. It's hard to explain. I just want you to try and understand."

Gidga remembered his sister and thought of how she must feel, also his Ma's pain which she never got over. So he quietly told Nick that he understood.

"When you know what happened and find your real Ma, will you come back?"

"Yes, one day, I promise. You have my word, but I might not stay long. I just don't know about the future," Nick replied.

Gidga was satisfied. The rain stopped as suddenly as it had started and the sun was left to clean up the mess. Within minutes steam rose from the ground and the roof tops.

16

Anne Spalding had been confined on her back to a stiff mattress in a hospital bed for almost nine months, which had seemed an eternity. Boredom was her biggest enemy. Books and her weekly Woman's Day Magazine did little to stimulate her for long. Listening to the radio through hard bakelite headphones for long periods was uncomfortable. She was constantly told to move as little as possible, not that she wanted to as when she did the pain was excruciating. She hated the periodic X-rays, bed washes and massage to prevent bed sores. All involved movement that she tried to avoid. After four months she was coached into gentle movement, and by nine months was ready to stand for a few seconds although it made her dizzy at first.

She was always worried about Robbie and desperately wanted to see him. Anne knew that Mrs. Sparrow could not care for Robbie on a full time basis so under bureaucratic pressure, she had authorized him to be taken into care at a Dr. Barnardo's home in Cambridge until she was able to take him home again.

When the day came to be released from hospital a shiny black St John's Ambulance took her home to Mepal. It had been almost a year since she was last there. The hospital insisted that she go from her ward to the ambulance in a wheelchair. This disappointed Anne, as she had always vowed to walk out of hospital unaided. Even so, according to the ambulance men, the regulations had to be adhered to. Similarly, when she arrived home, the Saint John's men insisted they deliver her to the cottage in a wheelchair. They helped her to a lounge chair, placed her walking sticks within easy reach and left. Her good neighbour Mary Boon was there to greet her saying,

"Hello dear, it's lovely to see you home again. I expect you'd like a nice cup of tea."

"Oh yes please, I'll get it," Anne replied.

Mary was quick to call back from the kitchen. "Oh no you jolly well won't. I'm going to spoil you until you're a bit stronger."

Anne smiled emotionally when she noticed fresh flowers in a vase on the sideboard. The house was almost as she had left it on the day of her accident. Mary had been in, aired the rooms, lit a fire and, without being asked, she had cleaned and dusted. Then just that morning, she had thoughtfully put some basic foods and milk in the cupboard. The only obvious difference that Anne could see was that her bed had been brought downstairs and placed in the corner of her front room. Mary said it could be put back upstairs later when she was stronger and could manage the steps.

She called in every day to check on Anne to see if she needed anything, often bringing her an evening meal and sometimes taking or returning washing. But the main thing Anne really wanted was her Robbie and to bring him home as soon as she was strong enough to travel to Cambridge.

As the days passed, Anne became increasingly mobile, and after two weeks she was able to slowly make her way to the village shop three hundred yards away. It took a lot of time and effort but was a major achievement that gave Anne confidence. Village folk greeted her and wanted to stop and talk, but Anne found standing for long was painful. She had difficulty carrying her shopping home because of her walking sticks. Anne had also been told not to carry heavy items that would put extra pressure on her back. Fortunately Maud, who owned the shop, had a small daughter.

"Where's that girl o'mine, never around when you need her," she would say before calling.

"Daisy! Come and carry Mrs. Spalding's bags home for her."

Anne was desperate to see Robbie and arrange to bring him home. As she missed him dearly. Sometimes standing uneasily at the kitchen sink for support, she'd gaze out of the window to the orchard, then squinting, so in her mind's eye she could see Ross pushing him on the swing.

Her trips to the shop were a painful struggle but a major milestone, raising her expectations that she could soon go to Cambridge to bring him home. He would be a year older now, and she trembled with emotion at the thought of first seeing him whilst regretting the year they had lost.

When the big day came Anne and Mary took the bus to Drummer Street, near Cambridge city centre and then a taxi to the Dr. Barnardo's Home. Anne was excited and hoped she would not cry too much or be silly when she held her darling Robbie.

Mrs. Boon knocked on the door and after a minute a woman came.

"Yes?" she asked.

"My name is Anne Spalding, I have come to see my son Robert Spalding."

The woman's demeanor seemed impersonal and complacent to Anne's request as she said, "you'd better come in then and see Mr. Robertson. Take a seat and I'll tell him you are here."

They waited for almost five minutes before the woman returned to usher them into Mr. Robertson's office. He stood, greeted them warmly with a guarded smile and invited them to sit. Anne's back was painful so she moved slowly. After introductions Mr. Robertson said, "now Mrs. Spalding, I understand that you have come to see one Robert Spalding." Emphasizing his name. "I'm afraid that will not be possible."

Shocked Anne asked, "why not?"

"He is not here Mrs. Spalding." Mr. Robertson answered awkwardly, knowing it was not true.

"Then where is he?"

"I'm afraid I can't tell you that."

Before he could say anything more, trying to stay calm through her panic, Anne demanded, "I'm his mother! I have a right to know where he is, and I want to see him right now!"

A cold shiver of fear then went through her as she added a little more calmly.

"Is he alright, he's not sick is he? I want to see him."

Mr. Robertson paused awkwardly again.

"Mrs. Spalding, I can assure you that your son is perfectly well, but you should understand that I do not keep track of our boys once they leave here. Their records go with them."

"What do you mean 'leave here'? I didn't give permission for my boy to be moved! Nor was I advised. I want to know where he is. I demand to know. I'm his mother, and I want to know where he is!" Anne insisted.

"My dear Mrs. Spalding, you did not come and see your son for in excess of six months and we received no communication from you. Therefore, according to the law, he was formally made a Ward of the State. You no longer have any rights or jurisdiction over him."

Mr. Robertson said in a condescending manner.

Anne was furious and flabbergasted.

"Don't you 'My Dear Mrs. Spalding' me!"

She said as tears welled in her eyes.

"I was in hospital with a broken back for almost a year, unable to move a muscle, let alone come to Cambridge, as much as I wanted to. That's why he was brought here in the first place. It's only now that I can even walk a little. You knew it was only temporary, that's what was arranged. I thought he would be safe and cared for here. I came as soon as I could!" Anne exclaimed as tears of frustration filled her eyes.

Mary reached across to hold Anne's hand in a gesture of comfort and restraint while trying to cope with her own alarm at what she was hearing.

"Your son was, and indeed is, well looked after and I'm very sorry to hear of your incapacitation Mrs. Spalding. However, you signed Robert into our care and we did look after him as you had hoped we would. We have fulfilled our obligations to you and the boy. There is nothing more I can tell you. You will have to take the matter up with the Home Office. They make these rules."

Mr. Robertson pronounced with a defensive air whilst folding his arms.

Anne and Mary were stunned into disbelief. Both had tears running down their cheeks as they left Mr. Robertson's office. Anne shuffled around in the doorway to look back saying. "you have not heard the last of this!"

She had no way of knowing that her precious Robbie , was there in the same building.

Mr. Robertson didn't answer.

After a much-needed cup of tea at Lyons Tea House, Anne and Mary took the bus back to Mepal. They debated the behaviour of Dr. Barnardo's with shock and disgust whilst considering what Anne's next action would be. She could do nothing before tomorrow and needed time for her emotional reactions to settle, to avoid doing anything that might damage her chances of getting Robbie back.

That evening Anne scrutinized her copy of the document she had signed approving Robbie's admission to Dr. Barnardo's in Cambridge. She could find nothing that said she would automatically and legally relinquish her son to the state if she did not make contact within any six month period. Nor was there any reference to what might happen to him after that period. She was still in denial that she could lose her son to bureaucracy seemingly forever.

At nine o'clock the next morning Anne made her way to the telephone box in the village, taking with her the document she had read and re-read the night before. In the top corner was an address and telephone number of what she presumed to be the Dr. Barnardo's Head Office in London. She nervously dialed zero for the operator, gave the number she wanted and waited. After being instructed to press button 'A', the pennies dropped and she heard a woman say,

"Dr. Barnardo's. Who do you wish to speak to?"

Anne said she was not sure but that her call was in connection with finding her son in one of their orphanages.

"I'll put you through to one of the secretaries who will help you."

After a short pause Anne found herself explaining her circumstance. The secretary cut her short saying, "I'm sorry Mrs. Spalding, but all enquiries of this nature must be in writing."

Anne pleaded to speak to someone in authority but only received the same instruction. She was given the address to write to but no contact person's name. Anne was still talking when the pips went and the call was terminated. Frustrated, Anne returned home to compose a letter.

Six weeks passed before she received a reply, during which time she had telephoned twice to chase the matter. The response was always the same.

"Your case is being handled by one of our managers, and you will receive an answer by post in due course."

When the answer arrived, it was courteous but to the point. It stated that she had signed the care of her son into the hands of Dr. Barnardo's, that she had not fulfilled her obligations of contacting them within any six monthly period of his stay, and as such, she had automatically relinquished all her rights governing her son's care. Also that he was now formally and legally a Ward of the State. The final paragraph read:

"Like all child care institutions, Dr. Barnardo's Homes are not permitted, or obligated, to divulge information pertaining to those in its care. Please be assured that your son is well looked after, and his future is carefully considered and monitored."

Anne cried. The letter she had so anxiously waited for only repeated what she had already been told. The next day she took the letter to her local vicar who was sympathetic but doubted he could do much to help. He offered to call Dr. Barnardo's Head Office to see what he could discover. Like Anne, he was told they would not discuss the matter on the telephone, and that he should write in to enquire. The eventual letter of reply was almost word for word the same as Anne's. The vicar committed to talk to the Bishop of Ely on the matter, "to raise the anti" as he put it, but nothing eventuated.

Anne didn't give up and went to see her local Member of Parliament, the Honorable Harry Legg-Bourke. Anne thought he was the epitome of a retired army officer. Immaculately dressed, clean cut, very correct in his manner and with an accent she thought was a little too upper-crust for a Fen man. So she was not surprised to discover that he had been a Major in the Royal Horse Guards. Anne was comforted by his sympathetic and understanding manner. He was clearly disturbed by her story and asked if she could have misunderstood any part of what she had been told. But on seeing the letter from Dr. Barnardo's Head Office it was clear that she was telling the truth. Frowning heavily he said, "I will do what I can Mrs. Spalding, but please understand that I can't promise anything except that I will do my best for you."

He explained that now the war had ended, there were many thousands of displaced children, even adults, throughout Britain and Europe. Also that the organisations involved in tracing and repatriation were severely stretched and under resourced. So there was unlikely to be any quick responses.

"It could be a minefield fraught with problems and disappointments, but we'll see what we can do," he said with a sympathetic frown.

Anne was appreciative of any help she could get. Mr. Legg-Bourke said he would get in touch with her via his secretary as soon as he had something to tell her.

Five anxious weeks passed before she received a short note on official letterhead, inviting her to contact his secretary to make an appointment to see him.

Anne arrived at his office eager and a little early. She waited for another person to leave and was shown into the MP's office. Mr. Legg-Bourke stood behind his desk, smiled a warm greeting and invited her to sit. Clutching her handbag with white knuckles she waited. He opened a file on his desk and after a few moments looked up to say.

"Well Mrs. Spalding, I have some comforting news for you but also some less so. It is a surprisingly arduous task to trace the whereabouts of misplaced children these days. You see, there are so many departments and organisations involved.

It may be a little comforting for you to know that extensive searches have found no trace of the hospitalization of your son. Further, Births, Deaths and Marriages have no record of him passing away. So we may assume that young Robert is fit and well. On the other hand Mrs. Spalding, we investigated the actions of Dr. Barnardo's in making Robert a Ward of the State, and I have to say that they acted perfectly within the law. In your circumstances it certainly does not seem fair, but the law will have its way. They claim that files relating to children in care are confidential, even to Members of Parliament, putting me in my place, so I could ascertain nothing more."

He stroked his mustache a moment before continuing.

"Their reasoning is that in the event of adoption, the information contained in files may cause distress and disruption for all concerned. There are also legal connotations. I regret to say they could not be moved on the matter, firmly holding their ground. So unfortunately, the only information I can give you now is what they were prepared to divulge, being that Robert is currently well and in good hands.

I have also been in touch with people at The Home Office who claim not to be at liberty to reveal further information, not even to me. Apparently, it's the law again I'm afraid. So there we have it Mrs. Spalding. I only wish I could do more to help you, but my hands are tied."

"So where do I go from here? I want my son back. No matter what, I mean to have him."

"The problem is Mrs. Spalding, even if you were to locate him, you may not have access to him whilst he is a minor. So you may have to wait until he passes from the jurisdiction of the law before you see him. It's very hard I know."

"That's not fair," Anne said.

"Well, I suppose you could mount a legal challenge, but that would be expensive and judges administer the law, not always justice, clearly for fear of setting precedents. But we have to find your son first."

The M.P. leaned forwards and spoke in a manner suggesting a degree of confidentiality.

"Mrs. Spalding, a suggestion was made to me, on the quiet you might say. I wonder if you are aware of a Government programme entered into with various Christian child care organisations and commonwealth governments concerning repatriation?"

"No," Anne replied.

"Well you see, even before the war our orphanages were bursting at the seams with children without homes or parents. There was nowhere for them to go and nobody to look after them in the longer term. Yet, some Commonwealth countries like Australia, Rhodesia and Canada needed to populate. So many of these orphaned children are now being sent to welcoming families there to give them a new life and a real future. I'm told the selection process is quite stringent to avoid sending any child other than a legitimate orphan or Ward of the State. Now we can't get any information such as names and family details. However you might try to get permission to review some of the passenger manifests of the migrant ships to see if your son was inadvertently swept up in the selection. It's only a slim chance, but it may be the first step in tracing him. Of course it may lead nowhere, but it is a possibility and might be worth a try."

Anne was reluctantly obliged to live with the circumstances but she never accepted them. Over the following years she made many attempts to trace Robbie through church and government organisations. The Red Cross and Salvation Army both claimed that a lack of records were a major obstacle. She checked many passenger lists of migrant ships which she had battled to get but did not find Robbie's name.

So Anne concluded that he was still in England. All her efforts came to nothing due to a lack of information or uncompromising bureaucracy steeped in regulation and apparent secrecy. Of great frustration to Anne was being repeatedly referred to other organisations, some of which she had already contacted. She was getting nowhere and felt she was going round in circles. The whole experience was surreal. Anne believed she was deliberately being kept from her son but could never prove it or comprehend why. Out of frustration she often said aloud, "someone must know where he is!"

In time Mepal held too many painful memories. This was where she had lost both Ross and Robbie. So after a few years she went to New Zealand to stay with Ross's family on a sheep farm not far from Christchurch. Anne was made welcome and enjoyed the Canterbury Plains. The flat expanse reminded her of The Fens, but it was somehow different. There were thousands upon thousands of sheep in vast fields instead of potatoes, wheat and sugar beet. Or maybe it was the backdrop of the distant mountains that made it different. She got a job working as a librarian in Christchurch and stayed with Ross's family until she found a small timber cottage, not far from town, to call home. Yet she never stopped fretting over finding Robbie. Every day she prayed that he was safe and well.

Ross's parents were also anxious to find their grandson and were in a state of disbelief at what had happened. To have him close would comfort them for the loss of their son. They thought they would see something of Ross in him and honour Ross's memory by loving and caring for his son.

In their efforts to trace Robert, they had written several times to authorities in Wellington with no satisfactory result. Replies either said that they had no jurisdiction over the matter or referred them to other associated, non-political organisations all of which had already been approached. The Red Cross had been sympathetic but referred them to organisations in the United Kingdom which Anne had long since exhausted. In desperation, a letter to the Prime Minister had only resulted in a reply, from a Permanent Secretary, suggesting they contact the Department of Internal Affairs in the United Kingdom.

One summer evening after work, Anne sat alone in a soft chair on her small timber veranda watching the sun go down. A local grower had given her a bottle of wine from his vineyard to sample. She sipped gently from her glass consciously savouring the taste knowing she would be asked her opinion. The owner had prophesied a new flourishing business based on it. After an hour and two glasses, she was feeling unusually relaxed. Her mind inevitably drifted back to Robbie and the great injustice she felt. There was a huge void in her life. She didn't know where he was, whether he was fit and well, if he was being properly looked after, if he missed her or even thought of her. The tears welled in her eyes as she cried deeply emotional tears for her son. For some reason she felt closer to him than usual, which she put down to the effects of wine making her melancholy.

The alcohol had made her tired so she went to bed early, quickly falling asleep. At some time during the night, she didn't know when, she woke feeling a presence in the room. As she opened her eyes, she heard a woman's voice with an unfamiliar accent saying, "don't be afraid lady. Your son is safe, but if you want to see him again you must go to where he can find you."

Anne focused her eyes in time to see the image of a tubby black woman with a round button nose, wearing a flowered print smock, gradually fade away, leaving behind a faint smell of eucalyptus. After several confused minutes, Anne fell asleep again but woke earlier than usual the next morning. Now in the cold light of the day, she was troubled by her experience, and was not sure if she had seen a ghost or had been dreaming. She tried to rationalize the event by blaming it on the wine, but it didn't work, and she was disturbed for many days afterwards.

Eventually, she came to the conclusion that if Robbie were to look for her, he would not look on the South Island of New Zealand. No, he would surely go to The Fens of East Anglia. So she decided to return and six months later was renting a small terraced cottage in Mepal. From the day that she went into hospital, not one had passed when she did not think about reuniting with her Robbie. Now she had raised hope that one day he would knock on her door.

17

Gidga secretly didn't want Nick to leave, but was philosophical and understood that Nick had no choice if he was to find his real mother. They spent their last evening sharing food and their deeper thoughts, both withholding their emotions from the other, as though admitting them would be a weakness or unmanly. Nick was reluctant to leave his friend and the people who had so graciously accepted him into their lives, an acceptance sealed by formally making him one of their own. Yet he was compelled to go and start the search for his mother and to find out who he really was, even though he didn't know where to begin.

After packing meagre rations of bread, bush fruit, some dried meat and water for Nick's trek, the boys slept. The air was chilled in the early hours of the morning when Nick quietly left the hut, trying not to wake Gidga. He felt they had said their goodbyes the evening before. His stealth did not prevent Gidga from waking, so in the still darkness he quietly watched Migaloo leave.

Nick retraced the steps he had taken previously, when he had gone for the doctor, but it was much hotter now. For the three days on the track, he was alone with his thoughts, a time to nurse his sorrows, to accept Arana's death and ponder his own purpose. The heat of the second day was severe. It played tricks on his mind and created illusions, turning the distance into rippling lakes that never came nearer. His mind drifted to where he could not be sure if he was awake or dreaming. In the heat he wandered along the track muttering like a drunk with the determination to get home before he falls over. Yet he was aware that he should find shade by midday and rest a while. Unfortunately there were no trees to be found, just low scrub. The sun was directly overhead and burnt his shoulders through his shirt. In moments of awareness, he saw how far he had travelled and was pleased, although surprised at not having previously noticed the many miles he had walked. When hungry, he chewed on the stale bread as he walked, but did not eat the meat, knowing the salt in it would only add to his thirst. He couldn't afford to drink all his water in case he was unable find any replacement for the next day. So Nick had to make it last, no matter how thirsty he was. The washed Scrub and fresh plants had given the outback a green veneer after the rain of a few days earlier, but it did not mean there was water to hand.

The coolness of the evening was welcome and helped him to think more clearly. Only then did he eat some of the meat whilst admiring the night sky and the brilliance of a million stars. He could understand why Aboriginal people believed that stars were holes in the sky where the spirits of their ancestors had passed through, to a bright dreamtime light on the far side. The biggest and brightest holes would be those made by Elders, the smallest were children, each hole marking their passage. It all seemed so logical and Nick wondered which one was Arana's.

Confused and depressed he was unable to make sense of her death. If only he had gone for help sooner, or asked the men who maintained the windmill to radio for help before they left. Nick felt guilty and it made him wonder how many people had died out here due to a lack of communication.

It seemed as if part of his mind worked independently of his will, falling back to former times that Nick hated, and then to the anxieties of finding his real mother. His thoughts were like a song you can't stop singing until it annoys you, yet still find yourself singing it in unguarded moments. He talked aloud, asking many questions, as if expecting someone else to give him logical, acceptable answers. Anxieties, optimism, reality, purpose and opinion openly contradicted each other as though there were two or three people holding a debate in his head.

The next morning he started out well before the sun began to heat the day to an almost unbearable temperature. His mind played tricks again, as for a moment he turned to look back. He was sure he'd heard Arana calling his name. He wished Gidga was with him now. The hours passed while his mind drifted again and again, allowing him to ignore his thirst and the persistent flies. He didn't count the number of times he had to stop and close his eyes when a dust devil blew over him.

It was past mid-afternoon when he stopped at a feature which had not been there on his last trek, to bring him back from his daydreaming. The storm had obviously caused flash flooding to create a torrent of water which had washed a channel four yards wide and a yard deep across the track and into the distance. As it was not too old, the newly uncovered rocks were washed clean. He noticed the angle of the afternoon sun had created a ragged strip of shade against the far wall of the cutting. Convincing himself he deserved a rest after walking for so many hours, he took the opportunity to stop a while in the shade's relative coolness. Exhausted, he took a sip of water, closed his burning eyes and unintentionally fell asleep.

It was almost dark before he woke and was annoyed with himself for losing so much time. Then considering the time of day, he decided the gully would be a good place to spend the night. The sand was fresh, clean and firm so there would be no scorpions or bugs hiding beneath. Now more refreshed, Nick spoke aloud as if disciplining himself.

"Well Nick, it was probably for the best. You might not have found another place as good as this to sleep. You've already had some rest, so you can jolly well get up before light tomorrow and start walking early."

As he drank from his bottle, Nick noticed Whitchetty bushes further down the edge of the gully where it was shallower. Parts of their roots were washed away and the grubs would be easy to find. While digging for them, he spotted a small Casuarina tree further along at the side of the washout. He had learned that Casuarina trees like lots of moisture, so he could expect to find water a few feet below its base. That evening Nick had a high protein meal of Whitchetty grubs with the fatty juices soothing his cracking lips. He smiled as he remembered the first time they were offered to him. He was also able to refill his water bottle in the hole he dug at the base of the Casuarina tree. The water was surprisingly clear but it would not stay there long even though the ground would remain moist. Nick filtered the water through his shirt to remove the grit and to collected enough to drink now, and to keep him going through the next day if he was careful.

Nick reached the station towards the end of the third day. He was very tired, his eyes were red and sore, his lips were cracked, and being covered in dust he looked like an urchin in his ragged shorts and shirt with no shoes and only the remains of an old sun hat on his head. He was sure the boss would let him stay the night with the station hands. Travellers were never turned away in the outback, so he was optimistic of a cooling shower, a good meal and a comfortable night.

As he wandered past the sheds, he heard Jess's familiar voice.

"What you doing back here mate? Ya dun'arf look a sight."

Jess's huge smile was pumped wider by a vigorous handshake. After talking to himself for almost three days, the sound of another voice welcomed Nick back to normality. Before he could say anything, Jess asked.

"How dy'a go with the doc. and ya Ma?"

"Ma died before we got there. Doc thought it was pneumonia."

Nick said quietly, not welcoming the reminder.

Jess's expression changed.

"Gees mate, I'm real sorry to hear that. The doc didn't say nothin to us black fellas on his way back."

Jess put a sympathetic arm around Nick's neck and steered him towards the sleeping shed. After a moment or two of respectful silence, he said cheerfully.

"Well it's bloody good to see you again mate, come on let's get you cleaned up before we see the boss."

Nick stood naked behind the rusty corrugated iron screen and looked up ready to welcome the falling water. He pulled the string to hear a gurgling sound followed by a splutter of rusty water. A second later he jumped out in shock as the scolding water hit his tender sunburned shoulders. The water in the pipe had been heated by the sun, but when it cooled to just below body temperature he stood in ecstasy under its flow. Again he raised his face, but this time to drink.

Jess shook Nick's clothes and brushed them off as much as he could then gave him a towel. After he was dry Jess said.

The boss is back from the pens now so we can let him know you're here."

As Nick was about to mount the timber veranda of the house, Jess put his hand across Nick's chest halting him and called.

"Hey Boss, Boss!"

They waited a moment before he appeared behind the fly screen at the door.

"Yeh what?"

"Young Nick is back Boss, bloody walked all the way here again. Is it okay if we look after him for a bit?"

"Yeh, sure," the boss replied.

Nick thanked him, but didn't think the boss heard.

"Bloody Bonza mate, he's a good sort is the boss. Don't say much but he's a fair dinkum bloke," Jess said as they went towards the shed that he and the Jackaroos called home.

The boss watched them walk away from behind the fly screen and again wondered about Nick, trying to fathom his story.

"Bet you could do with some tukka hey?" Jess asked, already knowing the answer.

"Yes please," Nick nodded.

"Come on then, grub will be up soon."

They sat in the shade on a crude timber bench next to a couple of saddles that hung over a fence rail. Jess gave Nick a tin mug full of water. It was not until he began to drink that Nick realised how thirsty he still was, gulping it all down in one go. Jess took the mug saying, "don't drink too much too soon Bro, it'll make you crook. I don't wanna pry mate, but what are ya doin back here again?"

Once more, Nick instinctively felt the need to hide his identity. He also remembered the story he had given previously so improvised using Gidga's experience.

"Over three and a half years ago my sister was taken by the white fella bosses to live in town. I promised Ma I would find her one day and bring her back, but I never did. Now I have to keep my promise and tell my sister that Ma is gone, if I can find her."

"I thought you said that your old man buggered off when he found out your Mar was pregnant – so how come you got a sister?"

Nick suddenly realised his predicament and quickly, thinking on his feet said, "Well, Ma was married and had a girl before she met my father. He went walkabout and was never seen again. She never married after my father cleared off, so she is really my half-sister."

"So your Ma had a rough time then. I hope you find ya sister mate."

"Thanks."

"Where is she?" Jess asked.

"I'm not sure but I think near Perth."

"So that's where you going hey?"

Jess was thoughtful for a moment then excitedly said.

"Hey, the boss is gonna to fly to Perth in a couple'a days. Maybe he'll give you a lift. I'll ask him if you want. Like I said, he's a good sort'a bloke."

Nick was apprehensive about flying, especially in a small aeroplane, so partly hoped the boss would refuse to take him. Yet knowing it would be a Godsend.

Without prompting Jess continued.

"When the doc come back through from your place he looked at the misses. The boss said she'd been getting pains and doc said she had to see a special bloke at a hospital in Perth. The missis is upset with the boss cos she wasn't gonna say nothing to the doc."

That evening Jess told Nick the boss would take him to Perth.

"You'll be there in three days from now mate. The boss already knew your Ma died cos the doc had told him. Anyway he feels a bit sorry for ya. Especially after I told him about your sister and after what you did to help ya Ma, he reckons you got guts. Said it's no inconvenience to take ya, an better than you going walkabout where you don't know. Could take weeks otherwise he said, safer too. He's a good bloke, not like the misses. She don't go much on us black fellas."

After sausages, baked potatoes and beans they relaxed in comfort with a few juckaroos around an old pot belly stove, grateful for the warmth in the evening chill. Nick thought Jess had taken a liking to him, making him feel guilty, especially as Jess had so obviously noticed his blue eyes and different features. He became pensive and decided to trust Jess with the truth, hoping he would not be too offended that he had mislead him earlier. So Nick apologized to Jess for not being totally honest with him before and explained why. After Jess had promised not to tell anyone, he then told him something of his past. Jess listened intently, partly from fascination and partly out of sympathy.

He sucked air through his teeth while gently shaking his head and said, "my little bro, I always knew there was somethin different about ya. You done more living than most people have but in less years. So you gonna find your real Ma hey. Good on ya mate, that's something you gotta do, and not leave it too long neither. A lot can happen to a person in no time at all. And don't worry mate your secret is safe with me."

Nick was relieved at Jess's discretion and being called 'little brother' made him feel good. He knew that brotherhood had a special meaning for Aboriginal people. It came with trust, comradeship, commitment and responsibilities, all he had learned from Elders, Gidga and Arana without it ever being spoken of.

Nick sat apprehensively in one of the two rear seats of the single engine Cessna. He was told to fasten himself in and put the headphones on, but the misses didn't want him to wear them because he would hear their conversation, but the boss said, "no, he has to wear them in case I need to talk to him in an emergency."

The missis didn't like it and pinched her lips while reluctantly accepting her husband's directive.

Nick waved to Jess as they disappeared ahead of a cloud of red dust. He was both fascinated and a little afraid, spending much of the time looking out of a small side window. The outback looked quite different from up here, and the sky was a much darker blue. Strangely, at times, it seemed they were not moving at all. He remembered what the Elder had told him about the boomerang and saw that same profile in the wings. There were times when the little plane bumped and bounced in the turbulence, making Nick afraid. The boss and his wife didn't seem to take any notice, so Nick assumed it was normal and relaxed his grip on the seat.

The boss asked Nick if he had flown before?

He replied with a simple "no."

"Well don't worry young fella, you're safe enough."

Before long they descended to land on another dusty runway.

"Is this Perth?" Nick asked.

The boss smiled in amusement.

"No son, this is Mount Magnet. We are stopping here to see someone and top up the fuel. We'll be about an hour. If you want to stretch your legs or take a pee, you'd better do it now. There's a bit o' tucker in the box behind you if you want something." It'll be a longer flight to Perth with no more stops till we get there.

He was right, it took almost four hours. On the way a flask, sandwiches and muffins were produced. Nick was hesitant to accept, but the woman said she had packed enough for all of them. He especially enjoyed the muffin but was not too keen on the sandwiches. There was little talk on board and the flight was thankfully uneventful, apart from Nick's ears popping as they climbed and descended. He dozed much of the way, not totally sleeping or being fully awake.

As they circled Caversham airfield on the northern outskirts of Perth, Nick could see the wide expanse of suburbia that reached to the ocean a few miles away. The boss spoke to someone on the radio asking if it he could land. The reply was lost to Nick in crackling noises, but the boss seemed to understand and called the man "Roger." Now, Nick more earnestly considered what he would do after they had landed, coming to no definite conclusion, other than that he would make his way to the city.

Before Nick walked from the airfield, he thanked the boss who gave a single nod saying, "I don't know about you, young fella. I'm certain there's more to you than meets the eye. I bet there's a lot we don't know. Now have you got any money?"

"No," Nick replied.

"Well then, I'd best pay you for the work you did at the station these last two days." The boss said as he pulled notes from his wallet.

Nick had done odd jobs to show his appreciation for being allowed to stay and for being fed, but had not expected to be paid. He hesitated.

"Go on take it, you earned it," the boss said.

Nick took the notes and stuffed them into his pocket.

"Good luck mate, with whatever it is you're up to," the boss added.

Nick thanked him again, no further conversation was possible as a man came to ask the boss if he wanted to refuel now or later.

Nick didn't really know where to go when he left the airfield and was a little afraid, yet fascinated, by the streets, houses, buses and cars. This was the first time he had ever been alone in a town or city, and he felt a vulnerability which he had experienced only once in the bush, on the day he first met Gidga. The way some folks stared, looking him up and down, made him feel even more uneasy and acutely aware of his shabby appearance.

Soon it would be dark and he needed somewhere to sleep. At a park he noticed a shelter and went to investigate, finding toilets at the rear. Sitting on his blanket in the shelter, he ate the leftover sandwiches from the flight. Then examined the crumpled bank notes with fascination, considered what they were worth and what they would buy. He had never held money before.

The air was beginning to take on a chill as the sun lowered to the fence at the opposite side of the park. A man walking his dog gave an enquiring glance and nodded. Nick returned the gesture but the man didn't speak, much to Nick's relief. Deciding this would be as good a place as any to spend the night he spread his blanket along the wooden seat and laid down. Nick then pulled the surplus blanket over himself and settled for an uncomfortable sleep on the bench.

It was cold and he was thirsty when he woke the next morning. Water from a tap at the rear of the shelter was cool and clear. Nick noticed its lack of taste and the absence of grit, reminding him of the water at Boys Town. None-the-less, water on tap was still a novelty.

He knew no one here and didn't know where to go, so walked in what he thought was the direction of the city. Nick wondered if he had done the right thing by coming here after all.

He thought he could afford to take a bus to the city but didn't want to bring attention to himself or waste his money. So he decided to make his way on foot by following ' the bus routes. The buses going that way had 'City' or 'Perth Central' posted on the front. He followed them as best he could, knowing he would eventually get there. When there was no bus in sight at a main junction he waited for the next bus to pass to see which way it went. Sometimes the way was signposted making it easier.

He came to a baker's shop where the smell of fresh bread was tantalising, so after some hesitation, Nick plucked up the courage to buy a loaf of bread, eating much of it as he walked. He had no idea of the change the baker had given him from the Pound note he had presented. But he was pleased to leave the shop after the enquiring look he had been given on presentation of so much money.

By lunch time he had arrived at the Swan River, just where it widens to take on the appearance of a lake. The buildings on the far side were tall and imposing. They were the same ones he had seen in the distance from Boys Town.

The sun was almost directly overhead, so Nick sat by the river for a while enjoying the shade of a tree. After eating the remaining bread, he laid back and drifted off to sleep. It was mid afternoon when he woke and it took him a few anxious seconds to remember where he was. Then his apprehension returned. This was the town where he'd spent so many unhappy years at the hands of the Christian Brothers. Part of him felt an urge to leave, but then he considered how close he might now be to Chris.

"Where are you Chris? We must be so close," he murmured as his urge to see Chris increased.

Going to Boys Town was out of the question since he was afraid of being detained again. Not to mention any punishment he might receive. Nick was already feeling like a fugitive, hiding and turning his back when he saw a police car or policeman. He had to leave here and so decided to go to Fremantle. Being a port, he thought there would be lots of different nationalities, strangers and types of people there. Naively thinking he would not stand out. If someone thought he looked different, they might consider he was from one of the ships which had come from foreign parts.

Crossing the river he looked down from the bridge. While staring at the water, he remembered little Craig who he and Chris had tried to protect. Craig had come to a sad end in this water simply to escape the clutches of the Brothers.

Nick's attention was then taken by long necked turtles lazing in the muddy shallows. Some were clinging to rocks, others floating lazily with their snouts protruding just above the water. Aboriginal instincts came to the fore as he wondered what they would taste like.

Now on the city side of the river he walked to where he could see timber buildings by the water's edge with boats nearby. At a timber wharf was an assortment of small craft, the largest of which were two fishing boats tied side by side. Then another vessel that looked like a pleasure boat and a little further a river cruiser with a small motor yacht next to it.

Two men were working on the furthest fishing boat and Nick stopped a moment or two to watch. A white man in his fifties was giving orders to a younger Aboriginal man. After a few minutes, a heavily built man with black greasy hands, wearing a dirty blue boiler suit, appeared from a hatch in the deck of the closer boat.

The older man on the far boat called out.

"We're just heading down to Fremantle, then to sea. See you when we get back mate."

The man in the boiler suit nodded, waved and shouted, "OK."

Before Nick realised what he was doing, he had called out. "can I come with you?"

All three men turned to look at him in surprise. Nick immediately became self-conscious and took a step back having surprised himself.

"I'd just like a lift please Sir, if I can?"

He said more quietly out of embarrassment.

"Cheeky little beggar hey!" someone said.

The men laughed. Then the white man on the far boat said, "Come on, hop over here then. We'll give you a lift just for your bloody cheek."

Nick felt awkward but thanked him as he crossed the deck of the first boat.

"You look like shit but you talk nice and polite, otherwise I'd have told you to clear off. You can untie that aft line while you're there young'n," the older man said.

"Then you can scrub the deck," the Aboriginal added in jest, making all three men laugh.

Nick, uncomfortably, did as he was told and relaxed a little knowing they were pulling his leg. Casting off was a small task, but a gesture that made him feel useful. As he climbed over the gunnels to the far boat he thanked them again.

The white man smiled at him saying, "at least you got manners, which is more than I can say for the rest of this motley crew."

The smaller, darker man glanced over his shoulder and scoffed at the remark. The deliberate twinkle in his eye betrayed any offence as if to enjoy the playful banter.

Nick hoped they would accept him without too many questions.

The small fishing boat slowly slipped away from its mate at the wharf to head out at a steady four knots diagonally across the Swan River. Nick surmised that the larger man was in charge, but you could not tell from their appearances. Both wore grubby dark blue boiler suits and wellington boots. Neither had shaved for some days and their hands were cracked and calloused. While their faces recorded a history of hard work and exposure to the elements. To Nick, they seemed like men who would not knowingly do anyone harm, yet not the types to cross.

"This here is Charlie. He's the First Mate, deck hand, head fish gutter, chief cook and bottle washer. He's part Abbo, and part, well a whole bunch of other stuff we don't want to know about but mostly Abbo. I suppose he's all right though. I might just keep him on for a bit. I am, well you can call me Skip or Skipper, whichever you like. What do we call you young fella?"

"Nick, just Nick."

Adding "just Nick" aroused the skipper's curiosity, seeing there was more to this lad than he wanted to let on. He respected Nick's right to privacy so didn't ask any more.

"OK Nick, were gonna run up to a little jetty in the Canning River first to pick some stuff up before we go down to Fremantle, so it'll be a couple of hours before we get there. Nick only had a vague idea where the Canning River was from here and even less where Fremantle was. So he simply nodded his vague understanding. Skip pushed past Charlie in the wheelhouse to grab a clean white paper bag. Opening it, he offered the contents to Charlie, who took out a brown ball shaped bun covered in sugar. He immediately held it in his mouth, freeing both hands to allow him to manouevre the boat to the port side of another craft coming up river.

"Want a Donut young'un?"

The skipper offered the open bag to Nick.

"Want a donut?" Skip repeated.

"Charlie grabbed these on the way in. Bloody nice too."

Nick was hungry again so eagerly took one with a quiet. "Thank you."

He didn't know what a donut was, and this would be his first. As his teeth sunk into the soft texture, sugar stuck to his lips as sweet red jam oozed from a hole to run over his fingers and across the back of his hand; he involuntarily murmured with pleasure as he licked his fingers clean whilst savouring every morsel. Nick took another bite, closing his eyes to focus his senses on the exquisite sweet taste. It was wonderful, and this would become one of those moments he would always remember.

As Skip ate, he watched Nick lick his fingers, hand and lips.

"Dear God, it's gone already. Enjoyed that didn't you son?" Skip asked by way of a statement while grinning.

"Here you'd better have another one, and watch out for your fingers! You'll bite them off if you're not careful."

Both men laughed.

With a restrained eagerness that was obvious, Nick put his hand in the bag to take another and once again said thank you. This time he ate more slowly relishing the experience. Skip was quietly impressed with his politeness, and a tinge of liking for the boy had begun to develop. He edged past Charlie again to enter a small galley, where he discarded the paper bag and put a kettle of water on a simple gas ring. Turning back to Charlie, he expressed his concern speaking in a low voice so Nick would not hear.

"I don't think that poor little beggar has eaten for a while. Not much of him is there. Nice kid though. I wonder what the hell he's doing here all by himself? Looks like a trainee swagman! C'ept he's got no swag apart from that old blanket."

Charlie gave a wry grin to acknowledge the notion and the sad comparison Skip had made.

"Do you reckon he's running away from somewhere or someone?" Charlie speculated.

"Probably, who knows?"

Then raising his voice Skip called.

"Want a mug a tea Nick?"

Surprised at the warmth in Skip's voice, he answered with a simple but enthusiastic, "yes please."

"Bet you take sugar and a lot of it, hey?"

"Just the normal amount Sir, two spoons please," Nick replied.

Skip almost fell over. Nobody had called him 'Sir' in years.

"He's got manners that kid has, I'll give him that."
Skip said to nobody in particular as he thought aloud.

The boat was entering the Canning River mouth by the time Skip gave Charlie his tea then appeared on the aft deck with two chipped enamel mugs. Giving Nick one, he then leaned back on a winch rope to enjoy the day. They didn't speak at first but Skip was curious and gave inquisitive glances towards Nick, somehow hoping he could decipher the boy's circumstances with clues from his appearance and a few comments.

He was a puzzle. Ragged and tanned, feet stained red to match the colour of the outback, but he was fit and healthy. Although a bit skinny for his age, he spoke nicely and had good manners. Unlike any other street urchin Skip had come across.

Nick sipped the strong sweet tea, noticing that the inside of the mug was stained to only a lighter shade of the tea itself. Once or twice he had noticed Skip looking at him inquisitively. He instinctively looked away in those awkward moments, pretending to scan the river banks for points of interest. Skip turned away feeling a pregnant silence. As they neared the jetty, Nick looked at the opposite side of the river and stood rigid, in a transfixed stare. Skip watched him stiffen and could see Nick's eyes widen. Nick pinched his lips and subconsciously gripped the mug hard, turning his knuckles white. Skip immediately felt he was learning more about Nick, if only from his pained expression as he looked at the white stone buildings across the river.

Dreadful feelings and near panic engulfed Nick. In a moment of alarm, he realised he was looking at the place he knew as Clontarf Boys Town, where he had spent so many years. His mind raced in fear as his memories came flooding back like a tsunami. 'Chris, was Chris still there?' He wanted to go and find out but didn't dare. He felt drawn like a moth to the flame. Were the Brothers still the same? Was the food still as bad? The beatings, sexual and mental abuses that went on in that place came flooding back to fill him with a mixture of dread and outrage. Did it all still go on? Was it even real?

Skip read Nick's body language and expressions confirming his speculation of a troubled past. In a moment of compassion he approached Nick from behind, gently put his hand on his shoulder and quietly said.

"It's okay son, don't worry, no harm's gonna come to you."

Nick, trembling, dropped the empty mug and in a quick single movement turned to face Skip, grabbed his open lapels with both hands and pressed his forehead onto the front of Skip's dirty blue boiler suit. Nick was hardly aware of what he was doing as his actions were almost a reflex.

This was a new experience for both and each was unsure how to handle it. It was a defining moment that would have lasting results for both man and boy. This show of emotion, and whatever had prompted it, made Skip feel uncomfortable, but he allowed Nick time to gather himself, quietly saying.

"It's okay son, it's okay."

Nick felt suddenly awkward and confused at his own actions. He had not expected those buried emotions to rush to the fore as they had. Such was the legacy of Clontarf Boys Town.

Skip was feeling awkward so gently eased Nick away, holding him by the shoulders at arm's length, then stooping to be at Nick's eye level to distract him, he said,

"come on Nick my mate, we got a job of work to do right now and I need your help. We'll have a chat later. For now, just let me say that you are safe here with us."

Then, after a long pause, he released Nick.

"Here, grab that forward line and when Charlie goes in, hop onto the jetty and throw a few loops over a bollard. I'll do the same down the stern."

The distraction worked. Nick took a deep breath and gave two gentle nods of understanding.

With a single wave, the skipper indicated to Charlie to go ahead and dock. The task at hand was a welcome distraction for all three aboard. Through his concern and compassion, Skip did not realise he had just emotionally adopted Nick, or at least his problems. Charlie had seen it all and although inquisitive, he was discrete, knowing that sometimes it was enough to simply observe and say nothing. In Nick's confused state, he warmed to Skip as he had never done to any other white adult since before arriving in Australia.

The only words spoken for the next half hour were Skip's instructions for loading the boat, mostly with food, water and supplies. Nick felt a renewed energy and enthusiasm, enjoying being allowed to help while occasionally glancing to Skip for signs of approval. Skip smiled and winked when he noticed. Nick struggled to avoid staring at the white buildings across the water, failing a few times to quickly look away again.

"OK young fella, untie that forward line and jump aboard when I tell you." Skip commanded.

Nick grabbed the heavy rope and waited while Charlie started the big diesel engine. A rattle and shudder went through the boat as a cloud of blue smoke appeared aft and slowly drifted across the river.

"Ready Nick?" Skip shouted.

"Yep!"

"Cast off then!"

Charlie nodded to Skip, who called.

"OK Nick, let's go."

Both Nick and Skip climbed aboard at the same time.

"You did alright son." Skip said to deliberately motivate Nick.

To reinforce Skip's compliment, Charlie turned and gave a big approving grin and a nod which carried the message 'I think the boss likes you.' Nick felt safe.

Once the motor had settled into a steady rhythm, Skip said, "We deserve another mug of tea after all that work, don't you think Nick?"

Nick grinned in agreement.

"Okay then young fella-me-lad, the kettle and all the stuff is in the galley. Let's see if you can make a decent brew of tea!"

The two men laughed aloud when Nick asked how they liked it.

"Bloody Hell Skip, that's the first time I've been asked that on this old tub. Things are looking up," Charlie said with a grin. Then continued, "Come on mate, I'll show you where everything is."

They relaxed, sipping their hot sweet tea from large enameled mugs while on the way down the river to Freemantle. Skip reminded Charlie they should fuel up before leaving and to head for the pump. They were going to sea and Nick was anxious. He didn't want to leave them to find himself alone again, and be faced with more uncertainty.

"I don't suppose you got any plans have you son? I mean, what are you gunna do, where are you gunna stay?" Skip asked.

Nick looked down and responded with a gentle shake of his head quietly saying, "no, I don't have any plans."

"So where will you stay?" Skip asked again.

"I don't know."

Skip took a breath and shook his head. Charlie sensed the delicacy of the ensuing conversation and deliberately appeared to concentrate on navigating the estuary channel. However, the wheelhouse door was left open for him to hear what was being said. He knew his skipper well enough to know what was coming. Skip stroked his chin as he stared down at the deck in thought.

"Can't let you go wandering off by yourself in the big city, can we? An I bet you've got no means of support, have you?"

Then without waiting for an answer and looking straight at Nick, he added. "I suppose we could take you to the Sally Army. They'll take care of you."

Skip saw Nick's eyes widen and quickly added, "narr, that won't do will it? Well, you'll just have to tag along with us for a day or two until we sort something out."

Nick was pleased. Charlie grinned while gently shaking his head saying to himself, "you can be a hard old bastard boss, but really you are just a big old teddy bear."

"Do you know anything about boats and fishing young fella?" Skip asked.

"No, but I can learn." Nick hurriedly replied. "But I can cook and clean."

"Well then, I suppose you'll make someone a great wife one day."

Skip and Charlie laughed.

"That'll have to do for now. You gotta earn your keep somehow, the Kingfisher don't carry no passengers!"

Skip said, only partly in jest.

The Kingfisher reached a timber wharf reserved for small boats close to the main docks where the larger ships berthed. By the time their conversation had finished, Charlie was guiding the craft close to the diesel pump.

"OK, Nick, you know what to do."

Now with some confidence, Nick leapt onto the jetty dragging the stiff hemp rope over his shoulder. A few wraps around a bollard and all was secure. Skip secured the stern, then checked the pump meter reading and disappeared into a tin hut close by. Charlie maneuvered a heavy hose across the deck, unscrewed a fuel cap which sat slightly raised above the side of the deck, then went and switched the pump on. He repeated the process on the port side where a second tank was located. After what seemed an eternity to Nick, who wondered where all that fuel was going, Charlie stopped, squinted at the pump dial and called aloud, "657 gallons."

Skip confirmed the reading and went back into the hut again to reappear in less than a minute. After climbing back on board, he checked that the fuel caps were tightened down. Now with the refueling completed, they were on their way.

"Been to sea before Nick?" Skip asked.

"No, well sort of, a long time ago when I was small. But it was on a really big ship with lots of other people. A liner they called it."

"Where were you going?"

"I was coming here from England."

Skip thought this lad had a strange story to tell. Looking like a tramp, no home, no belongings or means of support, and he came here on a fancy cruise liner? It didn't add up and he would ask about it later.

"Okay then, there are four things you gotta know. First, the life jackets are in that locker by the wheelhouse. Charlie will show you how to put one on. Second, if you're gonna throw up, make sure it's over the lee side and hang on tight when you do. The lee is always the side with the wind to your back. If you are not sure, go to the stern. We don't want your breakfast on the deck. Third, that's the starboard side, and this is port side he said as he pointed. Last and most importantly, do exactly what you are told, when you are told. Got that?"

Nick gave a serious. "Yes."

The sun was heading for the western horizon as the little vessel slipped out of the Swan River estuary. Once they were past the cargo and Navy ships that lined the wharves, they reached open water and Nick began to feel the movement of the swell. He'd had no thoughts of sickness until Skip had mentioned it. Now he hoped he would be okay.

The evening delivered a beautiful multi-coloured sunset that reminded Nick of the big outback skies. Thankfully, the sea was calm making it a perfect evening. He was content for now, but apprehensive about tomorrow. Skip took the wheel and told Charlie to give Nick a tour of the Kingfisher, showing him where things are and what they are for.

18

The rear deck took up almost half the length of the boat and was mostly clear but for two large winches at the stern. Back towards the wheelhouse stood a heavy wooden boom strapped in a vertical position against a short mast. Nick asked what it was for?

Playfully Charlie said, "In the old days they used it to hang cabin boys by the feet from it if they were no good or did something stupid. They'd swing him out over the water, and let him dangle there for hours. If he was really bad, they'd drop him in the water for the sharks to have a feed."

Charlie saw the shock on Nick's face and laughed. Nick swallowed and smiled on realizing his leg was being pulled. Charlie then explained that the boom was part of a hoist used to load and unload heavy gear and their catch. That it was also used to hoist the net high before pulling the release cord.

The gunwales were low and uncluttered except for a large plate on both port and starboard sides. Charlie showed how a part of the gunwale could be removed to allow access to the ocean.

"It's called a sea door. You betta make sure you don't topple out or over the gunwale mate. It's easily done, especially when we are beam on and the deck's wet. You should wear a life jacket when it gets rough, at least until you get your sea legs. Even then Skip might not let you take it off. She's a solid old tub, got a thick timber hull that sits well, and she don't roll too much neither. She's called the Kingfisher. That was her name when Skip bought her. He don't like it much but won't change it. Bad luck you see."

Nick nodded.

"And that reminds me, don't ever bring bananas on board. It's really bad mojo on fishing boats, and Skip will go ape-shit. Yeh, and that goes for suitcases too. Kit bags, duffle bags and rucksacks are alright but no suitcases, right!"

In front of the boom was a hatch about a yard and a half square that led down into the hold. Charlie lifted the cover for Nick to see below. It was dark and Nick had to wait for his eyes to adjust before he could see what was inside. The space was larger than he had expected and smelled. Back on deck, to the port side amidships, was a large platform like a table with raised edges, which Charlie explained was the gutting table.

At the back of the wheelhouse was a protruding portion, about a yard square, with a narrow full-length door.

"That's the Head, Dunnie to you mate. When you've finished you gotta give the handle a few cranks to flush it out. Nothing goes down there except human waste and toilet paper right!" Charlie said.

"Don't throw up in there either. It makes a stinking mess, and the skipper will get really pissed off and make you clean it up. I will too."

"You'd better remember these names I'm telling you mate, or you won't know what we're talking about later on."

Nick nodded and immediately began to make a more conscious effort to remember. The wheelhouse was small with a bench seat to one side. It was just big enough for four people, maybe five to stand at a squeeze. A few dials and a compass were set in front by the helm and to the right a large lever. Badly folded maps were pushed into a rack above the forward window. Others were wedged between the two-way radio and the cabin roof. Above the bench seat was a small cupboard with a red cross painted over a white circle on the door.

"I'm sure you know what that is?" Charlie said.

"The flares are in there too. Night and day ones, I'll tell you about them later."

To one side of the forward bulkhead were two small narrow doors, each held closed with a brass hook where they met in the middle. Behind them four steep wooden steps led down to a small galley on the starboard side. A little gas cooker with two gas rings atop sat next to a dirty sink and a small work space. Nick had seen this before when he made tea.

"We don't use the cooker or them gas rings with the doors shut cos if ya get a gas leak or one blows out, we could all be paying Davey Jones a visit."

Nick looked very serious.

"See this cover you're standing on, that gets us down to the engine room, such as it is. Shan't open it now, it stinks like hell of diesel. Gets hot and stuffy down there too."

On the port side was a cold locker with cupboards to one side. Fixed to the floor in the middle of the galley stood a table with raised edges. It was just big enough for four people to sit at with a squeeze. Forward was another bulkhead and door with more steps that led down into a triangular shaped cabin with sloping sides that followed the contours of the hull. In the gloomy light Nick could see four bunks, two on each side. Those nearest the door held ruffled blankets and pillows.

"This is the folksal where we sleep. You can put your blanket on one of them forward bunks if you like. We usually have a crew of three but Mick went crook and has never come back. That's about it for now mate. If you got any questions you better ask. It's too dangerous to pretend you know if you don't, especially when we get busy or are in big seas. The boss says you can cook a bit and help sort the catch. Don't worry, I'll show you how to do that."

Nick was quietly excited and couldn't wait to show his worth. He didn't have long to wait. As they returned to the wheelhouse, Skip turned to Charlie and, deliberately for Nick to hear, said, "how about we get the young fella to fry up a few snags?"

"Good idea, I could eat the ass off a donkey," Charlie said with a grin.

"Come on mate, I'll show you were the tucker is kept."

Half an hour later a plate of sausages, fried potatoes, baked beans and bread with butter were on the table.

Nick called. "Grub up!"

Skip and Charlie were surprised, as much for the confidence in Nick's voice as the presentation of the meal. Clearly Nick had done this before. He watched their faces for signs of approval.

"Not bad, not bad for a first go mate," Skip said blandly.

Nick looked at Charlie for his comment and missed Skip's wink.

Skip and Charlie took turns at the wheel. After they had eaten, Skip sat at the stern dragging deep breaths through a cigarette. Charlie turned to Nick with a smile quietly saying, "you did alright mate, the skipper liked the tucker. Looks like you might'a got a permanent job as chief cook."

Charlie was only half joking.

"Tell you what, go make a mug of coffee for him to have with his fag and he'll think you're a bloody star."

Nick put the kettle on the gas ring and made coffee for each of them. Charlie was right, Skip was surprised and impressed, saying.

"Ta mate, you're doing all right."

Then without expression, Skip reached out to put his big calloused hand on Nick's shoulder giving it a squeeze. Nick felt a wave of pleasure as the gesture spoke volumes.

The fifty-foot craft chugged on at a steady eight knots heading W.S.W. The evening was spent talking about fishing matters and some other idle chatter. Charlie had a good sense of humour, as did Skip, although he had a more serious nature. Skip occasionally made amusing yet mildly sarcastic comments to Charlie while keeping a straight face. At first Nick was apprehensive but soon understood it was all in jest once he had noticed the twinkle in Skip's eye. Nick had originally expected Charlie to get upset and respond, but he mostly laughed. At one time Skip made the comment to Charlie that all "black bastards" were lazy. Nick was offended and anticipated a robust, defensive reply from Charlie, but he just smiled saying,"tell you what Skip, I'm luckier than you."

"How do you make that out?" Skip asked.

"Well, I get to work with a hard working white fella. You get to work with a lazy black bastard!"

They all laughed. It didn't take long for Nick to see that Charlie and Skip had a deep relationship, and that a great trusting friendship existed between them. A friendship deep enough to allow smart, otherwise offensive, comments to be made in jest with impunity. Charlie was a little more reserved out of respect for Skip and his position as skipper. Skip had taken him into his life, given him a chance when others would not, and Charlie would always be grateful for that.

It would be morning before they reached the fishing grounds. As usual, Skip and Charlie agreed to man the helm each in four hour shifts through the night. Skip took the first watch. Charlie went to the folksal to sleep and suggested Nick to do the same, saying, "you gotta be up early to get the breakfast mate."

Nick felt strange in the small enclosed cabin and waited to see what Charlie did. As Charlie took his shirt off, he told Nick to take Mick's pillow if he wanted it.

"You can have his blanket too if you need it. He won't be back."

Charlie relaxed in his bunk as Nick took his shirt off. In the dull light Charlie saw Nick's tribal markings, and in astonishment, quickly sat up to rest on his elbows.

"Bloody hell mate! You're a brother! One of us!"

"We'll sort of," Nick said feeling comfortable talking to an Aboriginal person who he thought would understand.

"I lived up north in a village with Aboriginals for a few years. Arana, my tribal mother, adopted me and they made me a tribal member."

"Bloody Bonza mate, you and me sure got a lot to talk about."

"It was the best time of my life. Well, that I can remember anyway," Nick said.

"So why did you leave?"

"It's a long story, but I have to find my real mother, I think she might be somewhere in England," Nick said with anxious determination.

"When Arana, my adopted mother, died it made me want to find my real mother more than ever. But I don't know where to start, and I'm afraid of getting caught and being sent back to an institution. Especially if I go to the authorities for help."

"Tell you what bro, I don't think Skip would let that happen. He likes you, see. You remind him of his own boy what drowned out here when he was about your age. We never did find im."

Nick did not ask how or when.

"We'll have a bit of time to talk soon enough but we better get some kip now bro."

Charlie was intrigued and didn't fall asleep for an hour or more. His mind was too busy speculating about this boy who had walked into their lives only a few hours ago, making such an impact. Nick's mind was also racing. It had been a long and eventful day. He was tired and wanted to sleep. Yet although his bed was more comfortable than last nights, sleep evaded him for a while. But the gentle movement and the background rumble of the engine eventually lulled him to sleep with the soundness of a small child. He did not hear Skip and Charlie change shifts.

Nick was awakened before daybreak with the shake of his shoulder. It was Skip.

"Come on son, we have to get started. We're nearly at the fishing grounds. There's a mug of tea in the galley for you, now go splash your face and wake up. We could all do with a bit of breakfast. We got a long day ahead."

As Skip left the folksal, he turned to add.

"Me and Charlie will be getting ready to set the nets. We'll be about twenty minutes."

Nick took his mug of tea onto the deck relishing the crisp fresh air. He looked around noticing there were no distant lights or land to be seen. A light breeze and a grey hue were encroaching on the darkness of early morning. , Skip and Charlie were already busy under bright lights. The swell was minimal, and there was little chop.

Charlie greeted Nick.

"G'day young Joey, sleep alright? What's for breakfast?" Not expecting an answer.

Nick smiled. There was a hive of activity on deck as both men ignored him to continue with the nets and tackle. So he returned to the galley to prepare breakfast. In this one small task he was trusted and enjoyed the responsibility. He was happy, enthusiastic and felt a fulfilling sense of purpose and self-worth. Finally, he was proving the Brothers wrong and was not just society's burden, as he had been told.

Before he had finished preparing breakfast, he heard Skip shout.

"Let her go. Watch that line don't twist up Charlie."

There was a screeching of pulleys and rollers, as lines and net ran out to disappear over the stern, lasting almost five minutes.

"OK, secure it off," Skip called.

Moments later Skip and Charlie went to the wheel house.

"Keep her at about four knots on this heading mate," Skip instructed Charlie before calling to Nick.

"How's that breakfast coming on young fella?"

"Ready," Nick called back.

Skip raised his eyebrows in surprise.

"On-ya Nick. Perfect timing."

Skip ate his breakfast with gusto. Nick assumed it was to the skipper's liking and was pleased when he asked for more toast.

Partly to break the silence and partly from curiosity, Nick asked how he knew when to bring the net in?

"When the water comes over the arse end son," was the immediate reply.

Skip had that twinkle in his eye again, and after a suitable pause said, "No seriously, we keep the throttle steady at near to three or four knots, and when the net's full the old Kingfisher will start to slow, probably down to about two knots and the motor'll labour a bit. You'll know when you hear it. The stern'll drop with the weight so we know to winch the net in. We'll keep the motor ticking over just enough to hold our position and keep the net astern. We might need you to help with that later."

Skip could see that Nick was eager to do more.

"You have to keep an eye on it though incase the net gets caught on a bommie or a wreck or something. It'll stop us dead in our tracks and pull the stern under real quick. Many a good old tub has been lost that way. You just gotta keep watching and be ready to cut the motor or back up. If it comes to the worst, we,ll let the net go. Some of them newer vessels have safety devices and alarms but you still gotta be quick."

Charlie came down for his breakfast after Skip had relieved him at the helm. He was eager to get back on deck and ate his breakfast without more chat.

They trawled for almost two hours before the dripping bulging net was hauled above the deck. When Charlie released the drawstring, fish spilled in every direction, slithering, sliding, flapping and gasping. Nick had never seen so many fish before and was surprised at how many different species there were of all shapes and sizes. Charlie quickly pointed them out whilst giving their names to Nick: Aussie Salmon, Dory, Trevally, Ling, Tailor, Flathead, Eagle Rays and a variety of different Sharks.

While wearing wellington boots that were far too big for him, Nick put on a large rubber apron and gloves. Charlie showed which fish to pick out to be placed in boxes according to their type and size. It was a clumsy, slippery process at first, but Nick eventually got the hang of it.

"Watch out for the spikes at the back of them gills on the Flathead bro, and keep your fingers away from the Tailors' choppes, they got teeth like razors. Let the lit'luns slip out through the scuppers," Charlie shouted.

Skip straightened and cleared the net of weed and debry while he checked it for damage before feeding it back into the ocean after the drawstring had been tied again.

There seemed a lot to learn, but Nick absorbed everything he was shown and taught. Nothing had to be repeated. He was enjoying himself and was happier than he had been for a long time. His sense of contribution filled him with confidence. By the time the first catch was sorted and the by-catch returned, the net was already beginning to fill again. This cycle went on for almost eighteen hours, well into darkness. Nick was very tired, as they all were. They had occasionally taken hastily prepared food and drink, but not eaten properly or rested. Once the boxes were stowed below Skip was pleased saying.

"Well done lads. Let's call it a day. We'll give it another shot tomorrow. Put the kettle on Nick while I clean a Flathead or two for a feed."

Charlie tidied up the deck making sure everything was washed down and stowed correctly for the next day.

Nick had not tasted fresh fish before, and Skip knew how to prepare it so it melted in his mouth to reveal a delicate flavour, and Nick savored with every mouthful. As they ate, Skip listened to the short wave radio for messages that crackled from the wheelhouse. They told him how other boats were doing, where they were, if any needed help and importantly, the weather forecast. Skip raised a finger to call for quiet as he concentrated on an announcement. Nick could barely make out what was being said above the crackle, but Skip's tuned ear heard clearly.

"I don't like the sound of that," he said quietly.

"Storms, 90 mile an hour winds and twenty-five foot swells blowing in from the west tomorrow morning. Bloody typical hey! Just as we hit good grounds. What do you reckon Charlie?"

"The bigger boats could wear it alright, but I don't fancy our chances, it'll be bloody uncomfortable and risky to stay out here. There are no other boats within a hundred miles of us either. We'll be on our own Skipper," he replied.

"Okay, always better safe than sorry, we have taken enough to pay for this trip so we'll head back shortly."

"Come on Skip. You know I don't like being called Shortly. My name's Charlie," he joked making Skip grin.

Nick was up early again to prepare breakfast. Skip was at the wheel steering a course for home, and Charlie was in the hold securing boxes of fish should it turn as rough as the forecast had predicted. Skip had maintained a good cruising speed during the night to try and stay ahead of the coming storm. Nick noticed that the seas were already bigger, the water was now grey, and there were large white horses as waves broke around them as the wind got stronger. Both the chop and swell were picking up by the hour, and the sky was dark and threatening from the west. Nick was uncomfortable and apprehensive even though he felt he would be safe with Skip and Charlie.

"Here son, put this lifejacket on. I don't want to lose… just put it on hey," Skip ordered.

By mid-morning, the wind had picked up to gale force and a wall of water, twenty feet high, kept pace with them at the stern. To Nick it looked as though it might suddenly rear up above the Kingfisher to fall across the deck. Skip kept one eye on the compass and the other on the swell. No faster and no slower, just keeping pace with the mountain of water up forward, so as not to ride over it, and from the threat from behind. He didn't want to surf and nose into the next forward swell or be swamped by the one following. It was a slow steady trip that required the skill and patience of an experienced skipper.

Charlie could see Nick's concern.

"Don't worry bro, Skip knows what he's doing. Most other skippers would be tempted to run full ahead to get home quick and risk the lot. I've been out in worse than this with him, and he always gets us home safe."

By mid-afternoon conditions had seriously worsened, and Nick could see that even Skip was concerned with their situation. All three stood in the wheelhouse with the outer door shut for protection from the torrential rain that now pounded them almost horizontally. It was safer in there with no chance of being washed overboard. Nick was feeling sick but said nothing. Charlie told him to watch the horizon as best he could, hoping he would not throw up, but the horizon constantly moved. Skip radioed in every half hour to give their position and let the coastguard know they were heading back.

"Tell you what, let's anchor behind Rottnest Island for the night and get out of this stuff. I know it's not far to port, but I've had enough of this stuff," Skip said.

"But wouldn't it be just as easy to go straight in after we get to the island?" Charlie asked.

Skip gave a knowing look as he tapped the side of his nose with his forefinger suggesting an ulterior motive.

Three hours later the Kingfisher was anchored in Thomson Bay on the east side of the island. It was sheltered and the boat's movement was relatively gentle compared to the open water. Yet they still rolled and swung on the anchor.

"You did alright young'n. You didn't chuck up or nothing like I thought you were gunna at one time. You kept your cool too. Good job or you'd be on Crab Watch now," Charlie said.

"What's Crab Watch?" Nick asked.

"Ah, well you see, them crabs got a sixth sense, smart little beggers. When you got fish on board, they know and come up the anchor chain in hoards for a free feed. The only way to stop 'em is to bang the chain every few seconds with a steel rod or a bit'o pipe. They don't like the sound and fall off. Sometimes you gotta do it all night long."

Nick listened wide-eyed.

"Leave the boy alone Charlie, he's done fine.

Then turning to Nick. "You did all right son, don't take any notice of him, he's pulling your leg."

Charlie gave a big grin and put the kettle on.

For Nick these last two days had been a great adventure, and the storm had made it all the more memorable. However, he was relaxed now that they were in calmer water. Skip's motive for delaying became clear when, over mugs of tea, he turned to Nick saying, "well young fella, what are we to do with you?"

Nick was full of apprehension and did not know what to say.

"You did well today mate, that was a bad one. I mean you didn't panic or nothing, and the tuckers been good. That was some initiation you had too. I'd take you on if you have a mind to it, but I need to know a bit more about you first. I don't want to be in trouble with the authorities."

Skip paused then quietly said, "We could certainly do with an extra pair of hands on board."

Nick was excited, but said nothing, waiting to hear more. The two men saw the pleasure in Nick's eyes. Charlie leaned forwards to nudge Nick with his elbow.

"So what do you say young Joey?"

"Yes please, I'd like that," Nick replied.

"Well then, you better tell us all about yourself. Where you are from, what you have been doing and why you are roaming the streets alone looking like something out of Dickens."

Both men waited in silence. Nick felt comfortable and wanted to trust them, so began to tell his story from as far back as he could remember. Skip leaned forwards with his hands clasped, mostly looking down but listening intently. He occasionally shook his head as he watched his knuckles go white, occasionally giving his opinion with a gentle murmur or sucking air through his teeth.

"I bet the Department of Child Welfare don't know about this," Skip said in disgust.

"And that place over in Clontarf is supposed to be great for kids! Who would have guessed it?"

Charlie asked a few questions about his time in the outback, although they had little bearing on Nick's plight, but they were of interest to Charlie. Who concluded with, "Bugger me mate, you're more Abbo than me!"

Skip was more interested in the goings on at Clontarf and wondered if Nick was telling the truth or just exaggerating. Then remembering Nick's reaction to seeing the buildings again, he felt there had to be some truth somewhere in his story. Nick told them all he could remember of his mother and father, as little as it was. They seemed like a distant dream now. Then how he came to meet Chris, Gidga, Arana and finally, how he came back to Perth.

Skip still had doubts and tested Nick's story looking him in the eye.

"Now look here son. That Boys Town you were at has a reputation for looking after kids. They give orphans and other kids hope, a place to live and feed them, a Christian education and upbringing to set them up for a good life. What you are telling me is the opposite."

Nick found his tongue and indignantly raised his voice.

"I swear that what I'm telling you is the truth. You see, nobody ever wants to believe us. Nobody! They all think we are lying!"

Tears of frustration welled in Nick's eyes. He thought he had just damaged his relationship with Skip. He had raised his voice, burst out and spoken in anger. Then without pausing went on.

"I'll tell you what it was like. It was Hell. So bad that some boys ran away just like me. I knew one who killed himself. Others went feral, their minds were messed up from regular cruel treatment, so they became cruel and nasty too. I say cruel because it was! There were beatings with thick leather whips the Brothers had specially made. We all had cuts and welts. We got punished hard for just little things. Even for things we didn't do if they decided it was you. They never asked or investigated, just decided and punished. You were always guilty, and you never got a chance to explain. If you tried, they said you were cheeky and insolent so stuffed soap in your mouth. It didn't seem to matter just as long as they could punish someone, anyone would do. If something they considered really bad had happened, they thrashed you naked and in front of everybody. It was embarrassing and humiliating. They'd thrash boys in a sort of ceremony. You could see they

237

enjoyed it! When a boy knew in advance he was to be thrashed, he got into a bad state and was sometimes sick. The torment and humiliation was as bad as the whipping.

Most boys cried at night and wet the bed at some time or other, especially the younger ones. They made you stand in public with your wet stained sheet over your head for hours. You always got a cut or two with a whip, and sometimes the next night you had to stand by your bed all night long. Lots of boys had bad dreams and nightmares, you could hear them calling in the night. Some would sing to stop themselves from crying, mostly for their mothers, but it didn't always work.

The worst was when a Brother would take you to his room at night. For some reason I was never taken, but those who were would often come back crying. They wouldn't speak for days from shame. They had a haunted look about them, especially after the first time it happened. From then on they were terrified of being taken again. Some Brothers had their favourites who cooperated for special treats.

You wanted to own something, anything, just to have something that you could call your own. It didn't matter what it was, but it was impossible. They took everything off you when you arrived and that's how it stayed. You never had any privacy either, even going to the shower or toilet wasn't private.

The food was horrible and there was never enough. Any meal could be just one slice of bread with jam. Breakfast was usually porridge and coco. The Brothers got a proper fried breakfast with toast and tea! But not us. Then there was watery soup that had almost nothing in it, except maybe a piece of potato or cabbage. Sometimes you got a piece of bread with it. There was rarely any meat, and when there was, you hardly got a mouthful and it was mostly old and smelled bad! But you were never allowed to leave anything or you'd get a cut with a whip! Sometimes it made you ill, so they gave you warm Epsom Salts which made you worse or be sick. We liked mashed potatoes because it made you feel less hungry. Sundays was a big treat. We might get a small piece of cake or some broken biscuits and occasionally an apple. It was better on the church farm because we could steal the pigs' food that came in from the town. It was better than what we were given. Oh yeah, and denying you food was a punishment too."

Skip gently caressed Nick's arm quietly saying, "take a breath young fella."

Skip gave Charlie a look of shock and disbelief, yet he knew from Nick's demeanor that he was telling the truth. Charlie was staring at Nick with his mouth open and eyes glazed.

"But they boast about schooling and education. Did you go to school?" Skip asked.

"Yes, but I could read before I went there, which was a big help. The younger boys went to school and the older ones went to work, either on the farms or building work. That was hard graft, long hours of heavy work in the sun. No shoes, and we all had cut feet and hands with callouses. They said we had to work to repay our debt for being brought to Australia. And that a Christian Education developed a Christian character. But there was nothing Christian about it. If there is a God, he must have forgotten about us."

Nick began to calm down and spoke more quietly.

"I promise you Skip, I'm telling the truth, with my hand on my heart, really I am. It's a terrible place.

"Yes, I believe you son."

Skip's words were comforting.

Charlie added, "unbelievable, bloody unbelievable my little Joey. The bastards!"

Skip could see that Charlie was getting angry so cut him short.

"And what do you want to do with yourself now and in the future son?" Skip asked.

239

"I only have faint memories of my mother and even fewer of my father, I was a nipper when he died. But I know I have a mother, and I'm sure she must have loved me. I remember that I was to go to the children's home only until she was well again, but I must have done something very bad because she never came for me and I haven't seen her since. I don't understand why this all happened, and I don't really know who I am or where I'm from. But I have never believed that she stopped loving me, she might have even been trying to find me. So I have 'got' to find her. Arana said she went and spoke to her in Dreamtime, so I'm sure she's still alive, but I don't know where, and Arana couldn't tell me. I don't quite understand how Arana could do that, but I know she wouldn't lie to me."

Charlie gently nodded with a knowing smile. He understood, but Skip did not. He'd ask about it later.

Nick's eyes glazed over as he spoke. Skip reached for his arm again, giving it a gentle reassuring squeeze saying, "it's alright son. It's alright."

Without looking up, Nick took a deep breath, sniffed, rubbed his forefinger under his nose and continued.

"That's all I've ever wanted to do, to find my Mum. But I've never had the chance. Anyway, I'm not sure where to start or what to do. It will probably take a lot of time and money. I've got plenty of time but less than three pounds to my name. That's the most I've ever had. I'm afraid that if I go to the authorities and they find out that I ran away from Boys Town, they will send me back. So I have to wait."

Skip leaned back and said, "don't worry about that son. We won't let that happen, but we have to think about what to do next."

Nick felt a weight had been lifted from his shoulders. It was the first time he had told his full story uninhibited with emotion, telling more detail than he had to Jess, Gidga or Arana. The last half hour had been an exorcism of demons, leaving him no longer afraid to show his emotions or speak openly. He felt Skip's warmth, liked being called 'son' and wanted to hug him. The feelings were mutual but the moment was allowed to pass unfulfilled.

There was a long pause while Skip considered.

"Alright then, here's what we'll do. Before we can do much, we have to get you sorted out with the authorities, so that's first. Then we have to get you established and working so you can earn enough to go looking for your mother. In the meantime we can make a few enquiries and take it from there. You can stay here on the Kingfisher and earn your keep by cleaning her up and doing odd jobs when we are not at sea and helping out when we are. Just keep your head down for a week or two until folks get used to seeing you around. Charlie will bring you some better clothes. We can't have you looking like a bloody swagman. I'll find out how long them Christian Brothers have a call on their kids. So until we work a few things out , you can be my nephew from up north who wants to take up commercial fishing. So when folks are about, call me Uncle Bill. How old are you Nick?"

"Just turned sixteen, Uncle Bill," Nick said with a grin. They all laughed and the atmosphere lightened.

Nick slept well that night, but Skip did not with too much on in his mind. When Nick woke, the storm had passed leaving rain in its wake. They were already tied up at the fish market wharf, and their catch was being unloaded. He didn't attempt to help with the unloading as he didn't know what was needed, and it seemed to be going well without him. Noticing the mugs were still where they were left the night before, Nick washed them and made tea. He then poked his head out of the wheel house and called,

"Tea up."

Skip called back, "good lad – be there in a minute or two."

Charlie grinned in appreciation. Once unloading was completed, Nick and Charlie washed out the hold with water and Bicarbonate of Soda before scrubbing the deck with stiff brooms and water from a hose. Skip was away for almost half an hour debating the price of the fish and said very little when he returned. Then on firing up the engine he called, "OK lads, cast off."

The motor produced its customary cloud of blue smoke as it shuddered into life before settling into a regular rhythm.

"Take us back up the Swanny Charlie. Me and Nick need to talk."

"I've been thinking some more about what's to be done. Now as I understand it you've got nowhere to go, nowhere to live. Am I right?"

"Yes," Nick confirmed with a pang of inadequacy and embarrassment.

"Well then, as I said, you better spend the next few days right here. You know your way around this old tub by now. There's food in the locker, and we'll bring you some more to keep you going until we go to sea again in three or four days. You can fill the water tank with a hose at the wharf. Oh yes, and like I said, your 'brother' here will bring you some fresh clothes. Now don't go wandering about, and don't touch anything in the wheel house you don't understand. Got that?"

Nick agreed.

"Like I said before, I'm gonna try and find out how long those Christian Brothers reckon to keep you lads. Don't worry mate, I won't give you away, and I won't see as any harm comes to you. I just can't afford to get into strife over you, so I need to know how things are before we get too involved."

19

Nick was more optimistic and confident than he could ever remember. Feeling he really was becoming somebody at last, and had a real future.

"Now stay here until we can get you sorted out with somewhere to stay. I suppose you could eventually stay at the Seaman's Refuge."

Skip hesitated then quickly reconsidered.

"Perhaps not, a young lad like you could find yourself in a bit of bother there. Best we find you somewhere else. But before we do anything, we'd better get you cleaned up and looking respectable. I bet them clothes of yours haven't been washed in a while?"

Seeing that Nick was embarrassed, Charlie stepped in.

"We'll get you some new ones bro, not too many threads left on them what you got on."

As they prepared to leave again, Skip reminded him not to wander about.

"We don't want questions being asked. Think of this old tub as home for now, okay? We'll be back in the morning."

As Skip and Charlie walked from the jetty, it looked as though Charlie was getting instructions. Nick stood by the stern rail for a time watching them disappear. The clouds had cleared and the warm sun, with the gentle swaying of the Kingfisher, lulled him into drifting speculation about his future. He was more relaxed than he had been for a long time. His daydreaming inevitably took him to his mother, then to Chris who he had missed for so long.

He wanted his mother badly, but missed Chris more and felt there was something wrong about it. It didn't seem right as part of him said he ought to miss his mother more, since she was his flesh and blood. Yet he remembered little about her now as he was so young when they were separated. So he could not possibly know what he might have missed. It satisfied his conscience but it did not affect his yearning for her. He just knew he needed her and had to find her. Chris, Gidga and Arana were the only family he had any real memory of, so he had more to miss with them. When he was twenty-one he would go to Sydney and meet Chris again. It seemed such a long time to wait. In finding his mother, he would discover his roots and know who he was. The two were inseparably entwined, so each would surely enhance the other.

Charlie arrived the next morning just as Nick was making his first mug of tea.

"Plenty of sugar in mine," announced his arrival.

Offering Nick a large brown paper bundle he added. "The boss said to give you these. They are not new, they belonged to his son."

Then, while taking a grocery box to the galley, he quickly said.

"Don't let on I told you that bro. We didn't know your shoe size, so we'll have to get you some when we are out together."

Nick impatiently undid the string to the parcel. There were shirts, socks, underpants, trousers, a jumper and a jacket. Nick was thrilled. He had never had so many clothes at one time before.

"Where is Skip?" Nick asked.

"He's gone on a bit of an errand, might be along later or maybe tomorrow. Now let's get you into some of these togs," Charlie said deliberately to distract Nick from asking where Skip had gone, so as not to spoil the moment with talk of Boys Town. But he need not have bothered as Nick was now more confident at not going back.

He tried the clothes on. All were a little too large but it didn't matter. He was overjoyed.

"Are all these really for me?" he asked.

"You bet bro," Charlie said with a grin.

Later in the day, and trying to show his appreciation in the only way he could, Nick enthusiastically cleaned and tidied the galley, washed every plate, pot and mug he could find. Then started on the folksal. Blankets were hung in the breeze to freshen and pillows puffed up.

Skip arrived early the next morning saying, "You look almost human in them new clothes son."

Nick felt proud and presentable.

"Thank you Uncle Bill. They are the best clothes I've ever had."

Skip smiled with a little pain as he remembered his son wearing them.

"It's my pleasure son, my pleasure." Then he said, "I went to that Boys Town over the water yesterday afternoon, what boys I saw stopped and stared at me like I was strange or something. I didn't get to talk to anyone who matters, but I was asked my business by one of them Brothers – a bit arrogant if you ask me. I explained that I wanted to enquire about a boy that once stayed there. He cut me off saying that all enquiries had to be made in writing and would be responded to in due course. I said that wouldn't work for me as I was a seaman and away most of the time. Half a 'porky' I suppose. But it made no difference. He said they don't keep records of boys once they had left. Said it like it was the end of the conversation. So basically that was the end of any serious conversation."

Nick was disappointed, but then Skip added.

"As this bloke escorted me to the gate, I think he wanted to be sure I left. I casually asked a couple of questions and got a bit of what might be good news. It seems them Brothers are not much interested in lads once they hit fourteen or fifteen. Just before that age, they start looking for families, farms, stations or anyone else that will take 'em on. If they don't have any luck, they send 'em to one of their own farms until they do. They seem eager to get the lads off their hands."

Nick listened intently.

"So does that mean I'm free now!?"

"Can't be sure son. You see you left in a fairly unusual way, and it must have been a bit of an embarrassment to 'em."

"I'll find out who the head honcho is and write a formal letter asking about you. I'll do it before we cast off later in the week. Don't worry though, I won't let on that you are here."

Nick went to sea on the Kingfisher five times over the following few weeks and loved every minute. His tasks were mostly supportive of Skip and Charlie's activities. He was declared in charge of the galley, cleaned and did simple maintenance jobs. His greatest joy was to take the helm to hold the Kingfisher steady when the nets came in. Gutting fish was not much fun, but he did it without hesitation. Skip had noticed that he never complained, no matter the task. On one trip a small pod of dolphins rode their bow wave for almost ten minutes. Nick was enthralled at the spectacle, watching as they effortlessly kept pace with the boat. On another occasion they spotted a pod of whales. But each time they returned to Fremantle, Nick wondered if Skip would find a reply waiting in his mail box.

After each trip's catch was landed and sold, Skip gave Nick his wages. On the first occasion he asked what it was for.

"You earned it son. Don't look a gift-horse in the mouth. Now put it in your pocket."

Nick was astonished. A month ago he would have considered it impossible.

"Have you still got them three pounds you had? Cos you better get 'em changed to this new decimal money we got now or they won't be worth nothing," Charlie advised.

The day eventually came when Skip arrived at the Kingfisher with a letter in his hand.

"Okay Nick, I got this letter here from Boys Town. They don't say much except they want to talk to me and suggest the day after tomorrow. I think it's because I mentioned your name as the boy who ran away a few years ago and had never been found. Got them curious hey! Don't worry son, I won't dob you in or let them know where you are."

The next two days were agony for Nick as his mind was rampant with the possible consequences of being discovered. He hardly slept at all, and when he was not busy, the tension was worse. But he knew he could trust Skip.

Two days later in the mid-afternoon he returned to the Kingfisher. Nick saw him coming as he hurried with a spring in his step. Charlie was already there expecting Skip would go to the Kingfisher immediately after Boys Town.

Greetings were short. Skip spoke as soon he was on board.

"I was right. You are a bloody embarrassment to em, and they think sleeping dogs should be left alone because they don't want any bad publicity. Well, that's my interpretation of their mumbo-jumbo anyway. They're a funny lot full of pious, self-appointed importance. They wanted to know what had happened to you and where you are now. They didn't even know if you were still alive. So I told them you're okay just to satisfy their curiosity and that's all. I added that, all being well, I wanted to take you on as a sort of apprentice. That seemed to please them since they could finally wash their hands of you. But they got shitty with me cos I refused to say where you were. I got the impression you were not very popular there. You can take that as a compliment mate."

Nick smiled, eager to hear more.

"Anyway, we seemed to go round in circles, a bit of cat and mouse. Once they confirmed they no longer have, or want, any call on you, I just said you are safe and well. They were surprised and said they thought you might have snuffed it in the outback, and that dingos had carried off with your bones. Cynical beggars, hey. Naturally they wanted to know where you are but I said they'd know as soon as other formalities were completed, if they are still interested. I asked to see your records, but they said they don't keep records after a boy leaves them. They don't give anything away, do they? I had to ask were they went. They said all records were sent to The Catholic Migrant Centre who, they believe eventually sent them to The West Australian Department of Child Affairs. Saying that given your, I quote, 'mode of departure', there may have been other destinations for your file. There might still be police involvement since they had been alerted to search for you, and they may still have an open file on you."

"Was that all they would tell you?" Nick asked.

"No, they let a thing or two slip that could help us. I asked when and how you got there, but they were cagey and estimated an approximate year 1947, suggesting you were part of the Child Migrant Scheme from the UK. Then I asked how children are registered, and what paperwork came with you? They said it's a simple process. The courier hands over the files, children are identified, fingerprinted then taken to Boys Town."

"So I must have a history on file somewhere!" Nick stated excitedly.

"Probably, but I suspect it's going to be a devil of a job getting it. We can start by finding out exactly when you arrived by going through ships Passenger lists for 1947. Now that may give us a lead where you were before you got shipped. Do you remember the name of the ship you came on?"

"No, sorry," Nick replied.

Skip was as enthusiastic as Nick at unravelling the mystery.

"So what do we do next?" Nick asked.

"I've already done it. I went to the WA Police Headquarters and after they had checked, they confirmed they had been asked to find you up country. The file showed that you were never found and it was finalized as 'Presumed Perished'. So as far as they were concerned the matter was now closed and they had no further interest. Although they said that, just for the record, they would make a note on the file to say you had eventually turned up. But they did suggest I should report your discovery to The Department of Child Affairs to make you official again.

Nick could not suppress his joy. He clenched and raised both fists to the sky and yelled. "Yes! Yes!" It was as though the greatest weight on earth had been lifted from his shoulders. Then looking Skip in the eye he said,

"Are you really sure Uncle Bill?"

Skip nodded and laughed as he shared in Nick's joy.

"Yes, my little friend and you don't have to call me Uncle Bill anymore."

"But I'd like to, if you don't mind. You and Charlie are the only family I've got now. That is until I find my mother and Chris again. Then I'll have a family of four."

"That's fine son," Skip replied quietly.

Charlie was delighted and gave Nick a bear hug.

"Bloody bonza mate! You beat the lot of 'em. We gotta celebrate boss. The beers and cokes are on me. We'll have a barbeque on deck."

That evening was both a celebration and a milestone in Nick's life, one he would never forget. He would never again have to look over his shoulder in fear of the authorities. The snags and lamb chops were sensational.

Nick drank Coca Cola for the first time and didn't let on that he had never eaten lamb chops before.

20

Nick knew this was an important time in his life but one where he had to tread carefully, especially in the coming weeks. On rationalizing his situation, he decided there was little or nothing to be afraid of. He had done no great wrong that he could be reprimanded for. The police might want to tick him off for leading them on a wild goose chase, but that was all. The Christian Brothers could tell him off for running away but that was all. He smiled thinking they would be more annoyed that he had successful escaped them, and thought they wouldn't make a fuss because someone was eventually bound to ask why he ran away. Nick could not have imagined the extent of what a defining period this was, how it would influence his future and bolster his confidence.

Skip was protective of Nick and careful to do the right things in establishing him as a legitimate person in the eyes of the authorities, taking care of the formalities between fishing trips. While Skip was busy with Nick's official processes, some of his other shore bound chores fell to Charlie.

From now on there would be many milestones along the way for Nick. One of the first was the day Skip took him to the Commonwealth Bank to open an account in his name.

Skip had said, "You can't leave your pay laying around in little hiding places forever can you?"

The first document he had to sign took Nick by surprise. He had never been asked to sign anything before and squiggled his name. Skip laughed.

251

"You'd better remember how to do that again, you'll need it before long."

As Nick handed over most of his cash, the clerk had said. "Thank you, Sir."

It took Nick a second or two to realise who the bank employee was addressing. When the penny dropped, he grinned from ear to ear in amusement. He was now a person of substance and no longer a miscreant as he had so often been told. He was a legitimate person and his worth was recorded.

Then, just as he had been advised, a week later an envelope arrived from the bank. It contained a review of banking terms and conditions, a welcome letter that started "Dear Mr. Thorne" and a cheque book. Nick was enthralled at being addressed as Mr. Thorne, and this perfect little book had his name printed on every page and was his exclusively. Nick felt he was growing up and beginning to take his place in society.

During their next voyage, Skip suggested it was time he found a more permanent home than the Kingfisher.

"I got no problem with you staying on the Kingfisher son, in fact it's good for security. But I just think you should have a place of your own, somewhere to put your things and make your own nest."

Nick agreed since he was now finding the Kingfisher a little cramped. Later they debated the best locations, and the most suitable for what he could afford. It was agreed that somewhere within walking distance of the berth was best, otherwise some sort of transport would be needed. Public transport might not always be available as they could leave or dock at any time of the day or night. Skip said they will be forced to move to Fishing Boat Harbour before long but would face that when it happens.

Within three days, Skip and Nick were searching the local newspaper advertisements. It soon became clear that accommodation close to the wharf was too expensive, so it was necessary to look further afield. The pair travelled to inspection appointments in Skip's rusted old utility truck. It rattled and squeaked, having suffered the fate of a vehicle left to stand in salt air for long periods. The side windows were permanently stuck in the half way position, so ventilation was good, even if you did get wet when it rained. Yet for all its casual ventilation, it still smelled of old fish nets and diesel oil.

"One of these days someone will steal it while you are away."

Nick had suggested. Skip laughed saying, "who do you think would want this old wreck?"

Nothing suitable was found on the first expedition, so their details and requirements were left with two letting agents. On their return from the next fishing trip a message was waiting for them. An appointment was made to view and a decision made. There were reservations concerning Nick's age, stability of employment and his ability to pay the ongoing rent. Nick had now saved enough for the deposit and Skip said he would stand as guarantor, so the application form was completed. The agent thanked them saying he would do his best with the landlord and let them know his decision. Later in the day Skip got a call saying the landlord had accepted Nick as his tenant. Charlie declared, "This calls for a celebration."

Nick was now old enough to drink but had never been in a pub and knew nothing about alcohol. He had no idea what to order so followed Skip's lead with a stubbie of larger. He drank too fast and he began to feel light-headed. After the second one, he was surprised to lose a little balance. It amused him enormously and he found it difficult to stop giggling.

"It's like being at sea," he told Skip and Charlie as he sat with a permanent grin. Try as he might, he could not remove it, it seemed stuck there and got bigger the more he tried. He felt silly but didn't really care.

"I'll get him a meat pie to put something in his stomach," Charlie said.

The pie arrived with a big blob of tomato sauce atop. Nick ate it making a mess of his fingers, much to his great delight.

"Better not give him any more to drink or we'll have to pour him into bed later," Skip said with a smile.

The accommodation was modest, consisting of two rooms on the second floor of a large converted older style house. There was a small kitchen, dining space and lounge room all in one, and a small separate bedroom. The agent said it was what they now call 'open plan', a new trendy concept.

The toilet and bathroom were down the hall, both shared with another tenant from the other side of the house. The ground floor was configured in a similar way into two units. Gas and electricity were not individually metered, and the house rules were that bills would be shared equally amongst the tenants. Nick thought this was unfair as he would not be there for much of the time, but that was the arrangement so he had to accept it.

After the next fishing trip, Nick and Charlie climbed into the old ute to search the second-hand furniture shops. The sight of the vehicle parked in front of the shops helped their bargaining for lower prices. Before long they were struggling up the stairs with sections of a single bed and a mattress, three chairs and a small folding table. Skip arrived carrying a box of assorted cutlery, plates, dishes, cooking pot and a frying pan. The next day Nick cleaned his rooms and organized the furniture to its best advantage. It looked smaller now but a lot cleaner. Nick was proud of it, his first proper home, humble though it was.

"So when is the house warming mate?" Charlie asked.

"What's that?"

"Well, when you move to a new place, you invite your mates around for a bit of a feed and a few beers, to sort of christen the place."

"Okay then, let's do it tomorrow," Nick immediately said.

"Right bro. Me and Skip'll bring the beers. You can get a bit of tucker in."

This was a special occasion for Nick. He would be entertaining his friends in his own home for the first time. It was a strange feeling, but one that made him proud, and he was pleased to return their great kindness. Everything was caringly prepared, and Nick's little flat was christened with a toast to the future.

Nick had always been anxious to see Chris again but was too afraid to go to Boys Town and ask for him. Since Chris was a little older than himself, he knew he may no longer be there, so decided to write and ask where he is. It was four weeks before he received a short reply saying.

"Christopher Norman Cole is no longer at Clontarf Boys Town, and this institution is not at liberty to divulge his whereabouts."

Nick was disappointed and frustrated, but not too surprised at having received such a blunt reply. Forty-eight hours later he was aboard the Kingfisher heading south west out of Freemantle. Nick always found the first hours exhilarating and full of anticipation. Yet every time they passed the mouth of the Canning River he stopped to consider Chris, and how he had never really said a proper goodbye. Once they were settled and underway, Skip gave the helm to Charlie and suggested that a mug of tea was in order. The 'Fremantle Doctor' was blowing steadily as Skip and Nick sat together at the stern.

"Nick, I've been thinking that you ought to learn to drive."

Nick was taken by surprise but agreed.

"When we get back, you can apply for a learner license, and we'll get a copy of the Highway Code for you to study. Me and Charlie will show you the ropes and sit with you while you practice. Of course it'll be in my old ute. Then laughing Skip said, "but you can't take your test in it. The examiner will crap himself at the sight of it and probably refuse to get in."

They both laughed.

"I reckon that if you can drive that old heap, you'll be able to drive anything. Later we'll get you a couple of professional lessons to polish your skills and provide you something decent to eventually take your test in.

21

Nick was both restless and anxious to find out why he was orphaned, why his past was the way it had been, but mostly to find his mother. There was always an underlying fear that he might eventually be too late, and never meet her, which added to his urgency. He didn't dare think of the scar it would leave, one that would last until his own final breath. He even questioned if he would be able to cope with the knowledge. Certainly he would never forgive himself for not trying to find her sooner.

After discussing his feelings with Charlie and Skip, it was suggested that the Red Cross or The Salvation Army might be able to help.

"I know they have helped a few of my people find their families they were separated as kids," Charlie said.

He thanked Charlie for the suggestion saying it was a good one and would do that if he had no luck with the authorities. Nick decided to contact the child care organisations and relevant government departments first.

He began by writing to The Government Immigration Department in Canberra asking for a copy of his records or any information they could provide. A reply arrived four weeks later with the most significant part reading:

"Since you came to Australia as an unaccompanied minor, and part of a Child Immigration Scheme, records will be held by those organisations which sponsored you. Although the Australian Government approved the Child

Migrant Scheme, it has had no operational involvement. Therefore we suggest you contact Dr. Barnardo's, The Catholic Church Migrant Centre or The Christian Brothers organization where you were a ward."

Nick had been more hopeful of a better response. He showed the letter to Skip and Charlie whose opinions were that Canberra didn't want to be involved, a notion which had already grown in the back of all their minds, but not one they had wanted to voice earlier for fear of depressing Nick.

They agreed it was of no use going to the Christian Brothers. Skip had already tried them and been fobbed off with precious little. So they agreed to contact the Catholic Migrant Centre. On finding their address, Nick discovered they had offices in Perth so decided to go there in person.

At reception he met a pleasant middle-aged lady to whom he explained his purpose. She asked him to wait a moment in the reception area whilst she found someone to help, then returned a few minutes later.

"Mr. Carter will be with you in a moment or two."

Nick thanked her. It was only minutes before a flustered Mr. Carter announced his arrival with,"how can I help you Mr. Thorne? Please take a seat. Now what can I do for you?" All said in a single breath.

Nick got the impression he was not pleased to be interrupted, so was as polite and friendly as he could manage.

He gave Mr. Carter a brief account of his history saying, "so you see Mr. Carter, I have no idea where I'm from, who my family is or even if I have one. I believe I have a mother somewhere. I might have a brother or sister, aunts and uncles, but I just don't know. Mostly I want to find my mother, and I was referred to you for help."

"Who referred you?" Mr. Carter sighed.

"The Australian Federal Government's Immigration Department."

"Yes typical. Unfortunately I don't think we are going to be able to help you Mr. Thorne. You see our organization was set up just after World War II to assist Catholic Children from The United Kingdom, Ireland and Malta who had been brought to Western Australia without their parents. Our role was simply to 'monitor the placement' of these children into various institutions and homes. Once that was achieved, like you, they became the wards of that institution, and whatever records and notes we had on individuals were passed on with each child."

Nick was clearly disappointed at yet another negative response so in frustration said, "But I have already contacted The Christian Brothers, who say they don't have any records either. I'm going round in circles here. I'm getting the impression that nobody wants to help, or even cares."

Mr. Carter replied abruptly saying.

"As I said Mr. Thorne, our job was to 'monitor the placement of children' not record and retain their ancestry or future movements. I'm sorry, but I can't help you further."

In drawing the discussion to a close Mr. Carter stood, extended his hand saying.

"Have you tried The Department of Community Services, they might know something? I can only wish you luck Mr. Thorne."

They shook hands and parted. Nick returned to the lady at reception and asked to borrow a telephone directory. He found The Department of Community Services and noted their address. There was no time like the present, so he set off immediately, stopping along the way for a coffee and one of his beloved donuts, which allowed him to gather his thoughts.

He found himself talking to a young receptionist who greeted him warmly with a big smile. She was pleasant and friendly, but her femininity unsettled him. He didn't understand why he felt this way whilst knowing she was only being nice to him. He explained why he was there.

"Ah, you will want Child Protection then. You might need to make an appointment if they can't see you just now. They go out a lot and get short-handed. I'll see what I can do, maybe one of the secretaries will come down," she said maintaining her smile.

After making a telephone call, she looked back at Nick.

"Someone is coming down to see you."

An attractive young lady, only a little older than himself, approached. She made him feel even more awkward as he was unsure how to behave in the company of females, especially pretty ones.

"Are you Mr. Thorne?" She asked.

"Yes I am." Nick said as he tried awkwardly to return her smile.

She extended her hand to shake his. He immediately noticed how soft and warm her hand was.

"My name is Rose. Can you tell me what your enquiry is about please?"

Nick briefly said that he had been an orphan and needed help to find his family.

"Well that is the sort of thing we try to help people with here. We do a bit with native Australians and used to do a lot with returned servicemen, so I'd hope we can help you too. But unfortunately none of the officers are available at the moment. They do a lot of field work you see. It's best if we make an appointment for you."

This was the best response Nick had had in his search for help. He was pleased and liked Rose. She was kind and sympathetic. He wanted to be equally as nice to her but didn't quite know how to match her warmth, feeling both awkward and inadequate.

Rose carried a desk diary which she opened saying,
"How about the day after tomorrow, say 3 pm?"

Nick agreed.

"Alright Mr. Thorne, we'll see you then. You will meet with Mr. Hawkins, who knows his way around these searches. You should make as many notes on things you consider helpful and bring along any official documents you might have, such as your birth certificate, etc."

Nick was pleased that a little progress was at last being made and looked forward to seeing Rose next time. However he didn't quite understand why. She had disturbed him in a way he had not experienced before.

The next day and half dragged by, full of nervous anticipation, especially at seeing Rose again. He took a writing pad and started to make notes for Mr. Hawkins. There was less than half a page and much of that provided few real facts to go on. Nick had no birth certificate to present. Despondently, he saw these pitiful few lines as a review of his life so far. He allowed his thoughts to slip back to Boys Town; maybe the Brothers were right after all. Perhaps he was worthless. Then he gathered his thoughts and said angrily out loud,

"No! Bloody no! I am somebody, and I can prove it. I have friends, good friends who care about me. I can read and write, I have a bank account, a proper job, a home, a future and I can drive. There are just a few gaps, that's all! I'll show them!"

Nick was full of trepidation as he entered the offices of Child Protection just before 3 pm. He introduced himself to the receptionist who advised Mr. Hawkins that he had arrived. Rose appeared a minute later with a big welcoming smile which he nervously returned, causing himself to blush. Rose escorted Nick upstairs.

"How have you been keeping Mr. Thorne?"

"Fine, thank you."

He wanted to say more but became tongue tied before awkwardly adding.

"Please call me Nick, everyone else does. Would you mind if I call you Rose?"

"Please do," she said.

"Everyone else does!"

"They laughed, and the ice was broken."

Rose formally introduced Nick to Mr. Hawkins who came from behind his desk to shake Nick's hand. Mr. Hawkins had a professional, yet warm and understanding manner that Nick responded well to. They sat on chairs away from the desk while Mr. Hawkins rested a notepad on his knee.

"Well Nick, how can I help you?"

Nick explained his past as he knew it, that he needed help to trace his origins and especially to find his mother. He apologized for not having any official documents as he handed over the meagre notes he'd made.

"But it's not for the want of trying to provide more," he quickly added.

Mr. Hawkins frowned as he rubbed his chin.

"It's a pity we don't have any formal documentation to go on, so it might make things a little tricky, but never mind, we can sometimes open doors and find things others can't. It's amazing what a little authority will do."

He said with a smile to encourage Nick's optimism.

"Leave it with me, and I'll see what I can do. I'll get Rose to give you a call when we have some news. It's nice to meet you Nick and I look forward to seeing you again before too long."

Nick found his own way out, saying goodbye to Rose as he passed her desk. She smiled at him giving a cheerful "Bye Nick."

He was buoyant with the hope of getting somewhere at last; he had also seen Rose again and was on first name terms. He liked Rose, but was unsure about what to do next and could not get her out of his mind.

Four weeks and three fishing trips passed without a call from Mr. Hawkins. Nick told Skip the suspense was killing him.

"Why don't you call in and see him. Tell him you have been away at sea, so he wouldn't have been able to contact you. You'll get to see your little filly again too."

Skip said with a wink, making Nick blush.

At reception he asked to see Mr. Hawkins. They met in the entry hall three minutes later and went to a reception room nearby. Nick had wanted to go to his office to pass Rose on the way.

"I hope you don't mind me calling in unannounced, but I have been at sea for a week or two and you might not have been able to contact me," Nick said apologetically.

Mr. Hawkins said he didn't mind.

"Well Nick there is not a great deal to tell you at the moment. Briefly, we first contacted The Christian Brothers who rather quickly referred us to The Catholic Migrant Centre. Frankly speaking, they were no great help. I know you had spoken to them before, but we tend to be a little harder to fob off, so it was worth a try. I'm afraid everyone seems to be passing the buck. Dr. Barnardo's here in Western Australia had no record of you or anyone else by the sound of it. All very strange." Mr. Hawkins said wryly.

"But don't fret, we have involved the Red Cross and also written to Dr. Barnardo's in the UK. We'll let you know just as soon as we hear back from them. Otherwise, since you are away a lot, you can phone or call in again in about three or four weeks' time.

Nick was disappointed, but not too upset as he had expected a protracted process. Yet he was still guardedly optimistic.

"Otherwise Mary will give your skipper a call to let you know when to come in."

"Oh, where is Rose?" Nick asked in surprise.

"She's on honeymoon, won't be back for a couple of weeks."

Nick was speechless and looked at the floor for a second before facing Mr. Hawkins, offering a simple "thank you" before turning to leave.

He had difficulty coming to terms with what he had just heard and surprised at how upset he was. How had he become so attracted to Rose? He didn't know why, but he felt a heavy lump in his chest. It was all so emotionally painful. Had he presumed too much? He felt he had made a fool of himself and hoped Rose would not think the same of him. Nick was very hurt, couldn't stop thinking of her and decided not to allow himself to get carried away that way again.

After a number of anxious weeks, news eventually came from Mr. Hawkins.

"Well Nick, I'm sorry to say we have not had much luck. An official of Dr. Barnardo's replied saying that all records of child migrants from the UK had accompanied them to their destinations and were given to the organization the children were assigned to. The Red Cross took longer to respond, but it was clear they had researched further into the matter. They said it had been a difficult investigation given the limited information provided. Unfortunately, their research revealed that some Child Migrant files had been destroyed, accidentally or otherwise. Their assumption was that yours must have been one of the unfortunate ones since others of that era were missing too. However, they said they would keep your information on file should anything eventually be discovered or someone come forward looking for you."

Nick was very despondent, feeling there was little more he could do. He collected a carton of stubbies on the way home where he drank too much before falling asleep.

22

It was late September when Nick reminded Skip of his promise to meet Chris in Sydney on his twenty-first birthday.

"I was wondering when you would mention that. How do you plan on getting there?"

"I've a bit tucked away so I can afford the fare, but I expect I'll need most of it for food and accommodation. I thought I'd try and get a lift on one of those freighters that go into Sydney or Port Botany, maybe as a deck hand. That way I'll get a free ride, and I might get paid as well."

"Good idea son," Skip said.

"My only concern is that by leaving, I'll be letting you down. You'll be a man short," Nick added.

Skip smiled and shook his head.

"Don't worry about that. The old Kingfisher is overdue for a bit of work on her, so it'll be a good time to pull her up a slip, get her anti-fouled, have the motor overhauled and replace some of the worn rigs. That'll take a week or two, so you can take your time. Charlie and me could do with a bit of a break anyway. I expect he'll go off and see his folks."

Nick looked at Skip's old weather-beaten face and agreed that a break would do him good.

"I might take the time to go and see my brother up in Carnarvon. It's been a while. That is if the old truck'll get me there."

Then after a minute Skip said, "I got a couple of contacts at the Port Authority. One of 'em might know a

265

skipper who could sort you out, maybe on one of them new container ships."

Nick thanked him.

They did two fishing trips in October, the last one was for eight days returning in the last week of the month. Skip always radioed the Port Authority when he was leaving, reporting where he would be heading, and when he expected to return. It was routine for one of them to radio in once a day to give their position. Then he or Charlie would announce their safe arrival back in Fremantle. On this occasion the wireless operator said he had a message asking Skip to drop into the office after landing. Once the catch was unloaded and Skip had dealt with the fish wholesaler, he made his way to the Port Authority office. Charlie found a large box of Bicarbonate of Soda for him and Nick to scrub out the hold. An exhausting task that neither liked.

Eventually, Skip reappeared on the quay with a grin on his face and news for Nick.

"The bloke in the P.A. said there is a freighter due to depart on 3rd November bound for Sydney. She's the Panama registered Orion, arrives the day after tomorrow. She's not putting in at Adelaide or Melbourne, so you'll be there in plenty of time. You'll need to have a chat with the First Officer when she arrives to see if he'll take you on. I think you got lucky son. One of their deckhands has gone crook, and they radioed in to get an ambulance here for when she docks."

"The timing sounds perfect. Thanks Skip," Nick replied.

"Don't thank me until you've got a berth son."

The interview was short and sweet. It was a one-way trip, and Nick would be paid cash in hand. "To keep it simple," as the First Officer had put it.

Skip and Charlie were a little sad at his leaving but wished him well. The Orion slipped out of Fremantle on the high tide at 5.30 am and headed south. Nick was given a tour and shown the ropes by the Bosun. Work was not hard, but the hours were long. Nick had never spent so much time painting as he did in those next three days. He was surprised and impressed with the facilities on board; a dedicated cook to prepare all the meals, a full kitchen and recreational facilities for off duty entertainment. Also, the folksal had enough room to swing two cats.

All too soon they had picked up a pilot and were passing between The Heads into Sydney Harbour, high cliffs to starboard and low ones with a lighthouse to port. As the Orion entered and turned south, the cliffs gave way to rolling bush that reached to the water's edge, interrupted only by small secluded beaches separated by cliffs. Nick was in awe of this magnificent harbour. A multitude of small craft and ferries only added to the spectacle. Further down the harbour, buildings began to appear until the city was in sight. Nick thought the Harbour Bridge was amazing. He had never seen a structure so big and it looked even larger when they passed beneath it. Within minutes they were being ushered by tugs into a berth. Everyone on deck was occupied, and Nick did what he was told to do.

After almost two hours the Bosun gave Nick a thick brown envelope saying,

"The boss said to give you this and say thanks."

Nick didn't need to be told what was inside and didn't check. An hour later he was walking through the historic Rocks district of old Sydney, heading in the direction of the city. The smell of stale beer and cigarettes wafted from an open door of The Lord Nelson. It looked inviting, and Nick felt he deserved a beer. Dropping his kitbag by a stool, he seated himself at the bar and watched as his beer, cold and clear, was pulled from one of the taps.

"There you go Sport," the barman said with a smile.

"Not seen you in here before have we?"

"No, I just arrived, came in on a freighter from Perth a couple of hours ago. I need to find somewhere to stay for a few nights that's not too expensive. Got any suggestions?"

"Blimey Sport, you just landed with your bum in butter. We got a few rooms upstairs, not the Ritz of course, toilet down the hall, but you'll get a clean bed and a pub with cold beer and good tucker downstairs. What more could a seafaring man ask for, apart from a pretty girl!"

After his beer, Nick looked at the rooms and decided to stay. They were old style and basic, but clean just as the barman had said. The next day he found Martin Place and thought it must have been a street for traffic at one time, but was now paved over for pedestrian access only. He easily found the Central Post Office. A grand Victorian building with a row of arches covering the walkway across the front. A few bench seats were placed intermittently along the back wall. High above was a clock tower with a statue of Queen Victoria at the front. Nick sat for a while and noticed the cenotaph in the middle of the walkway. Two bronze statues guarded the memorial, a soldier and a sailor standing one at each end. This is where he would come tomorrow to meet Chris. His heart was already racing with excited anticipation.

The next day Nick was early at the Post Office and waited on one of the benches in the shade. Martin Place was constantly busy with pedestrians. He heard the clock above strike the half hour, then again at a quarter to twelve. The next quarter hour seemed an eternity. He began to search the faces of the people hurrying past as they went about their business. A few hesitated a moment at the cenotaph while some entered the Post Office. Everyone seemed to be in a hurry, but nobody stood around as though they were waiting for someone. In his excited tension, doubtful thoughts ran through Nick's mind. Would he recognize Chris now? Would Chris recognize him? Did Chris remember to come? His search became intense as he now stood by one of the columns ready to step out and embrace his dearest friend. The clock struck twelve midday. Nick spoke aloud. "OK Chris, where are you my dear brother"

Then after ten anxious minutes said.

"You must be here somewhere Chris? You have to be!"

Nick was becoming worried as the clock above announced the quarter past, then half past and still Chris was not to be seen. Nick's steps quickened as he paced up and down like a caged tiger staring at men's faces. Taking a deep breath, he decided that there must be a rational explanation. To calm himself he sat again, watching and waiting, pleading for Chris to appear. At 3.30 pm Nick finally accepted that Chris was not coming. His deep disappointment brought bewilderment and a lump to his throat.

There was a café only a few yards away where Nick sat by the window with a cup of coffee, hoping he might still see Chris. Half an hour passed before he decided to return to the Lord Nelson.

On leaving, he glanced around the café for the first time. By the door was a pin board where postcards, sent by patrons holidaying around the world, had been displayed. Out of idle curiosity Nick stopped to look at them. One in particular caught his eye as it showed attractive old buildings by a river. On the river were punts being maneuvered by men with long poles; it struck a chord and he felt a mixture of excitement tinged with surprise. He read the words printed along the bottom. "The Backs, Cambridge."

He stood motionless as memories flooded back in a way they had never done before. Goose pimples sat proud on his neck and arms as he sat again to gather his thoughts. Had it not been for Chris's near drowning, and the odd name of 'The Backs,' he might never have remembered the place. Now inwardly excited, here was a clue as to where he came from. Also he had not forgotten the name Barnardo's since it had periodically come up with other boys at Clontarf. It took only seconds for Nick to conclude that must have been in a Barnardo's home in Cambridge, England as a small boy.

He wanted to tell Chris and would come back tomorrow, hoping he had mixed up the days or that he had been delayed. In his excitement and preoccupation, Nick forgot that the next day was Armistice Day, and Martin Place would be busier than ever. Trying to identify anyone amongst so many was near impossible, but he stayed and searched the faces for two hours before leaving in despair. He walked a few blocks to the Botanic Gardens where he strolled, speculating on where Chris might be. The significance of the day reminded him that Chris had wanted to join the army. If he had, there would certainly be a record of him. Perhaps he had been posted away or was on an assignment somewhere and unable to return on time.

That evening Nick went to the bar of The Lord Nelson but only stayed for a short time. It became more rowdy as the evening wore on with old diggers celebrating, singing and playing Two-Up. They were enjoying themselves and letting their hair down whilst getting noisier as the evening wore on, and the beer took effect. Nick was not in the mood for revelry and decided there was little point in staying on in Sydney. Unfortunately, the next day was Sunday and no travel agents would be open. So he took a bus to Bondi for the day. On Monday morning he booked a cheap flight back to Perth. The cash he'd earned on the freighter more than covered this fare. He called Skip from a phone in the pub where he was staying, telling him when he would arrive in Perth.

"I didn't know if I'd get you, thought you might be up ' north," Nick said.

"I didn't go, I never got on with my brother's misses so decided not to rock the boat. She's a strange Sheila."

It was good to hear Skip's voice again.

The flight reminded him of his flight to Perth many years earlier, even though it was on a much smaller plane. Skip met him at the airport and, as they walked to the ute, Skip asked how it went. Nick explained what had happened while they drove into town. The disappointment in Nick's voice was obvious, and in an effort to see a bright side Skip said, "So it wasn't a totally wasted trip then, you had a stroke of real luck. Now you know where you came from in Blighty. That's a big step in the right direction son."

Skip paused for a moment.

"Tell you what mate. We'll drop your kit off and find a decent café, have a bit of a feed and a good old chat about what to do next."

Nick agreed as he felt he needed some cheer and to explain the events of his trip in more detail. After listening patiently, Skip said, "I wonder how we can find out if your Chris actually joined the Army. I suppose we could ask the Christian Brothers where he went after Boys Town. Narr, they won't be helpful. I remember you tried them before."

Skip then came up with another idea.

"I'm not sure who we should contact, but if we write to the Minister of Defence, he'd pass it on to the right place. Let's do it first thing in the morning."

Nick was heartened that they were going to do something positive.

True to his word, Skip appeared all smiles at Nick's flat in the morning saying,

"I got the bloke's name and address to write to mate."

They were unsure how to address the Minister, Sir Shane Paltridge, so simply wrote politely and respectfully hoping they had got the protocol correct. By lunch time the letter had been posted to Canberra.

After two weeks had passed, Nick was getting anxious for a reply. Yet another week passed, and his hopes were waning. Nick told Skip that he thought it had been a waste of time.

"You can't expect government departments to work very fast. They are all a bit 'pedestrian' across there in Canberra you know. Let's leave it a bit longer and see if anything comes back."

Nick shrugged and agreed.

Three weeks later a short letter arrived from the Department of Defence.

Dear Mr. Thorne,

Please accept our apologies for the delay in responding to your request. Your letter has been passed to the Honorable Jim Forbes, Minister for the Army. You may expect to hear from him in due course.

Yours truly.

Office of the Minister of Defence.

Part of Nick was encouraged, but he was left with a twinge of disappointment that no positive information about Chris had come now. Skip was quietly optimistic that news would eventually arrive and told Nick so, even if it be there was no record of Chris having joined the army. He tried to console Nick again by saying that he had to be patient with government departments, assuring him of an eventual get a reply.

"We just have to wait and see, son. Waiting is always hard."

After almost another six weeks, which seemed like an eternity, an envelope arrived with the words 'National Australian War Memorial' printed across the top. Given its origin, Skip fearfully suspected what it might say and prepared Nick who had already thought of the same possibilities. Skip suggested they sit. Nick fumbled in anticipation as he opened the envelope, but was too nervous to read the letter so asked Skip to. Sensing it was going to be difficult, Skip took a breath and read quietly:

Dear Mr. Thorne,

Re. Cpl. Christopher N. Cole

Your enquiry has been passed to us at the National War Memorial Records Department. A lack of precise information did not facilitate quick identification, hence our delay in responding. However it has been concluded that only one soldier of that name and profile had enlisted.

It is with great sadness that we must inform you of Christopher Cole's death on 3rd July, 1966.

Following two years on a farm for orphans run by The Fairbridge Society in Western Australia, Mr. Cole volunteered for service in the Royal Australian Army. In 1962 he joined 1st Battalion RAR 6 and underwent training in Townsville, North Queensland and other locations. He saw active service in Vietnam, where in July, 1966 he made the ultimate sacrifice.

His commanding officer's report describes him as an exemplary soldier who served his country with great distinction. Throughout his induction and training he had adjusted well to discipline, enjoyed the comradery of his peers, and as an operational soldier was highly respected for his professionalism and valour.

We are unable to identify his specific cause of death, but can confirm that he was wounded and died in hospital a short time later. He rests in Tarendak Military Cemetery in Malaysia, and his name has been added to the wall of remembrance here at the National War Memorial in Canberra.

Lest we forget.

Yours sincerely.
R.J. Sullivan.

National War Memorial Archives
Canberra, ACT.

Skip looked up at Nick who sat with his face in his hands. Then carefully putting the letter back into the envelope, he placed it on the table. Neither spoke for several minutes. Skip reached over and held Nick's shoulder, rocking him gently. Nick slowly uncovered his reddened eyes saying,

"It's okay Uncle Bill, it's okay. I'll be fine, you can leave me now please."

Although Skip did not want to go, he did not object, just nodded and left, understanding Nick needed time to grieve in his own way, by himself.

"Okay son, I'll check in with you tomorrow evening."

As Skip left, he found it hard to resist the urge to turn back and hug Nick, feeling he was deserting him at a time of need.

Although Nick had tried hard to make things appear normal, it was two weeks before Skip and Charlie no longer felt the need to tiptoe around him. Chris was not mentioned again.

23

Charlie and Nick had long shared the onboard duties, Nick now being Charlie's equal in ability and knowledge. The pleasure of being called 'son' and 'bro' never wore off. These were people Nick had bonded with, and who had become his surrogate family. He called Skip 'Skip' most of the time but 'Uncle Bill' in playful moments. At least once every day he would think of Gidga and imagine him back in the settlement.

During a short period of relaxation, while returning from a voyage, Nick told Skip and Charlie,

"I have to find my mother, you know. I must find her. I've been thinking about it a lot lately. I really need to go to England and see if I can find her, or at least see what has happened to her. I might even find some information about my father while I'm there."

"That'll cost a pretty penny son," Skip cautioned.

"Yeh, I know, but I've been putting a bit by for a while now. If our next few catches are as good as this one, I should have enough in a month or two."

Charlie was taken by surprise, but Skip had known it was bound to happen sooner or later. He was pleased for Nick that he might be able to put some of his demons to rest, believing he would not settle until he did. Yet at the same time he would be sad at his leaving, knowing he would miss him. Nick had become the son he had lost. As much as he wanted him to find his mother, he was inwardly afraid he might not come back if he did.

"What do you think the chances are of getting a lift to England the same way I did to Sydney?" Nick asked.

"Dunno son. It'll be a bit different from one of them freighters, it's all regulations and container ships now. Yeh, and I bet there's a truck load of regulations and formalities, especially as you'd be going international. We'll probably have to register you as a Merchant Seaman, and you might have to join a Union. Even then, I think it'll be pot luck if you can get a berth. They take a lot of these Asians on now cos they work for a lot less money."

Five weeks later Nick was registered as a Merchant Seaman and waiting for his Australian passport to arrive in the post. Getting the passport had been an arduous task as he was unable to provide accurate information about his origins and had no official documents.

He had been persuaded by an official to join a Seaman's Union, much against his will. He resented paying fees for no conceivable benefit as he saw it, especially as it was only a means to an end, and he'd not be staying on. The union official implied that no captain would allow him on board if he didn't have a union card arguing that if union members at the ports of call and the destination discovered he was not a member, they could boycott the ship. So the captain would be in strife with the owners. Nick detected veiled intimidation in that the official would make sure that word went ahead of the vessel. Nick concealed his feelings of manipulated entrapment and cash was handed over for his membership.

"Thanks mate, I thought you would come to see it my way."

The smugness in the union official's manner annoyed Nick. He had not felt so controlled or maneuvered since the Christian Brothers, and became angry when he later discovered that what he had been told was not entirely true. Yet Nick consoled himself knowing the union fees were a good deal less than the regular fare to England, especially if he was to fly.

In the meantime, Skip had managed to line up a casual deck hand to temporarily stand in for Nick after he had left. The next few weeks were uneasy for all three.

"It's a bit like waiting to go to the dentist. You know it's gotta happen but you don't want it to," Skip said.

A month later, after embraces and sad goodbyes at the dock side, they watched Nick walk up the gangway of a 19,000 ton container ship headed for Southampton. Nick was deeply touched that Skip and Charlie had followed the giant vessel out of Fremantle to see him off. Then just as the ship picked up speed, he was given a final farewell with two long blasts of the Kingfisher's horn.

"Do you think he'll come back Skip?"

"I don't know Charlie. All we can do is wish him well and hope he finds what he's looking for. Yep, I really hope he finds his Mum. You know what, I'd like to meet her."

The voyage was interesting at first, but it soon became routine. Most tasks were cleaning, painting and checking shackles. The more experienced deck hands took the plum jobs. Ports of call were interesting, but they were never there long enough for Nick to explore since that was when they were the busiest. The crew was a mixture of nationalities. Deck hands were mostly Filipino, making him a novelty amongst them, and he never really felt accepted. He didn't understand why they treated him with suspicion, even though he told them why he was there and had tried hard to be friendly. There were times when he knew they were talking about him, in front of him in their native Tagalog, even though they all spoke English. Nick found it unsettling and asked the first officer if he could put his valuables in the ship's safe.

More senior ranks were European, with a Scandinavian Captain, German First Officer and a Dutch First Engineer.

Nick was surprised that this huge ship only had a crew of fifteen.

After twenty-one days at sea and four more in ports of call, Nick watched the south west coast of England slip by on the port side. He knew he must have seen it before but was unable to remember it. His anticipation grew, knowing he would be ashore by this time tomorrow.

During the voyage he had been befriended by the Second Engineer, an Englishman named Tom who had been away from home for over two months. They had met in the ship's laundry and started chatting. Tom noted with curiosity that they didn't get too many European or Australian deck hands on board, and that Nick was a little 'on the outside' amongst his peers. Nick explained his mission, that this was a one-off trip to get him to England to find his roots. Tom asked where he was headed in the UK.

"London, then on to Cambridge," Nick had said.

Tom explained that he was taking shore leave for a few weeks and that his wife was to meet him in Southampton before driving to Hammersmith in West London. Nick didn't know where Hammersmith was, but when he heard West London, he eagerly accepted Tom's offer of a lift.

Nick was surprised at how green the countryside was as they drove through Hampshire, and although grateful for the lift he felt uncomfortable. His introduction to Tom's wife had been clumsy; having shook her hand and said "Hello" rather awkwardly. He had seldom been in the close company of women, apart from when he was in the outback. But that was somehow different, and he was a boy then. Now he was not sure how to behave, especially with a relatively sophisticated European woman. When Tom told her they were giving Nick a lift to London, her cool response was enough to convey that she was not impressed. She had clearly expected to have her husband to herself for the first hour or two after being apart for more than two months. Nick felt the resentment, and their conversation was stilted. Adding to Nick's discomfort was that it had become obvious that Tom and his wife had much to say to each other and were clearly reluctant to do so in front of him. Consequently, they felt obliged to make small talk and wait until later for what mattered.

Tom asked Nick where he wanted to be dropped off.

"Wherever it's convenient for you. I'll be looking for a small hotel for a day or two. One that's not too expensive," Nick replied.

"Okay, we'll drop you at Ealing Broadway Underground Station. You can get the tube straight into the city from there. Mind you, I'd think of getting a hotel further out if I were you. They are darned expensive in the City and the West End. You could look somewhere like Holland Park," Tom advised.

After being dropped at the station, Nick studied the underground map and found Holland Park. This was a completely new experience and quite different to anything he had experienced before. He felt like a child, fumbling and carefully reading the instructions as he bought a ticket from a machine, and then had to explore his way to the right platform. Being unable to find a timetable on any wall, he waited on the platform for a train to arrive. He didn't have to wait long.

Nick was amazed as the train rumbled and rattled into the station. It was not like anything he had ever seen, dirty, painted red, squat and wobbling, causing the driver to sway from side to side like a toy. It squealed to a stop in front of him, then the doors opened by themselves. Following the lead of other passengers, Nick stepped into the bowels of this noisy monster. The doors closed behind him, and soon the train rushed into a subterranean world like a giant red worm panicking to escape a predator. Given the closeness of the blackened tunnel walls, they seemed to be going even faster. He got off at Holland Park feeling relieved, but quietly pleased with himself.

Standing outside on the pavement for a moment, he was uncertain which way to go. Then, spotting a café and remembering he had not had a drink since he was onboard the ship, he decided a cup of tea was in order, and it would give him time to gather his thoughts.

"Yes Guvnor?" The man behind the counter asked.

"Tea please," Nick said just as he spotted the jam donuts, which were far too tempting. "And a donut please," Nick quickly added.

Nick waited while the tea was poured and the donut delivered from the glass case. He was amused by the man's accent but struggled to keep up given his speed.

"There you go Guv, one tea, one donut, and Bob's your uncle – unless your auntie's queer?'

There was a full two seconds before Nick realised what he had said. It was quite long enough for the humour to be lost, so he smiled and quietly said, "oh yes," giving the man a weak response.

After a short conversation about possible accommodation, Nick was advised to walk along Holland Park Avenue towards the city where he might find a small inexpensive hotel amongst the more expensive ones. He was bemused at the thought that café owners and publicans are a mine of information, and seem to know where everything is.

Nick found the streets of London unpleasant. Too busy, too noisy, claustrophobic and the air was laced with traffic fumes. There was no similarity to Perth. No big bright sky and super wide streets, only an oppressive grey covering that didn't seem to change. After a few blocks, he came to a small terraced hotel that had clearly been created from two, once elegant five story Victorian houses. In one of the lower windows, an illuminated sign read simply "Vacancies." At the front desk Nick was assured the rates were reasonable, although rather more than he would have liked and as he was not bothered that they only served breakfast. He took a room for four nights.

The next morning Nick bought a London Street Map and found his way to Somerset House in the city, where he intended to search through the births, deaths and marriage records. He arrived to find one of the grandest buildings he had ever seen. There was a printed message taped on the inside of one of the glass doors saying 'The Family Records Centre has been relocated to St. Catherine's House, 10, Broadway, London, WC2.'

Nick found Broadway on his map and was pleased to see it was close, and he would have no problems finding it. On the way he bought a postcard picturing Trafalgar Square. He'd send it to Skip and Charlie letting them know he had arrived safely in London. To his amusement, he eventually found himself passing the Australian High Commission and hesitated at the front door, then smiled to himself before walking on. He had never seen so many old, elegant, important looking, yet austere buildings before. There were no tall, bright shiny buildings like Perth.

On entering St Catherine's House he was hesitant, standing for a moment before going to reception where he explained why he was there and to sign in as a visitor. He was directed to a very large room which almost resembled a warehouse, containing rack after rack of large volumes. Where to begin? His confused look was noticed by a lady whose job was to advise how the volumes are set out, what details are recorded and how to search. Within a few minutes Nick had found a heavy volume containing records of births in the year and calendar quarter of his birth. Out of curiosity he searched the name Nicholas Michael Thorne which appeared twice, but he was able to quickly discount them. Then more importantly, he turned to finding Robert James Spalding. It did not take long. There he was, it had to be him! Robert James Spalding, born 10th November

1940 at Ely, Cambridgeshire. Mother's Name, Father's Name, Airman RNZAF. It was all there. Nick just stared at the page, overjoyed, emotional and speechless.

He wrote down the details and went to the reception office to ask if he could have a copy. He was told he would have to fill in a pink form and pay a fee. Then a copy of his Birth Certificate would be posted to him in a day or two. Desperation was in Nick's voice as he explained that he was in the country for only a short time, and that he didn't know any future addresses yet. Without further discussion, the lady at reception passed him the pink form saying,

"If you fill that in and pay the fee, I'll see what I can do for you. I'm not making any promises though. Can you come back later this afternoon?"

Nick said an appreciative, "yes."

Thanking her enthusiastically, he left. Outside he checked his list of things to do and places to make enquiries. The Australian High Commission was on his list and stood just across the road. So it would be next. No great hope of gaining information was held, but he felt he had to try.

In front of him was a row of old style bank teller windows where visitors spoke through holes in the glass and passed documents beneath. Above each window was the word "Visas." At each position stood half a dozen people queuing with passports and other documents in hand. To the side was a general enquiries desk where Nick asked a young lady if he could speak to someone about Child Migrant Scheme records. She was not friendly and he thought very negative. Talking into a telephone she said,

"We don't know anything about Child Migrant Scheme Records, do we?"

Nick was taken aback.

She listened for a moment before saying "I see." Then with her hand over the mouthpiece, she asked Nick what he wanted to know.

"I want to know what records you keep, and if I am on them?"

She repeated Nick's request, listened a moment, then put the telephone down. Speaking as though she was repeating exactly what she had been told, and with mannerisms implying there would be no further discussion, she said, "we don't know anything about a Child Migrant Scheme to Australia, and if there were such a thing, we would definitely not keep any records here."

Nick was indignant at the abruptness of the response to such simple questions.

Next he decided to walk to The New Zealand High Commission in the Haymarket. It was not far, and Nick was fascinated by the sights and sounds of London, so would enjoy the walk. The streets were never totally devoid of black cabs, big red buses and tourists. He was amused by an elderly man selling newspapers and stopped a while at a discrete distance to watch. The man wore an old threadbare cap, held a dozen folded newspapers under his left arm, and with the newsprint blackened fingers of his other hand, waved a newspaper in the air. His face was unshaven and a thin, half-smoked, hand rolled cigarette hung precariously to his bottom lip. Even when he shouted to attract attention, it failed to dislodge. With a slick twist of his wrist, he could perfectly present a newspaper to his customer and receive payment all in the same movement with one hand. Even after saying "Thanks Guv'ner," the dead cigarette still clung to his lip.

As Nick stood watching, he wondered what Gidga would make of this place and felt that it would be difficult to describe to someone who had grown up in the wide expanse of the Australian Outback. Gidga might even be afraid.

At the enquiries desk Nick asked about personnel records of New Zealand airmen during World War II and was politely told,

"I'm afraid you have come to the wrong place Sir. The New Zealand High Commission does not hold any of those records. You might like to contact the department of Defence in Wellington. If they don't have them, they should be able to point you in the right direction."

Nick thanked the man and said he would take his advice when he got back to Australia.

Then in a softer, more thoughtful, tone of voice the man added,

"It's just possible that your father's name might be recorded somewhere at the Imperial War Museum here in London. You could try there since you are already here. Who knows, you might get lucky."

Nick thanked him again and decided to follow it up later if he had time. His main objective now was to find his mother and discover more about himself.

At 3.15 pm that afternoon Nick returned to St. Catherine's House to find a brown envelope waiting for him. The lady slid it across the desk and smiled saying,

"There you go Mr. Thorne. Luckily, I was able to call in a favour or two."

He was elated and thanked her many times over, feeling he had identified himself and was now finally on his way to finding his mother. In his excitement, he didn't wait to leave the building before opening the envelope to inspect the certificate. He held the most precious piece of paper he had ever had and was full of emotion. Nick could hardly believe it. So much so, that he was uncertain what to do next. He gathered his thoughts as he read the words over and over.

"Name: Robert James Spalding.
Date of Birth: 10th November 1940.
Place of Birth: Ely, Cambridgeshire.
Mother's Name: Anne Sarah Spalding. Housewife.
Father's Name: Ross Spalding. RNZAF.

That evening Nick looked up the location and phone number for the head office of Dr. Barnado's. Since it was located far on the eastern outskirts of London, he decided to telephone the next morning to avoid the possibility of a wasted journey, but he'd go if need be.

Nick spoke to the receptionist.

"My name is Nicholas Thorne. I wonder if you could help me please. I would like to talk to someone who has access to the records of children who were in your care in the early part of the 1940's."

"Hold on please."

There was a click followed by a short pause.

"Good morning Mr. Thorne. My name is Roberts, how can I help you?"

Nick was deliberately as polite as he could be, hoping to encourage a helpful response.

"Thank you for giving me your time Mr. Roberts. As a child I was at Dr. Barnardo's, I believe in Cambridge where, I must say, I was well looked after. My father had died in the war and my mother went to hospital, so I was taken to Dr. Barnardo's. It would have been from about 1943 for four years. I subsequently lost contact with my mother, and now I'm trying to find her. So I wondered if you might have her address at that time tucked away somewhere in your archives?"

"Were you an orphan Mr. Thorne?"

"No," Nick replied.

"Well I was never actually an orphan but may have been recorded as one later."

"Ah well then, it sounds as though your mother may have passed away while you were with us, making you an orphan. It was not unusual in the forties."

"I understand Mr. Roberts, but I have never believed that to be the case."

"Well, how did you eventually lose contact with your mother?" Mr. Roberts asked.

"I was sent to Australia as a Child Migrant, and I have come to England to try and find her. Or at least find out what might have happened to her."

"Oh, I see," Mr. Roberts said thoughtfully.

In those three words Nick detected a change from his friendly tone to authoritarian. He was beginning to understand that The Child Migrant Scheme was a delicate topic which nobody wanted to talk about.

"Well then Mr. Thorne, we will have no record of your move to Australia," Mr. Roberts added.

"I didn't think you would Mr. Roberts, but I hoped you would have a record of my stay with you in Cambridge that may contain some background details," Nick pleaded.

"We may have had at one time Mr. Thorne. However it is almost certain that you would have been entrusted to another institution and your entire file would have gone to them for continuity. So I'm sorry, but I can't help you."

Trying hard to stay polite, Nick persisted.

"Well, can you tell me if you actually had a children's home in Cambridge during the period I mentioned and where it was?"

Sorry Mr. Thorne, I can't right now, it would require an hour or two of research. We have a home there now but I have no idea if it's the same one."

"Could you give me the address please?" Nick asked.

Mr. Roberts was getting flustered at Nick's persistent questions.

"You will find the address in the phone book. Now Mr. Thorne, I really must get on."

Nick was frustrated and annoyed by the time the conversation ended. He could not believe that Dr. Barnardo's would not keep even a brief record of the children in their care. Even if it were just names, date of admission and of departure. Given Mr. Robert's comments, the exchange prompted him to think of the worst case scenario, being that his mother may not still be alive.

He went back to St Catherine's House and spent the rest of the day there searching for a death certificate in the name of Anne Sarah Spalding, which he did not want to find. It was a difficult search as he was not sure of her birthdate. He found a number of entries carrying the name Anne Spalding but discounted them all. Although he was tired and his eyes sore, he was relieved and satisfied that he had eliminated the possibility of his mother's death.

Tomorrow would be Saturday and all official offices would be closed for the weekend. Rather than waste time, he decided to make plans to visit Cambridge and Ely next week. In the meantime, he would do a little sightseeing in London. Using the telephone, he was able to check train times to Cambridge and reserve a hire car. He also found the address of Dr. Barnardo's.

Nick spent the remainder of the weekend relaxing as a tourist. He had used a lot of nervous energy in the past few days and needed to unwind. By Monday morning he was refreshed and eager to make two more enquiries before going to Cambridge on Tuesday.

First was to The Home Office. The address was London SW1, not too far from Holland Park. Everywhere seemed so much closer than in Australia. London was huge compared to any Australian city he had visited, yet all that seemed important was compacted into short bus or train rides. A seat at the top of a London bus to SW1 was a new experience. Nick made a point of going to the front. Childish he thought, but interesting and a fun experience not to be missed.

He arrived early, and when the doors eventually opened he was greeted by an immaculately uniformed commissionaire sporting gold sergeant's stripes on each arm. A wide black polished leather strap rested diagonally from one shoulder to his hip. As Nick approached, the man saluted saying, "good morning Sir, can I direct you somewhere?"

No one had ever saluted Nick before.

"Thank you." Nick smiled.

"I'd like to go to the main reception please."

"Certainly Sir, just step inside and turn to your left."

Nick was quietly impressed as the commissionaire had made him feel important.

After explaining that he was enquiring about Child Migration records, the attractive young receptionist said with frown,

"I'm not sure if we keep those records here Sir, but I'll ask for you."

Nick watched and admired her as she made a telephone call. He was frustrated with himself for not being able to relax with women, especially attractive ones like this. He was attracted to them but didn't know how to deal with it. After a short conversation on the phone, she turned back to Nick.

"If you go over there and pick that telephone up Sir, someone will talk to you."

This time Nick went into more detail about his search while the lady at the other end listened patiently.

"I'm very sorry Mr. Thorne, it seems you might have had a wasted journey today. You see we don't keep individual records here or personal details involved with any sort of Migration. The only records we keep cover government policy on these matters. However, I suggest you contact the Public Records Office in Kew. I'm certain they will be of more help to you."

Nick thanked her and replaced the phone. He then asked the receptionist if she knew the Kew address, which , she looked up and wrote down for him. As she handed it over, she looked straight into his eyes and held his gaze. Nick felt himself blush and silently cursed himself for being so inept with women.

Checking his map, he could see that he was already on the western side of London so took the tube to Kew Gardens, then a short walk to the Public Records Office.

By now he was getting used to talking to receptionists and explaining what he wanted.

"Do you have an appointment with anyone, or have you come to conduct your own search?" she asked.

"I'm sorry but I don't know the procedures here. Should I look for myself or does someone search for me?"

"If you have not been here before Sir, I'll get someone to help you."

A cheerful young lady appeared and offered to help.

"Now what are we looking for Mr. Thorne?"

Nick's abilities with women were being severely tested today.

Together Nick and the woman searched for any records relating to his family, but were unable to find anything of significance. Disappointed, he said, "well I'd like to know about my father too. I'm afraid I don't know much at all about him or where to start looking, which is why I came here.

He was frustrated with himself and again a little tongue tied.

"Not to worry, let's start with what we know."

"All I can tell you is that he was in the Royal New Zealand Air Force during WWII and was killed. His name was Ross Spalding."

"Do you know what he did, how or where he died?"

"I can't be sure, but I believe he flew bombers from East Anglia."

Within half an hour, Nick was holding a photocopy of a War Graves Registration Form dated 17th July, 1956. At N° 5 on the list he saw his father's name:

Ross Spalding, RNZAF.
Service No. 401642.

Rank. Seargent, Flight Engineer.

Unit. No.75 Squadron RNZAF.

Date of Death. 3rd June, 1943 – Germany.

Place of Burial. Hamburg Cemetary, Ohlsdorf, Germany.

The word 'Death' struck home with Nick, upsetting him even though he now felt a little closer to his father, who was becoming less of a mystery. There was comfort in knowing where he was.

The young lady discretely said nothing for a minute or two, then.

"Will that be all Mr. Thorne?"

"Yes thanks. Thank you very much."

Nick replied without stopping to think, as at that moment his mind was preoccupied with his father. He hoped the archives of the RNZAF in Wellington would have more details about where he was based and how he died.

Nick now had two documents to treasure. He was happy that he was making progress with his research into both his mother and father, yet wondered how life might have been if his father had survived. Almost everything that had happened to him would be different. His destiny was changed in that one fateful night. He would have been raised by loving parents in a caring home. Maybe he would have had a brother or sister, known his aunts, uncles and grandparents. Then it occurred to him that he may still have a distant family, perhaps in New Zealand or, as yet, unknown relatives in England. It would be wonderful to meet his grandparents. He could ask them so much about his mother and father. They might even have photographs to show him.

Nick gathered his thoughts whilst strolling through Kew Gardens. Not that he took much notice of the botanic exhibits, he just enjoyed the tranquility. After an hour or two he returned to his hotel and prepared to make the trip to Cambridge.

Nick rose early, washed, shaved, packed his case and left before breakfast to be sure to catch the 09.10 train that went to Kings Lynn via Cambridge. He had paid his bill the evening before and had no extras to settle, so was able to leave quickly. He waited on the underground train platform, facing the rush of warm air which announced the approach of every train. Twenty minutes later he was at Liverpool Street Station, took the escalator up to the main line platforms and bought a ticket to Cambridge.

To Nick's surprise, the journey had only taken about an hour with stops. He was still adjusting to the small size and scale of England. Cambridge station was not what he had expected, thinking it would be larger and grander, not the scruffy, somewhat grubby place it was. There was a faint smell of fish, but not the same one he was familiar with. He thought it a poor introduction to a prestigious university city like Cambridge. At the news kiosk he bought a basic street map, which was mainly intended to locate various university colleges, but it served Nick's purpose.

He saw that the address for Dr. Barnardo's was not far away, and it was an easy walk into town from the station. Nick walked along Station Road, then into Hills Road to take him to the city centre. Two blocks along he noticed a window above a shop with a sign saying 'B & B'. Someone had taped a paper strip beneath it with the handwritten word 'Vacancy'. A door at the side of the shop was marked 'B & B Entrance.' Nick entered, making his way up the narrow stairs that creaked on almost every step. He knocked on a door and waited. Eventually, a plump, elderly woman with frizzy grey hair answered the door.

"Yes?"

Nick was not sure if it was a question or a statement given the way it was said, and he was taken back by the abruptness.

"I saw your sign from the street. Do you still have a vacancy?"

In a raised monotone and without stopping for a breath she said, "yes, I've got one room at the front. The young man who was there left this morning – I charge five pounds a day in advance that includes breakfast at 8 o'clock sharp – be late and you'll miss it – no pets – no parties, the front door is locked at 10 pm sharp and definitely no women!"

Amused, Nick responded with half a smile, thinking she was a caricature of herself.

"I'll only be here in the evenings, and I'm very quiet," he said.

"You're not a student are you? Pon my life, they are more trouble than they're worth, up to all sorts of things and sometimes all night long. My son runs the shop downstairs, and we don't want no bother. Oh! And you share the bathroom with a man at the back."

Nick was caught off guard by her manner, but quickly regained his composure whilst struggling to keep a straight face. He was unsure if he really wanted to stay here. After considering that it was within his budget and he may not find other lodgings at that price, he accepted. It occurred to him that cheap accommodation might be hard to find in Cambridge, given the demands of students and others.

"I'm visiting from Australia, and I'm not sure how long I'll need the room for. It could be a few days, maybe a week."

Then adding tongue in cheek.

"I promise to be quiet, clean and tidy."

Nick thought of asking to see the room before committing himself but quickly discounted the notion rather than risk the woman's acrimony. She had clearly placed herself in command with a 'take it or leave it' attitude.

"So you're Australian are you?" she rhetorically asked.

"I had an Australian here once before. He used to drink and swear a lot. He kept calling me Sheila. My name's Marge, not Sheila. I had to ask him to leave in the end."

Nick laughed.

"I promise you I'm not like that Mam, not all Australians are the same."

Nick said to deliberately to ingratiate himself and offer her respect, and to contrast with her previous experience of Australians.

"Yes well, I'll be the judge of that." Marge said wryly.

He didn't tell her that he was born in England.

"Well then young man, you better give me two days rent now and we'll see how we go."

After paying Nick followed Marge up a second flight of narrow wooden stairs. As before, almost all the steps creaked. Nick smiled, believing she would know exactly when her guests came and went. There's would be no way for anyone to sneak in or out of here.

It was an old building, but it had character. The room was on the second floor. He could see down to the road through a small dormer window high above the shop, and the thin faded curtains did little to dim the room. A single bed that was sunken in the middle took most of the space. An old dark wooden wardrobe with two drawers beneath provided just enough space to hang a few clothes, and a Windsor chair stood in a corner of the room next to a mirror. Nick was pleased with his decision since it was clean and homely, perfect for just a few days.

"Knock on my door when you come down and I'll give you a key. Mind you, don't lose it or I'll charge you a bob or two to replace it." Marge said as she left.

When she was gone, he lay down on the bed for a few minutes. It creaked with every movement, but it was comfortable. He unpacked his clothes and decided to go for a walk. Within ten minutes he was in town, standing by an ornate fountain in a busy cobbled square. It was market day. Nick had read about English markets and was fascinated. All manner of goods were being sold from canvas covered stalls. An Indian gentleman sold silk ties, scarves and clothes brushes. A young woman offered folks samples of her home made fudge. A vicar sold jars of honey to raise funds for a church restoration. Clothes of all shapes and sizes, home grown fruit and vegetables, ornaments, books, gramophone records, music tapes and second hand tools were all changing hands in a good natured atmosphere. Nick was enthralled at the scene. He picked up a tasty looking apple.

As he inspected it a lady said, "Coxes Orange, lovey."

Nick nodded, and decided to try it.

"Just the one my love?" the lady said.

Nick smiled at her affectionate manner.

"Yes thank you."

"Five of them new pennies will do it lovey. Need a bag?"

Nick thanked her but declined as he polished it on his arm, saying he would eat it now. As he wandered, smiling and wide-eyed, through the market he almost had to pinch himself to be sure this was real.

That evening as he lay in bed, he considered that it had been an enjoyable day. Tomorrow he would go to the Dr. Barnardo's address to see if it looked familiar. Then to find The Backs and later locate the car hire company. He knew there were regular trains and buses to Ely but wanted the freedom to come and go in his own time. He could not suppress his inexplicable feeling of being close to discovery. But of what, he didn't know. He felt uneasy, even a little afraid of what was to be discovered. It might not be good news, and he wished Chris could have been there with him. It took some time to fall asleep but when he did, he slept soundly.

There was a table set for two at breakfast in the small parlour, but he was the only guest there. The full English breakfast was more than he had expected and much better than he'd had in London. Marge fussed over him to ensure that he had enough of everything, repeatedly offering him more toast.

Tea came in floral china cups that looked too delicate to use, but Nick contentedly sipped. Marge made a point of saying it was her best china, a wedding gift from many years ago.

His mind's eye was elsewhere as he leaned back and stared at the ceiling. He decided to send Skip and Charlie another postcard, hoping to find one with a picture of 'The Backs'. They would surely smile at the irony and know where he was now. To add to their amusement and let them know he was in good humour, he would address it to 'Uncle Bill and Bro.'

After a second cup of tea, Nick pushed his chair back.

"That was positively the best breakfast I have ever had." He told Marge.

She looked embarrassed at the rare compliment, while wringing her hands in her apron. Although clearly appreciative, she pinched her lips and held her head back with satisfaction saying,

"Just so long as you liked it. Can't send you out on an empty stomach, can we?"

Nick thanked her again and smiled as he thought. 'She's softening. I bet she would make a lovely mum.'

That thought brought him back to his task, so he checked his map to find Fitzwilliam Road and was there in only a few minutes. No.1 was the first in a terrace of tall Victorian homes that Nick thought must have been grand when they were built. He stood across the road staring at the building for almost five minutes as he considered if this was the place where he had spent four years of his life. Although there were similarities, he could not be sure as his memories were faded. It looked as though two houses had been merged into one to create a larger building. He wanted to go in and ask questions but was hesitant while his heart was beating much faster than normal. On deciding that nothing would be gained by standing on the street just looking, he crossed the road.

With a feeling of trepidation, he made his way to the front door and knocked. It was opened by a young man who asked if he could help him. Nick heard the happy sounds of children coming from further back.

"Yes, if you can please. My name is Nickolas Thorne. Have I found Dr. Barnados?"

"Yes, can I help you with something?" He replied.

"Err, well you see, I was a Barnardo's boy, and I think this might be the place I stayed for a few years during the war and for a while after. I'm hoping there is someone here who could help me find a few answers about my family?"

"You had better come in. I'll see if Mrs. Wright can help you."

Nick was ushered in and led down the hall to a doorway with a chair standing outside. His eyes scanned the surroundings looking for something familiar. Although it was similar to what he vaguely remembered, this was brighter and lighter, a far more cheerful place.

"Wait here please."

The young man asked as he tapped on the door and entered without waiting to be invited. The door was firmly closed behind him, so Nick assumed he was clearly not meant to hear the conversation.

The minute he waited felt much longer. Two boys of about six years of age happily ran in his direction, one chasing the other and clearly oblivious of his presence until only a few feet away. They slowed suddenly, lowered their faces towards the floor but casting their eyes upward to see Nick's face as they shuffled silently past with their arms straight down to their sides. Nick instantly recognised that look; it was engrained in his deeper memory, grabbing him as if a hundred demons had dragged him back in time. A chill ran through his body as he took a deep breath. The periphery of his vision darkened, and he thought he was looking down a tunnel at distant images. It was the haunted look that orphans have in their eyes and the greying beneath from fitful sleep that captured them, irrespective of how well they were cared for. Nick knew that when their heads touched their pillows at night and their eyes were closed, anxieties returned. They would just want their mother, nothing and nobody else would do. They want to be held, loved and made to feel they belonged to someone. Nick knew their pain only too well. He wanted to reach out, tell them not to be afraid, that he understood because he had been an orphan just like them.

The young man re-appeared saying that Mrs. Wright would see him now. Nick walked into a room that had been converted into an office. It was bright and cheerful. Mrs. Wright was a slim, middle-aged woman with greying hair and nicely dressed, wearing only lipstick and small pearl earrings to enhance her appearance. Standing behind her desk, she extended her hand and smiled saying,

"Good morning Mr. Thorne. It's lovely to meet you, please have a seat."

Nick was nervous about being back in a Barnardo's Home and unsettled by his experience in the hallway. He attempted to smile as he shook her hand and sat down. Mrs. Wright quickly detected Nick's discomfort and tried to settle him.

"Well Nick. May I call you Nick?"

"Yes of course," he replied.

"I understand that you were once a Barnardo's boy yourself. Where was that?"

"I believe it was here in Cambridge. I came in 1943 and left in 1947."

"And what brings you here now?"

In spite of her efforts she could still see Nick's unease, so before he could respond, she cheekily twitched her nose and smiled saying, "I think it must be time for a cup of tea, don't you? Shall we have one?"

Nick's mouth was dry with nervousness so it was music to his ears, and he eagerly accepted. Mrs. Wright picked up the phone and politely asked for two teas to be brought in.

"So Nick, what brings you here now, and how can I help you?" She repeated with a smile.

"When I left here I was seven years old and went to Australia with other children. As a result, I lost contact with my family and relatives. So I guess you'd say I'm on a pilgrimage to find them, especially my mother."

Nick deliberately spoke in a calm, friendly manner to avoid the impression that he might be here on a mission of complaint.

"The memories I have of my time at Dr. Barnardo's are all pleasant, and I made some good friends here too. One in particular lasted for many years afterwards, even while in Australia. We had some fun times here together."

"Oh, don't you see that person anymore?" Mrs. Wright asked.

Nick looked away as a wave of sadness flushed through his face.

"No, I'm afraid not, he died in Vietnam."

Mrs. Wright looked at Nick's face and then wished she had not asked.

"Oh dear, I'm so very sorry. You must miss him."

"I do, very much."

Wanting to move on from those memories Nick asked,

"Do you know if this home is the same one that I would have come to in 1943?

"Gosh Nick, I really don't know. To the best of my knowledge there has only ever been one Barnardo's Home in Cambridge at any one time. But I'm afraid I really don't know if it was here or somewhere else. I have only been here for two years and was in my teens in 1947. I would have to ask our people in London. Maybe someone there would know, but it might take a little while to get an answer.

Tea arrived with a biscuit in the saucer. Nick immediately sipped, trying not to look too eager. He was pleased to have something to do with his hands.

"What leads you to believe you were here in Cambridge?"

The tea was helping to relax him.

"My Birth Certificate shows I was born at The Grange in Ely, so I believe I lived somewhere in the area. Also, I have distant memories of an event that happened by the river at a place called The Backs."

"Well, that certainly sounds as though the Cambridge home was the one you would have gone to."

"I was wondering if you have any records from my early years which would help me find my mother or perhaps anyone who might be a relative, even if there is just an address where I had lived before?"

"Dear me, no. When a child leaves Barnardo's, say for adoption or to be returned home, their records are sent to London. Or if the child is to go to another care centre, their records go with them. In any event, we are not permitted to show the records to anyone else, not even the child or later as an adult. It's government legislation you see. I hope you understand that, in some circumstances, it could cause all sorts of problems. If you went to Australia from here, your file would probably have been given to the first organization that cared for you there. Not even the adopting parents get to see those files. There are very strict rules about that," she said apologetically.

"I asked in Australia and got absolutely nowhere. No organization would admit to having my file, only to say they had passed it on to somewhere else. It was hard to get some of them to admit that I had even existed, and I was referred from one organization to another without any luck."

Nick had come half expecting this result, so was not surprised. Nonetheless, he was still disappointed.

"So what would you suggest I do Mrs. Wright?"

After a moment of thought, she said,

"Well since you are here, if you plan to go to Ely, you could find where you were born and see what records they might have. Maybe even your mother's address at the time."

"Yes, I was planning to do that," Nick said.

The conversation fell into small talk about life in Australia while they finished their tea. Nick thanked her and excused himself saying he had other errands that day. Mrs. Wright apologised that she had been unable to help and walked with Nick back along the corridor towards the front door. As they approached, he said,

"I hope you don't mind my curiosity Mrs. Wright, but do you have a loft room at the back of the building that's used as a bedroom or a dormitory?"

"Why yes, we do. Was that your room?"

"If it has a high dormer window that overlooks the rear gardens, then it probably was."

"Would you like to see it, just to be sure, and for old times sake?"

"Oh, yes," Nick enthusiastically replied.

"Come on then, let's go up," she said as if to imply they were being mischievous.

As Nick followed her up the stairs, it seemed familiar, and he felt a strong surreal sense of déjà vu. On entering the room he knew for certain this was the place. The room was brighter than he remembered, and the furniture was more modern, but this was it. The sloping ceilings on each side somehow made it appear smaller now, and he no longer had to stand on the bed to see out of the window. He walked to where his old bed had stood and looked across the room to see if Jeremey's bed was there. Silly, he thought, but in a flash of distant memory he saw a young

Jeremy sitting on the bed smiling at him. Nick's mouth immediately fell open, and in shock he blinked hard to clear his vision. Within a second or two the image disappeared as quickly as it had come.

Mrs. Wright watched Nick's body language and his face go white.

"Are you alright Nick?" she asked.

"Err yes, fine thank you," he said with difficulty.

"I'm certain this is the place. It's lovely to see it again, and it brings back so many memories. Thank you for bringing me up here."

Still disturbed, he didn't tell Mrs. Wright what he had just seen. They went downstairs to the front door where Nick thanked her again while she wished him good luck with his search before saying goodbye. As he left, Nick took three deep breaths.

He decided to walk into town and find The Backs. It was not far according to his map. Before long he was standing on an ancient stone footbridge over the river Cam. Memories came flooding back as he watched punts being gently pushed along with long wooden poles. He could not help but think of Chris and the events of that day all those years ago. He thought how wonderful it would be if Chris was standing beside him now to share this moment. Crossing the bridge into the park area, he looked back and saw it was exactly as he had seen it on the postcard in Martin Place. The river, the old buildings in the background and grasslands were picturesque and worthy of a postcard.

After dwelling for a while with his memories, he decided it was time to contact the car hire company. Returning to the market square, he was directed to Drummer Street where he would find telephone boxes next to the bus stops. After confirming that his car would be ready, he would collect it in the morning.

That evening he decided to find a pub for a meal and a quiet beer. His landlady, Marge, said The Crown was only two blocks away and did a decent meal. Before long it was smoky and loud with enthusiastic students whose main ambition seemed to be to outdo each other in abstract intellect or the ability to drink, sometimes both. Nick ordered a pint of bitter believing it was a traditional English beverage. But he drank only a few mouthfuls, as it tasted awful, was flat and warm. With some amusement, Nick thought that a pub in Perth or Fremantle serving beer like that would not last long. To be adventurous, he ordered Toad in the Hole without knowing what it was since the name had intrigued him. Foregoing the bitter, he took a glass of larger back to his table. It was more like Australian beer and served cold. He sipped gently trying to relax and take in the long, emotional day.

24

After breakfast Nick went to collect his hire car. There were so many questions and documents to sign that he felt he was signing his life away. A map of East Anglia was in the car, making it easy for him to get to Ely. However, finding the A10 north was a challenge due to the number of confusing one way streets. He thought it fortunate that in England people drive on the same side of the road as in Australia. Finding his way on the wrong side of the road would have been extremely difficult.

Nick eventually found himself heading out of Cambridge to pass Milton, then Waterbeach. He was amazed at how close towns and villages were to each other, unlike Australia where they were sometimes hours apart. Here the roads had twists, turns and corners that seemed unnecessary. There were no direct, straight roads out to the horizon or from one place to another. It didn't make sense to him. It was so flat, like much of the outback, so why not have straight roads.

As he left the village of Stretham, he stopped at the top of a slope by the roadside, not far from the remains of an old windmill. That feeling of déjà vue came over him again. Looking across The Fens and seeing Ely Cathedral in the distance was eerie. He had seen it before but had difficulty remembering exactly when. Strong, cautious, feelings of anticipation of what he might find came over him. He felt close to discovery, very close and it made him nervous.

As Nick drove into Ely he passed a church, then the cathedral on his right. At the Lamb Hotel he turned into the High Street, believing it would take him to the centre of town, not knowing he was already there. He found a parking place at the end of the street just before it sloped downhill between rows of shops.

Anxious for a cup of tea or coffee, and wanting to know where The Grange was, made him decide to find a cafe. Unable to find one in the immediate area, he thought they are as rare as hen's teeth here', and decided to ask someone if Ely had a café at all?

"Down the hill, turn right and there's one on your right."

Spoken in another accent Nick had never heard before.

"Called the Kimberly, they do a decent bit'o dockey there too."

Nick had no idea what the man was talking about and didn't ask, just thanked him before he set off to find it.

A strongly built young lady served at the counter. She was not pretty but not unattractive in her own way. She smiled at Nick as he approached. He asked for tea which she poured from a large metal teapot. It was dark and strong, reminding him of Skip's tea. Only these mugs were unstained. She was friendly, had a warm personality but looked tired. Her appearance suggested she needed a holiday and that she was putting on a brave face for her customers.

"Sugar's on the table. Is there anything else?" She asked.

"No thanks," Nick said with a smile, feeling a little empathy.

"Could you tell me where The Grange is in Ely please?" He asked.

"Do you mean the maternity home?"

"Well I suppose that's it, if it's called The Grange?" Nick replied.

"Yes, it's just a few minutes' walk, not far away."

The young lady gave directions, saying it was almost next to the police station.

"A big old place set back on the corner by the traffic lights. You can't miss it."

Nick smiled.

"Now when people tell me that, I usually do."

They both laughed.

It was a plain, grey, brick building with no outstanding features or any appeal. So this is it, where I was born, he thought. It was a strange feeling to be there now, and unsettling to be so close to where he had come into the world. He believed this may be his last chance to trace his mother and hoped they could help him.

The inside of the building did nothing to endear itself to visitors or patients. The walls were painted a pale clinical green, and the hall lighting was poor. A notice board, to the left side, displayed Health Department announcements and thank you notes from former patients.

There didn't seem to be a formal enquiry office or desk, just a hall with doors off to each side. Nick could hear the distant cry of babies. A woman in a nurse's uniform appeared from a doorway and asked Nick if he needed help.

"Yes, thank you," Nick replied.

"I'd like to talk to someone about your records please."

"Oh, are you from the Health Department?" She said in surprise.

"No, no. According to my Birth Certificate I was born here in 1940 and wondered what records you might have. It's a long story, but I was separated from my mother during the war, and I'm now trying to find her. I'm hoping you might have a file in you archives that would give me some clues, even if it's just where she lived at the time."

She thought for a moment, then replied.

"I'm really sorry, but we don't keep any of those older records here, only the more recent ones. Eventually, they get sent to the Cambridgeshire County Records Office."

"Where is that?" Nick asked.

"County Hall. I think it's in Castle Hill in Cambridge. You'll find them in the phone book. I don't mean to be rude, so please excuse me. I've got a lot to do."

She walked away, leaving Nick no chance to ask more questions. Clearly, there was nothing more to be done here, and he was disappointed. He had achieved very little except the knowledge that a record might be held somewhere else. The story of my life, he thought.

The next hour was spent looking at the cathedral and being amazed at its size and grandeur. It impressed him as he had seen nothing in Australia that could match it. No building of any kind there was more than two hundred years old. While sitting on a park bench near an ancient cannon, he examined his options from here on. Then Nick had a brainwave and went to the local newspaper office where he met a young man from the classified advertisement department. He asked if it was appropriate to publish an advertisement in the paper to search for someone.

He was told it was. So together they drafted an advertisement:

URGENT
Would anyone knowing
the whereabouts of Mrs.
Anne Spalding who lived
in Mepal from 1940 to
1943 please contact Robert
Spalding at P.O. Box 3374
Perth. Australia.

"It will be about a week before we can publish it as this ' week's issue has already gone to press," the man explained. Nick said that he may no longer be in the UK by then, so they agreed to use his Australian address.

The advertising representative also explained that using URGENT would hopefully attract more attention.

He decided to go to County Hall the next morning. On his way to Ely, he had noticed a quaint looking pub by the river near Stretham. Thinking it would be nice to experience an English country pub, he stopped on his way back. Feeling depressed, he thought a drink might give him a lift.

25

Sitting at the bar of The Royal Oak nursing a glass of larger, Nick looked over the Old West River in despair. He felt he had all but exhausted his options and avenues. Now tired, frustrated and empty, his last ounce of hope seemed to drain from his fingertips like drops of water. Having done everything he thought was possible to trace his mother and find his roots, he had failed. Finally, he was beginning to believe that he may never find his mother, and the possibility that she may have already passed away became a reality, even though he had found no Death Certificate in public records. Now, on his way back to Cambridge, his only hope now was that she might have gone to New Zealand to be with his father's family. However, it was a very slim hope. At times he had become optimistic, but each turn had led nowhere, only adding to his frustration and disappointment.

The landlord could see that his customer was troubled and gave him space, but at the same time occasionally casting him a casual but inquisitive glance. He was a friendly, warmhearted man who clearly liked people and enjoyed chatting, especially to strangers as they usually had different, more interesting tales to tell, and he was always curious to know where they were from. He wanted to talk to Nick but instinctively waited for the right moment. His attention was diverted when a regular put his empty glass on the bar saying, "same again Bill."

As Bill pulled another pint, Nick lowered his empty glass, putting it gently on the bar mat, unsure if he would have another. He wanted to drown his sorrows but knew it would be silly as he had to drive back to Cambridge. Bill made his mind up for him as he approached Nick with a warm smile asking, "another one Sir? On me this time."

Before Nick could gather his composure, the landlord had taken a fresh glass and was pouring a larger. Surprised and impressed, Nick quickly said, "thanks very much, just a small one though."

Bill smiled and looked back at Nick.

"Just passing through?"

"Yes, I guess so," Nick replied.

He didn't particularly want to talk, but it was the polite thing to do as the landlord had just bought him a drink.

The glass was placed in front of Nick while Bill waited for the froth to subside before pouring the remainder of the bottle. Nick nodded his appreciation. The landlord extended his hand across the bar and, with a smile, introduced himself.

"Bill Burgess."

Comforted by the warmness in Bill's voice, Nick smiled back and shook his hand saying, "Nick Thorne. Nice to meet you Bill."

"Do I detect an Aussie twang there? On holiday?" Bill asked.

"Yes, well sort of. I've been living there since I was a nipper, but I've come back to look for my family."

Bill naturally wanted to ask if he was enjoying himself, but realized it would not be prudent given his earlier observations. As a student of human nature, Bill knew one of the best ways to get people talking was to say as little about oneself first and lead on from there.

"I'm not from around here either. I was stationed near here during the war with the Royal Air Force. The boys often used to drink here, especially on Saturdays. I liked it, so came back after the war and bought the place."

Nick picked up the line of conversation.

"My father was in England during the war with the New Zealand Air Force." He was on Stirlings, 75 Squadron."

Bill showed a lot of interest.

"I was in the RAF, a rear gunner on Lanc's.

"Dear God, that couldn't have been much fun," Nick said.

"Froze my bum off every night, but I was too terrified to worry about it. I can't bear to think about it now, makes me shiver with fright."

Bill looked down and shook his head for a moment.

"So your father was in No.75 Squadron, hey. Yes, that was a Kiwi outfit alright. Was he at Mildenhall or Mepal?"

"I don't know," Nick replied.

After hesitating for a moment, Bill asked, "when were you here?"

"I was born in 1940 and was here until I was three, then went to an orphanage in 1943."

Bill's mind was still on the war years.

"You know what, he could well have been at Mepal. No.75 Squadron transferred there in 41 or 42, if I'm not mistaken."

"I don't know. All I can say is that he went off one night and never came back. I was a toddler at the time, so I don't remember a great deal about him apart from his blue uniform and that he was always fun. It doesn't feel right, but I can't remember what he looks like, and I don't even have a photo," Nick lamented.

"He used to hold his oxygen mask over his face and chase me with the tube saying that he was an elephant and going to eat me. Of course, I'd run away screaming and laughing with excitement. It made my mother laugh too."

In amazement, Nick suddenly realized this was a new memory which had come to the surface without prompting.

Bill smiled as he imagined the encounter, then looking a little more serious asked, "Have you been out to Mepal since you have been back?"

Nick shook his head.

"There's a memorial in the village dedicated to the Kiwi blokes who flew from there and 'bought it' during the war. The locals look after it and keep it nice. If you have the time, you should take a peep, especially as your father was probably stationed there. It's not far from here."

Without being asked, Bill gave directions to Mepal, excusing himself twice to serve other customers before returning. It was early afternoon and Nick had the time, so allowed himself to be talked into going. They chatted a little longer, and Nick reciprocated Bill's gesture of a drink. Bill accepted, making a point of taking the top off a bottle of Indian Tonic Water in front of Nick.

"Not allowed to drink the real stuff when I'm behind the bar, but thanks just the same." Bill said with a wide appreciative grin.

"I always make a point of opening the bottle in front of the customer so they can see I've not just put the money in the till."

Nick drank up while Bill talked about life in the RAF during the war years but did not mention his missions. Moving off the bar stool to leave, Nick thanked Bill for his hospitality and conversation. Genuinely meaning it since it had cheered him up. Bill reached across the bar, they looked each other in the eye and shared a firm handshake, as Bill said, "good luck with your search my friend. I hope you find what you are looking for. Oh, and you really should go to Mepal, if you can. Pop in again some time, I'd love to know how you get on."

Nick followed Bill's directions back along the A10 to Stretham, then left through Wilburton and within a few minutes he found himself in Mepal, a small, quiet village, not especially attractive, but appealing for its peace and tranquility. It was the sort of place where the folks would typically be uncomplicated and good natured. Still following Bill's directions, it took only minutes to locate the New Zealand Air Force memorial.

As Nick stood in the memorial garden, he saw that towards the centre was a thick round plinth with a deep chamfered edge. It was raised above the ground on a hexagonal base. Engraved around the plinth were the words 'TO COMMEMORATE THOSE WHO SERVED WITH NO.75 (NZ) SQUADRON 1939-1944'. Bill was right, it was nicely kept.

Whilst looking at the memorial, Nick considered the sad irony that this was probably as close as he would ever get to his father, an epitaph that did not even carry his name. On reading the inscription, he was sure his father must have been here at one time. Once more he felt he was making a little progress.

Looking down the road he saw a village shop. Outside were bunches of yellow flowers in a galvanized bucket and a bundle of brooms leaning against the doorframe. Nick strolled to the shop, selected a bunch of daffodils, and went inside. A bell clattered above his head. The shop was like an Aladdin's cave. It seemed to sell everything from rubber boots, to saucepans, bread, fruit, newspapers, Aspirins and more. A lady, only a little older than himself, came from a room at the back.

"Yes dear?"

She asked in a strong Fen accent. Then noticing that Nick was holding a bunch of daffodils, she said. "lovely aren't they?"

Then again not waiting for a reply, she added.

"They grow up by the old airfield you know. Mum sent the paper boy up there to cut a few this morn'n a'fore he went to school. I'd goo meself if I weren't so bloomin busy here. Anyway, you get full'a slub up there on that old drove when it's wet. He brought too many for the house, so we stuck'em in a bucket out the front."

Nick said they were lovely before asking the price.

Without answering the lady said, "you in't from round here, are you?"

Nick smiled at her accent.

"No, I'm visiting from Australia. Is it alright for me to put these flowers on the Kiwi Airmen's memorial?"

"Ooo, yes dear," she replied.

Then, with a little hesitation and sensitivity, she asked if Nick had a relative who was stationed at Mepal during the war. The flowers told her that whoever it was had died, so she tried to be diplomatic.

"Yes. I think my father might have been stationed here. He was in the New Zealand Air Force, 75 Squadron. He died in 1943."

The woman frowned as though in thought. Then forgetting the inscription on the memorial said, "you know what, you might be right, I remember my mother talking about a Kiwi Squadron. I think they might well'uv bin here. Let me ask mum, she'll know for sure, she knows everything."

Without waiting for Nick's approval, she raised a finger in a gesture that asked him to wait a minute, and then she was gone. He could hear women's voices coming from the back room but could not hear clearly what was being said. Nick didn't want to start an enquiry that he already knew the answer to but had little opportunity to stop the woman without causing offence.

She soon returned saying, "a New Zealand Squadron was definitely ere in the war and stayed until the end. Mum said you are right, it was No. 75 Squadron. Got a memory like an old elephant she 'as. They flew them big bombers, you know. Nice lads, my mum said. She felt sorry for 'em cause they were a long way from ome, so the village people made a bit of a fuss of 'em. She was here all through the war, you know."

Before she had finished speaking, an elderly lady appeared in the doorway leading to the back room. Her curiosity had got the better of her, and she had come to see who the stranger was in her shop. They didn't see many strangers in Mepal, just one or two at duck shooting time on Welney Wash. She raised her voice to ask Nick where he was from.

"Australia," Nick replied.

"Oh, I thought Daisy said New Zealand."

"No Mum, his 'dad' was from New Zealand," Daisy insisted.

"Well it's near enough the same place." The old lady muttered to excuse her error.

Nick chuckled with a twinkle in his eye and said.
"Don't let an Aussie or a Kiwi hear you say that."

Then raising her voice again, she continued.

"Well you're a long way from ome, that's for sure. Would you like a cup of tea dear? I've got the kettle on."

Nick didn't really want a cup, but sensed that he should accept. He liked the old woman and thought she would be offended if he refused. Plus, he might at least hear something of interest about No. 75 Squadron, or at worst, old ladies' chatter about the war years in Mepal. So he accepted and was invited in with the wave of a hand to follow her into the back room. Her face was weathered, and her gray hair stuck out. She walked slowly with some difficulty, supporting herself on furniture as she went. Nick liked her direct manner as she tried to project the image of someone in authority, strong and forthright. Yet, it was easy to see through the veneer to a kind and considerate person who would feel vulnerable when complimented. The sort of person you could rely on when you needed them.

Still clutching the daffodils, Nick followed and put a shilling on the counter as he passed.

As she scooped it up to give it back, Daisy said. "don't you worry about that, not if they are for your poor old dad. It's sort'a nice that they come from up the old airfield, like they was his all along."

Nick agreed and was fascinated by her accent.

"We'll sit out here."

The old lady said as she led the way to a small conservatory at the back of the house.

The cane chairs creaked when they sat, and with every movement afterwards. A small, glass topped, cane coffee table stood between them.

"Put the kettle on Daisy."

The old lady called back to the shop.

Nick heard her daughter say. "yes mum."

Then in a much lower tone, but deliberately loud enough to be heard.

"How'd I know you were gunna ask?"

Nick smiled remembering the old lady had said the kettle was already on.

"That's not her real name you know." The old lady said.

"Her first name's Hannah. But when she were little everyone called her Daisy Chain on account of how pretty she were. So we call her Daisy now, always 'ave done I suppose. I'm her mum you know, but I expect you've already gathered that. My name's Maud. What's yours?"

"Nicholas Thorne. Everyone calls me Nick, but it was Robert Spalding in a former life." Nick added in a melancholy tone.

He was no longer looking at the old lady as Daisy had entered the room with sugar in one hand and milk in the other. Looking for a place for her to put them, Nick leaned over to make a small space on the coffee table for her. He didn't see the look on Maud's face when he gave his name, revealing a moment of extra curiosity. Daisy left quickly for the kitchen in response to the shrill whistle of a boiling kettle.

Maud paused for a moment, before saying, "Daisy's got a lad named David. He's a good boy, helps his mum n'that. Me too, sometimes here at the shop."

Nick smiled saying, "That's nice."

"So what brings you all the way from Australia then?"

"Well, I've been there since I was a boy, and I've come back now to see if I could find some relatives. Especially my mother, but I've not had much luck."

Maud's interest and curiosity increased.

"What about your family in Australia, can't they tell you nothing?"

"No, I don't have any family there. I went there as an orphan, although I wasn't one really. It's a long story."

"Well dear, you can tell me all about it over a cup'a tea. I'm interested to know."

Maud leaned towards Nick, fidgeted in her chair as though trying to get comfortable but without success. Her mind was running wild in anticipation of a real-life mystery. So Nick provided her with a few salient points.

Like galloping horses, some of Maud's almost forgotten memories came charging back. She was excited but tried not to show it as she pondered. 'His name were Robert Spalding, his father were in the New Zealand Air Force. He were stationed here in Mepal, died in 1943 and his mum had an accident. The boy went to Dr. Barnardo's, then Australia as an orphan! Somehow it seemed a familiar story, apart from the last piece. She wanted to know so much more but hesitated to ask too soon, not wanting to appear nosy, and afraid she might have already pried enough.

"Did you originally come from The Fens then?" Maud asked as casually as she could.

"I was born in Ely. It might have been because my father was stationed here during the war, I really don't know," Nick replied.

"Well, them daffodils'll look nice on that memorial. I'll get Daisy to put them back in some water for you."

Maud said to gain a moment to think, then continued as gently as she could.

"What did your father do in the Air Force?"

"I'm not exactly sure, but I know he flew in a bomber. It went missing one night, and he was never seen again," Nick replied.

"There were a lot of them what never come back you know. Blooming terrible things happened to them poor boys," Maud said as she looked down, gently shaking her head.

"They'd be in the pub one night all having a good'ole laugh an a sing-song, and the next day they could all be dead. How they coped, I don't know. I was here all the time you know. I saw lots of 'em come and go. If you didn't see one of 'em for a few days, you never asked where he was or nothin', cos you knew."

Daisy returned with the teapot, cups and saucers on a tray. "I got a son name is David, you know. We called him that after…"

"Daisy!" Maud abruptly cut in.

It was enough for Daisy to realise she was saying something that her mother didn't want her to. Maud saw the surprised look on Nick's face, pursed her lips, and with a gentle sideways rocking of her head she reprimanded Daisy saying she had forgotten the biscuits again.

"Sorry mum, I'll bring 'em now," she replied, embarrassed in front of their guest.

Nick couldn't see why Maud would need to embarrass Daisy over something so small. What did it matter? Maud realizing her impoliteness in front of Nick, felt obliged to explain in whispering tones.

317

"Daisy had a child 'from the wrong side of the blanket', if you get my meaning. Named 'im after his father, but he don't want to marry her, see. We don't want every Tom, Dick and Harry to know our business. Dunno what'll become of 'em both when I'm gone."

Daisy came in just as Maud was finishing, so overheard.

"Come on Mum, do you really think everyone in the village has not known since David was born? Any secret was gone years ago."

Maud clutched her apron, rocked her head and pinched lips.

Nick was not interested but nodded politely. His mind was elsewhere, pondering mixed thoughts of anticipation and resignation about his failing search. He had reached a point where he was grasping at straws of hope. Maud had said she was in Mepal all through the war, so he was eager to ask if she knew his mother. Or met his father? Nick had thought it was quite possible. Mepal was a small community and, no doubt, even smaller during the war, even with the airmen there. Everyone would know each other and everyone else's business. Nothing would have evaded village gossip. Nick was about to speak when Daisy held an open biscuit tin in front of him.

"Biscuit?"

"No thank you."

The shop doorbell rang, so Daisy quickly gave her mother the biscuits and left.

"So you have lived here all your life?" Nick asked as a lead into more important questions.

Maud chuckled as she said, "not yet dear!" Then more seriously added, "in a manner of speaking, I 'ave. Bin in the Fens that is, I was brought up in Chatteris as a girl along with my sister."

Maud changed the subject and talked about Australia. Both knew they were playing cat and mouse but not aware that the other knew. Maud wanted to hear rather more from Nick than to answer his questions, but she was inquisitive and her mind was already on her next question. Nick thought that Maud may have implied that she might know more than she really did and was now evasive due to a lack of detail.

"They tell me it gets ever so hot out there in Australia an it don't rain for years at a time?"

"Yes, in some parts but it can get very cold too, especially in the winter, down south and in the outback too. In some places it even snows," Nick replied.

Maud looked surprised.

"Well I never, I din't know that. You never hear about snow in Australia do you? You'd think it was all sunshine and kangaroos if you believe what they tell you."

The conversation continued with inconsequential chatter. Every time Nick tried to ask a pertinent question, Maud avoided a direct answer. Eventually, out of frustration he looked Maud in the eye and impatiently said,

"Maud, my mother's name is Anne Spalding, my father's name was Ross. He was in the Royal New Zealand Air Force, No. 75 Squadron here in Mepal during the war. My dad was killed in 1943. My mother became ill or had an accident and had to go to hospital for a long time. Did you know either of them?"

Maud was visibly taken aback and went red in the face from Nick's sudden directness and tone. Not for a moment did he regret his manner. He simply had to know. Nick was desperate and nothing else mattered. Maud looked straight at him muttering, "well I'll goo t'u Southery!"

Followed by more mumbling, which Nick could not hear clearly. He knew he had been too blunt and apologetically pleaded for an answer.

"Look, I'm sorry Maud. I really didn't mean to be rude, but I'm so desperate to find out about my mother and any family I might have. If you can remember anything at all, please tell me. I go back to Australia in a few days, and all I have for my trouble so far is a few bits of paper giving my mum's and dad's names, my name and birth date. Everything else about my life is missing. I don't even know who I really am. Please try to understand. I don't even know if my mother is still alive. If she is, she will be an elderly lady by now and could pass away at any time, with us never knowing each other. Please Maud?"

She heard the anguish in Nick's voice, saw the pain in his eyes and now understood his desperation. She became upset in a moment of compassion. Taking a breath, Maud reached across to gently hold Nick's arm and while trying not to blink and release a tear, she quietly said, "listen, I know everyone in the village and they knows me. They all come in the shop at some time or other. Most of the old'uns were here during the war. Well them what are left that is. I'll ask around and see what I can find out for you. You never know, someone might remember something. Did you say you gotta go back to Australia in a few days?"

Maud already had some ideas, and thought it cruel to raise Nick's hopes only to have them dashed with disappointment again.

"Yes, in four days," Nick said.

"Where are you staying?"

"At a small bed and breakfast place in Cambridge."

"Well then young Nicholas, you come back the day after tomorrow and we'll see what I've found out, if anything at all that is."

Nick knew this was the best he would get for now, so he thanked Maud saying that he would definitely come back.

"Come afore dockey," Maud said.

Nick agreed. As he went out through the shop, he asked Daisy what happens at dockey. With a smile and some amusement she said that dockey was the Fen name for lunch. Nick asked if he should bring anything.

320

"Only yourself," Daisy said with a smile.

"Your daffs are in the bucket outside."

Nick took the flowers as he left and walked back to the memorial to carefully place them. Stepping back he looked at the inscription again, but this time his mind was buzzing with possibilities and a little expectation. He felt the inner tension of anticipation and hated the suspense. On previous occasions he had become optimistic only to have his hopes dashed. This time it felt different. There were no officials, offices or documents involved, yet he thought that Maud, and maybe even Daisy might help.

With sadness he looked at the monument and quietly said, "God Bless you Dad. I didn't know you very well, but I'm sure we must have loved each other. I still do love you in my own way, and I'd really like to know you again."

At that moment he remembered Arana saying,

"Your father will lead you to your mother."

As Nick drove back to Cambridge, his mind churned over and over with the events of the day. He thought of calling in at the Royal Oak to tell Bill what had happened but decided against it. He would do it later when there was more to tell, and he really didn't want another beer.

Immediately Nick had left the shop, Maud returned to the conservatory where she sat pensively thinking about the last hour and poured herself a large sherry, her thoughts mingling with her memories of the war years in Mepal and the people she knew. After serving a customer, Daisy went to collect the cups.

"Are you alright mum? Don't you think it's a bit early for you to be on the sherry?"

Daisy studied her mother's face.

"You look as though you've seen a ghost."

"I think I might ave," Maud muttered.

Without stopping to comprehend what her mother had just said, Daisy continued.

321

"Sorry if I made you feel awkward when Mr. Thorne were ere."

She was not sorry but wanted to lighten the atmosphere between them.

"We don't want everyone to know you got an illegitimate child do we," Maud said.

Daisy became annoyed that her mother didn't accept her apology gracefully, and was indignant that her boy might be considered an oddity or inferior in any way because of the circumstances of his birth.

"Well like I said, it's hardly a secret in the village, never as bin, never will be, an nobody cares anyway. You are the only one who worries about it!" She snapped back.

Daisy was angry and went back into the shop. They didn't talk to each other for more than an hour.

Eventually Maud said that she was going to Ely first thing in the morning to see her sister. Daisy thought little of it since her mother usually went once a week, mostly on market day.

The next morning Nick made his way to County Hall to find the Cambridgeshire Archive Department. At the empty reception desk was a notice saying it was temporarily closed to visitors while decorating and refurbishment took place. He managed to find someone and asked if it was still possible to go in under unusual circumstances. However, as he might have expected, the doors were firmly closed to visitors.

"I'm sorry Sir, you will have to come back next week when we open again," was the best he could get.

Maud took the nine o'clock bus to Ely, all the way thinking of how she would handle her sister Sarah and her delicate mission. She knew her sister was not emotionally strong, and that she had many dark corners in her mind which she would retreat to in times of depression. Yet, she had to talk to her and get her help to solve Nicholas Thorne's mystery. Half an hour later the bus stopped in

Market Street opposite the local newspaper office. Maud got off and made her way across the market square, down Fore Hill and along Broad Street to a terraced Victorian cottage where her sister lived.

They were pleased to see each other and shared a quick hug in the doorway before Maud stepped inside.

"Is everything all right?" Sarah asked as she took her sister's coat.

"Yes of course dear, shouldn't it be?" Maud replied.

"Well, I usually only see you on market days, so I thought something might be up?"

"No, everything's fine dear."

Sarah didn't quite believe her but accepted what Maud said without further question, knowing her sister would tell her soon enough. As the two women went into the kitchen, Sarah said,

"I expect you could do with a cup a tea?"

"Ooo, yes please. It's proper parky out there." Maud replied.

As she sipped her tea, Sarah blew hers cool and slurped it from her saucer, which was precariously balanced on her finger tips. She tried to wait for Maud to tell her why she had come. But her impatience got the better of her and she said, "come on Maud, I know you better than you think. Now what's this here all about?"

Maud hesitated a few seconds and then looked into Sarah's eyes to hold her attention and said, "I've got something to tell you, and I don't quite know where to start. I'll just have to say it like it comes, but I don't want you getting upset cos it's all a bit sad."

Maud paused again.

"Well a man named Nicholas Thorne cum into the shop yesterday to buy some daffs to put on that Kiwi memorial in the village. Had a funny accent, said he were from Australia."

Sarah shuffled herself upright in her chair now paying more attention, her eyes wide as she waited.

"Now don't go getting all upset on me. I'm telling you cos I know you would want me to. Anyway, we don't know who he really is yet."

Maud continued more confidently now she had started talking, going on to repeat what Nick had told her.

"So you see the poor lad as bin separated from his mother since he were a lit'lun. He 'ad a real bad time an'all. Now he's come back from Australia tu look for his old Mum. Poor lad. The thing what worries me is that I remember something like this. If I remember right, Daisy used to carry shopping for a woman what got hurt. She were in the Land Army, you know. She went away, and I don't know if she ever cum back. Now can you remember anything like that dear?"

Sarah had no recollection.

"You gotta remember Maud, I wer'nt in Mepal as long as what you were."

Maud and Sarah talked for the rest of the morning. Later she asked again if Sarah could remember Anne Spalding from the old days, but she was definite that she couldn't recall anyone of that name. Maud told her that Nick was coming back tomorrow before dockey and she wanted to tell him something, anything to give him hope. Sarah suggested that the best chance of finding anyone who knew Anne Spalding would be to ask the women at the old folks home up on the main road.

"There's one or two up there from Mepal," she said.

Thinking this was a good idea, Maud went to the home before returning to Mepal. Walking up Back Hill was very difficult for Maud. It took almost an hour to reach Cambridge Road with frequent stops, but her determination kept her going. She was not permitted to enquire with the ladies as some were sleeping and others were being attended to by a nurse. Maud explained the situation to the matron, telling her that Nick only had two or three more days before returning to Australia. So a meeting at the home was arranged for the next day when Nick could meet the ladies himself.

Maud was pleased the bus to Stretham and Mepal came along Cambridge road and stopped almost outside the old folks' home. She didn't think she could have managed another long walk and was feeling stiff from the previous one.

Nick was keen to get to Mepal, waking early to prepare himself for whatever the day would bring. He had time on his hands and went for a walk, but he couldn't relax so decided to leave early and drive slowly. At least it would give him something to do. He drove north again on the A10, but by the time he reached Waterbeach, he was already exceeding the speed limit. So he forced himself to drive more slowly, deciding that if he got stopped for speeding, he could be late. It was 11 am when he arrived in Mepal. He looked at the memorial as he passed and saw the daffodils still laying there. He was early, but it didn't bother him.

The bell on the door bounced and clanged on the end of a spring to call Daisy to the shop. Drying her hands on the bottom of her apron as she came. Maud's voice could be heard coming from the back room.

"Shop Daisy!"

"Oh, hello Mr. Thorne," Daisy said.

Then raising her tone calling, "Mum, Mr. Thorne is 'ere!"

"All right, all right! I'm coming. He's early."

She called back, wanting Nick to accidentally hear. There was no possibility that he could not.

"Please call me Nick." He told Daisy, feeling that he had just been chastised by her mother.

A few moments later Maud waddled through the door wearing her hat and coat while clutching her handbag.

"You're early," she said, moderating her tone.

"We are going to Ely to meet some women that might remember your mum, or know something about what happened to er. We'll go in your car."

Maud stated as a matter of fact.

On the way Maud explained that a few of her old friends from the village, and one or two former Land Army girls she knew, were in an old folks' home in Ely. Not knowing what to expect, she cautioned Nick that nothing may come of the visit but it was worth a try. At least she was looking forward to seeing one or two old acquaintances again.

"That's where they get put when they can't cope no more or got nobody tu look after'em, poor old things."

Maud said, ignoring that she was the same age as many of the ladies she now pitied.

She talked all the way to Ely, mostly about village life and how the big shops in town were affecting her business.

"Problem is most people are getting cars these days, so it's too easy to get to town, and they don't 'ave to sit on the bus with a lot'a bags neither."

Maud directed them into a gravel drive which led to a large Victorian house that must have been quite grand at one time. The large bay windows and double front doors reflected an era of lost opulence. As they entered, the matron greeted them saying, "hello Maud, nice to see you again. I see you've brought your young man with you."

Then turning to Nick without introducing herself,

"You must be the man who's come to talk to the ladies."

Nick was surprised and replied with a simple. "Yes."

Maud had omitted to tell him what was expected when they arrived.

They were led to a big lounge at the front of the house where soft armchairs were randomly scattered in small groups. Two elderly ladies had looked out of the window with great curiosity after hearing a car arrive. They had watched Nick and Maud get out and now turned as they entered the room. Their curiosity was still not satisfied. Four other elderly ladies sat silently watching as they entered. They muttered to each other as Nick and Maud were brought towards them, with the request that they sit on a couch in front of the ladies.

The matron left the room. Nick smiled a greeting causing the old ladies to fidget for a moment in anticipation. One wrapped her knitting up while another clutched her walking stick as it leaned against her chair. There was a quiet greeting of "Hello dear," but Nick was not sure who had said it. Maud introduced Nick.

"This ere is Mr. Thorne. He's come all the way from Australia to find his mum and… Well I'd better let him tell you all about it."

Nick cleared his throat.

"G'day ladies, my name is Nick Thorne. Well, I was re-named Nick Thorne as a child. My birth name was Robert Spalding, and I'm trying to find my mother, who I have not seen since I was a toddler. I think she lived in or near Mepal during the war years but I'm not sure, and I'm hoping to find someone who might have known her or knows something about her."

Before anything more was said, the door was opened by a nurse escorting two more ladies into the room. 'Sorry, we are a bit late dear' one said as they joined the group. One had a walking frame and took a few moments to settle. The other, who looked a little younger, was pushed in a wheelchair by the nurse. None of the ladies had been introduced to Nick, and they stared at him intently causing him to feel uneasy. Maud lightened the moment with small talk as everyone settled down again. Then with an air of authority, and for the benefit of the late arrivals, she said, "This 'ere is Mr. Thorne. He were born in Ely and might'a lived in Mepal during the war as a boy. He's here from

Australia trying to find his family, especially his mum. Or at least find someone what might know something to help him find her."

Maud turned to Nick inviting him to continue. He had not known what to expect and hesitated as he gathered his thoughts again. Beginning by explaining how he came to meet Maud, and how she had given him hope of finding something out about his mother, he went on to tell as much as he could remember about his mother and father and the events of his early childhood. He did not say a great deal about his time in Australia other than that he had been in an orphanage in Perth, had worked on a farm and was now a fisherman, considering anything else of little relevance. The elderly ladies listened, concentrating hard. A real-life mystery was unfolding before them which added a spark of excitement to their otherwise mundane day.

There was visible unease amongst some of the ladies when Nick gave his mother's name.

"I don't remember any Anne Spalding," one frail lady interrupted.

"Shush Dot, you never remember anything anyway," one of the women said.

The body language and murmurings of the other ladies suggested they also felt Dot should be quiet. Yet there was a definite atmosphere that Nick felt but could not fathom. Did someone know something or were they just enthralled with the mystery? Perhaps he had simply given them something to talk about. But Nick's heart was racing with the hope that he had touched a nerve with at least one of them.

"What did they change your name for?" one lady asked, and before Nick could reply another asked, "Why on earth would they want to do that?"

They all fidgeted and looked at each other not knowing what to say. None offered any information or speculation.

After a second or two one lady said, "so what on earth did they do that for dear? What was wrong with Robert Spalding?"

Someone nudged the old lady suggesting she not pursue the question. But Nick explained that he was told it was the name of a family in Australia who would adopt him, and that it would be best for everyone if they all had the same family name. Then he followed this by saying he was not adopted after all. There was a short silence before the lady in the wheelchair asked him if there was anything more he could remember about his father. Nick said he had told them all he could remember.

Then after thoughtfully hesitating, he added, "one little thing that sticks in my mind was his gold Kiwi tie pin. It was his lucky charm, and my mother always treasured it."

The lady in the wheelchair didn't speak for about a minute and her eyes were fixed intently on Nick. She slowly put her hand inside her handbag. Then trembling, slowly and carefully raised herself to her feet. Other ladies suggested caution in surprise.

A nurse wanted to support her, but she was brushed away.

"Be careful dear, you know you're not too good on your pins," one of the ladies said.

The woman looked into Nick's eyes as she slowly held out a small, worn, gold Kiwi tie clip and asked, "did it look like this?"

The room fell silent while tears began to stream down Anne Spalding's cheeks.

No words were needed. They stared into each other's eyes as realization and emotion overwhelmed them. They embraced, holding each other tight. Robbie and his mother felt their tears mingle on their cheeks, just as they had many years before.

Epilogue

Nick formally changed his name back to Robert Peter Spalding and lived with his mother in a small village in the Isle of Ely, where he lovingly cared for her.

These were happy years, and on 3rd June each year they placed flowers on the New Zealand Air Force Memorial in Mepal. Robert also took his mother to Germany to visit her husband's grave. He discovered that his mother had been an only child and was brought up by her grandparents, that he had an aunt, uncle and three cousins in New Zealand.

Anne Spalding passed away on 8th January, 1997.

After meeting his relatives in New Zealand, Robert returned to Perth in Western Australia. Skip had sold the Kingfisher and retired. Charlie had signed on with the skipper of another fishing boat out of Fremantle. Robert and Skip, who he called "Uncle Bill," remained very close until his death in 2000 at the age of 86. Robert kept his promise to Gidga, who was now an Elder, returning to visit the village many times.

Robert Spalding's knowledge of Aboriginal culture and language enabled him to secure a position with The Department of Aboriginal Affairs in Western Australia where he specialized in locating and reuniting those of The Stolen Generation with their families. An early success was to reunite Gidga with his sister. He lobbied for every Aboriginal settlement to have a means of summoning medical help by telephone or radio. As a result of his efforts, many larger settlements also levelled and cleared strips of land to allow Flying Doctor access.

Robert Spalding retired at the age of 67 and lived in Perth. He passed away in 2014 while visiting Gidga. 'Migaloo' was highly respected and loved in Aboriginal communities. More than three hundred Aboriginal people attended his funeral where dancers performed ceremonial rituals in his honour.

Clontarf Boys Town was closed in 1983 and is today known as the Clontarf Aboriginal College.

The RNZAF memorial Plaque for No.75 Squadron is still maintained by the village folk in Mepal.

**Australian Senate Committee Report 2004
"Forgotten Australians."**

Quotations from 400 pages of atrocities:

"...the committee received hundreds of graphic and disturbing accounts about the treatment and care experienced by children in out-of-home care...Their stories outlined a litany of emotional, physical and sexual abuse, and often criminal physical and sexual assault, neglect, humiliation and deprivation of food, education and healthcare."

1.49 The child migrant inquiry revealed stories of child exploitation, virtual slave labour, criminal physical and sexual assault and profound emotional abuse and cruelty. Evidence was given of children being terrified in bed at night as religious brothers stalked the dormitories to take children to their rooms for sexual acts, and of children being severely beaten with leather straps, belts, wood and other weapons."

1.50 Depersonalisation occurred through the crushing of individual identity and changing of names.

Girls were not exempt from these regimes and suffered equally, mostly in convent care.

It was later discovered that many records had been destroyed to prevent tracing of origins and biological family. Yet some files were later recovered and posted, unannounced, to former orphans. For many these were emotional bombshells, bringing relief for some and devastation to others.

On 16th November, 2009, The Prime Minister of Australia, The Honourable Kevin Rudd, formally apologised on behalf of the Government of Australia for its neglect to the half million children, known as "The Forgotten Generation." On 24th February, 2010 The Honourable Gordon Brown apologised on behalf of the British Government. Most religious organisations, including the Catholic Church, have since issued formal apologies, provided support services and financial aid to many care leavers.

The Stolen Generation.

The Stolen Generation were children of Australian Aboriginal and Torres Straight Island descent, who were forcibly removed from their families by the Australian Federal and State Government agencies and church missions under acts of parliament.

The intent was to provide better education, health care and to facilitate assimilation into western society. In many cases it is true to say that psychical health and western education were delivered. But little consideration was given to the damaging emotional effects on children and their families, nor respect for Aboriginal culture, heritage and identity.

Some estimates show that over 100,000 Aboriginal children were forcibly removed from their families. On 13th February, 2008, the Prime Minister of Australia formally apologised on behalf of the Government to indigenous people.